FRACCIDENTAL
DEATH

WET WORK
(Book One of the Water Warriors Series, 2014)
Royal Palm Literary Award Winner, Florida Writers Association

"Evokes a Carl Hiaasen novel, crooked strip-mall investor replaced by crooked water-project developer. A fun read that has it all: Science for sale, regulators on the take, a lawmaker set to seriously embarrass his wife."
—Cynthia Barnett, author of *Blue Revolution* and *Mirage*

"A Florida environmental mystery of the highest caliber. The suspense will keep you turning pages well into the night."
—Doug Alderson, author of *Wild Florida Waters* and other books

Reading WET WORK is like taking a group canoe trip into the lush wild world of natural Florida and rowing with a cast of characters who might kill you—or save you."
—Claire Matturro, author of *Bone Valley* and other mysteries

With memorable characters, a lush Florida setting, and our most precious natural resource at the center of its plot, WET WORK is a frightening environmental thriller that will make readers think twice the next time they turn on their water faucets.
—Julie Compton, author of *Tell No Lies* and *Keep No Secrets*

Also by Donna Meredith

The Glass Madonna (2010)
   First Place, Women's Fiction (pre-published), Royal Palm Literary Awards, Florida Writers Association

The Color of Lies (2011)
   First Place, Women's Fiction (pre-published), Royal Palm Literary Awards, Florida Writers Association
   Gold Medal, Adult Fiction, Florida Publishers Association

Magic in the Mountains: Kelsey Murphy, Robert Bomkamp, and the West Virginia Cameo Glass Revolution (2012)
   Silver Medal, Florida Publishers Association

> Dear Gladys,
> Thanks for enjoying books. (I'm a retired English teacher.)

FRACCIDENTAL
DEATH

Donna Meredith

DONNA MEREDITH

Wild Women Writers
An Independent Publishing Company

FRACCIDENTAL DEATH

This book is a work of fiction. Names, characters, places and incidents are either the product of the author's imagination or are used fictitiously. Any resemblance to actual persons, living or dead, or to actual events or locales is entirely coincidental.

Copyright © 2016 by Donna Meredith. All rights reserved, including the right to reproduce this book, or portions thereof, in any form, electronic or mechanical without permission in writing from the publisher, except for brief quotations contained in critical articles and reviews.

ISBN: 978-0-9829015-3-3

Published by Wild Women Writers, Tallahassee, FL
www.wildwomenwriters.com

Logo design by E'Layne Koenigsberg of 3 Hip Chics, Tallahassee, FL
www.3HipChics.com

Printed in the United States of America

For my mother

Most people say that it is the intellect which makes a great scientist. They are wrong: it is character.
—*Albert Einstein*

A mature person is one who does not think only in absolutes, who is able to be objective even when deeply stirred emotionally, who has learned that there is both good and bad in all people and in all things, and who walks humbly and deals charitably with the circumstances of life, knowing that in this world no one is all knowing and therefore all of us need both love and charity.
—*Eleanor Roosevelt*

One

November 14, 2014

BARELY MORE THAN AN EXHALATION, the whisper behind Summer Cassidy carried such force, such distress, that she let the AC adapter in her hands clatter onto the stage floor. Instinctively she stepped backwards and whipped around to face the source, her dissertation adviser. "No, no, no," Oliver Jennings breathed, the pitch of each plea rising higher than the last, his fingers pressed against bloodless cheeks. "He can *not* be here."

"Who?" she asked, tracking Dr. Jennings' eyes to a man in his late twenties near the entrance of Stansbury Elementary School's multi-purpose room. Instead of answering, Jennings bolted behind the curtain concealing the right wing of the stage. She could hear his hard-soled shoes clattering down a few steps backstage. Moments later he emerged onto the gym floor, his massive girth pounding along the left side of the gym until he disappeared into the boys' bathroom. Was he going to throw up?

Alone on the stage, Summer felt like a bride ditched at the altar. People were probably wondering what she'd done to send their speaker into such a panic. The bogeyman who had caused the freak-out didn't look the least bit scary. A copper-skinned fellow, possibly Indian, he hid behind hipster glasses with thick black frames and a stylish fedora cocked to one side. Well off. He hadn't yanked that fine gray suit off a rack at Goodwill like the faded cardigan Summer wore tonight. He remained standing near the out-of-bounds line to the right of the basketball hoop, a legal pad dangling from one hand. Two middle-aged men in puffy jackets and jeans shuffled past him toward metal chairs near the stage.

The room was rapidly filling with citizens interested in learning about the connection between hydraulic fracturing and the increase in low intensity earthquakes in Ohio. While Summer waited for Dr. Jennings to return, she set the computer projector up and launched the first slide of his presentation, identifying the topic and presenter. She settled into an orange plastic chair designed for rug rats. Her sit bones knifed into her glutes no matter which way she arranged her long legs.

Summer's throat contracted as she absorbed the room's atmosphere. Even if she hadn't noticed the serving area along the right side, the lingering odor of canned corn and hot dogs would have suggested this room doubled as a cafeteria, while undercurrents of sweat and the basketball hoop signaled phys ed. Some poor schmuck had to juggle the schedule for all these activities—a suck job, but she couldn't help thinking how lucky these kids were to have adults devoted to their needs. Summer had grown up in a home consumed by her twin's health issues. Instead of attending grade school, she read textbooks in hospital waiting rooms, which her mother passed off as home-schooling. It left Summer essentially in charge of her own education. No basketball games, no school plays, no notes or secrets shared among friends.

Metal clanged as a custodian set up another row of chairs. After five minutes had passed, Summer called Jennings' cell. He didn't answer. She was already annoyed that he'd demanded her help this evening. In the morning, she had to move her gear to West Virginia to begin her research. She could have used this time to finish packing. Could have used a good night's sleep.

Instead, she'd driven nearly three hours from Penn State to reach this elementary school in Ohio and set up his computer slide show—a simple feat anyone could have done for him or he could have done for himself. *You're the only grad student I trust with this task,* he'd told her.

What bull—but she could hardly say that to his face.

Three women and one man ambled in from the door across the hall labeled "Teacher Workroom." Very cool, their being here. The world needed teachers passionate about science. Summer approached the man and asked him to check on Jennings in the bathroom. The teacher returned with the message that the professor would be out soon. Hesitating, he added, "Dr. Jennings looks a bit shaky. Is he ill?"

Summer wished she knew. She checked her mobile: almost seven o'clock. Go time. She tried Jennings' cell again. No luck.

The buzz of citizens and officials—Summer counted forty-eight adults and seven children—rose in volume. Did they sound more aggressive or was it her imagination?

At two minutes after seven, the principal, a woman in her mid-forties, closed the hallway door, crossed the room, and mounted the highly varnished steps to the stage. She wore a blue pants suit that fit too snugly at the waist. After a brief show of frosty teeth, she leaned over Summer to inquire whether they might commence.

Summer hoped her smile conveyed a confidence she did not feel. "I'm sure Dr. Jennings will get started any moment."

The set of the principal's lips telegraphed an unmistakable message: she'd heard every sorry fiction scallywags could invent for tardiness. As the principal's heels clicked back down the stairs, Summer fidgeted with connections between her laptop and projector. Was Dr. Jennings going to abandon her—expect her to give an unrehearsed presentation?

She blew a sigh of relief when the bathroom door opened and Jennings raced toward the rear stage entrance. He hissed at her from behind the curtain. With jerky motions, he beckoned her to join him. He had to be kidding—didn't he realize his audience was growing restless? As she ducked behind the curtain, she noted with alarm the man's physical deterioration: his face damp with sweat, respiration too rapid, eyes bulging.

"He's still here."

"Who?" she asked, though she was certain he meant the dude in the gray suit.

"Elliot Ral."

"Who's Ral?"

"Look in the back of the gym. Wears a hat. Always carries that damn legal pad."

Since when did a legal pad inspire fear? "He's here."

"Summer, you must carry on tonight without me. They are determined to destroy my research and my family. I'm sorry, but this must end. Right now."

"What the—" She caught herself. She didn't know this man well enough to WTF him. "Who's 'they'?"

"Don't trust anyone. Our phones and emails have been hacked."

"Sir, do you want me to call a doctor? Or your wife?"

Backing away, he shook his head. "Good luck." He exited, stage right.

What now? Studies had found a significant correlation between creative genius and mental illness, and Jennings fit the definition of a paranoid schizophrenic gone off his meds. Summer knew Marcia Jennings, the current state attorney general, was running for governor. Political campaigns could exert enormous stress on families. Summer had no desire to get Dr. Jennings in trouble—she liked the man—but his behavior signaled something dreadfully amiss.

She gazed at the sea of people, the individuality of their voices merging into bedlam, swelling and crashing in waves of sound. She would have to deal with his problems later. The principal lifted one eyebrow, meeting Summer's gaze head-on.

Her mouth felt dry as charred toast. What wouldn't she give to be banging back a cold one in her favorite booth at the Foos and Boos beside her good bud Dayita. Summer glanced at Ral. Was he from Bangladesh originally, like Dayita? They had similar facial features and skin tone, but he could just as easily be Indian, Pakistani, or Afghan.

She stepped to the microphone. "Good evening. Due to a . . ." *Don't look at her, no, don't*—Summer's eyes flicked to the principal against her own inner voice, the one that knew better. The woman's lips puckered and creases amassed along her jaws like a bulldog's chops—driving the words right out of Summer's head. *Get a grip, girl—look somewhere else.* She focused on a young mother in the front row. "Due to a medical emergency, Dr. Jennings will not be able to join us this evening." With dismay, she realized her pitch was vaulting up and plummeting down like a storm-tossed aircraft. She had to gain control. Had to do this for the university.

"Can everyone hear me?" As her voice steadied, people nodded. The geek-glassed bogeyman who had alarmed Dr. Jennings pulled the legal pad to his waist, pen poised to stab paper. His mouth turned up slightly, and she imagined she read satisfaction on his face, but she couldn't be certain.

Summer smiled, hoping the shine of her teeth would fool folks into thinking she was thrilled to be standing in front of them. "I'm Summer Cassidy, Dr. Jennings's research assistant, and I'll be speaking in his place tonight." When she clicked the laser mouse, the first content slide appeared. Though she couldn't remember much of what Jennings had said when he gave this presentation in class, she recalled verbatim the notes he'd distributed. Tonight, her near-perfect visual memory wouldn't mark her as a dork, the way it did in high school. Tonight, it was gonna save her ass. And the university's reputation as well.

A flash of insight slammed into her. Jennings had planned all along to bail if this Ral character showed up. What a sneaky, low-down—

Recovering her focus and her cool, she cleared her throat. Those people in front of her had come for information she could provide. She tried not to watch Elliot Ral's pen flying across that legal pad. Was he waiting for her to make a mistake? As she finessed each slide, her confidence jelled. Without any major snafus, Summer flew through the presentation.

Now, all she had to do was get past the Question/Answer period. She swallowed, forcing down a new bubble of fear. When it came to processing what people said, she sucked. Always had.

The principal offered a wireless mic to an audience participant, and Summer could have hugged her. At least she wouldn't have to make sense of half-whispered words obscured by chairs scraping against the floor and people fishing in purses for candy or keys. The first question concerned equipment used to monitor seismic activity. She could have answered in her sleep.

Next, the male teacher Summer had spoken to earlier asked if she would return to speak to his science class in December, a request declined because of her research deadlines. "But I could come back in spring," she suggested.

Ral's voice projected without need for a microphone. "How many jobs would you say Dr. Jennings has destroyed?" Strong British inflections suggested he'd been raised overseas or at least learned his English there.

Several men were grumbling. If Summer didn't counter fast, she would lose them.

She took a deep breath. "As scientists, our work is not about creating or destroying jobs. Our job is to ask questions until we find the truth. Our research didn't cause earthquakes. It only affirmed the probable correlation between injection wells and unusual seismic activity in the surrounding areas."

Ral persisted. "Two highly regarded scientists, Bauer and Ford, did a study in 2010 disproving any such connection. Isn't it true these quakes could be natural occurrences, acts of God, rather than man-made? Or are you one of those scientists that don't believe in God?"

Not taking his bait, she said, "As you are probably aware, Bauer and Ford's study was paid for by the oil industry, and they skewed results to show what they were told to find. All other studies—including those done in central Oklahoma, North Texas, and this state—found probable links between injection wells and earthquakes. That said, we don't know enough about the state of the ground before the wells were drilled to prove causation."

"So you can't definitely prove the wells caused these little tremors, can you?"

Summer felt heat rise to her face. "That's what I just said. But we do know something unusual is happening. Arkansas has banned injection wells after experiencing 1,200 small quakes near a fault line. Oklahoma experienced 250 small-to-medium quakes in the first half of this year. When you inject enough wastewater a mile below the surface, it is likely to provoke seismic activity. That's why the Ohio legislature introduced new rules to monitor injection wells."

"Sounds like typical liberal scare-mongering and government over-reach to me. You impose ridiculous rules and regulations—"

The principal stopped the back-and-forth. "Sir, let's keep the tone civil. You had your opportunity to ask a question. It's time to let others have their turn. And I would appreciate it if the audience waited until I provide the microphone to ask questions so everyone can hear."

Summer was certain no one had trouble hearing Ral, but was thankful the principal made an effort to control the meeting's tone. Setting off two pops and a screech of feedback, the principal passed the mic to a young mother in the front row.

"I'm worried about my kids' safety," the young woman said. "We've had a cluster of small quakes near Youngstown. Does this mean we are at risk now for more serious earthquakes?"

Elliot Ral wouldn't like this answer. Too eff-ing bad. "When earthquakes are induced by wastewater injection, large quakes typically do follow smaller ones. But Ohio now requires seismic monitoring during drilling, and if any disturbance originates near the well bore, operations will be suspended."

"Bull," Ral interrupted. "Injection wells have been used in this country since the 1930s and there wasn't any trouble reported until a bunch of tree huggers latched onto this issue."

The principal snatched the mic back and placed it close to her lipsticked mouth, causing every *s* and *p* to fart explosively. "Sir, *please*, you're *speaking* out of turn again."

Frowning, he waved a hand as if swatting away a bug.

Summer wasn't about to allow him to spread misinformation. "I'd like to comment on what Mr.—what's your name, sir?"

He hesitated. "Smith."

Why use a bogus name unless he had something to hide? "Well, Mr. Smith, in the early days, we didn't have to exert much pressure to store wastewater underground. But as amounts accumulated over time, we had to apply more and more pressure to force additional fluid underground. Also the number of wells multiplied faster than bunnies. The marshmallow kind that proliferate around Easter." Chuckles rippled through the room. "Besides all the new fracking activity going on here in Ohio, wastewater is being trucked here from Pennsylvania because their geology isn't as good for injection wells. So, what you've got is more and more stress beneath the surface. Something has to give, a simple fact of physics, and the fluids unclamp faults, making it easier for rocks to slip."

The principal tugged the front facings of her suit jacket together across her abdomen, reminding Summer of the missing button on her blouse. She snugged her Goodwill cardigan across her chest.

"Thank you, Ms. Cassidy," the principal said. "You have given us a lot of important information to digest. I know I understand better what's happening right around us." She addressed the audience. "I don't think Dr. Jennings could have done the least bit better, do you folks?" Her tapping of two fingers against her palm prompted an outpouring of applause.

Summer stepped down from the stage where audience members

swarmed her, some with private questions, some wanting to share their experiences, others simply wanting to say "good job."

A gray-haired woman Summer had pegged as an environmental activist pressed waxed-paper wrapped cookies into her hand. "Organic oatmeal with toasted pecans and raisins," she said. "I baked them for my family this morning. Enjoy."

For the first time since arriving at the school, Summer smiled because she was happy. "Oatmeal's my favorite. I'll devour these as soon as I get back to the motel."

"I'm sure you hear it all the time, honey, but you have the cutest Southern accent."

What? No she didn't. Summer pressed her lips together before she got sidetracked arguing that Florida might be in the South, but in no way did it resemble other southern states. Catching the eyes of those lingering nearby with cups of punch, Summer asked if anyone knew where Mr. Smith worked. One by one, they shook their heads, leaving the principal to declare him an outsider. "We don't treat our guests that way around here."

"I can see that—you've been terrific." Summer scanned the room for Elliot Ral, but he had disappeared.

Her major problem now: what to do about Dr. Jennings. She couldn't completely repress her anger over how she'd been played, but she supposed she'd have to excuse his clever deceit in getting her to come to Stansbury. Obviously he was terrified and quite possibly unstable.

Summer loaded equipment into her truck. In darkness only intermittently dispersed by street lamps, Summer zeroed in on a child's giggle and the slip-slap of rubber soles on asphalt. As her eyes pierced the dim light, she discerned the silhouette of the young mother, calling out to her toddler: "Rainelle, I'm not kidding around. Stop running away from me." Summer wanted to call out a warning of how quickly, how irrevocably a life so small and fragile could be stilled. Hadn't it happened to her own sister—gone in an instant?

A lump in her throat, she hopped inside the truck and yanked the door closed. Backing out of her parking space, she paused to wave at the woman, who had caught up to her daughter. Summer should concentrate on them. On all the people like them. Her research on water quality near fracking sites could benefit thousands of families.

Yet the downside Ral had mentioned nagged at her. If drilling stopped, those same families could lose their livelihood. Balancing those competing needs would fall to legislators and regulations. She had to concentrate on her own job: determining which drilling practices provided safety and efficiency.

When she arrived at the motel, she plopped down on the lumpy double bed and called Dr. Jennings' cell, but he didn't answer. He could still be on the road—or as upset as he'd been, he might have had an accident. She called his home, leaving a message for his wife, expressing concern.

Summer flung herself back onto the worn floral bedspread, staring at the pimply textured ceiling. A few months ago, she had been so excited about living away from Loblolly Lake, Florida, for the first time. Now, she was beginning to think she might have made a huge mistake in choosing Penn State.

When Summer had first arrived in State College, Pennsylvania, in June, she'd fallen in love with the mountains. They seemed womanly, like bosoms enfolding small towns between them for safekeeping. Almost overnight in late September the hillsides threw on a glorious shawl of copper, topaz, and garnet—only to shrug off the frippery a week later, exposing the desiccated bones of an ancient god, barren, remote, angry. Foliage had concealed the junk heap left behind on the mountains when earlier booms went bust: rusted metal, glass shards, warped and splintered boards—forensic evidence of families falling on hard times and whole industries collapsing into ugly piles. No one cleaned up the trash. The universe had faded corpse-gray, plunging Summer into an unfamiliar ennui. No wonder bears hibernated and snowbirds drove their RVs south.

But her fear she'd made a mistake had more to do with Oliver Jennings than with seasonal changes. During summer term, her professor had been everything she hoped for. He served up lectures with a wallop that matched the geology professor who'd been Summer's mentor in the master's program at Florida Sci-Tech.

Jennings's work had earned international respect. Summer had been especially impressed by his ethics. When a shoddy study claimed no link existed between drilling and a rash of small earthquakes, Jennings discovered the fracking industry had bankrolled the research and dictated results. By publicizing his findings, he had, no doubt, angered the study's authors as well as industry executives and stockholders. To Summer, he was a hero with the courage to do what was required of every decent scientist: ask questions and seek the truth.

But a month ago, the geology department had experienced its own tremors. Jennings stopped keeping office hours. He posted this loony notice by the lab telephone ordering students to hang up if they heard a click on the line. Even weirder, he videotaped even ordinary meetings. If you tapped him on the shoulder to get his attention, he startled as if you'd poured ice water down his back.

Most likely, Jennings was having a psychotic break, but she'd already had a taste of the lengths corporations would go to protect profits on her last project at Florida Sci-Tech. Her research had revealed that water drawn from Harewood Energy's million-dollar Aquifer Storage and Recovery wells contained high levels of carcinogens. The company went to extraordinary lengths to stop release of her data. They stole her computer and threatened to withdraw financial support from Sci-Tech. Before it was all over, she was actually forced to shoot an industry-hired thug named Jake Fowler in self-defense when he attempted to murder her and her friends.

What if Jennings was right and someone did want to prevent water tests near fracking sites?

She hopped off the motel bed and booted her laptop. Ral's profile popped up on the first professional social media network site she checked. Stretching back six years, his resume included a B.A. in public relations and communications technology.

Ral listed Allied Consulting as his employer. AC, a limited liability corporation operating out of Tulsa, offered information and security services to the oil and gas industry.

Obviously, Ral hadn't come all the way from Oklahoma to Ohio to harass her or Dr. Jennings for personal reasons. So who had hired Allied Consulting and why? Summer intended to find out.

~

CORKY ROGERS HOPPED OUT OF HIS TANKER truck and issued a two-fingered mock salute to Fairhope Energy boss Boomer Walsh, who was yakking on his cell phone at the far end of the bulldozed job site. Walsh, a tall man, but not as heavy as Corky, raised his chin in acknowledgment. Half a dozen fellas, Corky's bar buddies, paused in their various tasks to hail his arrival with a shout or a wave.

Behind these men, naked trees peppered the distant hills, their dark trunks rising like a farm of missiles aimed at the sky. So far, those hills had escaped clear-cutting in the mad rush to bring the vast deposits of oil and gas in the Marcellus Shale to market, but for how long?

Corky secured the upper end of a hose, gray as an elephant's trunk and twice as fat, to his tanker truck, a routine task requiring little concentration. His mind drifted toward his fiancée. Yesterday the wedding gown had arrived via UPS. One corner of his mouth twisted up in amusement as he remembered Sloane sashaying around the living room in her red dress, its sequins scattering flecks of light with every wiggle. He warned her that the local church-going women would gawp at those sequins clinging to her bouncy curves. She'd provide gossip fodder for weeks in that gown. Sloane shimmied for him, laughter bubbling from deep in her chest: "Honeypot, I aim to have a holiday wedding this town will never forget."

How a pudgy blue collar nobody had snagged a gal like Sloane still mystified him, but he thanked God every day for this unexpected gift. It had taken forty-two years to find her, but the discovery, at last, of the perfect woman for him made up for his miserable first marriage.

Corky checked the connection again, and satisfied it was secure, slapped the side of his tanker. It held a load of FloMoshun, a proprietary chemical compound used to fracture rock and release the natural gas trapped inside. Corky dragged the other end of the hose toward a containment tank. It snaked across a distance of about ten yards. The tank served as a blender, mixing and adjusting levels of chemicals before they were added to water and mixed with sand.

A bag of fast food trash blew across the expanse of dirt and caught against the tires of one of the dozen trucks lined up on the site. Their red cabs were the only color in an otherwise drab landscape. Corky shivered and turned up the collar of his jacket. Following protocol, he tested the connection to his truck again.

He threw the switch to blow off a portion of the tanker's load under full pressure. When he heard the grind indicating transfer had begun, he stepped a few feet away to spit a wad of chew onto the dirt. He was wondering what time Sloane would get off work when an unexpected hiss made the hairs on his neck salute. He pivoted on one heel toward the tanker. Some of what happened next, he only pieced together afterward.

A four-inch fitting which coupled the hose to his tanker's pipe split in half. The pressurized chemical cannon blasted him in the chest and slammed him to the ground. His hard hat fell off and skidded more than forty feet across frozen dirt. It came to rest against Boomer Walsh's boots.

On Corky's first attempt to stand, his legs skidded out from under him. He rolled sideways a couple of times, shielding his face as best he could, and finally bulled his way to his feet. On some level, he was aware that Boomer dropped his cell, catapulted over his pickup's hood, and sprinted to Corky's tanker. Walsh threw the switch to change the pump from push mode to off. Corky's buddies barreled toward him, dragging a freshwater hose.

"Good God, Corky, you all right?" Walsh asked.

Bent over at the waist, Corky could only respond with wheezes and hacks as he took stock of his condition. FloMoshun drenched his leather boots and was soaking through his jacket and jeans, icing his skin. He ran his tongue over the roof of his mouth and swallowed, trying to cleanse his mouth of a taste similar to gasoline and burned plastic. Why was he able to taste it? Not like he'd taken a swig of the stuff. A haze of lemon and pink grapefruit streaked the sky. Blinking barely improved his vision. The chemicals were hijacking his senses.

Walsh seized the hose from Corky's buddies and sprayed him off with a powerful flush of clean water. The boss ordered the crew to contain the spill, but his directions proved unnecessary. The more experienced men were already setting up a quick-throw containment pool. Others sprinted from the spill response trailer with absorbent booms, mats, and pillows.

"Gul-dern-it-all, Walsh, you're fu-freezing my nuts off," Corky yelled. "Gotta buh-be twen-twenty frigging degrees out here." His teeth chattered uncontrollably.

"Strip."

Corky peeled his clothes off and Walsh turned the hose on him again. Finally, Corky dodged the spray. "Enough, you lou-lousy, ro-rotten sumbitch, enough."

"You all right?" Walsh asked again, a question echoed by two men setting up additional vermiculite booms.

"O-k-kay." He hoped he was.

"Let's get you dressed."

As Corky followed Walsh into the trailer, a few of the crew lingered outside, recounting details of the accident among themselves. The odors trapped inside the trailer were nauseating. Corky wheezed, his lungs burning while the rest of his body froze.

Walsh threw him a rough towel. Corky buffed his cold-reddened skin, but the physical exertion of even this simple act taxed his lungs. Walsh rummaged through a box in the back of the trailer, coming up with a flannel shirt and jeans. "Try these on."

Corky managed to fasten enough of the buttons to keep the shirt in place. It fit fine, but mildew clung to the fabric. The smell curdled his stomach. He pulled on the jeans. When he let go of the waistband, they slid off his butt. Despite the size of his belly, the planes of his butt were flat.

With a box cutter, Walsh sliced off a piece of string trimmer line and looped it through the back belt loops. "For God's sake, hold still so I can knot this string. Can't have you mooning folks."

Finally, Walsh stared at Corky's feet, purpled from cold. He rooted through the box again and offered baseball socks. Navy and gold stripes circled the tops. "No spare boots. You're gonna have to put yours back on."

As chemical-laden as the boots were, there'd be no escaping those fumes. But if he didn't put them on, he risked frostbite. Corky couldn't even feel his toes as he shoved his feet into the sodden boots. His fingers had stiffened like icicles, unable to manipulate the laces. Walsh bent down and tied them. As a final touch, the boss found a quilted moss-colored mat, the kind a mechanic might lay on the ground for protection. Walsh tucked it around Corky's shoulders.

"Now what the hell happened out there?"

Anger had replaced Walsh's initial concern, and Corky understood why. "Fi-fit-ting broke," he said between shivers. "S-sorry. I know—headaches—OSHA and—EPA." The company despised government agencies for their regulations, rules, and paperwork.

An accident meant filing reports. It meant regulators visiting the site, asking questions, reviewing safety procedures, pointing fingers.

The room swirled. If Corky took one more diesel-tinged breath, he was going to throw up. He staggered past the open door and lowered his head between his knees. Fresh air arrived too late. His stomach emptied its contents in a series of violent thrusts, followed by dry heaves.

Walsh had followed him outside, hovering at a discreet distance, his lips pressed together.

Corky heard him asking someone how big the spill was.

Marky Markowitz answered. "About a hundred and fifty gallons, I'd guess."

A hiss followed. Walsh ordered Marky to move Corky's tanker out of the way, before turning back to Corky. "Guess you'd better head over to the hospital and get yourself checked."

Corky remained in a squat, sucking in deep breaths, clutching the mat tightly against his shoulders. Minutes passed before he felt steady enough to stand. "Thanks for the clothes, Boomer."

"No problem. Let me get someone to drive you over."

And let his boss call him a wuss behind his back? Corky shook his head.

Walsh pulled out his wallet and stuffed a handful of hundreds into Corky's shirt pocket. "No worker's comp. We'll pay for it. Whatever you need."

Though the boss might have intended the promise to be reassuring, it had the opposite effect. Could Corky trust Boomer to keep his word? He'd heard rumors the company was having financial problems though he didn't know if he believed the gossip. Boomer certainly still lived large, like a guy with no worries. Corky trudged over to his pickup and started the engine. There was a knock on the window, and he rolled it down a few inches.

Walsh pushed a blank check through the opening. "Use this if you have to. Let me know how much. Don't tell them what happened, okay? No accident report."

Boomer didn't say it, but Corky heard the unspoken threat: not if he wanted to keep his job. He didn't see how he was supposed to explain why he was at the hospital without mentioning the spill. Fifteen miles down the highway, Corky stopped at a red light not far from the hospital. He guessed he'd better call Sloane—though he dreaded what he knew was coming. Maybe the call would go straight to voice mail. But no such luck. He relayed the morning's mishap.

"Goddamn it all to hell, Corky, I told you Fairhope Energy was a rotten company to work for. Didn't I tell you that?"

She had, and he hadn't listened—any more than she had when he'd hinted she shouldn't take the Lord's name in vain.

"Bunch of cheapskates. They—" She broke off when his hacking grew intense enough to overtake her rant.

"I'll meet you at the hospital. Debbie can finish my client's haircut," she said.

"No need."

"I'm coming and that's that. And you're quitting that damn job. Today."

Over and out. Once Sloane Dumont made up her mind, no one could change it.

He looked up at the stop light, amazed by the wide halo ringing the red light. Even when he blinked, the haze didn't budge. The fuzzy ring bounced to the yellow light and flared around the green with an intensity that swamped his ability to process anything else. That glow expanded and became his world. He swayed in the driver's seat. Air. He needed air. Fumbling with buttons on his door, he lowered the window. Fresh air cleared his head. The hospital was only a few more blocks. He could make it. As he drove onto the hospital grounds, he aimed for the emergency entrance. Opened the truck door. Staggered two steps. Collapsed to his knees and vomited.

Up. He had to get up. He pushed himself off the asphalt. Stumbled a few more steps.

"What the hell?"

The baritone sounded as if it was coming from the bottom of a well. Footsteps pounded behind him.

"Hang on, buddy." This second male voice reminded Corky of the bass saxophone he'd played in the high school band—big instrument.

From behind, strong hands seized his arms, fitted themselves around his waist, and Corky felt himself propelled toward the entrance. Automatic doors slid open.

"Get a team over here—stat!" The man with the bass voice demanded. He seemed huge, even heavier than Corky. A black fella. "We found him outside," the bass continued.

Everything happened in slow motion and at warp speed—both at the same time. Was this how it felt when you were dying? They lifted him onto a gurney and wheeled him into a cubicle. Overhead fluorescents pained his eyes. He closed his eyelids, barely peeping out, while he answered their questions. His name. Age.

"Insurance?" someone asked.

"In my wallet." He reached toward his back pocket and panicked. These weren't his clothes. Where was his wallet? How stupid. In his glove box, of course. Someone went out to retrieve the wallet and park his truck. He'd left it under the portico. He didn't remember if he'd turned off the engine or shut the door.

A pretty gal with blond hair fetched up in a ponytail like a high school kid leaned over him with a stethoscope. "Heart rate one-fifteen."

"Way he stinks, it's amazing his heart works at all." That was the baritone again, a white guy with close-set eyes. It was meant as an aside to the black fella, but Corky overheard. He was struggling for every breath and this guy could make jokes—really? Didn't he understand how scared Corky was? So scared he could hardly think straight.

"Respiration, thirty-two," the woman said. "Get a drip going."

Didn't respiration have something to do with breathing? Was thirty-two normal?

The white guy wiped something cold over the crook of Corky's elbow. "I'm starting a saline drip and you'll feel a little prick." He flicked a gloved finger against that tender spot and jabbed a needle into Corky's vein.

The girl with the ponytail introduced herself as Dr. Bissett. "Can you tell us what happened?"

Without giving away the spill, he listed his symptoms: bad vision, headache, vomiting.

Hands moved along his abdomen. He cracked his eyes open enough to watch another woman cut away his borrowed clothes. Considerably older than the doc, she reminded him of his mother. He felt a tear forming, but dang it, he wasn't going to cry like some big baby. If his mom was here to take charge, she'd make sure he got the best care. But his mother had passed away four years ago.

"Any idea what caused you to vomit?" Dr. Bissett pulled one of his eyelids up and flashed a penlight directly into his pupil. Aghhh! He turned his head away. No accident report, Boomer had said. If Corky kept his eyes shut, the doctor would assume he couldn't remember or didn't know.

"Respiration increasing," Dr. Bissett said to her staff, before laying a gloved hand on Corky's chest and suggesting in the kindest voice imaginable that he should try to take deep, slow breaths.

"Get those boots off him," Dr. Bissett ordered.

The black fella who had helped him inside tugged on a boot lace. Corky's eyes flashed open. "Be careful handling them boots."

"Why?" Dr. Bissett scrutinized his feet. "They're soaked. What's on them? What happened to you?"

God, he was going to be in so much trouble. Boomer would never forgive him if—his thought got lost because a commotion erupted outside the cubicle.

"I don't give a big goddamn what your rules say, that's my fiancé in there and you ain't man enough to keep me from him. Corky, where are you?"

For the first time since the spill, the tension in his throat eased a little. He hadn't realized how bunched up his muscles had been until he unbunched them.

"Can you tell me what happened?" Dr. Bissett repeated, leaning over him.

Metal rings skidded across the bar holding the curtains that concealed his cubicle. Even though the lights overhead were painfully bright, Corky smiled as Sloane shoved her way in and clasped his hand.

"I'll tell you what happened." Her brassy voice filled the void. "There was a goddamn fracking spill. Now, who's in charge here?"

Corky squeezed her hand. Sloane would take care of him. The white guy was attaching a tube to the needle he'd poked into Corky's wrist.

The black fella stepped outside the cubicle and boomed his bass sax: "Code Yellow, Code Yellow." When he stepped back inside, the white guy with the close-set eyes reminded him that the first rule in the emergency manual was not to yell the codes.

"Well, forgive me all to hell. You aren't the one had his face right next to those nasty boots a minute ago."

"Wuss."

"Who you—"

Dr. Bissett silenced their bickering with a sharp look before asking again, "What exactly spilled?"

"Stuff's called FloMoshun," Corky said.

"You know what's in it?"

Corky shook his head and the room spun. Nausea stole any further evasion he might have offered.

The public address system blared: "Attention all staff—respond yellow alert, ER triage, cubicle C. Attention all staff—respond yellow alert, ER triage, cubicle C."

Sloane stroked his cheek. "Honeypot, shhhh, you're hyperventilating. You're gonna be okay, take deep breaths and calm down."

"Where do you work?" Dr. Bissett asked Corky.

Sloane answered for him. "He *did* work at Fairhope Energy. Today was his last day with those jackasses." More people streamed into the tiny room, pushing Sloane aside, insisting she had to leave, but she clung to his hand.

"Who are all these people?" Sloane demanded.

"Chemical emergency team, ma'am, we're evacuating and locking down the ER, you have to leave now." Dr. Bissett turned to the woman who'd cut off Corky's clothes. Her face was hidden by a respirator similar to the one he wore when cutting grass, her body enclosed in a hazmat suit that made her resemble an astronaut.

"Bag those boots and all his clothes," the doctor said while another worker helped her suit up.

Sloane swore she wouldn't leave, but Dr. Bissett stood firm. Maybe the little gal wasn't as inexperienced as Corky first thought—not if she could stand up to Sloane Dumont.

Over the doctor's protests, Sloane kissed his forehead. "I'll be right outside, Honeypot, promise."

While the white guy hung a bottle of fluid over Corky's head, the black guy phoned the fire and rescue squad. "Code Yellow. Chemical spill. You're gonna have to aerate the ER," he said.

Corky moaned. Boomer would have a spaz, and he could be one mean son-of-a-gun when he got riled, especially when he got drunk.

Two

November 15

THE BLAST SHORT-CIRCUITED SUMMER'S MIND, her fingers clutching the sheets. For a second, she smelled blood—Ty's, pouring out of his shoulder where Jake Fowler had shot him. She saw herself standing in her apartment holding a gun, pulling the trigger, watching Jake's blood stain the cream-colored carpet in her bedroom.

Gasping for air, she reared up from the pillow to unfamiliar smells and furnishings. An engine revved outside and she remembered she was in a motel in Ohio. What an idiot she was—the noise, simply an eighteen-wheeler firing its engine in the parking lot.

She raked her fingers through tangled hair, frustrated because she thought she'd left the nightmares behind. Sure, she'd had a couple of panic attacks right after she'd killed Fowler, but they had stopped when she'd moved north five months ago.

Her mother wanted her to see a counselor, but Summer saw no need to wallow around in the dark soil of the past. She'd thrown a wrench at Fowler and kept him from killing her friends. When he'd evaded the police and come after her, she had shot him with his own gun. End of the story.

Yet she knew it wasn't. His life had drained away on her carpet. She had no choice but to tramp back and forth across where his body had lain when she moved out her belongings.

Thinking about those stains, she shivered and rubbed her arms as if that would chase the ghosts away. She grabbed her mobile from the nightstand. Only four in the morning. Early to get up, but she'd never get back to sleep. She switched on the bedside lamp and checked to see if Jennings or his wife had left a voicemail.

They hadn't, but Ty Franceschi had messaged that he looked forward to showing her what real pizza tasted like once she arrived in Clarksburg—instead of that cardboard stuff that passed for pizza in Florida.

She humphed but had to smile. It had been five long months since she'd seen him. She had believed something meaningful was developing between them, but the day before he returned to West Virginia, he had become distant. And though he was cordial the few times they spoke on the phone, he had ignored her hints about getting together. She'd been disappointed, too, that he'd managed to rein in his passion, if he felt any, in emails. Yet on her birthday, a competition Frisbee had arrived special delivery at her dorm room. Swirls of emerald and turquoise decorated the disk. On the underneath, he had written, "This reminds me of your North Florida beaches." The gift, perfect in every way, said that he knew her. She had been captain of the Ultimate Frisbee team in college, could hit targets with almost anything. Her throwing skills had saved their lives once. And if he was thinking about Grayton Beach, he remembered the blissful day they strolled barefoot along the shore, fingers entwined. He remembered those kisses, which for her, had been off the chain.

If she was absolutely honest with herself, part of the reason she chose Penn State for her doctoral work was its proximity not only to the Marcellus Shale Formation, but also to the only man she'd ever loved, and she'd chosen Clarksburg as the base to gather water samples mostly because Ty lived there.

She hurried through the rest of her emails, deleting most, until she came to one from Dr. Claire Dunham, her former thesis adviser at Florida Sci-Tech. Claire hadn't found a job since moving to Boston with her new husband, but she was having a ball volunteering at middle and high schools encouraging girls to take upper level science classes and consider science careers. Dr. Dunham wouldn't have run out on Summer the way Oliver Jennings had. In light of Jennings' odd behavior, Summer wished Claire could replace him as her dissertation adviser. Fat chance the dean would approve of anyone not employed by the university in that role, but at least he had approved Claire as the outside reader on her committee.

Summer considered getting Claire's take on Jennings but held off. First, she owed the man a chance to explain himself. She left him another message, begging him to get in touch.

After a quick shower, she dressed and tossed her backpack into the truck. Soon after dawn, she arrived in Clarksburg and checked into the only motel she could afford. The moldy shower curtain and shabby bedspread sent her scurrying back to the lobby to ask the desk clerk to recommend a good real estate agent. He referred her to PJ Wine. Summer wasted no time in calling.

She explained she needed an inexpensive rental in Clarksburg for the next month while she arranged to assess water quality near fracking sites. Ms. Wine did everything but clap her hands and shout goody-goody. Besides running her own company, PJ Wine explained she served as a Harrison County Commissioner. "My neighbors deserve clean water," Ms. Wine said. They arranged to meet in half an hour in a downtown parking lot.

Hearing the commissioner's resonant voice on her mobile, Summer had imagined a young woman, sturdy and slim, someone fond of flannel shirts and hiking. Instead, the elderly woman in the red coat reminded Summer of a radish. Squat, thick, and rosy in the middle, toothpick legs, and a frothy patch of thin hair on top.

Unfortunately, after visiting five apartments in the space of two hours, Summer hadn't found anything suitable. She and Ms. Wine stood on the crumbling sidewalk in front of the final building, trying to overlook the blue tarp stretched across the roof. The real estate lady looked as disappointed as Summer felt.

"We're gonna find you something, honey. Let's take a break so I can show you a little something of our town," Ms. Wine said. "We'll start with the library since you might need its services as a grad student."

Ms. Wine drove, pointing out various landmarks in an attractive downtown, in particular a statue of Stonewall Jackson on the courthouse plaza. The county library was modern, a brick structure with expansive windows providing plenty of natural light. Once inside, the commissioner slipped out of her red wool dress coat and folded it over her arm. Perhaps in her early sixties, she wore cream stretch slacks pulled high over her middle, with a rose floral top she kept tugging down.

Summer followed the commissioner upstairs to view the computer stations. The half dozen users possessed the glazed-over eyes and slack mouths typical of deep immersion in the online world.

Ms. Wine flicked a hand toward a plumpish woman of middle age. In undertones appropriate for a library, she said, "That lady's learning landman technology. Beginning landmen earn $70,000. With experience they can pull down $200,000 a year."

Landmen were basically door-to-door salesmen, convincing landowners to sign over their mineral rights. Despite the money, the job didn't sound the least bit inviting to Summer. "Hasn't the rush to frack slowed down with the plunging price of oil and gas?"

"A little. Bound to come back up."

Maybe, but companies had already snapped up leases on land likely to be most productive. Summer's cell vibrated. She slipped it out of her coat pocket. Only a text from Dayita. She pictured her friend, legs crossed, the one on top jiggling impatiently, ankle bracelet tinkling, but Summer thought it would be rude to respond while the commissioner was devoting so much attention to her.

Talking incessantly, PJ Wine led the way down the staircase, eyes alternating between Summer's face and the foothold on the next step. The soles of her loafers echoed as sound bounced off the stone floor toward the high ceiling. "I steer a lot of our unemployed citizens toward this online course. They learn basic title research and everything you need to know about leases."

Finally she paused for breath, allowing Summer space to ask a question. "How long does training last?"

"Two weeks."

Summer forced herself not to sputter. The average hydrogeologist only made $49-80,000, maybe $100,000 with an advanced degree and experience. Here she was, knocking herself out to go after a doctorate in hydrogeology and environmental studies—and in a measly two weeks she could become a landman and make more money. The job would suck—but still. She tuned back in to the commissioner, who was slipping her coat on while she walked.

"The demand for a whole range of jobs has shot through the roof because of the oil and gas boom. Makes me wish I was a young woman starting out again. Believe I'd grab a career in energy instead of real estate."

Summer wondered if she'd second-guess her own choices one day. As they walked through the lobby, she tried to imagine herself as an elderly woman. Married to her career—or married to Ty? Useless speculation. She didn't even have a clear vision of where she'd be two or three years from now with the PhD behind her.

Ms. Wine held the door to the street open and Summer slipped past, deliberately expelling a lungful of air just so she could see her visible breath. How cool was that? She managed to suppress a laugh since she didn't want to appear childish. Visible breath wasn't something you often experienced in her hometown in Florida.

Summer could tell there'd be no slowing the commissioner's enthusiasm now. The woman talked so fast Summer couldn't interject a single word. PJ spoke to a lardy fellow in a West Virginia University ball cap, and after he'd passed by, PJ told her the man was a trucker. "There's so many kinds of trucking jobs it boggles the mind. Big tankers haul water, chemicals, and sand to well sites and carry it away after it's used. Eighteen-wheelers drag oil rigs to the sites. Cement mixers pour pads for rigs. There's trucks going every which way."

Estimates varied, but Summer knew trucks made, on average, over a thousand trips to each well, causing serious wear and tear on roads and bridges.

After rushing through descriptions of other jobs the boom was creating, the commissioner pronounced the Marcellus Shale the greatest thing ever for the local economy.

Summer stayed a half step behind on the narrow sidewalk. "For your real estate business, too, no doubt."

"You're exactly right, honey. We never experienced the downturn with the rest of the country when the housing bubble burst. And you can hardly find an empty motel room in these parts."

Tell her about it. Summer wouldn't be surprised if they rented her room by the hour for horizontal dancing. But what would happen now that oil and gas prices were falling so drastically from a flooded market? It didn't look like the Saudis were going to relent any time soon and reduce production. Nor were American frackers.

A steady barrage of cars zipped by, their tires crunching against cinders and salt left behind from treatment after an anticipated early November snowfall that hadn't amounted to anything. A truck chugged along, puffing diesel exhaust into the tainted air hovering over Pike Street. By now the moisture in Summer's nose had actually frozen and her cheeks felt as if tiny needles were piercing exposed skin.

With a flourish of a chubby hand, Ms. Wine directed Summer's attention to an impressive white columned building. Pausing on the sidewalk, the commissioner clasped her hands against her middle and eyed the building with reverence. "This is Waldomore, a jewel in our county crown. When I was a little tyke, the building housed our entire library. It has the most wonderful creaky wooden floors." She turned and headed back the way they had come. "We outgrew the space in Waldomore, so we built the new library. But Waldomore houses special collections you may find useful."

Summer suspected the commissioner couldn't resist showing off the antebellum home. "What kind of collections?"

"The West Virginia collection and the Gray Barker UFO collection."

A laugh rippled up Summer's throat, quickly transformed into a discreet cough. UFO—was that considered science around here? Perhaps Ms. Wine only meant the state collection, which would likely contain the local history of energy exploration.

When the commissioner learned Summer hadn't had a bite to eat yet—and it was nearly one o'clock—she toddled down the sidewalk to The Ritzy Lunch. "Best chili dogs you'll ever eat," she said.

PJ ordered two with mustard only, holding the onions. Summer followed suit but said onions were okay. After all, she wasn't going to be kissing anyone. At least not anytime soon. Thoughts of Ty flitted through her head, but she pushed them away, annoyed that they had surfaced over something as mundane as a chili dog with onions.

After lunch, the commissioner insisted Summer hop back into her super-sized SUV.

She started the engine and set the defroster on high. "I'm gonna introduce you to a happy landowner. He can be the first one you sign up for those water tests you wanna do. This fella's been able to keep his farm because of fracking. The press only tells you about the one unhappy landowner, never about the hundreds thrilled by the benefits gained from selling their mineral rights."

Summer's stomach churned, not because of the chili dogs, but because Dr. Jennings' words were replaying in her head: *We can't afford the slightest appearance of bias. We must ensure science—not greed, emotion, or politics—determines the best procedures in hydraulic fracturing to carry forward.*

The more Summer considered what PJ Wine was offering, the more she felt Jennings would frown on it. She grasped the seatbelt, fighting an urge to unbuckle immediately and end this unexpected side trip. "I appreciate the offer, Ms. Wine, but I have to conduct a random sampling of water located near sites slated for future drilling, not pick and choose landowners because they are happy or unhappy."

Ms. Wine accelerated as they entered the Expressway. "You stop with that Ms. Wine stuff. I'm just PJ. You won't be taking sides at all. Consider this a friendly get-together. Besides, I already told Joe Glover I'd be out to see him this afternoon. His wife was my best friend, and since she passed away four months ago, he's been lonesome. He doesn't get out enough, so I like to check on him once in a while."

Summer relaxed into the comfortable curves of the passenger seat; Glover's name had appeared on the list of landowners in her sample.

"Whether you test his water or not," PJ continued, "is up to you two. Now, you didn't hear this from me, but if you want to get on Joe's good side, admire his remodeling job. Use the word *gorgeous*."

Her monologue continued almost the whole way to Glover's farm. "The Marcellus Shale formation is gonna take this country a long way toward energy independence. We're talking about revolution. A resurrection of American manufacturing, especially plastics. And West, by God, Virginia is gonna thrive at the heart of it."

An odd expression—*West, by God*. She thought West Virginians used it to demonstrate pride in having their own state, to emphasize their historic split from Virginia during the Civil War years.

Anyway, the commissioner didn't need to tell Summer how important the Marcellus Shale Field was. As a hydrogeology student, the opportunity to study the Marcellus is what drew her to the area for her doctoral work. Important or not, recovering the oil and gas would have consequences. "Do you worry about encountering problems like those in Pennsylvania?" No sooner had the words left her mouth, than she wished she could take them back. It sounded as if she were taking sides.

PJ's forehead furrowed. "Coming to the party a little later has its benefits. We can learn from their mistakes."

The road ahead savaged its way through the mountain, leaving barren cliffs on both sides, an abomination Summer was still not accustomed to after months of living among the Appalachians. Once, these mountains had stretched as far into the clouds as the Himalayas. In the 470 million years since their birth, the old crones had shrunk considerably. Like everything else in the universe, they were in the process of dying. A single stream could level a mountain in 500 million years, one spoonful at a time—unless bulldozers and explosives reduced them to rubble in seconds.

It was interesting, though, the way road cuts exposed the sedimentary structures resulting from deposits in stream beds. You could sometimes spot plant fossils and the remnants of early trees in the layered cliffs running alongside the road.

Downshifting, the SUV turned off the asphalt onto a one-lane country road, tires crunching over sparse gravel. A two-foot ditch channeled each side of the road, leaving it devoid of shoulders. They crept along for nearly a mile. As the commissioner rounded the next bend, a two-story white farmhouse came into view. The house sported two recent additions: a single-story wing to the left, and a long L-shape extending from the right. The material and architecture of the additions didn't quite match the central part of the house. On the front door hung a wreath of orange and yellow plastic daisies. A whiskey barrel overflowing with matching plastic flowers guarded the entrance. Hideous as they were, Summer could understand how the short growing season left people hungry for color.

Joe Glover greeted them on the porch, one thumb tucked into an empty belt loop of his jeans. "So you're the scientist—a whaddayacallit?"

"Hydrogeologist." Summer shook his hand, noting calluses, liver spots, swollen knuckles, prominent veins. A hand exposed to sun and manual labor.

He scratched one side of a prominent nose, its hook suggesting American Indian or Italian heritage. "Odd job for a gal, ain't it?"

"More men than women in the field, that's a fact." She handed him a color pamphlet explaining her project.

PJ nudged her with an elbow, and in a fake whisper said, "Thought you had to stick to those random samples you were going on about."

She fake-whispered back that Glover was on the approved list.

If Joe heard their exchange, he didn't let on. "World's changing. Girls don't stick to the kitchen anymore. We weren't blessed with children, but if we had been, I would have encouraged my girl to learn a career. Won't you have a cup of coffee?"

"Thanks, but Ms. Wine was kind enough to buy me lunch, and I don't need a thing." She followed him inside. He tossed her pamphlet on a catch-all table by the telephone. A landline with a rotary dial. She'd only seen phones like that in reruns of old TV shows.

"Doesn't she have the cutest Southern accent?" The commissioner said to Joe, helping herself to coffee.

Summer's lips parted, a protest already formed in her mind, but Joe was faster. "Noticed it soon as she opened her mouth."

She supposed her voice marked her as an outsider. Speech patterns around here had distinctive traits, too.

PJ took cream from a small pitcher in the refrigerator without asking. Obviously she knew her way around this kitchen. She eased into a chair at the table. "You two go on about your business. I'm gonna sit here and check email."

Joe bobbled his head, teasing that the commissioner wasn't half as popular as she let on. To Summer, he said, "Gonna give you the ten-cent house tour. If the Missus was still alive, you'd get the twenty-dollar tour. She was mighty proud of the new additions. Shame she didn't live long enough to enjoy them more." Joe showed off the movie room where a wide-screen television dominated one wall and beautifully crafted oak shelves showcased a collection of porcelain angels. One wall of the new room was nearly all glass overlooking a meadow and hill. It looked as if fracking had paid off big time for the Glovers.

About five-foot seven, Glover was on the short side for a man, but the way he moved reminded Summer of those spry shorties on the basketball court capable of blitzing past taller opponents. He trotted her back through the remodeled kitchen, dressed out with black appliances that sparkled like polished onyx. He smiled at her expectantly.

"This kitchen is even prettier—more gorgeous—than the ones in ladies' magazines," she finally offered, but how would she know? She only read popular periodicals when stuck in the waiting room at the auto repair shop. The whole nesting obsession other girls enjoyed didn't interest her much.

"My wife would be so tickled to hear that. She designed it all herself, and I built all the cabinets right in here." He held a door open so she could enter the L-shaped wing, which housed a workshop full of woodworking equipment. The far side of the space was a two-stall garage.

"The sale of my mineral rights paid for most of this equipment and all the remodeling," Joe said.

As she stepped over a pile of sawdust and the hose of a wet-dry vac, the pungent odor of gasoline and dried grass clippings loosened Summer's moorings. She detested the smells, which reminded her of the shed where Jake Fowler had held Dayita hostage. She had to quit dwelling on that stuff—what the devil was wrong with her? Despite the cold, sweat beaded on her forehead as she stared at the shiny wrench hanging on the pegboard in front of her.

"Ms. Cassidy, you all right?" The words drifted in from far away.

The wrench dangled so close—another inch and her fingers would close around the handle.

"Ms. Cassidy?"

She gripped the edge of the workbench. Her first landowner encounter—and here she was jeopardizing its success. Joe Glover would think she was a total ditz.

She let go of the workbench and shook off the jitters. "Yes, sir, I'm fine."

"Good, we're gonna ride out to my back pasture so you can see where the drill site's gonna be." Joe tugged rubber boots over his shoes. "I'm glad PJ brought you out here. See, fracking's getting a bad rap. Fairhope Energy has done my family a world of good. Many a year we teetered on the brink of bankruptcy till this windfall came along. You can set the record straight."

His expectations anchored her on familiar ground. "I'm a scientist, not a reporter, Mr. Glover. My dissertation will involve testing water near drill sites. The only way to scientifically assess environmental impacts is by collating samples with the casing and cement standards used for each well, examining the erosion and sediment control plans in place, and the planned disposition of wastewater—"

Joe Glover's eyes glassed over like an alcoholic's on a bender. In Summer's mind she could hear Dayita chiding her: *For crying out loud, don't you dare get into all that syncline/anticline textbook stuff. No one else has a clue what you're talking about.*

She started over. "The only way to prove whether fracking leaves your water as harmless as mother's milk or makes it as cruddy as used motor oil is to test it. Before, during, and after drilling."

"Ain't a bit necessary." Joe pulled on a heavy pair of work gloves and stepped toward the door. "I'd know if my water was bad."

"Maybe, maybe not, but testing's the only way to prove it's safe." Once she had test results for individual sites, she could determine whether particular ground features influenced migration of methane or chemical contaminants. She followed Joe outside. The sky seemed colorless, backlit by an invisible wintry sun. "A solid scientific study could help erase that 'bad rap' you say fracking is getting."

Joe pulled the garage door closed harder than necessary. "You bet it's a bad rap. I'd sure like to get certain people off my case for signing over my mineral rights."

Who were certain people? She supposed neighbors might not want fracking operations near their property even if Joe didn't mind having it on his. She lengthened her stride to keep up with him. "Do we have time to ride out to the drill site? Ms. Wine is waiting—"

"It's not far, and don't you worry—that old gal likes to yak all day on her fancy smartphone. Don't mean anyone wants to listen to her." Joe winked to emphasize he was joshing a longtime friend.

Her mobile vibrated, but she ignored it. Probably Dayita again.

A gate wide enough to accommodate farm equipment groaned as he swung it open. Patches of bare metal shone through the faded paint on the metal bars. Joe latched the gate behind them and headed into the new barn. "Hope you don't mind—I'm gonna take care of my chores on this little tour." He slung a plastic bucket labeled protein supplements onto a wooden trailer attached to his tractor, then tossed a dozen bales beside the bucket. He wiped his hands on his pants and told her to hop on the trailer.

As Summer settled in, musty straw prickled through her jeans. Occasionally the trailer wheels bumped over rocks, jangling her bones. The tractor groaned up the first hill. Hereford cattle mooed and drifted toward them.

They stopped beside a pond nestled in the valley. Joe scattered the hay and sprinkled powdered supplements on top, while responding to her volley of queries about bovine care. With what he called a metal spud bar, he broke up thin ice along the pond's edge. Already, cows were congregating near the feed.

Summer studied the slope of the land. "In addition to your well, I'd like to test the pond."

He refastened the spud bar to the trailer with bungee cords. "Shouldn't be a problem. You can walk back here any time."

One landowner's permission down. Only ninety-nine more, and her dissertation would be on its way.

The tractor rumbled to life. They cut across a meadow, then veered onto a narrow trail ribboning through deciduous trees, bare of leaves. Summer smelled smoke and heard a faint buzz. The droning grew increasingly shrill as they rambled through Glover's rear acreage. Abruptly the trail intersected with an access road covered in chunks much larger than regular gravel. Piles of trees and brush smoldered alongside the road. Joe stopped on the hilltop where several acres had already been flattened. They got off to walk around. A pall of ash and dust hung in the air. Stakes marked about seven acres for demolition. Beeping as it backed up, an earth mover positioned itself behind yet another pile of debris. When the chainsaw operators finished, this mountain would be emptied of every living thing—except men and their machines.

"Them yellow stakes," Joe pointed about a quarter mile away, "are where the drill pads gonna go. They tell me they tunnel down about seven thousand feet, and then shoot out horizontally in parallel lines about a mile long, like the tines on a pitchfork."

Summer surveyed the devastation. So, this was the Marcellus Shale Formation. Over 350 million years ago, a shallow inland sea covered the spot where she stood. Over time, sediment and organic matter compressed and heated deep within the Earth, gradually transforming into the natural gas everyone was fussing about today.

About half a mile distant, Summer noticed a spacious log cabin with floor to ceiling windows nestled into the valley below the drill site. On one side of the house, thin fingers of mature pines cast long shadows on an amoeba-shaped pond fed by a shallow creek. She couldn't imagine a more delightful site for a home.

Except for what was happening on this hill.

Indicating he was ready to leave, Joe gave her a hand climbing back onto the trailer.

"Who owns that cabin?" she asked.

Every trace of friendliness left his face. "My brother."

That must be the E. L. Glover on her possible test list. "He's okay with the drilling?"

"It's my hill." Joe stomped to the front of the tractor and fired the engine. "I can do any goddamn thing I want with it."

Summer supposed she knew the identity of at least one of the "certain people" giving Joe a hard time over fracking. They better not try to drag her into their feud.

~

A MOUSE-LIKE DISTURBANCE near the door drew Boomer Walsh's eyes away from his breakfast sandwich. Holly Stone stood there, dangling the morning newspaper from one hand, tapping lightly with the other—though Boomer had assured her on several occasions she didn't need to knock when it was open.

"Come on in, Holly, a good-looking young lady shouldn't be so shy." She seemed to cringe. He didn't know what to make of his new secretary.

"About the morning paper, sir? You asked me to let you know if anything might concern the company?"

Her inflection lifted on the last word of each sentence. Everything a question. Boomer felt sure she would grow more confident after a few more months on the job. He smiled encouragement and held out his hand to receive the paper.

Right away he zoomed in on the story Holly wanted him to see. The spill made the front page. What a crock—if Corky Rogers had elevated liver levels, it was because he drank too much. FloMoshun wasn't on his body long enough to damage a skinny ballerina let alone a big hulk like Rogers. Boomer ought to know—hadn't he gotten soaked himself hosing the big idiot down? Hadn't Corky insisted on driving himself to the hospital?

This country didn't operate fair anymore. The ones at the top were always trying to hold guys like him down. Guys who worked hard for everything they had. Unlike the former publisher of the newspaper, Arnold T. Corbett, Jr., who had inherited coal mines from his daddy. Unlike Arnold's son, Kit, who had the keys to Corbett Energy handed to him. Boomer would be glad when he'd paid back the money Kit loaned him to buy controlling interest in Fairhope Energy. Once Boomer owned the company free and clear, none of these rich bastards could thumb their noses at him. Hell yes, his fingernails were dirty. He worked for a living.

He continued to read the story until he came across a quotation from Corky's fiancée, Sloane Dumont. What on earth did she see in that big lug? For years she'd cut Boomer's hair, and for years she had turned him down no matter what invitation he issued, and he'd issued plenty before he married Nadine.

Last night Sloane had the nerve to call and say Corky quit. She hung up before Boomer could get a word in edgewise. The wuss didn't have the balls to quit himself. Had his fee-awn-say do it for him.

"If he'd kept his mouth shut about the spill—caused by his own incompetence—Fairhope wouldn't come off like a villain," Boomer said to Holly.

She poured coffee into the over-sized travel mug Boomer favored and tightened the lid. "Surely everyone knows we're not the bad guys?"

Boomer turned to the inside of the newspaper where the spill story continued. The article rehashed Fairhope's sins before Boomer had taken over the company, especially details of that explosion that burned three workers back in 2012. The story circled back to yesterday's spill. "Listen to this: 'Providing appropriate treatment to Rogers has been complicated by Fairhope Energy's refusal to release a complete list of chemicals used in FloMoshun, according to Ty Franceschi, CEO of a well-known nonprofit environmental group.'" Boomer snorted. "Imagine calling that fella a CEO. It's downright funny."

Holly frowned. "Why's that?"

"His organization has all of one employee—himself," Boomer

said. "Fairhope has over a hundred full-time and many other contract employees, and we're growing all the time, but the reporter gives our comments equal weight. I thought once I'd explained that the spill hadn't amounted to a hill of beans, she'd drop the story and find some real news to write about."

But no, she'd reached out to the most radical environmental activist in the area, trying to make a big deal out of nothing. He wished he could discredit Franceschi, but saying anything bad about a decorated wounded vet would only add to Boomer's PR nightmares.

Well, at least now he had ammunition, in case Old Lady Kirby complained about her water tasting funny again. It wasn't Fairhope's fault, thank you very much. Another company's rig operated closer to her property than Fairhope's, but he had agreed to go halves with them on bottled water for her. Call it good public relations.

And now Boomer held the proof in his hands that Fairhope's closest rig to Mrs. Kirby's water was hunky-dory, thanks to blowing a wad on filet mignon and top shelf bourbon at the Wonder Bar last night to entertain Freddy Chambers. Boomer had plenty of reasons to keep Chambers happy. Five million reasons—the number of shares Boomer had purchased to become majority owner of Fairhope Energy after Harewood's death. Chambers inspected wells for the Office of Oil and Gas, a division of the Department of Environmental Protection in West Virginia.

Following dinner, Boomer had written a thousand-dollar check to Chambers' daughter as a wedding gift. So when Boomersuggested to Freddy he should find a way to misplace the previous inspection paperwork for one Fairhope well, Freddy hesitated less than half a second before signing his name to the new papers Boomer laid in front of him.

With studied nonchalance, Boomer slid the stapled document across the desk. "Holly, got something here for you to file."

She left with the papers, but returned shortly, her forehead corrugated. "Sir, I file documents by date? Should this be filed by today's date or the date it says this inspection took place?"

"The date it took place would be fine."

Holly's mouth formed an "O," then closed. She looked as if she might leave, but instead asked, "On the outside of each folder, you know I keep a list of the documents inside?"

When she hesitated, Boomer raised his eyebrows, prompting her to finish. "The folder says we already have an inspection on that site, but, well, could something have happened to the document? Because I can't find it."

Sometimes Holly could be too damned efficient. "I spilled coffee on the original, so I had Mr. Chambers sign a new one."

Finally she left to do as he asked. He should have filed the damn thing himself, but what else was he paying her for?

Boomer grabbed his hard hat, ready to ride out to the Glover job site, but as soon as he stepped outside, a man he didn't recognize blocked his path.

"Boomer Walsh?" he said.

"Yeah?"

The man slapped an envelope in his hand. "You've been served."

~

JOE GLOVER FLICKED HIS FINGERNAIL against the caterpillar creeping along his front porch railing. "You got the blackest, thickest coat of any woolly worm I've ever seen, little feller."

With purpose, he strode to the barn and opened the doors wide. Cows moseyed inside, a few mooing appreciation for nighttime shelter. A terrible hard winter was coming, for sure—the woolly worm never lied. Neither did the once-broken bone in Joe's left hand. It had been aching for weeks now. The weatherman was predicting only seventeen degrees overnight.

Joe fired up the tractor and headed for the site being cleared for drilling. As the tractor lumbered up the hill, he noticed that grind in the engine again. Either it went into the shop for repairs, or he was going to have to buy himself a brand new machine. He passed by the fields he usually planted in potatoes, beans, tomatoes, squash, and cucumbers. No more, he thought, not without his wife to can or freeze the surplus. No more wild strawberry, raspberry, and blackberry jam either. He wasn't eating as much anyway. What was a meal if you couldn't share it with someone else—even if you'd been married so long you had little conversation other than giving thanks for the food?

On top of the ridge, Joe could make out Boomer Walsh's black SUV parked next to a pile of smoldering brush. Excellent. Now he could get some real answers. Seemed like this whole project was moving along mighty slow. Down at the feed store, he heard one of the neighbors got $8,500 for the first month of drilling. That kind of cash would come in handy if he decided to buy that beaut of a John Deere he'd been eyeballing.

Leaving the tractor beside Walsh's vehicle, Joe crossed the barren ground on foot. Walsh and a bunch of other men stood around yakking. An earth mover sat idle. Not a lick of work going on.

Walsh frowned as Joe approached. "You aren't supposed to come up here."

Heat crawled up Joe's neck. If that didn't take the cake. "Why not? It's still my land."

"Don't go getting your dander up. We don't want anyone wandering around where they might get hurt."

The other men, all wearing hard hats, stared at Joe with unfriendly faces. He felt like an intruder, not part of the tribe.

"I want to know when the drilling's gonna start. When am I gonna see one of those royalty checks you promised?"

Walsh put his hand on Joe's shoulder and tried to herd him toward the tractor as if he were a stupid cow. "We were supposed to pour the pad this afternoon, but we've run into problems."

"Like?" Joe asked.

"Your little shit for a brother filed a temporary injunction claiming our survey stakes are actually on his land, but don't worry. We'll get it straightened out."

Joe stomped his boot into the dirt. He should have guessed.

His parents had always been "Early this" and "Early that," holding him up like the family trophy. Their college-educated son. So what? His nose was always buried in a worthless book. Never done a hard day's work in his life.

When Early had come home from college one Christmas, he'd stolen Joe's girl, the one he wanted to marry. Didn't love her—stole her out of spite. Joe had followed them to the drive-in, watched the windows steam up. He could never have held her in his arms again after that, could never have forgotten what happened in that back seat. But the memory of his fingers trailing through Lacey's silken hair still could make Joe tremble, even after all these years.

He had married Barbara, a fine Christian woman, and they'd had a good life, but she did not have silken hair and they had not been blessed with children. All that amounted to nothing next to the way Early screwed Joe out of the deal of a lifetime. He'd worked so hard to cobble together a consortium of neighbors to negotiate a better deal with the oil companies. They could have bargained as a group, gotten much more for their mineral rights, but Early had to spoil it. He wouldn't sign on and even talked others out of the deal.

His brother was nothing but trouble. Always had been. Always would be.

~

WHEN SUMMER INSISTED SHE NEEDED To find a cheap rental that very day, PJ Wine reluctantly mentioned a hunting cabin right outside of town that had belonged to her father.

"No one's lived there for the past five months," she said, "and it's really not suitable for a young girl."

This attempt to reduce girls to weaker-sex status ignited Summer's inner rebel. "Let's go look at it."

The two-room cabin was partially furnished, a boast earned by a saggy plaid couch, olive green easy chair and ottoman marred by two prominent cigarette burns, and a sad double bed and chest of drawers. A spider had established squatters' rights inside a shower stall the size of an upright coffin.

The kitchen had a set of melamine dishes and a couple of chipped coffee mugs—enough gear that Summer wouldn't have to move more of her own belongings down from storage at Penn State.

An ax was propped beside the fireplace, prompting visions of cozy embers on cold nights.

She squatted to inspect the telephone and TV receptors on the wall. "You sure there's broadband service out here?"

Taking one step back, PJ seemed to take offense at the question. "Course there is. This city's a certified business location."

"I'd like to explore the property," Summer said.

PJ's eyes cut to her own shiny loafers, a regretful look transforming her face for less than a second before the professional smile returned. "Sure, we can do that."

"No need for you to come along. I'll be back in a jiffy."

Summer wandered through the open door onto the buckled porch boards and hopped down the steps, avoiding the third one, a victim of wood rot or termites. She trekked to the cabin's rear, rustling through masses of fallen leaves. A wisp of red flashed by and settled on a barren branch—a cardinal. She smiled.

The thinnest of melodies trickled through the chilly air like distant song. She stood still, peering through the denuded woods. About a quarter mile away, a sliver of a creek meandered through the trees, disappearing from view as the terrain dropped away. It likely fed into the larger stream she'd noticed beside the road on the drive over.

She jogged back to the porch. "I'll take it."

PJ's eyebrows steepled. "Gonna be hard getting in and out when it snows. County won't maintain the road way back in here."

"My trucks a four-wheel drive. It can handle a little snow." It had to be less than half a mile to the highway. How difficult could that be? Besides, the rent was cheap. She needed to wrap up this chase after a rental unit so she could line up landowners. She signed a contract, handed over one month's rent, and PJ drove her back downtown to retrieve her truck.

They shook hands in the parking lot, but before Summer could leave, PJ fished around in her pocketbook and came up with a notebook. "I've got some more contacts lined up for you," she said.

Bless PJ's heart, she meant well, but she didn't know jack about scientific studies.

PJ scribbled something on the top sheet, ripped it off, and gave it to Summer. "Talk to Kit Corbett. Local fellow using top-notch drilling practices and a good man all around. Tell him PJ sent you."

Summer pocketed the info with thanks.

"Check out Fairhope Energy, too," PJ said. "They do a lot of work in this area."

Summer held onto her smile, though her lips ached from the effort. It would be difficult to maintain objectivity where Fairhope was concerned. That company had been a subsidiary of Harewood Energy, the folks who'd worked relentlessly against her research in Florida. But Fairhope had been sold off, and she supposed it wasn't fair to blame whoever ran the company now for Harewood's unscrupulous behavior.

Waving goodbye to PJ, Summer pointed the truck toward the motel. At the last minute, she executed a right turn without signaling, earning a honk from the car behind her. Turning like that was stupid. Where she was going was even stupider, yet she didn't seem to be able to stop herself from cruising past Ty's apartment building. She nearly missed the red brick structure because it had appeared tan on Google maps.

The sidewalk was deserted, but she spotted his van angled into one of the spots designated for the building. She was glad he wasn't outside, because she had no rehearsed speech to explain how she managed to find herself on his street like a foolish schoolgirl with a crush. For now, she would have to hold onto the implied promise in his last email: that he would take her out for pizza. Not the declaration of undying love she'd hoped for, but at least he hadn't written her off completely.

At the end of the block, she braked to a rolling stop and hurried toward the motel. As Summer gathered speed on the highway, the truck developed a severe case of hiccups: accelerating, and then stopping in a series of jerks. Before the trip north, she'd bought new tires and replaced a broken door latch and an exhausted battery. What else was the ancient beast going to demand to stay on the road? Her speed fell to twenty miles per hour, and the engine sounded like an out-of-balance washing machine. The car behind her blew its horn and hurtled past. The driver shot her a bird. She returned the kindness. Finally, she accepted that the truck wasn't capable of limping into a service station. Eventually she located a shoulder wide enough to pull off the road and searched for a tow service on her mobile.

"That'll be $70—how do you want to pay?" the man on the line said.

She couldn't afford this extra expense, but she had no choice but to pay. She read him her charge card number and arranged for the cheapest rental available, a rear-wheel drive Chevy. Nearly three hours later, she transferred belongings from the truck to the rental.

It looked like peanut butter sandwiches for the rest of the week.

A little past two in the morning, Summer finally made it back to the motel. Exhausted, she fell asleep in her clothes.

~

Hard hat dangling against a lean thigh, Boomer Walsh closed his eyes and kneaded the back of his neck with his free hand, the crewcut stubble prickling against his fingers. The day had started off rotten with that newspaper story on the spill and gotten worse with that injunction. Joe was ticked off, of course, whining about royalties. But what was Boomer supposed to do? He was only going ahead with the well on the Glover site as a favor to PJ Wine. Well, that, and the geologist was so sure the site would be the most productive in the region.

Glover's was the only new well Boomer planned to bring online right away. Oil prices were too depressed to make additional new investments feasible. When the price per barrel hit $112 in June, Fairhope Energy's books looked fantastic, but this month the price had plummeted to $62 per barrel and suddenly expenses exceeded income, forcing Fairhope to produce all the gas they could nudge from the oldest wells first. It wasn't without risk. The materials used on these conventionally drilled wells weren't as robust as what the company would use to construct ones designed specifically for horizontal drilling, but the old ones were faster and less expensive to bring online. Boomer hoped to add new leases slowly, maximizing early returns. Gas needed to flow into the wells fast, so cash could flow into his bank account even faster. Before Kit Corbett pressed him for repayment on the loans.

As if the injunction weren't trouble enough, Joe Glover told him a bunch of hoity-toity academics wanted to test water—not only water wells, but lakes, ponds, creeks. Boomer had countered by having Holly email an offer to landowners for free tests. If any wells tested positive for contamination resulting from drilling, Fairhope would deliver free bottled water. In return, landowners agreed not to have their water tested by other entities. That way Fairhope could control which labs did the testing and manage any negative results—not that Boomer expected any.

For ten hours, Boomer had been on one job site or another today handling problems. Made a fella thirsty for a beer. Or hungry for a big rack—either deer or dear would do. Until he thought of Sloane Dumont's rack and his smile turned upside down.

When he'd gone to get a haircut around lunchtime, he'd asked Sloane how Corky was doing and she seemed friendly enough. Boomer figured Rogers couldn't be too sick if his fee-awn-say had gone into work. Halfway through the haircut, Sloane dropped the comb. She leaned across his body to pluck a replacement from a Barbicide container and had practically stuck her boob in his mouth. What normal man could resist squeezing a cantaloupe that size? She kicked him out of her salon without even finishing his haircut, said she'd rat him out to his wife if he ever came near her again. He might be a fool for big tits, but not foolish enough to argue with a scissor-armed bitch.

That didn't stop him from imagining a different ending, though. Like shoving Sloane Dumont against the wall and showing her what a real man felt like. Something she'd never learn from that fat slob Corky Rogers. Her loss.

Boomer scraped his fingers across his scalp one last time and resettled the hat on his head. Time to head home. If it weren't for the temporary license in his wallet—the result of a cop trying to act like a big shot by issuing a DUI—he'd head for a bar instead. He wasn't looking forward to a confrontation with his wife. In this small town full of gossips, Nadine might get wind of the incident at Sloane's salon.

He strode across the gravel toward his SUV. At the sound of a motor approaching, his steps slowed. He groaned when Kit Corbett's vehicle appeared under the bright spotlights. What the hell? Corbett had never visited one of Fairhope's sites before.

The sooner Boomer got this over with, the sooner he'd get a beer. "Kit," he said as the big money man got out. Corbett ignored Boomer's outstretched hand. Wuss didn't like to get his hands or his spit-shined shoes soiled.

"I've been trying to track you down for hours, Boomer. Why didn't you answer your cell?"

Boomer glanced at his passenger seat, where he'd tossed the phone after the battery had died.

"Sorry. Must not have heard it." Besides, Corbett might have loaned him money, but that didn't give him the right to expect Boomer to be at his beck and call.

"Why on earth did I have to learn about a spill from the newspaper instead of you?" Corbett asked.

What—was Boomer supposed to let Corbett know every time a problem arose? The man gave him a business loan, which would be repaid with interest. It wasn't like they were best buds.

Boomer whipped off his hat and propped it against his belt

buckle. "Rogers drove himself off the site. More cold from being hosed off than anything else. No big deal."

"A big enough deal they locked down the emergency room and called in the fire department to handle possible contamination. The hospital is calling all the local oil companies requesting the chemical composition, which you know I can't reveal under contract agreements with FloMoshun. This is going to hurt all of us in the business, Boomer, not just your company."

"Sorry. Thought I'd handled everything when I gave Rogers a check for his medical bills."

"You'd better notify the EPA right away. Get ahead of the blowback bound to hit from this incident."

Corbett could bring the EPA down on his own head if he wanted to, but Boomer would bear the brunt of their ire. No way was he notifying those Muthas.

"So how's Rogers?" Boomer asked.

The harsh spotlights made the lines of Corbett's face appear hard, and his eyes even harder. "A decent human being would have already checked on him," Corbett said.

It took every ounce of restraint Boomer possessed not to punch that self-righteous prig's face in. Some people had to work for a living. Besides, he had checked on him. He'd asked Sloane.

"Rogers is improving," Corbett added. "They'll monitor his liver levels again tomorrow. If he continues to improve, they may discharge him the following day. When I called half an hour ago, he was sleeping and his girlfriend said she didn't want to wake him up."

If the hospital planned to discharge Rogers already, why was everyone making such a fuss? Though aggravated, Boomer tried to sound sincere. "That's good."

As soon as oil prices rebounded, Boomer was going to pay off all his loans and stuff a bank account so full of money it would make Corbett look like a lightweight. Boomer couldn't wait for that day. The first thing he would do: tell Kit Corbett to kiss his ass.

3

November 16

SUMMER FELT AS IF SHE'D ONLY BEEN ASLEEP a few minutes when a call from the garage woke her. Still groggy, she listened to the diagnosis: a clogged fuel pump. She sighed when she heard the repair would siphon another $450 from her bank account. Peanut butter sandwiches might be too extravagant. She imagined a future of microwaved ramen noodles.

As she pushed the plastic-lined motel curtains back, brittle light streamed into the cheerless motel room. She never ever slept in this late, clear evidence of the stress of the past two days.

After she checked out of the motel, she drove to PJ's cabin, where she unloaded her meager belongings from the rental car. She'd only brought essentials along: clothes, computer, the Frisbee Ty had given her.

She still hadn't heard from Dr. Jennings, which alarmed her more than she liked to admit. Requesting immediate reimbursement on her motel room and cabin rental, she emailed him her new address. If she didn't hear from him soon, she would have to contact the dean—a last resort that might harm Jennings' career and their research project.

Munching on a granola bar, she studied Allied Consulting's website, drilling through various menus. Beautifully designed, the site loaded efficiently, yet she was surprised by how little specific information it actually revealed. The website glittered with generalities. If Shakespeare had been around to see it, Summer figured he'd declare it "Full of sound and fury, signifying nothing."

Determined to uncover some specifics, Summer called Allied's contact number, indicating her company would like to engage their services. She hedged on exactly what her imaginary company wanted done. "We're ready to engage your services if your references are acceptable," she said. "I'd like to contact a few recent clients."

She was placed on hold. An office administrator came on the line to explain the company strove to protect the identity of their clients and the nature of work performed for them. "Industrial espionage is rampant, today, Ms.—what did you say your name was?"

"Doesn't matter. I don't think we're going to be able to do business together. We don't hire any firm without references."

"We offer a money-back guarantee if you aren't satisfied with our work. Which of our services do you require?"

Summer disconnected. Too bad she hadn't been able to learn more about Allied Consulting's client list. Still, nothing about the company Elliot Ral worked for triggered alarm bells.

She no sooner hung up than the garage called again. The fuel pump clogged because the gas tank had rusted. The mechanic had to flush out the whole system. The good news? They didn't have to replace the gas tank. They could spray special gunk inside to seal it better than new. The whole operation would only cost a thousand bucks.

Frigging truck wasn't worth that much.

When the mobile trilled again, she winced. Surely the garage couldn't have found something else wrong already. The familiar number on the screen triggered memories of walking the trails at O'Leno State Park and crossing the dunes at Grayton Beach State Park, hand in hand. Ty Franceschi's simple "Hi" sent tingles from her thighs to her throat, a sensation the scientist in her dismissed as a flood of chemicals set off by the timbre of his voice. Not magic, just biology.

"I'm so glad you're in town." Ty's tone conveyed relief, rather than desire to cover her body with love bites, much to her disappointment. "You know where the university hospital is?"

Summer's heart raced. "What's wrong?"

"You need to drive up here. Morgantown's about forty-five minutes up the interstate. There's someone you should see."

Summer sucked in her bottom lip. "Want to give me a hint what this is about?"

"It's important or I wouldn't ask. I'll be waiting at the main entrance of Ruby Memorial." She could imagine his eyes darkening, the way they did when he went into Navy SEAL mission mode. No nonsense.

On the drive to the hospital, her mittens skated around on the steering wheel so much she finally ripped them off. Better to suffer the cold than wreck. As she pulled into a parking place, she spotted Ty waiting under the covered walkway.

When she got out, bitter wind blasted her face and made her eyes water. She turned up her jacket collar and dashed across the asphalt.

He wore a heavy navy parka and Steelers baseball cap. She drank in the familiar details: broad shoulders, trim jean-clad hips, the hint of beard. He looked good. Too damn good. The magnetism she felt at seeing him again exerted a pull so intense, she was certain they would be drawn together.

Instead, he blinked, took a step backward, and gave her a quick hug with plenty of air between their bodies. "Good to see you again, Summer."

"You, too." Lame, but she had to say something to mask her disappointment.

Casually, he steered her toward the automatic doors, stepping aside to let her go first, even though the entrance was wide enough for three to pass abreast. Gentlemanly reflexes, she supposed. Or an excuse to keep his distance from her.

Once inside, Summer rubbed her hands together to generate heat. "What's with the urgent message?"

He explained while they waited for an elevator. "A friend of mine was involved in a fracking spill."

His words scraped out her insides, leaving behind a hollow shell, where loss echoed in an empty chamber. He was going to ask for a favor, pick her brain, use her.

The elevator doors whooshed closed. A familiar half-second of inertia told Summer they were ascending. The doors slid open and she followed a half step behind him. They turned a corner and traveled a long corridor, turned again, and walked what seemed like a quarter mile but probably wasn't. When Ty pushed open the door to a private room, a bear of a man lying in the bed startled awake. Yellow stained the whites of his eyes. His skin was jaundiced too.

"Summer, this is Corky Rogers," Ty said, adding to Corky,

"Summer's the hydrogeologist I told you about."

"Nice to meet you." Corky fumbled with the remote control and raised the head of his bed. "Thanks for talking to that reporter," Corky said to Ty. "She's going to get this into the paper, right?"

"First piece ran yesterday morning, and Alexis said she'd keep the follow-ups coming as long as her editor would allow it." Ty pulled a chair up to the bedside, offering it to Summer but she took a seat further from the bed. "How you doing, big guy?" Ty asked.

"Better, they tell me. I want to go home."

One corner of Ty's mouth lifted in that familiar half-smile. "I bet you do. That's one beautiful lady you're engaged to."

Corky smiled. "I'm a lucky man."

"You are, my man, you are. And lucky to be alive after what happened. I want you to share your story with Summer."

The details of his accident gave Summer goosebumps, especially the part about being sprayed down with cold water. Even grimmer was Corky's description of the vomiting and subsequent swelling. Since Summer didn't know how large he was before, it was difficult to judge how much of the hump beneath the sheet was extra bloating, and how much simply his previous girth.

"I felt like I couldn't breathe, kind of like I was drowning from the inside," Corky said. "Our local hospital life-flighted me here."

"Liver damage caused by chemical poisoning?" Summer asked.

"Yeah, they've done hemodialysis and whole bowel irrigation. I'm a whole lot better, but they say they're flying blind because they don't know what chemicals I was exposed to." A slight tremor of the bottom lip revealed his fear. "They don't know if down the road I'll get cancer."

Ty stood and paced the floor. "No one wants to take responsibility. The fire department aerated the ER, but says the incident wasn't significant enough to trigger a report. I called OSHA, and they said Fairhope didn't report a work-related accident. The Environmental Protection Agency said they have no record of a spill."

His voice had ballooned way above the volume acceptable for hospitals.

A custodian, pushing a buffer along the linoleum corridor adjoining the room, paused, no doubt weighing whether he should send for security.

"Did the hospital ask the drilling company what chemicals are in FloMoshun?" she asked.

Ty's fists clenched. "Yes, but what they provided was incomplete. They claim they have the right to withhold trade secrets because it would hurt their ability to compete."

She winced. He referred to the so-called Halliburton loophole. Energy companies were exempt from the standards of the Clean Water Act and from revealing the composition of fracking fluid.

"Everyone says it's too sad, too bad, nothing they can do." Ty's voice thrashed the air.

"Why'd you want me to come here?" she asked.

"Can you figure out what's in FloMoshun?"

For heaven's sake, she wasn't a chemist. "Didn't the hospital run blood tests?" she asked.

"Sure, but they haven't been able to pinpoint what caused Corky's meltdown," Ty said. "They can't say if there will be long-term effects."

"I might be able to help a little." Locating the composition of FloMoshun would be difficult, but Summer, already pulling her laptop from her backpack, would try.

Natural gas occurred in fractures, in the pore spaces between individual mineral grains. To produce gas commercially, drillers used water under high pressure to form fractures in the rock. The fracking solution usually contained sand or gels to prop the fractures open so gas could move to the well. The trouble was, drillers added a wide variety of chemicals to the water they pushed into the shale. Some, like hydrochloric acid, helped to crack the rock. Chlorides might be used to keep the fluid free of bacteria. Some stabilized the liquid; others kept it from overheating in summer or freezing in winter. Still others prevented scale from forming in pipes or adjusted the pH level of the fluid.

FloMoshun, according to the company website, was a proprietary phosphate ester capable of increasing well production up to thirty percent. One in five of the 84,000 chemicals used in fracking was exempt under federal law from disclosure of its name, properties, and sometimes even the manufacturer. The identities of the chemicals were known to a handful of EPA employees, who were legally barred from sharing that information with other federal officials, state health and environmental regulators, emergency responders, and the public. FloMoshun, she learned, was one of those protected patents.

Along with typical hype, the website listed methanol and two undisclosed proprietary compounds as ingredients. She jotted down physical properties like freeze point, density, and specific gravity. They might prove useful later on. She wrote down the company's phone number, too, and suggested calling them.

Ty grimaced. "You think they are going to hand over their trade secret?"

"It's worth a try."

She punched in the number. The receptionist passed her on to someone else, who listened to Summer's request and passed her off to a third individual, the official spokesperson.

Summer repeated her request, adding, "Look, the guy in the hospital is really ill. I'm trying to find out if FloMoshun contains ingredients that could be connected to his liver failure. If we can identify the chemicals, we might be able to help him. This poor man's hanging on by a thread, and I know you don't want to let him die without trying to help." She winked at Corky to let him know that she was exaggerating to prod loose the information they needed.

The spokesperson responded with more than a hint of irritation in her voice. "I can't reveal the ingredients because it's against company policy, but of course you have to be careful around it. Anything can be a health hazard. If I ate too much chocolate, that would be hazardous to my health too, wouldn't it?"

Having half a brain ought to be a qualification for company spokesperson. "The patient was involved in a spill of FloMoshun. He didn't eat it, for God's sake. And you'd have to eat one hell of a lot of chocolate to die from it." Summer punched her cell off.

One corner of Ty's mouth lifted. "That went well."

"Very funny."

As Summer's mind returned to the problem, she knew they needed to get their hands on a Material Safety Data Sheet and all the chemicals in FloMoshun. Twenty commonly used chemicals were known to cause acute liver damage, while over a hundred and fifty caused elevated liver profiles.

"What drilling company's involved?" she asked. "They might

be able to tell you the composition."

"Fairhope Energy," Corky said.

Those people again. She remembered Ty had filed a lawsuit against the company for polluting private water wells in Pennsylvania. He'd been arrested during a demonstration for blocking access to their headquarters. And now he was trying to drag her into his vendetta.

"Fairhope isn't gonna tell you squat," Ty said. "They're a bunch of cold-hearted bastards."

Because she was facing the door, Summer was the first to notice a man snailing his way into the room. How long had he been standing there? For an older fellow, maybe late fifties, he was good looking in a rugged way. He held a hard hat in his hands, so Summer assumed he was one of Corky's co-workers. Surprise washed over Corky's face as the man stepped all the way inside.

"Hi, there, big guy," the man said. "How you doing?"

"Better, they tell me," Corky said. "Liver function's improved, but they won't let me go home yet."

"Corky, I'd tell you what was in FloMoshun if I knew," the man said, "no matter what our contract with those people says. I'd tell you, but I really don't know."

"I know." Corky's eyes teared up and he swallowed visibly. "I owe you a big thank-you, Boomer. You probably saved my life, hosing me off fast as you did."

"Not worth mentioning," Boomer said. "I did what anyone would have done."

"No, plenty of guys would have stood around with their fingers up their—" Corky broke off, his eyes shifting toward Summer. "Boomer, you already know Franceschi, but this pretty gal is Summer Cassidy. She's a scientist who's gonna try to figure out what's in FloMoshun. Boomer Walsh is my boss."

Walsh frowned. "Your former boss. Sloane told me you quit. That right?"

Corky nodded, but he didn't look happy about his resignation. "Sorry, Boomer, I gotta file for worker's comp."

Walsh's lips compressed. "I'm sorry too."

His expression denied his words. He was furious, though trying hard not to show it.

Summer could only see Ty's back from where she was sitting, but there was no mistaking the contempt in his voice. "It's awfully nice of you to spare the time to check on your employee, Mr. Walsh. We all know how busy you are tearing up everything that's green and clean in this state."

Ty's blatant hostility shocked Summer. Sure, a coal ash spill near Ty's family's farm was linked to his mother's death from cancer and his half sister's disability, but Boomer Walsh could not be held responsible for crimes he had nothing to do with.

Boomer stiffened and side-stepped to the door. "I hope you get better real fast, Corky. Let me know if there's anything I can do."

Summer didn't blame him for leaving. After that rude display, she was out of here, too. She packed up her computer and stood, refusing to look at Ty. "I'll try to find the composition of FloMoshun, but I can't get involved in any way that compromises my research." She laid her hand on the crisp sheet near the big guy's arm. "Corky, hope they spring you from this place soon."

He tried to smile. "Me too."

Ty rose to leave with her, putting his hand against the small of her back as they moved down the corridor. She edged away. Only an hour ago she'd have given anything to feel his touch. When they got in the elevator, she rammed a fist into his abs, but other than a grunt, more from surprise than pain, he gave no sign of injury.

"What was that for?" he asked.

"You can be such a jerk. That man did a decent thing coming to check on Mr. Rogers, and you attacked him for no reason."

"I had plenty of reasons," Ty said. "You don't happen to know them."

No way was he getting off that easy. "You were inexcusably rude."

They left the hospital. At her rental car, he leaned his backside against the door, effectively blocking her escape. "Summer, did you ever talk to someone, a professional, about the stuff that happened last spring?"

Like she couldn't see right through his tactic. Instead of dealing with his own issues, he wanted to talk about hers. "Nope, you know how I feel about counselors."

"Tougher guys than you—soldiers trained to take lives—have

had issues after actually doing it."

Just because he experienced PTSD episodes didn't mean she had them. He had lost part of a leg in an explosion that killed his comrades. Her situation was entirely different. "I'm fine."

"Think about it, okay? Stuff like this can come back and kick you in the teeth later."

She turned his suggestion around. "You should probably get some counseling yourself. Learn anger management skills."

"Touché."

When he moved aside, she slid into the car, poised to shut the door—after slinging a final admonition his way: "Every human being involved in energy production isn't evil."

A brief mouth shrug served as his response, but he held onto the door, preventing her escape. In an attempt, perhaps, to part on better terms, he tried a safer subject. "So, how do you like Penn State?"

"Fine."

He swung her door back and forth a few inches. "What happened to your truck?"

"In the shop."

He stared at her a few seconds. "Okay then," he said. "I'll be in touch. There's that pizza I promised."

"Fine." She started her engine and he closed the door. Now that he was letting her leave, she didn't want to. She watched him stride away without a trace of unevenness in his gait. He had completely adjusted to his computer-controlled prosthetic. He'd made progress physically, if not emotionally, to the pile-up of tragedies in his life.

She had made progress, too. She didn't need a counselor because work served as therapy. The background research chapter of her dissertation was nearly complete. Now the Christmas deadline to sign up a hundred people for water tests loomed. She vowed the afternoon would not get away from her without making progress toward her goal.

~

FROM HER HOME IN LOBLOLLY LAKE, Dayita Patel had news, something Summer needed to know. Thank goodness this time she accepted Dayita's call. "Helloooo? About time you answered your phone," Dayita chided her friend.

Summer apologized and claimed she'd been busy. To Dayita,

she didn't sound very sorry, but she didn't sound like herself either.

"Yeah?" An explanation better be forthcoming. Like she'd been quarantined after Ebola exposure. Or abducted by aliens.

"My dissertation adviser's gone bonkers, a nasty guy heckled me at a presentation I got conned into doing, my truck died, and it's going to cost a thousand dollars to get it fixed. The Chevy I rented won't cut it on country roads once it snows. I gotta have my truck or there's no way I can get a hundred landowners signed up before Christmas. I'm screwed."

Whoa—Dayita had never known Summer to have a case of the blues. Was she homesick? "If anyone can do it, you can. Have you seen Ty?"

"Yeah." A few beats of heavy silence followed.

Weird—Summer didn't sound the least bit thrilled about being reunited with the first big love of her life. "A date?"

"Not exactly."

"What happened?"

"He had me drive forty miles to a hospital to see a man whose liver was damaged in a fracking spill. Ty wants me to find out what chemicals are in the compound."

Ty's obsession with all things environmental was no secret. "So you feel used instead of loved."

"Yeah."

"You make plans to see each other again?"

Summer sighed. "More of a promise to get together for pizza. *If* he follows through. I blew up because he was rude to a visitor at the hospital, the CEO of Fairhope Energy. You know how intense he gets."

Intense? Anyone willing to live for months with a half sister in a van just so he could shut down an energy company was more accurately described as *fanatical*. Dayita remembered how Ty had pleaded with Summer to work with him at Water Warriors instead of continuing grad school. He didn't know Summer very well if he thought she would abandon her dream of earning a PhD. But he was the first guy Summer had ever fallen for, and Dayita figured disappointment in that relationship was more to blame for Summer's blues than troubles with her old truck. If only Summer were back in Florida, they could meet for a smoothie or spend the evening at the Foos and Booze—anything to cheer her up.

"Can't be all bad up there," Dayita said. "Tell me one good thing that's happened to you."

"Okay, Suzy Sunshine. I signed up a landowner for testing."

"Awesome—you're the rock star of research projects. You'll make that deadline." Dayita hesitated. With Summer sounding so whipped, Dayita hated to dump more bad news on her. Maybe she already knew the skinny on Dr. Jennings—after all, she had called him *bonkers*.

"Summer, have you seen the latest issue of *Trending Times*?"

"Which part of 'I've been busy' did you miss?"

"Aren't we bitchy today? I thought if you were too busy to call your best friend, you probably hadn't read the article on Dr. Oliver Jennings. He's overseeing this project of yours, right?"

"Yeah." Summer sounded scared, as if she already suspected something. During two seconds of silence, Dayita thought she could hear Summer's heart racing.

"What's it say?" Summer asked.

"It pretty much calls him a fraud. I thought you'd want to know."

The *shit-shit-shit* Dayita barely made out was so soft she figured Summer must have moved her cell away from her face. But then Summer was back.

"I gotta read it ASAP. Can you send a link?"

"Sure—working on it now." The article was already open on her phone. She hit SEND. "On the way."

"You're the best. Can you summarize while I wait?"

"The people quoted in the article question Jennings's research methods and hint about his secret ties to a radical underground environmental group."

"That's plain flat-out freaking wrong. His research is solid—and no way is he tied to radicals. Not the way he preached ethics to us. What group—does it say?"

"Unnamed. The article quotes someone who supposedly infiltrated the group and wants his or her identity protected."

"Great. A hatchet job by an unseen assailant. Either Dr. Jennings has experienced a psychotic break or someone's got it in for him. I have to find out which."

"In your spare time."

Summer laughed. "In between signing up ninety-nine more landowners and finding out what's in FloMoshun."

Dayita heard a ping over the phone line.

"Your email arrived," Summer said. "Let me hang up and read it."

"Okay. I'll see if I can find out what's in the compound that spilled—that FloMoshun. If there's anything else I can do to help, say the word."

"Thanks, Dayita. You're the best friend ever."

"I know."

Summer laughed again. A good sound.

Now, time to put her computer skills to work—Dayita couldn't wait to get back in the game. As she fired up her laptop, she wondered if Summer had ever gotten around to installing encryption on her equipment. Dayita emailed her friend another reminder. People outside the security business gave little thought to how vulnerable all their personal information and communications were.

Through regular channels, Dayita was able to learn quite a bit about Signal-Muller Chemical Corporation, the makers of FloMoshun. Founded in 1962, it manufactured and distributed hundreds of chemicals, ranging from cleaning agents like chlorine dioxide to components of polyurethane like aniline. It produced refrigerants, fire suppressants, and of course, the compound Summer was interested in, FloMoshun. In short order, Dayita compiled a list of their board of directors, stock prices, career opportunities, and contact information. She clicked a link "Creating a Sustainable World," laughing out loud as she scanned the overblown hype. Even a child would know not a word of this bull rang even remotely true.

Now for the work requiring her unique skill set. She drove to Tallahassee, a bigger city than Loblolly Lake. At three in the afternoon she entered the Black Dog Café, a small coffee shop nestled along one bank of Lake Ella. It was the kind of place where you weren't likely to find your face on security videotapes.

Over the next few hours, she set up a fake email account and rudimentary website for a nonexistent drilling company. She set up four additional email accounts using fake names and arranged for incoming email to be forwarded from one to the other through an anonymizer. If anyone tried to trace the IP address where this day's work was done, they'd only find the café.

A familiar rush swept over her. God, how she'd missed this. After the university administration learned she'd hacked their server to help Summer expose Harewood Energy's corrupt practices, they'd held up her paperwork. Eventually, they would process her transcripts, but they were dragging their feet while they conducted a "review." The government job she'd lined up wanted the official paperwork in hand—crazy bureaucracy—so her life hung in limbo.

Unless she got tired of waiting.

As Summer Cassidy rounded a curve on the narrow two-lane road, a flagman in an orange vest stepped into the road in front of her. She stomped the brakes, peering into her rear view mirror anxiously. No one better plow into her in this tiny rental car. Since the visit to the Morgantown hospital had consumed her morning, she needed to get cracking on landowner visits, starting with E. L. Glover, Joe's brother.

While she waited at the intersection, she mulled over that article attacking Dr. Jennings. The allegations of ties to radical environmentalists had to be false. She should ask Ty. Being such an activist himself, he might know if Jennings had connections to any groups.

To her right, a tanker pulled out from a dirt road. A second and third emerged. She rolled down her window and motioned the flagman over. "What's going on?"

He rotated his neck and spit out a wad of chew before he leaned toward her window. "Trucks are picking up loads of water."

"Are you county employees?"

"No, ma'am. I gotta get back to work." He strode back to the red stop sign.

A pick-up parked off shoulder sported the Fairhope Energy logo on its door. How odd that a corporation had the right to stop traffic.

Her mirror revealed three cars backed up. Others might remain hidden beyond the bend. Eleven tankers total lumbered out before the flagman let her proceed.

She felt foolish for being surprised by the number of trucks, yet it was one thing to read about fracking in a textbook and another to experience its effects firsthand. The typical well required about three million gallons of water over its productive life, and more than eighty percent was pulled directly from rivers and streams. Nearly all that water was forced deep underground during drilling and remained there, completely removed from the hydrologic cycle. Not a good thing for areas suffering from drought.

The road to the Glover brothers' farms was pitted with potholes. Were they caused by winter freeze and thaw cycles or increased truck activity? As Summer pulled into the driveway, she admired the clean lines of E. L. Glover's two-story cedar cabin. Abundant windows were situated to make the most of the views. Something moved near the pond—not horses, but of a similar size. She parked and slid out of her truck, squinting to make out details. Shaggy. Elongated ear flaps. Llamas! Half a dozen, at least. What were they doing here—didn't they originate somewhere in South America, like Peru?

Hitching her bag to her shoulder, she trotted over to the wooden steps, which were in much better condition than those at her cabin. Before she could knock on the door, it opened.

A male figure stood on the other side, gaunt rather than wiry like his brother. They shared a hooked nose and deep-set eyes. His bushy eyebrows resembled a prickly caterpillar as they crinkled together over the bridge of his nose. "If you're another one of them landmen, you can haul your fanny back to your truck right now. I got a rifle in my other hand, and that's the only answer you're gonna get."

He opened the door the rest of the way. Her eyes dropped from his face to the gun and her breath caught. The man looked down at a tiger-colored dog standing by his stocking feet. It wasn't as big as a tiger, but neither was it small. Its head nearly touched the man's hip.

"Don't bite her unless I say so."

Summer looked into the dog's eyes and her panic evaporated as quickly as it had overtaken her. The dog wasn't going to bite. Something profound dwelt behind those eyes. Checking the man's eyes, she knew he wouldn't shoot anyone anymore than the dog would bite. Nonetheless, face-to-face meetings without a prior phone call might be a bad idea here in West Virginia unless you had a police escort or toted a gun of your own.

"I'm gonna count to three and shoot. One—"

In a breathless torrent her answer poured out. "Don't shoot—I'm not a landman, Mr. Glover, swear to God."

"What do you want?"

"My name's Summer Cassidy. I'm a hydrogeol—" Perhaps this was a good moment to follow Dayita's Keep It Simple Stupid rule. "I'm a scientist trying to make sure fracking isn't harming the local water supply."

Glover's face grew so scarlet Summer took a step backwards—he looked ready to blow an artery. Or a rifle. "Course it's hurting people's water. Tried to tell my fool brother that, but you think he'd listen?"

"No, sir."

"Hell no. He sold those outsiders his rights and they blasted the top of the hill where Joe doesn't have to look at it. Sumbitches are gonna set one of those eyesores right on the edge of my property."

"Yes, sir. I saw where they were clearing the land." She wished he'd put the rifle down. It would make explaining her mission easier. But standing around all tongue-tied wasn't winning her any points. "I am a scientist so I have to stay neutral on the issue of fracking and make objective measurements of its effects. What I'm doing, Mr. Glover, is testing people's water before, during, and after the drilling operation."

She held out the flyer.

He leaned the rifle against the wall and threw the door open wider. "Should have said so right away. Come on in. I'm Early."

Early for what? Summer wished she had better auditory skills. "Excuse me?"

He chuckled. "I love watching the confusion on folks' faces when I say that." He chuckled again. "I'm Early Glover, Ms. Cassidy. Now, get on in here and give me and Wallace a hug."

Hug? A minute ago he was ready to shoot her. Was Wallace the dog? Early ushered her over the threshold and tossed his scarecrow arms around her. Not comfortable being hugged by strangers, Summer stood stiffly, arms pinned to her sides. As soon as possible, she slipped away and followed him into his living room.

Early Glover's furnishings were as modern as the exterior of his home. Leather sectional sofa. Several good reproductions of Impressionist paintings on the walls. Cherry bookcases loaded with volumes, their edges out of alignment here and there. Clearly read, not purchased just to display.

He motioned for her to sit in an ergonomic recliner. Wallace sniffed her boots and licked a shoelace, then a patch of bare skin between her boot and jeans. Absently, she scratched behind his ear. He propped his snout on her thigh and she would have sworn he sighed.

"How odd," Early Glover said.

"What's odd?"

He shook his head as if puzzled but didn't elaborate. "So, you're a hydrogeologist. A fine profession, one of increasing importance around these parts."

"I—" She hadn't finished telling him what her career was. She considered the art, the books, the furnishings, revising her initial impression. Not a redneck. "Yes, I'm working on my doctorate."

He leaned forward. "Really? Where?"

"Penn State."

"Good school. I teach at West Virginia Wesleyan. Philosophy."

Summer couldn't repress a smile. "Which philosophy advocates shooting strangers at your door?"

He cackled. "Gun's not loaded, but playing whack-a-mole with all the salesmen gets tiresome. A new one pops up every day demanding the right to rape my land."

She squirmed in the leather chair, careful not to kick the stack of books on the floor near her foot. This, she realized, was where Early Glover sat when he read at night. His favorite chair.

"The word *rape* is a little harsh," she said.

"The history of this region bears out my view, Ms. Cassidy. Coal and gas operators have always taken what they wanted, grown wealthy at our expense, and left behind a trail of destruction. Drive along our country roads and observe the strip mines."

Curious, the way he switched between backwoods vernacular and formal English with ease. "Natural gas wells aren't quite like strip mines."

Early canted his head to one side. "Not particularly attractive either. This farm has been in our family for three generations. Except for my college years, I've never lived anywhere else—never wanted to. Until now. The racket those trucks make 24/7 is bad enough, but it will only get worse once they start installing the rig."

"I gather the drilling has caused some trouble in your family."

One corner of Early's mouth lifted but you couldn't call it a smile. "Maybe you should ask my brother."

Summer admitted she'd met his brother the day before.

"So, you met Joe. What'd he say?"

She hesitated, opting for a slight edit. "It was his hill and he could do whatever he wanted with it."

Early sighed. "It's a little more complicated. The view, the peace in this valley—they belonged to me. But perhaps it would be more accurate to say I am the caretaker of this land, and it has been completely altered by what my brother chose to do."

"I imagine that makes you pretty angry."

Early's head turned in the direction of the pond and pine trees, clearly visible through his picture windows. "You bet I'm angry. And we can only speculate on how that rig might change my water. They plan to drill right under my pond and there may not be a thing I can do to stop it legally. My lawyer is trying to get another injunction. Our best hope now is proving the company does shoddy work. We already have a deposition from one former employee and I think I can twist the arm of another who finally wised up and quit."

Summer wondered if the one who quit was Corky Rogers. She was no lawyer, but she figured a judge might be inclined to dismiss testimony from a former employee as someone getting revenge against a boss. The more who testified, the more weight the complaints would carry. But what was she thinking? She shouldn't be discussing injunctions and shoddy work.

"I'm sorry, but I can't get involved in legal issues," she said. "I need to stay neutral."

As he stood, his bones cracked and popped. "Please accompany me to the kitchen." Wallace stayed right on Early's heels. Early didn't wait to see whether Summer would follow.

Like the living room, the kitchen was modern: stainless appliances, glass-topped table, a bay window with five exquisite art glass vases, all in different colors and shapes. A shelf with dozens of prescription meds caught her eye. She could make out part of the labels turned toward her. Mitomycin C, Sunitinib, Fluoroura-something-or-other—cancer drugs! She recognized two her grandmother had been prescribed, drugs that had failed to prevent her death. Serious illness explained why Early Glover resembled a coat hanger covered by loose skin, his fat and muscle consumed by disease and the chemicals used to treat it. What kind of cancer? How advanced? Didn't matter. She was here to further her research, not to form personal attachments, but she hated to think of the suffering this man probably faced.

He filled an ordinary juice glass with crystal clear water. "Taste it." As he handed her the glass, she made her expression as blank as possible, masking thoughts of cancer and mortality.

The water seemed colorless, odorless, chlorine and chemical free, but you couldn't judge its quality without tests. She drained the glass and returned it to him.

"That's what I stand to lose once they start drilling on my brother's hill, Ms. Cassidy." He set the glass down. "A group of professors at West Virginia University published an article in the Morgantown newspaper on fracking. They made recommendations for those with wells near drill sites. How often do you think they suggested having your water tested?"

Summer shook her head. "No idea."

"Every day."

Great—and she just drank his water. How many wells were nearby?

His eyes strayed to the kitchen window, peering up the hill to the future drill site. Two plumes of smoke rose from piles of burning trees. "How easy do you think it would be to sell my land after that story was in the paper?" He shook his head. "You can test my water any time." He signed her form. "I own several hundred acres and drillers already have rigs operating around the perimeter of my land, so you can test my pond, the river, and Glover's Lake. The more testing the better."

"Guess the number of rigs nearby explains all the water haulers I saw down the road."

Early Glover's face reddened. "How far down the road? I've chased those truckers off my property two or three times. They've been stealing from my lake and the creek running through the lower acres. Dang, that ticks me off." He paused and seemed to be counting to ten—Summer couldn't be sure. Gradually his face assumed a more normal color. "It takes millions of gallons to run a fracking operation—but you already know that. What you might not know is this: truckers get paid for every tank they deliver. If they can suck up water close by drill sites, they have faster turnaround times. They stand to make more money. Besides the temptation to take water illegally from whatever source is closest, they drive too fast. One of them barreled through town, took a corner too fast and overturned the tanker onto a car. Crushed two children and their mother."

He sighed again as he returned to the living room. Summer followed him and resumed her seat. Wallace nosed her leg, letting her know he would love another round of ear scratches.

"I don't really blame Joe for what he did," Early said, settling onto the couch. "He doesn't know anything but farming, and as he rightly points out, I have my salary from the college. I don't have to make a living from my land. Small farms all across this country are struggling to survive. Most have already been bought out by mega-farms. The money my brother got from selling mineral rights will let him stay on his land, but it won't ever be the same. Fracking will be the end of a whole lifestyle. We are witnessing, Ms. Cassidy, the end of rural America."

Summer thought about the trucks, the access road, the flattened hilltop. But she also thought about the additions to Joe's house, how the financial windfall had already improved his life. "Are you suggesting change is inherently evil?"

"Not at all, but I like to consider all the consequences, both intended and unintended, before making a decision that will alter everything I cherish."

Considering all the books in the room, Summer commented that he cherished reading.

"I cherish ideas, Ms. Cassidy."

They talked about books for half an hour, discovering they shared five or six favorite titles. Summer jotted down the names of two philosophy books he recommended.

Eventually Early led the discussion back to hydraulic fracturing. "Joe tried to build a consortium of local landowners to negotiate a better price per acre. He pitched a fit when I refused to sell my rights. My brother no longer speaks to me, Ms. Cassidy, so I have lost more than my view and quiet life. He can't bring himself to let go of his anger. He's taking my opposition personally. I have forgiven him for the choices he made, even though I intend to use every legal means possible to defend my land."

"If I were in your shoes, I don't know if I could forgive him."

"It takes strength to forgive, but it's the only path to peace. I don't know if you can appreciate what it means to lose a brother—you are still so young—but I can tell you it isn't easy."

Summer's eyes closed. She knew what it meant to lose a sibling. Neighborhood kids splashing each other in a swimming pool, a stray giggle floating from the cereal aisle at the grocers—ordinary occurrences sometimes reminded her of Chrissie and caused the floor of her chest to collapse inward.

Beads of moisture dotted the corners of Early Glover's eyes as he escorted Summer to the front door, his stocking feet whispering against the heart-of-pine floors.

He hugged her. This time, those unshed tears moved her to return the gesture.

"I like you, Ms. Cassidy. More important, Wallace likes you, and he doesn't cotton to many people. I think he's a brindle-coat hound/boxer mix, but he's a rescue, so I'm only guessing. Promise I won't greet you with the gun next time."

She bent down to scratch Wallace's head, surprised by how much she looked forward to another visit. "I'll be back soon."

"You see Joe, tell him 'hi' from me."

~

THE WIND HAD PICKED UP by late afternoon, and the rental car, a lightweight compared to Summer's truck, shimmied every time a vehicle passed in the oncoming lane. She bought groceries, and then stopped at Gabe's, a discount store, where she bought a set of sheets to cover the furniture.

As she turned off the highway onto her dirt road, a family of wild turkeys toddled across the dirt road a few yards ahead of her car. She watched until they disappeared into the woods.

Inside the cabin, she stashed the groceries and tucked the new sheets around the couch cushions.

By phone, she contacted five landowners in her sample. Three gave permission for water testing and provided directions to their homes or offices where she could drop off the release forms. The fourth and fifth hung up on her, mid-spiel. Rude, but she hadn't expected one hundred percent acceptance. The sixth call went straight to voicemail. She got partway through her pitch and the machine cut off. She redialed and left only a callback number.

If the couch could be described as lumpy, the cabin's bed might be described as a trough. No matter where Summer lay, she rolled toward the middle where ancient springs poked like rusty nails through the ticking. In the end, she made a pallet on the floor and turned off the lights.

At first she attributed the noises outside to an over-active imagination, jitters sparked by Dr. Jennings' paranoia. Her cabin was surrounded by woods full of foraging critters. She tried to close her eyes, but they flew open again when she heard a click far too similar to one that had awakened her when Jake Fowler broke into her apartment in Loblolly Lake. *Don't be ridiculous*, she told herself. *It's a critter.* But after a few more clicks and scratches, she turned the lamp on. Arming herself with a chef's knife, she flipped the switch for the porch light. It didn't work. Probably needed a new bulb. She remembered seeing a flashlight in the kitchen drawer closest to the door. She retrieved it, unlocked the door, and stepped onto the porch. The stillness of a wintry night surrounded her. No clicks. No scratches.

Carefully she made her way down the steps. She flashed the light about, but no other vehicles had arrived, no figures lurked in the dark. The flashlight flickered and went out. She smacked it with her hand and it blinked on. Then blinked off. Crap. Didn't anything work right in this cabin?

As she approached the front porch, she froze. Against an ebony sky, a large shape crept along her roof. Closer to her. She held the knife by the dull edge, ready to hurl it at the intruder. The form edged closer and stood upright as the moon peeped out from behind a cloud. Squinting, she could make out a pointed nose and black mask.

She lowered the knife and laughed. "Hey there, Rocky Raccoon. Plenty of room for both of us here but try to keep the noise down, will ya?"

4

November 17

SUMMER SAT IN KIT CORBETT'S TRUCK, wiggling her foot frenetically. To make herself sit still, she uncrossed her legs and planted both feet on the floor mat. If PJ Wine was right, Summer was minutes away from observing one of the best companies working in the Marcellus Shale Formation. Corbett Energy Site 132 was located in nearby Doddridge County.

While Corbett drove, Summer studied him in brief sideways glances. Short dark hair with a touch of gray near the temples. Probably in his thirties. The narrow face and patrician features might be deemed too pretty for a man had they not been balanced by a distinctive brush of eyebrows.

The red drilling rig rose far above the tree line and foretold that they were nearing the fracking site. It looked like something you'd build with an erector set. Or a small version of the Eiffel Tower. Summer shuddered, remembering the piles of smoldering trees all along the approach to Joe Glover's hill. Corbett's company had cleared land for their rig and equipment, sure, but the site didn't look like a bomb had detonated on it.

Trees and understory growth remained in thick masses along Corbett's access road and site perimeter. He pointed out various patches of forest they'd made an effort to retain by shifting the road a fraction here, a smidgen there. "It not only makes good environmental sense; it will make it easier and more cost-effective to reclaim the site when drilling is complete. A year after we cap the well, you will hardly be able to tell we were here."

Summer suspected that was an exaggeration. At the top of the hill, they parked on a massive concrete pad. What became of the concrete after drilling ended? Did they bust it up and haul it away?

She inclined her head toward five tractor trailers to the left of their parking spot and yelled to make herself heard over the noise of compressor engines. "Chemicals?"

"Yes. They're disclosed on our company website and FracFocus. All local hospitals and first responders have been provided with the specifics. We use three basic kinds. Polyacrylamide as a friction reducer. A phosphonate to inhibit scale. And a surfactant, similar to household soap."

The Corbett approach definitely trumped Fairhope Energy's. Summer raised her eyebrows. "No biocide?"

"Bacteria are definitely harmful to any fracking operation. We kill most with ultraviolet radiation. Sometimes we have to use a little iodine, which is less harmful than chlorine. We try to be industry leaders in our methods."

"Diesel?" she asked.

"Absolutely not. No responsible company would use it in fracturing fluid. We don't even use diesel to run the rig engines. We're using liquefied natural gas instead. Why ship it to China when we can use it ourselves?"

That *was* impressive.

As they made their way across the drill pad, he shook hands with and, practically screaming to be heard over the machinery, introduced her to half a dozen men, whose names she promptly forgot. He directed her attention toward three green vertical gas condensate tanks. Metal stairs angled up the first one and a horizontal platform connected the tanks. Corbett elaborated on their function, finishing with a sheepish smile. "Stop me if this is too technical and you don't want to hear it. I tend to rattle on."

Summer returned his smile. "I'm here to learn all I can." And it was a pleasure to meet a man who didn't assume she would be too dumb to understand. She turned her face away from him as she remembered PJ Wine giving her the lowdown on Corbett: *You didn't hear it from me, but Kit Corbett's near about the most eligible bachelor around here.* Everyone assumed at her age she needed to find a husband. Quick—before the good ones were all taken.

"My wells were designed to capture all the methane released during the drilling, rather than burning it off for weeks before production begins like some operators."

"Yes, between 3.6 and 7.9 percent of the lifetime production of shale wells has been escaping into the atmosphere as methane. At least, that's what Cornell professor Robert Howath says." She blushed. Corbett was going to think she was some kind of show-off. Why couldn't she shut up? "Good thing the EPA is now requiring everyone to handle the methane as you are."

"Yes, the EPA." Corbett frowned. "They have good intentions, but won't have the funds needed for adequate oversight and enforcement." He moved farther along the drill pad. "Our geologist mapped this whole area carefully before siting wells. He created a three-dimensional model of the subsurface geology so we could design a safe drilling plan for this specific site."

"I'd *love* to see the model." Oops—her voice sounded too eager, her wording too girly. But Corbett's eyes told her he approved. She had seen models, of course, but this would be real world, not a classroom exercise. When rocks were compressed, they could either bend, creating folds—or they could fracture, creating faults. If geologists mapped out the underlying rock carefully, they could help a driller find the oil and gas while avoiding the underground water.

"When we're done here, I'll take you back to our main office. The model is on display there."

He pointed out a panel of gauges. "We continuously monitor pressure and injection rates. There's also a webcam here, so back in the office we can see in real time exactly what's happening on the drill site. I can even check activity from my cell." He sounded like a kid with the best Christmas toys ever.

Finally he stopped in front of the one rig currently operating, leaning his palm against it. "The well housing itself is triple-cased in concrete extending over a hundred feet below the water table. I never want to find out Corbett Energy has contaminated our neighbors' water wells. My name and reputation are on the line."

"I can see you've made a real effort to use best practices." Of course he could talk a good game and turn into an ass when no one was around to impress. But he seemed like the real deal.

"One thing you haven't mentioned is what you do with flowback water," she said. You couldn't simply send used fracking fluids to the local water treatment plant. Pennsylvania found out the hard way when the Allegheny River became so corrosive not even steel mills could use its water. Sometimes frackers stored the toxic brew miles underground. Sometimes the flowback languished in plastic-lined impoundment ponds that resembled swimming pools full of sludgy water.

"We're reusing nearly all of it." Corbett's smile projected the kind of enthusiasm and pride that would make employees bend over backwards to help him succeed.

Summer raised her eyebrows. "I'm impressed."

"Recycling flowback is a no-brainer. Cuts down on the need to draw fresh water. We're also researching the possibility of using foam containing nitrogen, carbon dioxide, and relatively small quantities of water."

"If the fracking industry wants to realize its potential, it has to manage water resources more carefully than it has been," Summer said.

"Exactly. Some environmental groups want to ban fracking altogether."

"Like Vermont and New York. I understand their concerns."

Corbett directed her back to his truck. "Nothing is more important than protecting the aquifer and sources of drinking water, but unless we're all willing to give up our cars and sleep in uncomfortably hot or cold homes, we need energy. Natural gas is going to be a major source for the foreseeable future. Unless drillers get careless. Bad ones could ruin the industry for everyone."

They headed back to town. While driving, he responded to two calls, apparently to employees, with a Bluetooth device perched on his ear, his manner and tone congenial. When he finished, he apologized. She waved off his concern.

"I took the liberty of checking you out before I brought you here today," he said. "I talked to your lead professor at Penn State and the woman who chaired your thesis committee at Florida Sci-Tech. I hope you're not offended."

Depended on where he was headed with the scrutiny. She hoped Dr. Jennings hadn't sounded too whacko. "Should I be?"

"Here's what I was thinking. You already have your masters. Have you considered forgoing another degree and joining the workforce? Our geologist moved to North Dakota last month. We could use a bright young person like you on our staff. Both your professors highly recommended you. Said you learn fast."

Blood raced to her head. Quit school? She'd never considered it.

He parked his brand new badass Ford truck next to her rental. "Starting pay is $100,000."

"I—I—" Words wouldn't form—and what would they be if she managed to conjure them? She liked Corbett. Liked his operation. And the money was good. More than good. Great. No more peanut butter sandwiches and ramen noodles when expenses like truck repairs mounted. But still—give up the doctorate?

"You don't have to answer now," he said. "Think about it. Now, let's go see that three-dimensional model I was telling you about."

She put one foot in front of the other and followed him into company headquarters, a sprawling three-story red brick facility. She plodded her way through introductions to people whose names she would never remember.

But she would never forget this day when she received her very first real job offer. One she hadn't even applied for. Should she say yes?

No, of course not.

She thought about the 298,000 miles on her truck. Thought about the ramen noodles in her kitchen. Thought about Jennings' bizarre behavior.

How long would Corbett wait for an answer?

~

BARELY NOTICING THE SCENERY, Dayita Patel headed south on Route 19 as she passed through Lamont, Perry, Cross City, Crystal River, and Homosassa. Only as she approached Tampa, where the roads were more congested, did she focus her attention solely on driving. She was thinking about the steps she would take to hack into Signal-Muller's website to obtain their formula for FloMoshun without their ever realizing she'd been inside. She wouldn't need fancy equipment; a little "social engineering" would do the trick.

She chose a coffee shop bordering a suburban neighborhood and logged onto their network. She drafted an email request for information to one of Signal's top female sales people, Allyson Smallwood, posing as the CEO of the bogus company she'd created earlier.

On a disposable prepaid cell, Dayita called Smallwood's extension. Since it was after hours, it went straight to voicemail. She recorded the woman's personal message and listened to it several times.

Since she had already driven this far, Dayita headed into Ybor City for lunch at her favorite deli, La Segunda Bakery. She ordered their original Cuban sandwich and a guava tart. It wasn't as if you could get authentic Cuban food in Loblolly Lake.

Onto the next city on her list, Gainesville. On the drive Dayita practiced Smallwood's tone and inflections until she had them nailed. Twice she phoned Summer, dying to see if even her best friend could recognize her voice. Both times the call went straight to voicemail. The second time, she left a message. "You frigging forget how to use a phone? Call me."

Besides, she had news. Her contact at the college of journalism had scraped together enough information from a fellow reporter for Dayita to uncover a key unnamed source in the *Trending Times* article: a firm based in Oklahoma called Allied Consulting.

Once in Gainesville, Dayita drove to the Tower Hill Library. This step would be a little trickier, since there was video surveillance, and later Signal-Muller's security people might acquire that footage if they ever learned they'd been hacked from the library's IP address. With her braid tucked up inside a large hat that hid her face from surveillance, Dayita asked the front desk volunteer for the location of the computers. She asked in Allyson Smallwood's Midwestern voice. The volunteer, a charter member of the Blue Rinse Set, smoothed her hands down the sides of her granny sack before pointing Dayita in the right direction. Apparently the voice con sounded natural—at least to someone who didn't know Smallwood.

Just before five when Signal-Muller Chemical Corporation's employees were ready to rush home, to the gym, or to their favorite bar, Dayita phoned their help desk. Using the accent she'd practiced throughout the day, she claimed to be unable to access the company's intranet for information she needed to close a deal. "It's not accepting my password."

"Let's try setting a new one. I'll email you a request," the woman suggested.

"Thanks." Dayita provided an email address close to Smallwood's with one slight change diverting the message to another account Dayita had rigged to shuffle through several bogus accounts before landing in hers. The most serious flaw in most big companies' security systems had nothing to do with firewalls; the human element was nearly always the weakest link. With a little social engineering, skilled hackers could worm their way into any site. A little sweet talk. A good story. Only through rigorous training of every new employee could a company prevent this sort of intrusion.

Now, with the new password, Dayita assumed the saleswoman's identity.

"Yes!" She rose halfway off her chair and pumped her fist in their air. She was in.

Yes, she realized she was in—in the library. The homeless dude sitting at the station beside her was staring. She had to settle down. It was hard, though, when this was the most excitement she'd known since Summer went off to Penn State. Dayita owned Signal-Muller. She had everything—internal communications, work orders, test results, memos, emails, messages, photos, videos, and documents, directories full of documents dating back to the '80s, contracts, legal briefs, non-disclosure agreements. It was all there. Dayita escalated her privileges, giving herself unfettered access before replacing part of the site's binary code to disguise her intrusion. With her footprints covered, she began searching for something admissible.

In less than ten minutes she located the Material Safety Data Sheet for FloMoshun. She scanned through two pages of product hype before she found the warning at the very end of the document: *FloMoshun as a component of hydraulic fracturing fluid can be an immediate and chronic health hazard. Prolonged exposure can cause kidney and liver damage, irritate lung tissue, decrease blood pressure, and result in dizziness and vomiting.* She downloaded the PDF file.

Next she searched for all internal documents authored by the head chemist, whose name she'd snagged off the corporate directory. Even though the encrypted documents would be useless to her now, she downloaded them all to a flash drive. She could take her time to break the code and decipher the documents later. Nosing around inside too long risked triggering a security breach.

Before logging out, she located the name of a recently terminated employee and reactivated his email account and intranet access. If discovered, it wasn't likely to raise red flags, but even if anyone was getting unauthorized access to their system, a former employee would be the first person they would suspect. Dayita hoped, for his sake, Peter Bell was nowhere near a terminal or a hotspot or an Internet access point at the time of the breach.

During the ride back to Loblolly Lake, she realized this whole business of hacking for Summer was way better than sitting around reading *Wired* magazines waiting for the department head at Sci-Tech to get over being peeved.

Sometimes she felt as if people were lassoing her from all directions. The cousin in Bangladesh her mother wanted her to marry. Summer, who roped her into doing one quasi-legal thing after another with computer skills meant to catch perps, not become one. Her mother, who'd saddled her with obligations.

She was tired of waiting, tired of being tied down.

This was the only life she had. Nothing prevented her from launching a start-up without the university's stupid paperwork. All she needed was one or two good references. She grinned as she pulled into an empty parking spot in front of the Patel residence. How easily she could make glowing references appear on her start-up's website.

Great idea—except for all the frigging student loans the government would forgive if she'd work for them for a few years. It took time for a start-up to grow legs.

When she got home, she kissed her mother, climbed the stairs to her bedroom and called Summer. It went straight to voicemail again. "Call me, damn it." She threw her phone onto the bed. It bounced once and tumbled onto the floor.

On her laptop, she logged into her email account. Maybe Summer had gotten around to responding to her previous message. Lots of junk mail had accumulated during the day, but when Dayita found no word from Summer, she executed a noisy Bronx cheer. She emailed that she'd snagged all Signal-Muller's documents, and surely one contained the formula, but it would take a little longer to break the encryption. She attached a PDF file of the Material Safety Data Sheet and hit SEND.

After she read through the rest of her emails, she skimmed a couple of blogs. She was ready to shut down, when a message popped onto her screen: *Who sneaked in the back door when they thought no one was looking?*

Omigod! What did they know? How—?

She messaged back: *Who is this?*

The drawing of a lion-headed avatar appeared. *Ashoka* was typed underneath in a gamer's Gothic font.

Was *Ashoka* supposed to be a name? The man—if it was a guy—with an avatar you could never be sure—messaged again: *Find what you were looking for?*

Immediately she shut down. Damn. Her department chair said she was the best cybersecurity student he'd ever seen. She'd done everything right. She always used an encrypted browser on her own computer and she had used different IP addresses for every search. She should have been untraceable. How had anyone figured out she'd broken into Signal-Muller's site? This Ashoka character had to be a skilled hacker himself. What if he'd slipped malware or a keylogger or a trojan onto her machine?

And more important, what was he going to do now?

OLIVER JENNINGS CHECKED THE REAR VIEW mirror for the umpteenth time since he'd left State College. No one had pulled into the rest stop behind him. He phoned his newest doctoral student—the one he most dreaded contacting. He knew he had behaved shamefully at Stansbury, but perhaps Summer Cassidy would forgive him when she understood what they were up against.

"I'm sure you are wondering why I left so abruptly in Stansbury," he said.

"Yes, I've been worried, sir," Summer said. "Are you all right?"

"I need to talk to you in person."

"I can drive up there tomorrow."

It was a three-and-half hour drive, one he'd just made. "I was hoping to see you tonight. I'm ten minutes outside of Clarksburg, so if you'll give me directions to your place, I'll pop in for a few minutes and be on my way. I promise not to take up much of your time."

"My house? It's not really—I'm—" She broke off and dictated the route he needed to take.

He knew how these young girls were. She'd probably skitter

around in panic scrubbing week-old debris off dishes stacked in the sink, hiding the socks and bras littering the floor. He tried to forestall any efforts she might expend on his behalf. "Please don't try to clean up. I've seen plenty of college residences, Ms. Cassidy, and I assure you no amount of mess can shock me."

He ended the call before she could ask questions.

Though he'd never been to Clarksburg before, nothing about it particularly surprised him. It resembled most other small towns in the region. Two-story wood-sided homes rose in tiers up the hills. Roads were annoyingly narrow, especially in the residential sections, where parking consumed one lane, leaving motorists to share what was left of the road. Local government had made an effort to maintain an attractive two-block downtown though it was devoid of retail stores, which had departed long ago for the mall. Downtowns these days consisted of banks, parking lots, law and accounting offices, a library, government buildings.

Following the young woman's directions, he left town, traveling along a road where first, the houses were scattered more widely, then were separated by patches of woods and dormant fields. He eased onto a single-lane dirt road. His sedan bumped over the uneven ground; low-hanging branches whooshed and clunked against his roof and side mirrors.

Soon his headlights illuminated what she had called a cabin; the proper term was shack. He shook his head. Pitiful. A direct result of inadequate funding for this project.

The young woman met him on the front porch, shining a flashlight on his path.

"Be careful, third step's rickety," she called out. "Haven't gotten around to fixing it."

His peripheral vision picked up unexpected movement, and instinctively he halted. "Uhhhhh—something's moving on the roof."

She laughed. "That's Rocky, my resident raccoon. He's the curious type, likes to know what's going on."

Dr. Jennings chuckled. Summer had an amiable personality. Under other circumstances, teaching this young woman would be delightful. He took her up on an offer for coffee.

The inside of the cabin proved drearier than expected. Chinks in the wall let wind rush through, although he could see where she or some former resident had stuffed something into some of the gaps. He pointed at one rather significant wad. "Are those tissues?"

Her laughter pealed out. "Yes, sir. I stuff them in and Rocky steals them. I suspect he's making a soft bed up there in the eaves."

She delivered a cup she had reheated in the microwave.

He settled into one of the kitchen chairs and sipped. "Good coffee, thanks," he said, more polite than honest.

She looked at him expectantly. Yes, he had best to get down to business. "I'm going on sabbatical, and you deserve to hear this from me in person."

Two spots of color appeared on her cheeks as if he'd slapped her. Her body became absolutely still, her eyes losing their sparkle, accusatory. He couldn't blame her. He was letting her down, and it was important she understand the reasons behind his decision.

"Certain people have begun a campaign to discredit our research," he said.

"Elliot Ral?"

Jennings set the cup on the table. "Did he behave abominably at the meeting?"

She shrugged it off. "Nothing I couldn't handle."

If what these people were proposing to do consisted of a few antagonistic questions, Jennings could have handled it too, but they were far more unscrupulous.

"Ral's a hired gun," he said, "and I haven't been able to determine which company contracted him. They twist everything around so we look guilty when that couldn't be further from the truth."

"Guilty of what?"

"Bias against the oil and gas industry. Fabricating research results to prove a particular point of view. These people will use every means possible to ruin our reputations. If you had read the article in this month's *Trending Times,* you would have no doubts about the lengths they will go to."

"I did read it and dismissed it right away as shoddy reporting. Almost no named sources. All your research has received high marks in peer-reviewed journals. That's what matters."

He suspected she'd feel differently if it had been her name in the article or if she understood what was at stake. He tried to enlighten her. "You don't understand. We're going to lose more funding.

Probably all of it. I realize this puts you in a bind, but perhaps you should look at this setback as an opportunity to consider a different line of inquiry for your dissertation."

"I have no intention of quitting. I'm going to find out who hired Elliot Ral."

"It doesn't matter which oil and gas executive is behind this campaign."

Her tone was flat. "So you're leaving."

"Summer, they will expose information to destroy my family. If it were only me . . . but it's not. You need to move on, too."

She shook her head. "But it *is* just me. I don't have a husband or even a boyfriend they can threaten. If a company is this afraid of what our tests will reveal, they must be hiding something terrible," she said. "I intend to uncover whatever it is, with or without your help."

Brave words. They were trying to ruin him, yes, but he had years of published papers and established reputation behind him. He could rebuild after people forgot all about the *Trending Times* article. She, on the other hand, stood to damage her credibility before her career even began.

"The dean wants to see you within the next three days to talk about what happens next," he said. "You're to make an appointment. In any case, I have no more funds and can write you no further checks. So you'll need to pack up your things and head back to the university. My dear girl, *please* find another topic with a new adviser. Better yet, go home to Florida for the rest of this semester. Give these people a chance to realize the threat to their fortunes has passed."

As he'd feared, she sputtered nonsense about doing the right thing, saving the world. What a Girl Scout. He removed a folded paper from his coat pocket.

"This letter was in your college admission file. It is from your mother." He held on to it a little longer, reluctant to cause her pain.

She paled. "From my mother? You got it from my admission file?"

She looked shaken at the mention of her mother. He couldn't begin to fathom the family dynamics. He shook his head. "No, it's a copy they mailed to me so I could show it to you if you insisted on testing the water here in West Virginia."

"Who is 'they'? I don't understand."

He didn't either. Maybe they paid an employee in admissions to get their hands on it. More likely, a hacker broke into the university's database. Everything was digitized these days. "I don't know who 'they' is. Could be Elliot Ral or someone else hired to stop our research. But they sent it to me because on your own, you might not comprehend the significance of it."

She hadn't reached for it, so he placed the letter in her hands. Her lips trembled as she read it. He had to look away. What he was doing was wrong, so wrong, but if the letter became public . . . wouldn't it be worse?

The single sheet of paper fell from her fingers to the scarred wooden floor. A tiny spider scurried out of the way.

"My mother tried to discourage the university from admitting me? She thinks I'm too fragile to be trusted?"

He couldn't bear to look at her. He stared at the tiny window in the door, even though it was pitch black outside and he could see nothing through it—any more than he could see into the heart of this girl's mother. "I'm sorry. They'll use this letter to discredit your research, paint you as mentally unstable. You could expect a smear campaign like the *Trending Times* article they wrote about me. These people are ruthless. They'll search for every mistake you ever made and publicize it." The same as they threatened to do with his wife, the most decent woman he'd ever known. The abortion Marcia had all those years ago would torpedo her political career right when it looked as if the governor's office might be hers for the asking. These people intended to broadcast Marcia's one youthful indiscretion to the world, including their children. It was one thing to demonize him, but he couldn't let them hurt his family.

He didn't comment on the tears on Summer's cheeks. Who could blame her?

"Tell me," he asked gently. "You were catatonic?"

"Yes," she whispered. "For a few weeks. I was nine."

"After your twin . . . the hit-and-run accident. I did a little research after I received the letter. I hope you can forgive the invasion of privacy, but I wanted to understand. Your mother home-schooled you both before and after your sister's accident?"

As if she barely registered his presence, she nodded. The movement seemed to focus her senses again. She swallowed. "Once a week she let me take the bus across town to the university library. I studied on my own, choosing books and academic journals with the help of a sympathetic librarian, but I wanted to go to public school. At first, I rebelled in small ways. Our disagreement came to a head when I was fourteen." She barked a laugh that carried no shred of humor. "I stole my mother's car. Didn't have a driver's license, but that didn't stop me. I tent-camped near Goose Pasture and spent my days kayaking on the Wacissa River and Slave Canal. When my mother realized I had taken the car and disappeared, she sent the police looking for me. After two days, I called her and we came to an agreement. I could attend public school. In return, I had to leave a note to let her know where I was going and I couldn't ever cross the state line. She threatened to press charges for car theft if I didn't uphold my end of the bargain. I haven't ever told anyone I stole her car, Dr. Jennings. Not even my best friend. Guess anyone who judged me by the stuff I did back then would decide I was a nut case and lock me away for my own good."

"Or they might decide you were resourceful and used every tool at your disposal to get an education. Being a rebellious teenager doesn't mean you are fragile, mentally unstable, or emotionally damaged. I have thought about what would make a mother write those things. Even in the few months I've known you, I would swear on my life they aren't true. You are precisely the kind of person universities were created for. The letter, I believe, is an example of projection. You know what that is?"

"You're saying my mother is the one who is fragile."

"She doesn't want to let you go, so she projects her weakness on you. But you are not fragile, Summer. A mind like yours is a treasure. Get your doctorate. But not here. Go somewhere else. Somewhere safe."

"No place is safe," she whispered.

Thinking of her twin, he supposed. The child had died in the street a few blocks from the Cassidy home. "What will you do?"

It took her several seconds to respond, but then Jennings watched her features transform. As her chin jutted out, he knew he had failed to convince her. She declared she would continue the research.

"And the letter?" he asked, slipping his hand into his coat pocket to assure himself that the roll of antacids still had a couple of tablets left.

"If it becomes public, I'll figure out what to do about it. The letter can't hurt anyone but me, and the research can do a lot of good if I finish what we set out to do."

He clasped her hands in his. "I believe in you, Summer, and I still believe in the project, even if I can't direct it." From an inner pocket of his jacket he withdrew an envelope. "In the event your mother's letter becomes public, use this recommendation from me, but only if you can't find any other way to clear your name." He wished her good luck. Jennings let himself out the door, treading cautiously on the warped porch boards and disintegrating step. It ought to be replaced before someone got hurt.

If only that young woman's family could be fixed as easily as the rotten board.

~

SHOCKED BY WHAT DR. JENNINGS had revealed, Summer couldn't stand to stay in the cabin another minute, pacing and fretting, so she grabbed her keys and headed to a local bar called Knuckleheads. She propped her arms on the bar top and signaled the bartender for a shot of tequila and a beer. She wished she were back in Florida, where the bartender knew her brand without asking and steered easy marks her way so she never had to buy her own drinks. She simply beat some cocky guy at darts or foosball.

Across the room, a college-age guy yelled out an exuberant "yessss" when his ping pong ball landed in an opponent's beer cup. A stupid Beer Pong tournament.

Her cell vibrated. She pulled it from her jeans pocket, saw it was her mother, and punched it off without answering. She turned it back on and blocked all calls from her mom. The battery was almost dead again.

She imagined windmilling her fists against her mother's chest. Even though her rational mind accepted Dr. Jennings' diagnosis, Summer clenched her teeth to keep from screaming.

Of course her mother was fragile and unstable. Had been ever since Chrissie's death. Maybe even before. She blamed herself for giving birth to an unhealthy baby, and her self-hatred magnified ten-fold after Chrissie died. But it was no excuse for writing that letter.

No way in hell would Summer ever forgive her. Not for this. Not ever. While growing up, Summer had no choice but to endure her mother's behavior. The pills she took to dull the pain of losing Chrissie. The ones she took to get out of bed in the morning and to go to sleep at night. Her insistence on home schooling deprived Summer of the opportunity to interact with other kids. To learn what normal families without drug-addicted mothers looked like. The parents of other home-schooled kids made sure their kids took field trips and played team sports. Not Jordan Cassidy.

Summer accepted that she couldn't change her mother. She could only control her own reactions. Knowing this didn't make the betrayal any less painful. She was not a fragile child who needed her hand held. She was certain now that her mother had written letters to all the universities Summer had applied to, in an attempt to keep her in Loblolly Lake. Hurray for the schools willing to give her a chance despite her mother's allegations. At least now she understood why her number one choice, MIT, had turned her down.

When Summer had located this bar tonight, she thought whupping someone's ass at darts might distract her, lift her spirits. Only she couldn't muster the enthusiasm to drag herself off the barstool. And it was only partly because of her mother.

Summer twirled the bottle of Sam Adams around and watched the patterns of condensation on the bar top scatter. She tilted her head back and threw down a tequila shooter followed by another slug of beer. She had just succeeded in spending her remaining peanut butter and ramen money on liquid painkillers in under fifteen minutes.

Maybe her mother was right. Looked as if Summer had made a terrible decision in coming here. Her adviser had abandoned ship, leaving future funding in question. Why not tuck tail and run?

She tipped the Sam Adams again. Here she was, proving her mother's point. She was immature. No more stable than her pill-popping mother. A guy about her age with the kind of classic features Michelangelo might have sculpted leaned against the barstool next to hers while he waited on a draft. "Saw you watching the dart game," he said. "Want to join us?" He pushed bangs back from eyes that shone like polished jade.

The eyes, the bangs—suddenly she couldn't take in air fast

enough. *She was in the Foos and Booz and Jake Fowler loomed over her booth, green eyes smiling. Inviting her to play darts. She time-shifted to her apartment. Jake was calling her a slut. She saw him shooting Ty. Heard her head thwack the bedroom wall.*

"Hey, you don't have to. No pressure." The hottie with bangs wiggled his fingers in the air between them. "Name's Hank. Come on over if you'd like to play." He loped off without looking back.

She blew out air to reduce the adrenaline rushing through her bloodstream. Jake Fowler was ensconced in his casket. No sense in letting a silly similarity give her the shivers. She needed to get a grip before people started thinking she was crazy. No one would trust a nutcase to test their water.

Hopping off the barstool, she made her way over with a bit of a swagger. After all, she had reigned as the unchallenged queen of the dart board and foosball table in her hometown. These guys looked like amateurs.

Because her twin's heart defect and frequent surgeries had absorbed so much of their mother's time, their father treated Summer to frequent camping trips, teaching her to shoot, fish, and kayak. At home, Summer and her father had played darts in the den most evenings. Until the divorce two years after Chrissie's accident.

Even though Summer banged down enough beer and shooters to blur her vision a bit, she and Hank won enough money to pay for drinks.

Near closing time, Hank offered her a ride. He seemed nice enough, and she didn't pick up on any vibes that he expected anything at the end of the ride. Which was too bad because he was one fine specimen. On the other hand, all she wanted tonight was to crawl into bed and pass out. As she toyed with the idea of accepting the ride, Jake's face snaked its way between her and Hank. She extracted her rental car key from her jeans pocket.

The bartender stepped between her and the door. "I can call a cab. You shouldn't drive."

She shouldn't. It would be risky and immature. She flashed a weak smile at Hank, who had been far more restrained in consumption than she.

"Hey, Hank, you serious about giving me a lift?"

5

November 18

DAYITA'S MOTHER HAD LONG GONE to bed, the house silent except for the hum of electronics. Too wired to sleep, Dayita made coffee and drank three cups, as she set up apps on the pre-paid cell she'd purchased right after Ashoka had contacted her.

She kept her laptop nearby on the coffee table. What if Ashoka was there waiting for her? Who was he and what did he know? She'd looked for signs that he'd left behind a Trojan, keylogger, or eavesdropper, but hadn't located anything.

Whoever he was, this avatar could not only ruin her career before it started but maybe even send her to jail. Internet hacktivist Aaron Schwartz committed suicide because he faced a million dollars in fines and 35 years in a federal facility, and all he'd done was download some journal articles from JSTOR. What she had done, snagging proprietary documents for Summer, was worse. Way worse.

Yet all she and Schwartz—not that she could compare herself to him, he was an icon in the computer world—all they wanted was to release information that should be available to the public.

No, she had to act. This was war, and she intended to win.

On the new cell, she'd closed her email accounts and opened two new ones.

She waited until she thought Summer might be awake, going outside and sitting on the front stoop so she wouldn't wake her mother—still dark, stars fading, the morning quiet except for a few birds out for the early worms. Calm. Peaceful. Totally out of sync with her agitation.

By the fourth ring, Dayita was ready to stop trying, so she was taken by surprise when Summer answered.

"I wasn't sure you'd pick up," Dayita said.

"Me either. My God, Dayita, it's not even six o'clock."

Summer's voice sounded scratchy. The long boards on the porch creaked as Dayita paced across them. "I figured you'd be up since you're so busy with your research. Why haven't you called me back? Your mother said she can't even reach your voicemail. She's worried sick. You think your research is the only thing that matters. You think it will save the world, save all these people you don't even know. What about the people you *do* know, Summer? The people who care about you. When do *they* matter?"

A few beats of silence followed, broken by a blue jay scolding an unseen annoyance from the telephone wire across the street. Summer better be squirming with shame.

"Sorry, Dayita. It won't happen again."

"Right, like I believe that." When Summer got caught up in her research, she forgot the rest of the world existed.

"Really, I plugged my charger in yesterday to a dead outlet in the cabin. One whole wall doesn't have functional electric. Maybe it blew a fuse, but I haven't found the fuse box yet."

"Oh . . . sorry." Now what was Dayita supposed to say? She dropped abruptly onto the porch swing, which shifted backward and she nearly lost her balance. "I shouldn't have gone off like that. I didn't mean a word of it." Yes, she did, but she shouldn't have opened her big mouth.

"So, you going to call your mother?" she asked. "She's phoned twice to see if I'd heard from you."

"No."

"Why not?"

"We have nothing to say to each other. I blocked her calls."

The Cassidys' relationship had never been strong, but this seemed extreme. "What happened?"

"Had any luck tracking down the ingredients in FloMoshun?"

"Come on, what'd she do?"

"Drop it, okay? What about the FloMoshun?"

Okay, Dayita got it. Summer wasn't ready to talk about it. "I emailed you a copy of the data sheet last night. I wanted to make sure you saw it right away."

She described the warning at the bottom of the sheet.

"That's terrific, Dayita. It shows Corky's exposure certainly could have caused the liver damage and the company knows it. Any luck pinning down the chemicals in the trademarked ingredients?"

"Yep. I was able to decode the encryption."

"You're beyond fantastic. I'll let Ty and Corky know and send the information over to the lab running the blood tests."

"Fax or email them the sheet anonymously so it can't be traced back to me," Dayita said. "I don't want to get in trouble." Any more trouble, she amended mentally. Ashoka already spelled trouble with a capital T.

"Absolutely. I'll be careful." A beat of silence. "And I'm sorry I get so caught up in my research."

Dayita had been unfair. Summer was, after all, trying to help this sick guy. Her friend was task-oriented and persistent. Caring. The kind of person you wanted on your side when you were in trouble. "Glad I could help."

"Your voice sounds gruff this morning. Been drinking too much coffee?" Summer asked.

Her voice was gruff because she couldn't sleep for worrying about this Ashoka character. But if she sounded bad, Summer sounded worse—like she'd been run over by a truck. Dayita bet she'd been out drinking last night. "I've only slept a few hours since you called. Not easy to get this stuff, you know?"

"Dayita, you're the best."

"Best what?"

"Best computer genius." Summer hesitated only a second before adding, "And best best friend."

Dayita made a face. Yeah, right—this "genius" couldn't even manage to graduate. Better to be a friend. You pulled all-nighters and drove hundreds of miles and broke laws for best friends. "I miss you, Summer."

"Me too. Hey, why don't you drive up here over the Thanksgiving holiday? You can stay with me."

"Really?" Dayita squealed. "How fun—a holiday together!"

"Don't expect too much. My place is far from fancy."

As if Dayita cared—a vacation! They'd talk late into the night. She'd get Summer to spill whatever it was the Wicked Mother had done. They'd share Thanksgiving turkey with all the fixings. It would be perfect.

She ran inside and upstairs to tell her mother, who was now awake and brushing her teeth.

Mrs. Patel spit a mouthful of blue foam into the sink before responding to the news. "That's wonderful, honey. I hear West Virginia's beautiful. I'm so glad Summer won't be alone for the holiday."

How thoughtless—Dayita hadn't stopped to think of how her mother would feel. "Oh, Mumsy, I can't leave you alone."

"Don't be silly. I'll be fine."

Dayita hugged her mother from behind. "No, Mumsy, I would miss you too much."

Laughter met that announcement. "Nonsense. You and Summer will have too much fun to think about anything else. Of course you're going. Did you tell Summer to call her mother?"

Dayita frowned. "She doesn't want to talk to her. Something awful's happened, but she wouldn't tell me what."

Her mother's posture exhibited a weariness that concerned and annoyed Dayita simultaneously. Her mother was not responsible for every bad moment in the Cassidy family's life. It was time for everyone to get over an accident that happened thirteen years ago. It was tragic, yes, but time to move on.

Refusing to get sucked in by her mother's heavy mood, Dayita dashed into her room. A trip north definitely called for a new sweater, maybe orange for Thanksgiving. This called for online shopping. She was vacillating between a stylish cowl neck and a crew neck that could be layered when a lion avatar and new message popped on the cell screen: *You're coming to West Virginia! Goody! Let's meet.*

For a few seconds she couldn't breathe. How was this possible? Ashoka had overheard their conversation. How had he hacked her new phone?

With a quick intake of breath, she figured it out—Ashoka was ripping off Summer's contact list and reading all her mail. Both Summer's smartphone and computer had been compromised. He must have researched Dayita's background, and when he discovered she was a cybersecurity expert, decided to taunt her.

As she read the message again, her heart rate slowed. Someone who meant to report her to authorities wouldn't use the word *goody*. She wasn't going to jail after all. He was a fellow hacker playing a game—and she excelled at cyber games. Already, he'd left a clue in wording that implied he might be in West Virginia.

She hadn't wanted to worry Summer about the hacker, but now she needed to. She had to uncover Ashoka's true identity. She had an idea of how to turn this game around on him, and when they all met up in Clarksburg, she would expose him for the lowlife he was.

She messaged the avatar back: *First I find U, then I decide if we goody up!*

~

SUMMER'S HEAD WAS POUNDING as she hung up the phone. What had she been thinking inviting Dayita up here? Though well-intentioned, this Thanksgiving trip was not a good idea. The cabin was too rustic and that girl didn't even own any shoes sturdier than rhinestone-trimmed flip-flops.

Thank heavens Summer had let Hank drive her home last night. He had kept her Chevy's keys and promised to have one of his friends drive out to the cabin with him to return the car first thing in the morning. She peeped out the window and saw he had kept his word. The Chevy was parked safely near her porch. While making a cup of coffee, she thought about what a nice guy he was. He hadn't tried to take advantage of her condition. If only she'd gotten his phone number so she could thank him again. She didn't even know his last name to Google him.

She called Ty with Dayita's news. He promised to give the formulation to Corky's doctors, who could pass the information along to the lab, keeping Summer's and Dayita's role off the record.

"Pizza tonight?" he asked.

She hesitated, remembering how abominably he'd behaved toward Corky's employer, but in the end, she agreed. Eating every meal alone got to be a drag. But soon that would change, she thought with a smile. Dayita was coming for Thanksgiving. The two of them would find out what kind of trouble you could get into in this little burg.

Since Summer's head still felt like it was stuffed with cotton, she decided to wait until afternoon to line up landowners. Instead she headed downtown to the library. As soon as she mounted the staircase at Waldomore she knew she was going to love researching the history of mineral extraction in West Virginia there. PJ Wine had been right: the old building had delightfully creaky wooden floors. A helpful male librarian—thin, pale, bespectacled—directed her to the West Virginia collection.

She opened the first fat tome the librarian brought out for her, relishing the dusty fragrance of old paper. Quickly she learned oil and gas were first discovered in the Kanawha and Little Kanawha River valleys in the southern part of the state in the eighteenth century. By 1859 the world's first drilling operations were underway in Burning Springs, in what would become West Virginia; and the Drake Well in Titusville, Pennsylvania.

During the Civil War, General William E. Jones raided Burning Springs and torched the oil field, turning the Little Kanawha River into a sheet of fire. But the oil boom persisted, making fortunes for drillers like Michael Benedum and John D. Rockefeller of Standard Oil Company as oil production moved from the southern to the north central area of West Virginia. Rockefeller amassed the largest fortune ever accumulated, amounting to a greater percentage of the nation's GDP than even Sam Walton or Bill Gates.

Summer was blown away. Talk about serious moola—those dudes never had to worry about affording next week's groceries.

All that money soon migrated from oil fields into politics. John D.'s grandson Nelson became governor of New York and later vice president. Another grandson, Winthrop, became governor of Arkansas. John D.'s great grandson, Jay, became governor and U.S. senator, serving West Virginia for over forty years.

She skimmed over more history of mineral extraction in Appalachia. Finally, she slipped her laptop back into its protective carrying case.

The librarian, whose metallic nametag read John Gilmer, hovered over her. "Find anything interesting?"

A sad laugh escaped Summer. "Looks as if oil and gas exploration has always been tangled up with vast wealth, wars, and politics. And anyone who thinks you can't buy influence hasn't read about the Rockefellers."

Crinkles fanned out from the outer edges of his eyes. "Used to be billboards up along some highways around here that read 'Standard

Oil: Legal Thieves.' Some folks faulted Rockefeller for the money he made from our state resources. But despite John D.'s roughshod business practices, you have to credit him for his philanthropy. And he instilled in his children and grandchildren the responsibility that accompanies great wealth."

Summer eyed the man, suspected he would have a well-informed, relatively unbiased view of fracking in the region. "I know what local environmentalists and business leaders think of the Marcellus development, but I'm curious, what do you think, Mr. Gilmer?"

He hesitated as if considering how best to answer. "We're told this new method of drilling is safe, and I hope the experts are right. No question it's a boon for the economy, but if it damages our water supply. . . I wish we could slow down a little."

Gilmer's jaw lengthened, making his face appear even narrower. "I predict we can expect to read about more regrettable incidents like the spill that trucker had a few days ago and the bad taste in Patricia Kirby's water."

"I'm afraid you're—whose bad water?" The trucker she knew about, of course, but not the other.

The librarian located the news article where Mrs. Kirby complained about the water. He even helped Summer find the woman's address on Windy Hollow Road. She located it on a map and compared it to a map of gas wells in the county. Although there wasn't one on Kirby's land, several companies operated fracking rigs nearby. Summer grabbed a topography map, her fingers tracing the contoured lines representing elevation changes. "It doesn't look like chemicals would migrate into Mrs. Kirby's water well from the closest site run by Sunburst Energy. Of course, I would have to do tests to know for sure."

Mr. Gilmer looked up Mrs. Kirby's phone number and jotted it down. He offered the phone behind his desk, and Summer called, arranging to visit the next day.

This contaminated well could be the reason someone was determined to stop her research. Summer grabbed her gear, feeling far more optimistic as she left the library than when she'd arrived. If she found more solid evidence, she knew she could convince the dean and committee to let her continue.

~

The odor of fresh lumber and the bang of hammers greeted Boomer Walsh as he emerged from his Escalade. He peeled his work jacket off and traded it for the clean parka on the passenger seat. Boomer offered up silent words of praise to the Lord—and the consulting firm they'd hired—for sending him this opportunity for positive publicity.

Months ago, Corbett had recommended the consultants because he claimed he was concerned continuing bad press after an explosion at one of Fairhope's sites would hurt the whole industry. Huh—Boomer figured what Corbett really worried about was loan repayments.

Building a Habitat House would counteract those awful news stories this week on the spill. Three days in a row a reporter had kept stirring the pot. If only Corky had kept his mouth shut. At least other bad news had finally bumped the spill out of the paper this morning.

Boomer strode across the dirt and entered the partly constructed building. Already on the scene, his secretary, Holly Stone, handed him a Habitat for Humanity ball cap.

He tugged it on over his crewcut. "Photographer here?"

"Yes, sir. The racket you hear? About two dozen of our employees. They're pounding and sawing away already." In that halting way of hers, Holly filled him in on who was who. What had happened to his new secretary to turn her into such a scared little rabbit? He had paid her a compliment about her legs one day, and she scurried into her office and closed the door. He only meant to show a little friendly interest in an employee. Other than this tentativeness, she seemed competent.

As a matter of politeness, Boomer introduced himself to the man Holly had identified as site boss, then walked from one framed-in area to another, thanking his workers for contributing their day off to help a needy family in the community.

"Where's my son?" he whispered to Holly.

She shrugged. "Maybe he'll show up later?"

Boomer frowned. He'd made clear the importance of this project when he'd given his crews an extra paid day of vacation, with the understanding that they'd help build this house. It would look bad if the boss's son didn't show up.

Holly steered the photojournalist in his direction, and Boomer shook her hand. For half an hour he pounded nails and joked with his employees. During a break, they devoured the pumpkin cranberry muffins Holly had baked. From a giant silver urn, she dispensed coffee that steamed into the cold air.

"Thanks, Holly. You're a peach." Boomer raised his cup and turned to the photojournalist. "You can quote me: I have the best secretary in the world." That ought to boost her confidence. Once the reporter was ready with the digital recorder, Boomer spoke about the importance of giving back to the community and the Christian duty to help those less fortunate. In what would become the kitchen, he saw Holly adjust a Habitat cap on his son Hank's head, giving him a playful punch in the shoulder, which was more warmth than she'd ever shown to him, Boomer realized. Was she flirting? If so, she didn't realize she was barking up the wrong tree.

Boomer joined them. "You're kind of late."

"Sorry, Dad. I stopped by the office first and Mrs. Kirby called. She said even her laundry smelled funny. She wanted to know what we were going to do about it. I told her I'd have to talk to you. I wrote her number down and left it on your desk."

Acid kicked its way up Boomer's esophagus. He couldn't afford to do more for this woman when Fairhope surely had nothing to do with her water problems. She was old, probably taking meds that affected her taste and smell.

The television crew arrived with a videographer so young Boomer half expected her to pull a flute out of her black carrying case and trill the high school fight song.

"We'll talk about this later, Hank. I'll take you out to dinner tonight."

The videographer signaled readiness to tape Boomer's piece.

His son was already walking away. "Can't tonight. I have plans. Catch you later."

Boomer sighed, watching as Hank jumped in to help one of the guys lift a hefty piece of plywood onto sawhorses. His son didn't look like what Boomer had always assumed queers looked like: weak chins, pouty lips, squeaky voices. Boomer was at a loss to explain how this had happened. Hank had a normal upbringing. Boomer took him hunting, fishing. Hank took girls to the prom in high school. When his son "came out" his junior year in college, Boomer had offered to pay for counseling, for interventions. Anything would be better than the weight of knowing his only son faced a life of marginal acceptance. But Hank had only been angered by the offer to help, said he wasn't going to change, so Boomer had better get used to the way things were. He was trying, but Boomer found the whole situation embarrassing.

"Ready?" the videographer asked, drawing his attention away from his son.

As soon as the videographer finished taping, Boomer glanced at his watch and set down the hammer. A busy day lay ahead. He wanted to deliver season tickets to Mountaineer basketball games to PJ Wine: a little thank you for choosing the right sort of man when an opening arose on the Local Emergency Planning Committee. Ty Franceschi had lobbied for the position, claiming environmental interests should be represented, but thankfully, PJ had appointed a more business-friendly man instead.

Since a judge had already revoked the injunction delaying drilling at Joe Glover's after Fairhope moved the survey stakes an inch or two. Boomer wanted to check on progress out there, make sure everything was moving along. He would try to calm Joe down. Wouldn't be easy. Through the grapevine, Boomer had heard Early was plotting yet another obstruction. What would it be this time? Someday that jackass was going to take his stupid games too far.

THROUGH METICULOUS EXAMINATION of her laptop, Dayita found Ashoka had intercepted and infected one of Summer's emails. She isolated it and looked for any other changes on her hard drive that had occurred around the same time. But when Dayita tried to trace the infected email's source, she discovered Ashoka had covered his tracks well. No surprise: she already knew she was dealing with a highly skilled hacker.

After running two malware detectors, Dayita rechecked the tasks running on her laptop and parsed through lines of code where a hacker might typically hide keyloggers or back doors into a machine. Everything looked familiar, so Dayita felt confident that no one was watching her laptop moves from afar.

Next she located a strand of altered code on her phone and removed it. Time to turn the tables on Ashoka.

Signal-Muller didn't have a large in-house IT presence, so she figured they outsourced tech support and security. Payments would show up in their records. She set the computer to search through the thousands of documents she'd downloaded and quickly located recent financial statements. Scrolling through the last quarter summary, the name of one firm jumped off the page and practically bit her on the nose. Allied Consulting—the unnamed source for the *Trending Times* article on Jennings.

"I'll be damned," she whispered. This first step toward finding Ashoka had been almost too easy. She searched online for the company and learned they specialized in oil and gas company security needs. So Ashoka was probably employed by AC to discredit Dr. Jennings—and Summer too. Dayita had to warn her.

Rushing out to the nearest discount store, she bought an inexpensive cell and took it to the nearest overnight courier service. Inside, she included a terse message: *Call me on this phone only ASAP. Your phone hacked. Computer too.* Summer would have the clean device by noon the next day.

Back at home, Dayita set up a search of Signal-Muller documents for every mention of Allied Consulting. Any shred of information might narrow down which employee at AC might be Ashoka.

His chosen name could tell her something about him. While the computer sifted through documents, Dayita discovered online that Ashoka had been an Indian emperor around 220 BC. She searched again with the name plus the word *lion,* the avatar's graphic representation. Bingo—a sculpture of four-headed lion named Ashoka was an important symbol in India, sometimes associated with Buddhism.

So she was looking for a male of Indian descent. Gee, that narrowed it down to approximately a third of all the serious coders on the planet. AC likely employed a few dozen that fit that description here in the States, and probably contracted with freelancers in Bangalore. Yet she had no doubt she would ferret out Ashoka's identity. Both a money trail and an information trail existed somewhere, and she would follow the bread crumbs to the source.

Summer's devices would yield clues, too.

Look out, Ashoka, here I come.

~

SQUINTING THROUGH THE PEEPHOLE, Early Glover could see a redhead standing on his porch, beaming out at his pond as if dollar bills floated on its surface. What would it take for those gas companies to get his message? "No, thank you" certainly hadn't worked. He went back to his ergonomic chair and picked up his book, Jim Holt's *Why Does the World Exist?* Something Early had pondered most of his life and never come up with a viable answer. Existence, as far as he could ascertain, was a vast cosmic joke.

The doorbell rang again and again. Although his eyes saw words on the page, his brain fogged until he couldn't make sense of them.

"Mr. Glover, I know you're in there," a female voice yelled.

When the bell rang the fourth time, his teeth clamped together. On the fifth chime, he went for his rifle. The dog followed one step behind and sat by his feet as Early opened the door.

He held the weapon out of sight in case she was as harmless as the Cassidy girl had been. "Well?"

"Funny you should say that." The redhead laughed as if someone had let her in on the cosmic joke. She was scrawny, bones barely covered by pasty skin. Her eyes jumped; her face twitched. Had a long-sleeved jacket and jeans not completely covered her body, he suspected he would find the needle marks and bruises of an addict. If not, she might be anorexic or have cancer like him.

"Well?" he asked again.

"Mr. Glover, I'm Darlene Tucker, and I'd sure like to give you some money today. How would you like that?"

"Got all the money I need. Now, I'm gonna count to three." The door creaked as he opened it wider to reveal the rifle. "When I get to three, I'm gonna pull this here trigger." He held out the gun so she could see its mechanics. "One . . ."

"Now, Mr. Glover, I heard you're a cantankerous one, but I don't believe you're gonna shoot me. I don't believe it for a minute."

"Two . . ."

"Mineral rights on your land might be worth over half a million dollars, maybe even a million—especially if you allowed our company to draw water from that lake and river out there."

He raised the rifle, wedging it into his armpit, a move that placed the barrel close to Darlene Tucker's nose. She retreated a bit to the side but didn't leave the porch. Full of gumption—Early would give her that. "I already shot at a truck driver I found stealing water out of my lake." Wasn't exactly true—he'd only threatened to. Early stepped over the sill in his stocking feet, closing the distance between them once again.

A low rumble vibrated in Wallace's throat. "Don't bite her until I say so, Wallace."

Darlene backed up two more steps. "I don't want to steal your water, Mr. Glover. We will pay—"

"Don't want your money, and don't want to shoot you, but if you don't move your skinny butt down those steps and hightail it out of here, that's exactly what I'm gonna do. Two and a half . . ."

She sprinted toward her beat-up car.

"Property's posted, 'No Trespassing,'" he yelled after her. "Can't any of you fracking people read?"

As she hurled herself into the driver's seat, something clunked onto his driveway.

He set the rifle aside. He and Wallace bounded down his front steps. "Hey, you dropped something."

Darlene took one look over her shoulder and accelerated hard, her tires spraying gravel in a wide arc. She was gone, leaving a cloud of burnt oil behind.

Early bent to retrieve the fallen item, a booklet printed by a copier and bound with a metal spiral. So, Darlene Tucker *could* read. What kind of trash was it?

On his way up the drive, he flipped open to the first page of text, the words so mesmerizing he couldn't remember how he made it back to the porch or into the house. He staggered through the living room and settled into his favorite chair. The more he read, the tighter his teeth clenched, the redder the fog in his brain.

The document laid out an elaborate scheme to deceive landowners, beginning with a psychological analysis of West Virginians. Typical residents were patriotic, so landmen should point out that leasing mineral rights would help our country become energy independent. By starting with this point, residents would be more likely to let landmen stay and talk. The longer a landman talked, the more likely he'd leave with a signed lease. The guidebook advised saying the company was searching for oil rather than gas because people believed it less environmentally damaging. If the landowner brought up water contamination in Pennsylvania, the agent should emphasize that the Pennsylvania DEP still issued new drilling permits every year, and they wouldn't do so if the process were unsafe. They should hedge about the amount of land affected, about twenty acres, instead emphasizing the five-acre pad remaining after initial drilling takes place. They should stress that leases lasted for five years, without explaining if a well continued to produce, the lease automatically extended for the life of the well, which could be forty years. Land agents should avoid discussing property values, because they would decrease for land with oil and gas leases, and some major banks had stopped issuing mortgages on properties with leases. They should also avoid admitting that the company would likely drill multiple well heads.

"Un-frigging-believable," he told the mutt, who lay at his feet, unconcerned.

When Early finished reading, his teeth unclamped and a thin smile replaced his scowl. "My lawyer is going to *love* this."

He leaped to his feet and tilted his neck toward the ceiling and howled. He executed a happy dance and howled again.

Wallace raised his head from floor and regarded Early curiously for a moment, sighed loudly, and settled his head back between his paws.

~

ONE MORE TIME, SUMMER REHEARSED her pitch to get people to sign up for testing. Taking a deep breath, she punched in the next number on her list.

"Good afternoon, Mrs. Ammons. My name is Summer Cassidy and I'm a student at—"

"Who is this?"

"Summer Cassidy, ma'am."

"If you're selling something, I don't want to buy anything."

"I'm not selling anything. I—"

"And if you're calling for one of those politicians, I don't vote so you can save your breath. All of them are crooks."

If Summer could finish a sentence, maybe Mrs. Ammons would find out why she was calling. "No ma'am, I'm not a politician. I'm a student at Penn State and I would like to test your water, free of charge."

"Why would you want to do that?"

Remembering advice in an Internet post on phone marketing that a smile came through in your voice, Summer put on a happy face and explained the nature of her project.

"Missy, nobody does anything for free. Who's paying for these tests?"

"We have several funding sources, ma'am." At least Summer hoped they still did. "Several nonpartisan national foundations are underwriting our research. I would like to drop by your home with a brochure explaining what we are doing."

"Would you now." During a lengthy pause, Summer held her breath. At last, Mrs. Ammons conceded it sounded like a fine project and provided directions to her home. She suggested Summer come by the following afternoon.

When Summer hung up, she was exhausted. How did phone marketers do this all day long, day after day?

Two landowners on her list hung up as soon as they heard what she wanted. Why? She couldn't understand their reluctance.

The fourth person wasn't home, so she left a voice message. A fifth readily agreed for her to visit the next day, but the next three hung up on her. At this rate, she would never meet her Christmas deadline. Why was she putting herself through this aggravation when her whole project might disappear soon anyway?

She decided to call Claire Dunham, her former Sci-Tech adviser, for advice.

"Try face-to-face visits with your brochure in hand," Claire said. "It's too easy to hang up on people without hearing their pitch."

Face-to-face. Made sense, though after Early Glover had greeted her with a rifle, she'd grown somewhat reluctant to approach houses unannounced. Still, once people read the brochure, which explained the project better than she ever could on the phone, they'd realize getting water tested was in everyone's best interest. They would be protecting their families.

Now, for other pressing issues. She explained Dr. Jennings had gone on sabbatical, leaving her without an adviser, and possibly without funding. She toyed with telling Dr. Dunham about Jennings' fears for his family and about the letter from her mother someone wanted to use as blackmail, but she was afraid Jennings would sound crazy and she was too ashamed to tell anyone about that letter.

"Bummer," Dr. Dunham said. "Ask the dean to recommend a replacement for Jennings and see if he has suggestions on financing. I'm sure he can come up with a little bit of money to tide you over. They all have a stash of funds for emergencies. I'll see if I can scout out any grants you could apply for."

Summer groaned.

"Don't worry. I'll help you with the applications. Something's going to turn up."

Later, as Summer composed an email to the dean, she hoped Claire Dunham was right.

~

EARLY'S DAMN DOORBELL RANG for the third time. When he didn't answer on the first ring, why did people persist? Reluctantly, he put down the guidebook he'd been studying and retrieved his rifle. He trudged to the front door.

Through the peephole, the distorted face of PJ Wine came into focus. Early threw open the door with one hand and leaned the rifle against the wall with the other.

"Hell, PJ, I thought you were another one of those legal thieves knocking on my door. Come on in."

PJ laughed, her hands resting on the row of buttons on her red coat. As if mere hands could stop that over-sized belly from jiggling. The past few years she'd allowed herself to go to seed, but he guessed everyone deteriorated sooner or later. Before long, he'd be planted in the dirt himself.

When she bent over to greet Wallace, the dog growled and backed away. Her smile was already fading from this canine snub when she caught sight of the gun. "You planning to shoot someone?"

Early snorted. "No, but I'm tired of landmen trying to con me. I take stewardship of my granddaddy's land seriously."

PJ frowned. "I know you do. That's why I'm here, Early." She shifted her weight from one foot to the other. "See, the sheriff got a complaint about you chasing a truck driver off your property in a less than friendly manner. Then this morning this little girl comes tearing in, all breathless, claiming you nearly shoved a rifle up her nose. Turner Skidmore intended to charge out here on a white horse and arrest you, but I asked him to give me a chance to reason with you first."

Early crossed his arms in an effort to contain his temper. "Deputy Skidmore couldn't figure out how to mount a horse even if he had one. My property's posted with No Trespassing, No Soliciting signs."

"Sure, but you can't—"

"Hell, yes I can. That fellow was siphoning water out of my lake. Drove up my road, clearly marked as private, and stole my water. I told him to leave and he smirked and asked what I planned to do about it." No telling how long it was going on before Early had caught him. He retrieved his rifle.

"Whoa, now." PJ backed toward the door, tripping on the welcome mat. The irony wasn't lost on Early—one more example of the cosmos's warped sense of humor.

"Oh, for God's sake, PJ, how long have we known each other?" They'd been good friends since grade school and friends with benefits off and on for the past twenty years. Early unlatched the barrel breach and turned it toward her. "Look—not loaded. I've never even shot the darn thing—ever. Belonged to my granddaddy. I keep it for sentimental reasons."

The tension in PJ's stance melted away faster than ice on an August day. Early couldn't hold back his laugh. "Wouldn't be surprised to see a yellow stain running down your pants leg. You should've seen your expression."

The set of PJ's lips revealed her irritation. "Nothing funny about scaring people half to death, Early Glover. I thought some kind of dementia had taken hold of you. Brandishing a weapon is against the law, whether you have signs in your yard or not. I came out here as a favor to you, but next time you pull a gun on anybody, you're going to jail."

Early sighed. Wouldn't do to piss off the only county commissioner who would still talk to him. Or the only woman who'd sleep with him. "Sorry. Won't happen again. Come on in and have some tea before you leave."

PJ's eyes traveled to the glass-tiered hutch housing Early's liquor. "Got anything stronger?"

Out of habit, Early checked the wall clock. Only three-thirty, but he supposed, as the saying went, it was after five somewhere. He touched the switch to illuminate the shelves. Various colors of bottles and liquids captured light, and the display became a work of art in its own right. Sole reason he'd purchased this particular cabinet. He couldn't drink any longer, betrayed by his old body. It couldn't process alcohol on top of all the drugs he had to take.

"Name your poison, honey."

PJ chose Irish whiskey—always did—and Early scuffled to the kitchen for ice, his longtime friend following, slipping off her coat and easing it onto the back of a chair, revealing a rose blouse, a shade he'd once declared flattering on her. She had worn it exclusively ever since. They returned to the living room with drinks. After they settled down to reminisce about their high school not-so-glory days, Early presented PJ with a plastic bound copy of the guidebook. As soon as he had realized the value of what he had in his hands, he'd rushed to town to run off copies.

"What's this?" she asked, thumbing past the copyright page. He supposed he'd violated copyright laws, but he didn't care if they jailed him. People needed to wake up and see the truth about fracking.

He tapped his original booklet. "This contains proof your constituents are being swindled out of their rights."

Her mouth gaped open. She studied the first few pages carefully, pulling the booklet closer to her face as if she were planning to eat it. At last, she set it back on her lap. "Early, where did you get this?"

"That little gal who ran off whining to the police dropped it on her way out."

PJ said, "Because you held a gun on her!"

"Not at all. I had already set the rifle aside. The booklet fell out of her car as she got in."

PJ's lips pursed, and she resumed reading. From time to time, he pointed out significant passages and they discussed their meaning.

"I have to say, this material is disturbing." She pointed at the booklets stacked by his feet. "What are you going to do with those?"

"Send them to newspapers, commissioners, government agencies—everyone I can think of who might put a stop to this horrific rape of our land."

"Your language is inflammatory, as usual, but I agree the booklet raises several questions. Has your lawyer seen it?"

Early grinned. "He met me at the copy shop." The exhilaration of the day was wearing off. Suddenly he felt so light-headed he could barely walk. *Chemo brain,* he thought. Those pills scrambled his circuits and made him so tired his bones ached. He covered a yawn with his hand and PJ, bless her soul, must have noticed.

"I can take this with me?" she asked, holding the copy she'd been reading.

"Sure, but before you leave, I have a little job for you." Early retreated to his office. His fingers trembled slightly as he picked up his revised will. Writing one had been far easier years ago when death felt like a hypothetical event far in his future.

He returned, feigning nonchalance as he dropped the document into her lap. "I want you to notarize my will."

"You're too rascally to die," PJ protested.

"Wish it were true."

PJ had probably figured out months ago that his health had declined. Asking for her signature was his way of confirming her suspicions. Soon everyone would know. If his skin turned any sallower, they'd be calling him mustard and slapping him on a baloney sandwich.

~

THE SKY HAD ALREADY GROWN INKY by the time Summer reached Twin Oaks restaurant. When Ty had suggested meeting there, she let him know it had to be his treat. Paying for truck repairs and a rental car had left her strapped.

Summer knew Ty had to be careful with his money too, especially with Grace, his five-year-old half sister, to support, but he had *some* income. Even though his nonprofit, Water Warriors, couldn't pay a salary, he received disability from the mercenary outfit that had sent him to Iraq—the least it could do, since he'd lost his leg from the knee down while rescuing a diplomat. And Summer was certain he received social security survivor benefits for raising Grace.

Inside the restaurant, Summer easily spotted Ty's table. Grace had accompanied him, her coloring book already spread out, silverware bundles shoved aside to accommodate her giant box of crayons. Three water glasses were already weeping condensation, so he'd been here long enough to speak to a waiter. Ty started to stand, but Summer motioned for him to stay seated.

She pulled out a chair, resisting the impulse to hug Grace because the child sometimes flinched when touched. Dayita's mother was fairly certain Grace was autistic, but Ty had never shared a diagnosis if there was one. Grace's quirks might be caused by trauma from her parents' deaths and a brief stint in foster care until Ty could rescue her. If so, the unusual behaviors should disappear eventually.

"How you doing, Sugar Pop?" Summer asked.

For the first time since Summer had met the child, she made eye contact and responded without further prompting. "I go to school now."

Summer raised her eyebrows at Ty, before returning attention to Grace. "That's great. What's your favorite thing about school?"

"I get to color a lot."

Summer refrained from rolling her eyes. The kid was still crayon-obsessed. "What else?"

"Ms. Jones is nice, but she makes me talk."

Makes? Whatever the teacher was doing seemed to be working. This was the longest conversation Summer had experienced with Grace, and her speech problem with consonants had all but disappeared.

While they perused a menu, Ty said, "This town has the best pizza in the world, and this place serves up some of our best."

"Puh-leeze." No way this little burg had the best pizza in the world.

"Seriously, lots of Italians settled here, and you won't find better red sauce anywhere."

Laughing, she held up her palms and surrendered. "Okay, okay, bring it on."

Ty put in their order, half pepperoni and mushroom, and half plain cheese. The waitress set a couple of beers before them, and a Shirley Temple in front of Grace. Summer was pleased he had remembered her brand of beer. A small thing, but still. While they waited for pizza, he reminisced about Grayton Beach State Park. "Most beautiful beach I've ever seen," he said, which was saying something since he'd traveled all over the world during his military service.

She had never seen a beach outside Florida, but judging from photographs she'd seen, those near her home were exceptionally lovely, with spectacular sugar sand, sweeping dunes, and emerald-streaked turquoise water. Best of all, no high rises reminded you what century it was, so you could imagine the scene that greeted early settlers and indigenous people.

Ty reached for her hand, but almost as soon as his fingers brushed hers, the light in his eyes evaporated and he pulled away as if he'd been stung. What kept him from renewing the electrifying connection they'd experienced in Florida? During the meal, Summer felt awkward and heartsick; their conversation seemed so inconsequential, the stuff of long-married couples after romance had faded.

When the table had been cleared, Ty placed a document in front of her. "What's this?" she asked.

"A petition I want you to sign."

She read the heading: *Fight back, Say No to Frack*. "Unh-uh. No can do." She pushed it across the table.

Ty laid it in front of her again, jabbing an index finger against an empty line. "What do you mean you can't? You saw Corky. What happened to him is a direct result of the kind of shoddy maintenance and construction Fairhope is known for. We've got to stop these guys before they destroy everything important. When the cement in all these wells starts to fail—and it will, especially the older wells—the aquifer will be polluted with toxins."

"Triple-cased cement's a pretty strong safeguard against failure." She pushed her chair away from the table. "But that's not the point. No one is going to believe I tested this water fairly if I put my name on your petition. The validity of my research stems from having a total lack of bias—in either direction."

"No engineer can guarantee the wells are earthquake proof. Predicting disaster is a no-brainer. Everywhere the oil and gas industry goes, they betray American citizens, leaving a trail of air and water pollution in their wake."

"I still can't sign."

For several seconds, Ty's jaw remained rigid. Then his face softened and the anger left his eyes. "I'm not giving up on you. One of these days you're going to team up with me at Water Warriors."

A pang of longing swept over her at the idea of their being a team, but she pushed the sentimentality aside. There was a difference between a persevering hero and a stubborn fool. He often acted like the latter, blinded by a singular passion. Their desire to safeguard water had brought them together, bound them in a common fight, but their weapons differed.

"Don't hold your breath. I need to get paid for my work."

A wry smile twisted his face. "Guess I deserve that. I can barely keep a roof over Grace's head as it is." He signed the credit card slip, defusing the tension of the moment. "Where will you work?"

She'd been thinking about her future a lot since Kit Corbett's job offer, but still hadn't developed a clear vision. "Maybe a university, teaching, doing research. Or there are lots of jobs with the US Geological Survey. Or maybe I'll work in the private sector."

"You'd work for a fracker?" His contempt hung over the table almost visibly.

"I haven't ruled it out. A geologist can help a company avoid drilling near fault lines and locate possible hairline cracks in rock near aquifers. It's important to drill in places most likely to be productive without damaging the water supply."

He seized the hand she was resting on the table, squeezing the fingers tightly. "If you can't work with me, stick with the university or geological survey—please." He eased up on the pressure and pulled her hand up to touch his cheek. "No frackers."

She wouldn't promise—her future was a road with an unknown destination. "You mentioned Corky. Any word on his prognosis?"

Ty looked grim. "He will have to be careful the rest of his life. No drinking alcohol, ever, because it could send him into a tailspin again. And there are dozens of drugs he should never take because they tax the liver. The doctors also say, based on the FloMoshun formula Dayita was able to get, there's a possibility of cancer down the road. Several components are known carcinogens." He paused. "Sure you don't want to sign the petition?"

She shook her head. He was a warrior; she, a scientist. They attacked problems from different perspectives. Her cell jingled.

"Ms. Cassidy, this is Kit Corbett. Have you given my job offer any consideration?"

She laughed, her eyes flicking over to Ty, and she came off sounding brittle, rather than amused by the speed of his renewed contact. "I haven't had much time to think about it."

"Well, my staff and I were talking about you this morning, and we thought you might like to have dinner with a few of us. If you get to know us better, it might make your decision easier."

She felt awkward with Ty overhearing every word. "Uh, sure, sounds good."

Corbett suggested having the dinner five nights from then and said he'd pick her up.

The ramshackle cabin was a bit embarrassing. "I can drive myself."

"Oh, no, I won't hear of it. We're supposed to have bad weather coming. I'm not going to be responsible for putting a Southern girl out on our roads at night."

"Okay, see you then."

Ty eyed her curiously. "Big plans?"

"Not really." She hoped she didn't look as flustered as she felt. If the firm wanted to take her out to dinner, this was a serious job offer—and right now all she could think of was the way Ty had insisted, *No frackers.*

To deflect his interest in the phone call, she told him about Dayita's impending visit. "So what are the must-see places around here? Where should I take her?"

6

November 19

Summer set out for Patricia Kirby's home, eager to follow through on the lead she'd picked up at the library about a possibly tainted well. Eventually she realized she was traveling in the general vicinity of the Glover properties, though the road to the Kirby residence wound to the northwest side of the hill the brothers were feuding over.

When a delivery van approached from the opposite direction, Summer was forced to back down the one-lane country road about a quarter mile before locating any sort of shoulder wide enough to allow the two vehicles to pass. Summer held her breath, but she managed to keep her car out of the ditch. After the truck edged by, she set out again.

Patricia Kirby's brown and tan two-story was in a small tract of modest homes that backed up to the kind of rolling hills Summer loved. The heavy wooden door creaked open and Mrs. Kirby welcomed Summer with a froggy voice.

Was the elderly woman a smoker? Congested from a cold? Either way, she didn't sound healthy.

Mrs. Kirby's hair mounded softly in white clouds while her eyes blazed blue as a summer sky. From her posture and the cautious way she walked, Summer deduced she suffered from osteoporosis and spinal compression fractures, ailments her grandmother had suffered from. Summer followed Mrs. Kirby into the brown and gold living room, where every inch was covered with family photographs, mementos from vacations, dust-furred candles, decoupaged photos cut from magazines, slightly chipped teacups and saucers, miniature fairies—decades' worth of brick-a-brac. Though Summer wasn't a nester herself, she found the room warm and cozy, a welcoming place you could easily call home. Summer settled into an overstuffed chair, her back resting against a knitted afghan.

"I was so glad when you called yesterday," Mrs. Kirby said from a reclining lift chair. "You're the first person who acted like they really cared. Fairhope and Sunburst Energy Companies sent someone out here to test my water and assured me it was fine. Even though they said they were under no obligation to help, they delivered bottled drinking water. Good thing—I would have trouble squeezing that out of my budget." She seemed mortified by the admission.

"Could I see the analysis?" Summer asked. When the older woman operated the lift function to get out of her chair, Summer regretted asking. "I could get it for you if you tell me where it is. I don't want to be a bother."

"No bother. It's good for me to move around. If you don't use it, you lose it."

After rifling through a cardboard box sitting atop a dining room chair, Mrs. Kirby handed Summer a file containing water analyses on her well for the past ten years, including the one Fairhope had paid for. Summer frowned as she flipped through the report. The company had run the basic fecal coliform and bacteria tests, but only added in iron, manganese, copper, pH— not the full range of testing needed to detect chemicals used for fracking. The company knew better, but Mrs. Kirby didn't. They should be ashamed for taking advantage of her.

Unfortunately, Mrs. Kirby's well wouldn't fit the design of Summer's study, which required randomly selected sites and included a baseline test for chemicals not ordinarily run unless a problem was suspected. Among other tests, Summer would measure the dissolved methane and benzene levels present before fracking took place and compare it to levels after drilling.

But no one would know if she fudged the sample a little and included Mrs. Kirby's well. She knew what Dr. Dunham would say: science required adhering to strict standards. But that overlooked the human element, this woman who stood before her.

"Did you report your problems to the EPA?" Summer asked.

"The reporter said I should, but Mr. Walsh said if the EPA found medications had changed my taste buds, he'd quit supplying drinking water. I still use the well for everything else."

"Aren't you worried about exposure to harmful chemicals?"

"If I let things worry me, next thing you know my hair might turn white."

Mrs. Kirby maintained a deadpan expression so long Summer wasn't sure it was okay to laugh until her hostess finally let loose a raspy, phlegm-filled gurgle. The woman's spirited attitude tickled Summer.

"I figure I'm not gonna get out of here alive anyhow," Mrs. Kirby said. "Something's gonna get me. Before much longer, too."

Might be true, but Fairhope had no right to hasten that day along. What if Summer slipped this sample in with the others, testing it with university's funds? Fairhope didn't play by the rules—why should she?

Aw, crap. She couldn't bring herself to do it. But she could write a personal check to cover the testing—even though it would drain the expense money the dean had deposited to her account this morning. She was a stupid weenie, but Claire Dunham would be proud.

~

DURING TEN FACE-TO-FACE MEETINGS, no one greeted Summer with a rifle. But only Mrs. Ammons, the one who had invited her over after a contentious phone conversation, welcomed her into a home and signed the release to permit testing. The rest accepted materials and promised to get back to her.

It was nearly ten by the time she returned to the cabin with little to show for a day's work. Once inside, she pulled off her boots and padded to the pantry for ramen noodles. The cellophane crackled as she tore the packet open and dumped the contents into a ceramic bowl with water. The microwave beeped as she punched in the appropriate cooking time and pressed *start*.

Her phone jingled, and PJ's enthusiastic salesman's voice greeted Summer. After initial pleasantries her tone changed. "Look here, we got some complaints today about your house calls, and on account of county ordinances, you're gonna have to restrict your visits to between nine in the morning and six at night."

Great. How was Summer ever going to get enough people signed up—she wouldn't be able to catch working folks at home during those hours. She told PJ she would comply with the ordinance though it would really hamper her project.

"How about using the telephone instead?"

Summer endeavored to hold in a sigh. "Most people hang up on me before they even find out what I want. I really thought people would want to know their water's safe."

"If you tell me the names on your list, I could set up a little meeting at my church tomorrow night. We'll invite everyone to come on out and meet you after our Wednesday night church supper. You can eat with us first. We're a real friendly bunch. You'll see. I'll get our church secretary to help me call folks. And I have a little radio show I tape tomorrow morning and I'll invite those listeners to come too. We'll get the word out, so when you call or visit homes later, people will know who you are."

PJ's kindness touched Summer. "I don't know how I could ever thank you enough for this."

"Just part of my job as county commissioner. I want you to love West Virginia so much that you'll come back and visit after your project is over. Maybe you'll even want to move here."

If she'd been in the room, Summer might have kissed her.

After changing into the sweats she'd been sleeping in, Summer checked her email. To her surprise, there was nothing from Dayita, and she hadn't phoned all day either. Summer had expected her to be so excited about the trip that she'd pester her all day with plans and questions. In her mind Summer had been rehearsing ways to temper Dayita's expectations. This cabin was hardly the Ritz-Carlton. She dialed her friend, but it went straight to voicemail. While leaving a message, she heard a vehicle rumbling up her road. Who would be coming here at this hour?

Through the tiny window, she saw an overnight courier van. Summer watched the delivery man walk to the back of the truck. Even though she felt like a chicken shit doing it, she grabbed the ax by the fireplace and moved it within reach of the door before she opened it to receive the package.

"Sorry this is so late getting here," the driver said. "We had trouble finding this place. It doesn't exist in our GPS system."

Summer joked with him about needing to hang a red flag out by the highway. When she closed the door, she returned the ax to the hearth, poking fun at herself. Until she opened the package and read Dayita's message. Summer called her immediately.

"I've been worried sick," Dayita said. "What took you so long?"

"The courier just now delivered the phone. How'd you find out my stuff's hacked?"

"Because they accessed my phone and computer through yours."

Summer hadn't even known that could be done. So Dr. Jennings had been right about their devices being compromised. "Surreal."

"Nope, this is *very* real. I've tried to warn you about the dangers."

She had, but Summer hadn't taken the warnings as seriously as she should have, or adopted the extra security measures Dayita had recommended. No wonder Dayita hadn't answered a couple of text messages Summer had sent her. "My fault, Dayita. What should I do now?"

"First, damage control. The new phone gives you a way to communicate anything important or sensitive without the hacker eavesdropping. And two, I'm going to find out who he is."

"Dayita—"

"It's not as impossible as you might think. I already figured out he works for Allied Consulting and is probably—"

"It's Elliot Ral."

"What?"

"Elliot Ral. Bet you a million bucks."

Dayita snorted into the phone. "As if you had two bucks to rub together. How do you know this guy?"

"How did you figure out he works for Allied Consulting?"

Dayita explained the timing of the incident corresponded with her hacking into Signal-Muller and when she searched their financial records, Allied Consulting stood out since the company was the anonymous source for the *Trending Time*s article.

"Makes sense." Everything kept pointing to Ral. But who hired him?

"Your turn: how do you know this guy?"

Summer filled Dayita in on Ral's harassment at the Ohio meeting. "So what's next?"

"We beat Ral at his own game. He's probably installed a keylogger on your computer."

"How do I remove it?" Summer asked.

"Not yet." Dayita chortled with glee. "Put the old phone in your car if it doesn't matter if he knows where you're going. Leave it at home when you want him to think that's where you are. Keep using the old devices for routine or unimportant messages so he doesn't get suspicious. Meanwhile, I'll lay a trail to lure him in and when he follows it, boom!" Judging by the reverberation, she must have smacked her palm on a table. "I'm gonna trap him so fast and so bad, he won't know what happened."

Busting him sounded good to Summer. The sooner the better, so she could get on with her research unimpeded.

Dayita added one last warning: "Be sure to keep your laptop lid closed unless you're using it. Some hackers activate the built-in camera and watch you while you're changing clothes."

The laptop sat across the kitchen table from her right now. Summer yanked down the lid.

~

EYES DROOPING, BOOK CLOSED on his lap, Early Glover let his neck fall against the adjustable headrest of his recliner. The regimen of pills exacted a toll. He found himself drifting off in the middle of chapters.

Sloane Dumont burst through the front door without ringing the bell, arms pumping, hips thrusting, hair tossing, mouth traveling at warp speed. "I heard what happens to people who ring your bell, you crazy old outlaw, so I snuck in to catch you unawares. I dragged him over here," she jerked a thumb over her shoulder at her fiancé, "so you can convince him what's in his best interest."

They were still standing in the foyer. "Come all the way in and close the door," he suggested.

Corky Rogers stepped forward and held out a hand. "Evening, Early."

Early grabbed his arm and pulled him into a hug. "Get over that handshake stuff. It was okay when we were buddies, but not now that we're gonna be family. Boy, is it good to see you back on your feet. When did you get home?"

"This morning. I'm doing much better."

"So, he's really your dad?" Corky asked Sloane, his voice teasing.

"So he says, but my mother isn't around to confirm it."

Early could hardly believe it himself. He hadn't thought of Lacey

Dumont in years when her letter had arrived six months ago, posthumously informing him he had a forty-year-old daughter. "Your mother's word ought to be good enough. You want a DNA test?"

One hand on her hip, Sloane assumed a stance of defiance, which Early suspected was half real, half put-on. "How about a dad who was around while I grew up."

"Must we rehash this every time we're together?" Early asked. He was still trying to wrap his head around the recent revelation that he had fathered this woman. He had dated Sloane's mother briefly over one Christmas holiday before returning to his studies at Duke. Sloane was angry at him, and he didn't blame her, but Lacey had never told him she was pregnant. She went off to live with a great aunt, so how was he to know?

Wallace rumbled his displeasure and padded off toward the laundry room without a backward glance, headed for his cuddle bed. Smart dog. Naps were out of the question with Sloane around.

"Why don't that dog like me?" Sloane demanded.

Early rose from his chair. "Wallace doesn't like anyone but me." And Ms. Cassidy—an odd turn of events, one he was still pondering.

Sloane flicked her head toward the wall by the front door, making her thick mane even more unruly. "That the rifle I been hearing about? It's all anyone wants to talk about when they come into the salon."

Early grinned. "I've finally become infamous, West Virginia's latest incarnation of the Hatfields and McCoys. It's not loaded."

"We have business to take care of," Sloane said. "Let's sit down."

They moved into the living room, Sloane leading Corky toward the sofa, leaving Early his recliner.

Early scooped the book up from the chair. "I'd still appreciate the honor of giving you away."

"Hell, no. I'm not the property of any man, and I wouldn't let you even if you had come to my soccer matches."

The few times they'd met in the past, she refused all his attempts to get her to open up about her childhood. "Did you play soccer?"

Sloane pouted. "No, but maybe I would have if you'd been there to encourage me."

A memory floated up: her mother's expression when she'd asked him to take her to a chic flick at the drive-in. He'd been reluctant but when Lacey pulled that face, Early gave in. To think this young woman wouldn't exist if he hadn't.

Corky put an arm around her, pulling her closer on the couch. "Baby, quit beating up on Early or he's gonna take back the invitation to have a real family Thanksgiving together. None of us can help what's past. We gotta make the best of what we have today."

"A good philosophy," Early said. "You should listen to this man."

"So says the great philosophy professor." Sloane rolled her eyes, then her shoulders, the latter signaling a mood change. "Anyway, explain to my foolish man here why he needs to give a deposition against those assholes at Fairhope."

Early laughed. "Corky, I hope you know what you're in for, marrying this spitfire."

Corky grinned. "I do. Even if you didn't raise her, she takes after you more than she ever took after her mother."

"I believe you're right." Lacey, near as he could recall, had been far more sugar than spice, and she did like to sprinkle her sugar around.

"You're both full of shit," Sloane said. "Get down to business."

"Yes, ma'am," Early said with mock obedience.

Sloane got up and stomped toward the kitchen.

"Where you going?" Corky asked.

"Getting myself a beer. You want one?"

"Sure," Corky said.

"I'll bring you one this time, but don't get any ideas. I'm not gonna turn into a step-and-fetch once we tie the knot."

Early grunted. "If you don't stop being so mean, I'm gonna turn you over on my lap and give you a good spanking. Clearly your mama didn't administer enough of them."

Sloane whirled around, fury in her eyes. "Don't you say nothing about my mama."

Early didn't flinch from her gaze. "You have a right to be angry, but I told you before I didn't know about you."

"You should've married her." She started to leave the room, but with one hand on her hip, she swiveled back toward him. "I guess you can escort me, but it don't mean you're giving me away." With that, she left.

She sure had a penchant for drama, but he was determined to

love her in what time he had left. If she'd let him.

He turned his attention to Corky. "Grab one of those booklets off the floor."

"Aw, I'm not much of a reader, Early."

"Take it anyway. I think you'll find this more interesting than a New York Times best seller. As you know, my lawyer wants you to give a deposition about your accident. In case you aren't sure it's the right thing to do, you should read this little booklet. If you haven't already figured out these fracking companies are crookeder than Little Tenmile Creek, you'll know it for sure when you finish reading."

After skimming the booklet, Corky said, "Tell your lawyer I'm in. I'll give him everything I know about Fairhope."

Early got up and shook his hand. "You're doing the right thing."

Soon, Early hoped his lawyer would possess enough ammunition to shut down the whole business of hydraulic fracturing. And he hoped he'd live long enough to see it.

7

November 20

EARLY GLOVER COULDN'T HELP BUT SMILE as he watched Ty Franceschi brandish the guidebook like one of those evangelical preachers waving a Bible.

"This is exactly the tool we need to break the frackers' backs," Ty said.

"I knew you'd see its significance right away." Early rose to refill his guest's coffee. "I have copies printed up to mail to the newspaper and every commissioner and legislator in our district."

"If you'd like help getting them fixed up to mail, I'm your man." Ty said.

"Sure—tomorrow if you have the time to help address mailers."

They agreed to start around ten in the morning.

"What's the clipboard for?" Early asked.

Ty turned the board around to face Early. "While I'm here, I'd like to get your signature on my petition."

Early read aloud the heading. "'Fight back, Say No to Frack'—did you start this campaign yourself?"

"Yes, sir. It's only a matter of time until we'll face a disaster in West Virginia if companies like Fairhope continue their shoddy practices."

Early admired the young man's fervor for environmental causes. They often irritated the same people at county commission meetings. Early placed *Zen and the Art of Motorcycle Maintenance* underneath Ty's petition to prevent the pen from poking a hole in the paper. He added his name to the others and flipped through the pages to see who else in this community possessed a lick of sense. Quite a few, it seemed. Early returned the petition to Ty and walked with him to the door. "If you leave me a few copies, I'll circulate them to friends sympathetic to the cause."

Ty shook his hand. "I'd appreciate it. It's online, too, of course."

At the front door, the young man paused, inclining his head toward the gun leaning against the wall. "That the rifle I've heard so much about?"

Early grimaced. "Much ado about nothing. My granddaddy's gun. Not loaded. I've never used it."

"Mind if I—" Ty reached for the weapon and ran his fingers down the barrel. He hoisted the gun to his shoulder, sighting it out the window. "It's a beaut. My dad had one like it. Took me hunting a lot when I was a kid."

"Sounds as if you have good memories. Never took to hunting myself." His brother Joe, though, he was another story. He frequently brought home squirrels and deer for their mother to fix for supper.

Ty gently leaned the gun back against the wall. "My dad's rifle was one of many things the bank's thugs took from our house when they foreclosed after my parents died. By the time I made it back from Iraq and rehab, nearly everything my family owned was gone."

The young man's pain struck a chord. "That's a bitter greeting for a returning vet. My granddaddy carried that rifle over his shoulder so often, seemed like his third arm." Objects transmitted memories. They embodied emotions. Early's eyes slid toward a watercolor of street musicians he and PJ had bought on a visit to New Orleans. They had sung along with musicians like those in the painting, fed the orangutans in the Audubon Zoo, strolled along the Riverwalk to watch the sunrise. PJ should get the painting when he died.

Early followed Ty onto the porch, noting how the wind was picking up. Might rain later in the day, or snow if it got cold enough. "My grandfather would be honored if you would take his gun hunting someday."

"Thank you, sir. I might take you up on that."

The young man's smile was sad, and Early knew he would never come back for the gun. Any old gun wouldn't fulfill the need in Franceschi. We only cherished objects that bore testimony to the love we shared with others.

~

Wet stuff the cashier at the gas station termed "a little sleet" pelted the windshield as Summer pulled out onto the highway again. She hoped her buddy Rocky the Raccoon had a warm place to hole up for the night. Her old phone lay beside her on the seat, since there was no point trying to trick Ral into thinking she was at home. As PJ had promised, she'd promoted Summer's free independent tests and tonight's meeting at the church on her morning radio show. The commissioner thought folks would turn out. If she was right, Summer's job would be much easier, even though they wouldn't all attend, especially with this weather.

At least the sleet wasn't sticking to the asphalt. The Chevy, a lighter vehicle than her truck and one she wasn't used to driving, held the road okay, but the windshield wipers needed to be replaced. They squawked and only partially cleared a path; but if she ducked her head a bit, she could make out the road ahead.

A hundred yards past the gas station, a black SUV without headlights took his side of the road out of the center. She edged to the right and honked her horn. Instead of realizing his mistake, the SUV driver swerved even further into her lane.

Her adrenaline shot into overdrive.

"You dumbass," she yelled. To avoid a crash, she steered onto the shoulder, taking care not to over-correct. After a bump, thump, bump, and one thud where who-knows-what hit the underneath of the vehicle, she slowed to a stop. Her heart still bump-thumped ferociously. She loosened her grip on the wheel and tightened it again, shuddering as she saw what lay ahead: five yards past the front bumper, the shoulder dropped into a drainage culvert. If she had hit that drop-off at traveling speed, the car would have rolled. She might have died. It could happen that fast. Inertia, force, material strength—the laws of physics were brutal and unforgiving.

When she tried to back up, her tires spun futilely on the soft surface. She climbed out and surveyed the situation. If she had been in her truck, she would have had something to put under the tires for traction. Then again, if she had been in her own vehicle, her tires wouldn't have gotten mired. A truck pulled in behind her and two men got out.

The first one dragged long fingers along one side of a neatly cropped brown beard. "Looks like you could use some help, Ms."

"Yes, sir. I'd appreciate it." Maybe for every jackass creating havoc in the world, there were two kind people who strove to undo the damage.

Even though the ground was pocked with puddles, the other fellow knelt behind the Chevy, peering through glasses at the ruts. "Believe if you put her in reverse, we can push on the front end and get you out."

It worked, and she shouted thanks and waved as she drove on.

She glanced at her watch: too late for the supper now, but she could still make the meeting.

When Summer arrived, she easily spotted PJ Wine, decked out in a pink top adorned with blingy doodads. The commissioner introduced Summer to three couples and expressed surprise that she hadn't arrived in time for the meal.

Still rattled from her near-accident, Summer launched into an account of the way she'd been forced off the road.

Elliot Ral strolled in. Same cocky fedora. Same legal pad, or maybe it was a different one. But same guy all right. He had some nerve showing up here. Hacking her phone and laptop were bad enough, but trying to kill her was something else entirely.

Her hands shook. "Excuse me," she said to PJ.

She clomped toward Ral, leaving a trail of mud on the tile floor. "You drive a black SUV?"

His glasses were fogging so she couldn't see his eyes. "Yeah, why?"

"Did you run me off the road a few minutes ago?"

He raised his eyebrows until they arched above the frames of his glasses. "Now why would you think such a thing, Ms. Cassidy? Lots of people drive black SUVs."

She interpreted his cavalier tone as a confession. "Mr. Ral, I don't know which gas company hired you as a 'consultant' but I know you're only here to cause trouble. I'm going to make this as clear as I can." She whipped up the volume about six decibels, to make sure he understood she would tolerate no further interference. "Piss off."

The total silence of the room filtered into her consciousness. PJ Wine sidled next to her, pulled on the sleeve of her jacket, and whispered, "Summer, honey, you might want to keep your voice down. This is a church."

Appalled, she turned to face the dozen people who had come

in directly from the supper to attend her meeting.
   Well, shit, she thought—but at least she hadn't said it out loud.

8

November 21

THE RED DOOR SLAMMED IN SUMMER'S FACE, another landowner who'd sold rights to Fairhope, turning her down. She couldn't muster enthusiasm for any more face-to-face contacts today. Despite the discouraging progress, she cheered up when the garage notified her that her truck was repaired. She missed the old heap and knew its weight and size would hug the road better than the Chevy she'd nearly wrecked last night.

She was still ticked off every time she thought about Ral's showing up at her meeting. After her outburst, she was lucky PJ had provided such a glowing introduction while Summer passed out her flyers. Everyone had been friendly and interested in the testing, even though Ral tossed out a couple of comments meant to derail participation. The women had pressed enough leftovers from their church supper on her to serve as dinner for the next two days.

After she retrieved her truck, she headed across the Fourth Street Bridge to Glen Elk. PJ had told her about these cool things called pepperoni rolls, a local specialty at Tomaro's Bakery. The aroma inside the shop nearly made her swoon. The rolls themselves were about six inches long: Italian bread baked around long slices of pepperoni and they didn't require refrigeration so they would be the perfect quick lunch when she was out collecting samples. She was so hungry, she devoured one right there in the store and bought a half dozen to take home.

Back at the cabin, she was rehearsing tweaks to her spiel when her cell jingled. She answered, instantly nervous when she realized the dean of her college, Alonzo Kimball, was on the line. She'd never met him, had only seen his photo on the university website. Her only contact with him so far was her request for emergency funds, which he'd sent—and she'd blown on Mrs. Kirby's testing.

"How's your research going, Summer?" the dean asked.

Deans didn't call students to check on their progress. With a sinking feeling, she knew the direction this conversation would take. The situation called for truthiness, a useful word coined by comedian Stephen Colbert.

"Dr. Kimball—" What if Ral was listening? She didn't want him privy to this conversation. She hung up and called the dean back on her new phone.

"I'm sorry we got cut off a few minutes ago, sir. Everything's moving right along with my research. A county commissioner is arranging meetings with landowners, a local driller showed me around a job site, and my background chapter is now complete."

"Good, good." The dean cleared his throat. "I'm calling because the university has concerns about this project going forward. One major funding source has withdrawn, as I'm sure Dr. Jennings informed you, and now, with Dr. Jennings on sabbatical your project is in a real bind, isn't it?"

Summer chose her words carefully. "My outside reader, Dr. Dunham, is helping me find additional funding sources, and I was hoping you might help too. Dr. Jennings believes this research is vital, sir, but he isn't able to continue it himself."

"I suspect he found the article in *Trending Times* disheartening."

"Yes, but it's a terrible article. A hatchet job without named sources."

"Hmmm. Dr. Jennings believes a plot is afoot to stop your research. Do you have any reason to believe that's true?"

She had to tread carefully here. "The man who heckled him at public meetings has shown up here in Clarksburg as well. And last night, an SUV crossed the center line and ran me off the road. I'm sure it was the same man."

"Did you report it to the police?"

She had next to nothing they could work with. "All I saw was a black SUV. No face, no license number."

"The roads in this part of the country get slick this time of year. Isn't it more likely the vehicle lost control? Perhaps Dr. Jennings' case of nerves affected your interpretation. At any rate, I'm glad you weren't hurt."

"Me, too." Mentally she replayed the way the vehicle came at her. "The driver seemed to have full control of the SUV. And the heckler showed up at the meeting right after I arrived."

In the dean's silence she could hear skepticism. If she weren't careful, he would be recommending a sabbatical for her too. Or a softly padded room. Especially if he'd read that horrible letter in her admissions file from her mother. Summer realized she'd made a tactical error. She should have told him about the hacked devices, something she had solid proof of instead of the accident. If she tried to tell him now, she didn't think he'd believe her.

Still, Summer had no choice but to ask for his help. "Sir, I was hoping you might have an idea who might replace Dr. Jennings as my dissertation adviser."

"I'll be in touch, Summer. I'll let you know what we decide."

The dean didn't believe Dr. Jennings or her, but the SUV had deliberately crossed the double yellow lines. She didn't know if Ral had been driving, but if not Ral, who?

She texted Dayita about the road incident, asking if she had made progress in designing a trap for Ral.

Working on it, Dayita responded. No details followed.

Summer hoped she worked fast.

~

WITH ONE ARM RESTING ON KNUCKLEHEAD'S BAR TOP, Hank Walsh swiveled on the stool to watch two Fairhope employees align themselves at a proper distance from the target to begin a game of Around the Clock. Every time he visited this joint now, he looked around for that grad student who'd blown everyone away at the dart board, but she hadn't shown up again. He wished he'd gotten her phone number. Her dart skills certainly livened up the game.

The match-up Hank was watching now didn't look too promising. Marky Markowitz let the first dart fly. When it hit metal and clunked to the floor, Marky swore viciously. Hank knew better than to josh with him or cross him in any way. Markowitz had a reputation of taking offense easily. The fellow's opponent, his opposite in disposition as well as body type, lumbered into position. Corky Rogers' dart stuck one ring outside the bull's-eye. In uneven fashion, the match continued until Markowitz quit. He stomped to the bar and retrieved his bottle of Bud, pulling a long drink before slamming the bottle on the counter.

"It's not fair, Rogers," Marky said. "I could whip you with one arm tied behind my back if you were drinking beer instead of a fucking Shirley Temple."

Rogers took the comment in stride. "Afraid my drinking days are over." To the half dozen Fairhope employees present in the bar, he added, "Sloane's expecting me for dinner, but I wanted to stop by to thank you fellas for the flowers and cards you sent to the hospital." He extended his hand to Markowitz, who turned away as if he hadn't seen the gesture.

Appearing uncertain what to do with his rejected hand, Corky finally saluted his friends. "I'll miss you guys."

Hank hopped up to shake the big guy's hand. "Don't be a stranger, Corky, and stay well."

Others came over and slapped Rogers' back, walking him toward the entrance.

"Heard you quit," Lanny Elkwater said to Rogers. "What'll you do now?"

"Once the doc gives me the all-clear, I'll haul fresh water for Corbett Engineering," Rogers said. "Doc says even a whiff of chemical fumes might put me back in the hospital."

It was good of Corbett to offer Rogers a job, but Hank knew it would gall his dad. His father's inferiority complex flared at any mention of Corbett. It made him do stupid stuff, marrying Nadine being a prime example. Half her attraction, besides being younger than Hank's mother and in better health, had been the broken engagement to Corbett. His dad was sure he'd scooped up a prize Corbett hadn't been able to win. But Hank suspected his father had it all wrong. Corbett's wealth and upbringing engendered the confidence to let Nadine proclaim to all who'd listen that she'd broken off the engagement. It was far more likely that Corbett ditched Nadine when he discovered how devious the wench could be.

Hank ordered a second beer, watching another dart game underway. Someone slid onto the stool next to him. When he turned, he was surprised to find Holly Stone, his father's secretary, and she was holding manila folder. The taste of beer in his mouth soured.

She asked the bartender for a cold one. "You said you were worried about your dad—wanted me to let you know if I noticed any problems?"

"Yeah?" His father was hiding something, and Hank dreaded finding out what it was. When his father examined the company books at day's end, he looked like a man in denial about his terminal illness.

Holly's eyes flitted over those clustered nearby, her grip on the folder tight. "Let's sit somewhere more private."

Even though he knew he wouldn't finish a second beer, Hank carried it to a table far from Fairhope employees still hanging around near the bar.

Wasting no time, she slid the folder across to him. The document on top was an inspection on a Fairhope gas well. As he turned the page, he expected a list of infractions—or worse, evidence of a leak. Instead, the state inspector found no issues with the Domico drill site. Hank didn't get it—why had Holly brought this to his attention? He glanced at her, the question in his eyes.

"Look underneath," she said.

The single sheet under the inspection was a photo copy of a thousand dollar check from Fairhope to Alfred Chambers signed by his dad. The memo at the bottom said "Wedding Gift."

"Who's Alfred Chambers?" Hank asked.

Holly explained Freddy Chambers was a state well inspector. Two weeks ago, he had issued a warning about a potentially leaky wastewater impoundment on the same site. The original report disappeared, replaced by a new backdated one with no citations. From the beginning, the revised report seemed irregular, but when she reconciled the checkbook and found the gift, she suspected corruption.

Hank couldn't believe it. Didn't his father realize he was only making the situation worse by bribing a state regulator? The press would have a field day if it came out that Fairhope knew about a leak and didn't fix it. What if flowback water from the holding pond leached into the aquifer or ran off into people's water supplies? What if people got sick?

"Can you sit on this for now—not tell anyone else yet?" Hank asked. "I want to give my dad a chance to make this right. He's not thinking straight."

"Sure," she said. "That's why I brought it to you and not the authorities."

Considering the way his father had suddenly pink-slipped Holly, it was a wonder she hadn't immediately grabbed the opportunity for retribution as a whistle-blower. Hank tucked the damning evidence back inside the folder.

"This leaky holding pond explains why your dad is so gung-ho about stopping that university study," Holly said.

Word of the free water tests the university was offering was all over town, but Hank hadn't known his father was against them. Whatever was happening at the Domico site must have his father worried sick.

9

November 22

Joe Glover climbed on the tractor. It beeped as he backed up. Morning chores complete, he was anxious to learn what was happening at the drill site. Since the weather was supposed to cooperate, the crew was supposed to pour the pad today. He shifted gears, ready to ascend the final hill where Walsh's SUV and a dozen men had assembled on the hilltop. He pulled in next to them.

This was a big moment, one Joe had anticipated for months. Walsh promised he'd put the well into production the moment it was drilled even though oil and gas prices were depressed.

Joe's hopes rose when a vehicle entered the access road. As it came closer, his excitement faded. It wasn't the convoy of cement mixers he'd expected. No, it looked like a sheriff's vehicle. He killed the tractor engine and waited, his hands strangling the steering wheel. A deputy got out and strode toward the men in hard hats. Joe leaned forward to hear, though he knew what was coming.

"Boomer Walsh?" the deputy said.

Walsh stepped forward. "Yeah."

"This is an injunction ordering Fairhope Energy Corporation to stop work here immediately."

"Dammit sonofabitch." Boomer took out his cell. "Holly, call our lawyer and find out what the fuck's going on. We got slapped with another injunction on Glover's property."

Joe didn't need a lawyer to tell him what had happened. His brother Early had happened. Early and bad news were one and the same.

~

First thing in the morning, Ty called and invited Summer to go on a short road trip. She wanted to see him, but she had already scheduled appointments to collect water samples and she needed to persuade Dr. Dunham to contact the dean about additional funding sources. Summer couldn't let this research dry up from lack of money. She was sure there were others like Patricia Kirby who needed to know their water was safe.

"Why—what's up?" she asked Ty.

"There's someone I'd like you to meet."

Summer frowned. "When did you want to go?"

"Now, if you're not too busy."

She was tempted to refuse altogether, but could hear Dayita's accusing voice: *what about the people you do know, when do they matter?* She offered to go with him around eleven, after she collected the samples. She took the new phone to gather the samples, but planned to take the old one wherever Ty was taking her. The sooner Dayita trapped Ral the better. This figuring out which phone to use was a complication she didn't need in her life.

When Ty picked her up at the cabin, she asked, "Where exactly are we headed?"

"Amwell Township, Pennsylvania."

"Oh." Exactly what she'd been afraid of: this trip was another effort to enlist her support for his anti-fracking cause. She knew about Amwell, of course, the trouble they'd had with their water.

At the first stop light, he glanced at documents on the bench seat between them and suggested she read them while he drove.

The suave voices of NPR announcers faded into the background as she digested the manuscripts. The first paper examined the economies of two states, finding that although industry mouthpieces promised shale gas extraction would produce jobs and an economic boom, after gas production petered out, the industry had destroyed twice as many local jobs as it had created.

He turned the radio's volume down a notch. "What do you think?" he asked when she laid the study down.

"I don't trust reports unless I know the funding behind them and how they reached their conclusions."

"It's put out by a very reputable environmental group. They wouldn't lie."

He couldn't be that naive. "Everyone lies when it suits their purpose. If it was a solid scientific study, it would have revealed funding and how they reached their conclusions."

That little mouth shrug thing he did when he was annoyed flashed over his face. She doubted if he had any idea how clearly his face gave away his thoughts, even when he didn't say anything.

He slid the small bound booklet across the seat, closer to her. "Read this one."

It was titled "A Landman's Guidebook." Where on earth had Ty gotten this? She skimmed the pages, but wasn't impressed. People weren't as stupid as this book made out. She didn't think anyone would buy the argument that government wouldn't keep issuing permits if fracking were unsafe. Unless they were sleepwalking through life, people understood how politicized every government institution was today, including state or federal environmental agencies. Energy companies alone contributed over six million dollars to mostly conservative campaigns in the last election cycle, and for every dollar spent, they got about one hundred back in the form of subsidies. Quite a windfall. And that didn't even consider the influence bought with those contributions. It could result in appointments of energy-friendly department heads who shaped agency missions and controlled expenditures.

She deposited the booklet on the bench seat.

They left the highway and turned down a bumpy one-lane road. He pulled off beside a camper barely longer than his van. Only half of the camper's exterior was properly sided. Wind lifted random strands of shredded Tyvek on the damaged end.

Ty got out and announced, with his arms flung wide, "Welcome to Jennifer Roy's life."

Summer figured she might as well get out too, though she still had no idea why he'd dragged her all the way up here. Who the hell was Jennifer Roy?

"She lives here with three kids," he added before he strode off to knock on the camper door.

Summer surveyed the bleak surroundings. An SUV with a bumper duct-taped into place. A toilet and sink plunked down in the side yard for no apparent reason. A tire swing dangling from an ancient oak. A Big Wheel tricycle lying on its side. Assorted clothes, including a turquoise thong and matching lacy bra, dangled on a line stretched between two pines.

The door opened and a woman's exuberant voice hollered she'd be out as soon as she found her parka. She added something about darn kids always moving her stuff. As Jennifer Roy stepped down the concrete blocks that served as stairs, Ty planted a kiss on her cheek and got a hug in return.

Summer's stomach knotted. How good of friends were they? Jennifer was short, well-built. Hard to judge her age—maybe late twenties like Ty. Cute nose. Too cute.

Jennifer steered them to the faux redwood picnic table in the yard. "I'd invite you inside, but between Annie's and Bobby's toys and Jonah's guitar and school books, not much room left for visiting."

Ty straddled the bench next to Jennifer, so Summer sat on the other side. "Jen, I brought Summer here so she could hear your story firsthand."

Jennifer attempted to finger her chestnut hair into place, though the wind immediately kicked her locks into a frazzled mess again.

"Me and my kids didn't always live like this, Summer." Jennifer swept her hand to indicate her porcelain yard art. "Until two years ago we lived on a farm that had been in my family a hundred and thirty years."

Jennifer went on to explain how she supported her children by working as a supermarket cashier, and even after her divorce, she had been getting along fine. Until she sold her mineral rights. "When I signed that lease for $1,000 an acre, it felt like winning the lottery. Netted $95,000. Figured I could send the kids to college and still have some left to retire someday."

Jennifer's eyes watered and it took her a few seconds to regain control. "First my dog died. Alfie was old, so I didn't think too much about it. A few months later two goats and my horse developed these strange bare patches on their hides. They acted tired all the time. They wouldn't eat. Vet said he'd never seen anything like it. We had to put them down. Then my littlest, Annie, busted out in blisters. Doc gave me a steroid ointment, but it wasn't much help. She kept getting sicker. My neighbor gave us the first clue as to what was going on. The plastic pipelines that crossed his land were leaking like sieves. I tried to drive up to the drill site, but they had the road gated. I called and talked to someone in the company office. They said I couldn't go up there. On my own land. So I got suspicious of what else they were trying to hide."

Jennifer hired a lawyer, who finally gained access. "It took months of calls to state officials, but some fellas finally showed up. They found out aerators at the holding pond had quit working. No one knew for how long."

By then, Jennifer said, Annie was hospitalized, fighting for her life. Jennifer sniffled periodically as she related the rest of her story. "Now we can't live on my farm, and I can't sell it neither. Who'd want to live there? The water pipes are all corroded. Can't sell my cattle because they test positive for heavy metals. And all that money that was supposed to pay for my kids' college—it didn't even cover all of Annie's medical bills. Anyway, we were lucky my cousin had this camper setting on his property. He let us move in, rent free."

Jennifer looked off in the distance, her expression wistful. "Suppose I'll spend the rest of my life not knowing if my kids are going to come down with some crazy kind of cancer and die."

Summer's throat tightened, as she thought of her sister. No child should die. Ever. But what did they want from her?

Ty leaned forward on the bench and pulled Jennifer into a sideways hug. She stayed there for a minute, and then shrugged him off. It didn't seem an unfriendly shrug-off. More like refusal to give in to despair. Summer had to admire that.

"Oil lobbyists own the legislators," Ty said. "In 2012, Pennsylvania stripped funding from a bill to start a health registry to track respiratory, skin, stomach, and other ailments related to gas drilling. Legislators also inserted a requirement into the bill that doctors have to sign a confidentiality agreement to have access to chemicals used in fracking process. So they can't share information with other health care workers even if it might save lives."

Jennifer sniffled once again and visibly stiffened her spine. "Anyway, my lawyer's filed a lawsuit against Fairhope. I hope those people rot in hell for what they've done to my Annie."

Fairhope again. Once Ty decided a company was corrupt, he didn't give up until he brought them down.

~

Around four-thirty, Boomer Walsh waltzed into A Cut

Above. Over a week had passed, time enough for Sloane to cool off. She accepted walk-ins, and he couldn't be the first guy overcome by those bouncy jugs.

A bell tinkled as he opened the door. A Cut Above provided top to bottom service with five separate rooms off a long corridor. He touched his baseball cap and dipped his head as a greeting to Zenia, who practiced reiki and therapeutic massage in the first room. She didn't have a customer at the moment, so she was messing around with her own nails.

Throaty laughter tumbled from Sloane's room. He sauntered to the archway leading to the hair-wash area she shared with another stylist.

Lingering there, he watched Sloane blow-drying an old lady's damp hair. His eyes inhaled a double dose of Sloane: her lovely backside pointing toward him, her face and those gorgeous mammaries animating the mirror. In the midst of chatting with her customer, she smiled into the mirror, meeting the old lady's eyes. She used to smile at him that way, the reflected image of her lips somehow even more seductive than the flesh, her fingers on his scalp, skillful, intimate, arousing.

In the midst of his recollection, her eyes lifted from her client and locked on him, and the memory wilted as she whipped around, arms tense.

This wasn't likely to go well, but it was too late to back out. He removed his ball cap. "Hey, sweetheart, you got time to work me in for a trim today?"

"Don't you 'sweetheart' me. I told you not to show your sorry ass in here ever again."

The old lady's hand flew to her mouth, covering a grin.

"Aw, come on, Sloane. Nobody cuts hair as good as you. Tell me how I can make it up to you." He might as well go all the way. On tiles littered with hair trimmings, he knelt before her. "I'm begging for your forgiveness. I'll take you to dinner at the Wonder Bar. Anything you want. You name it."

"Out."

"Don't be like that."

"Out—or I'll press assault charges."

He got to his feet. "Assault? Just for—"

Sloane launched a hairbrush at his torso. The old lady's eyes in the mirror crinkled with amusement. His face burned. Bitches, the both of them.

A can of hairspray connected with his thigh and clanked against the floor. Sloane reached for the scissors.

"All right, all right!" He backed away. "You'll be sorry."

"You're the one who's gonna be sorry, you pitiful prick, if you ever come near me again."

He beat a retreat down the corridor, his teeth clenching as laughter reached his ears. And Zenia joined in. Well, fuck every last one of them. He just didn't get it. Why didn't Sloane like him? The woman drove him crazy.

~

Traffic racing up and down Bridgeport Hill created a steady rumble, but Commissioner PJ Wine still surveyed the parking lot of Twin Oaks to make sure she couldn't be overheard as she talked with Boomer Walsh and Joe Glover.

"You're asking too much." She didn't appreciate their double-teaming her.

"We wouldn't be asking if this wasn't in the best interests of the workers in this county," Boomer said.

As if he had ever been interested in any worker other than himself—a thought PJ kept to herself. "I've done more for the working man and woman than anybody else and you know it."

Joe roped a wiry arm around PJ's shoulder, which she promptly sloughed off. He needn't act all condescending toward her. Corbett was backing her as mayor, come next election. See if they thought they could push her around then.

The brush-off didn't slow Joe down. "Everyone knows how much good you've done for Harrison County. We think there's more you can do for your friends, that's all."

PJ waved to a couple from her church as they strolled by on the way into the restaurant. She waited until they were out of earshot. "Look, I've done all you asked up to now, but no more. I voted against those regulations because you thought they'd strangle further development of the gas industry. And I brought the Cassidy girl out to your place, Joe, before the anti-frackers had a chance to get to her. You had your opportunity to persuade her to your way of thinking. If it didn't work, too bad."

Boomer's face reddened. "You might not be willing to do more, but I intend to make these problems go away. I've worked too hard to see it all go down the drain. No outsider's gonna screw up all we've got going for this county."

"Who cares about the girl," Joe interjected. "What are you gonna do to stop my brother? Fracking's been the best thing to happen to this town for decades. You gotta do something about this latest injunction."

"Seems like you should have some influence there," Boomer agreed.

PJ wondered if these two had slept through their high school civics classes. "I can't interfere with a court order."

At least Boomer had the good sense to realize when the cause was lost.

Joe stayed on, pushing, yammering. "My wife wasn't the only Glover you been especially good friends with. Don't think I haven't noticed how often your car's been at Early's over the years. Make him see he's in the wrong." He gnashed his teeth and then turned away to spit onto the asphalt.

As if PJ could change Early's mind. Joe ought to know better, but he was like a dog with a bone he refused to let go of.

"You know he ain't gonna stop with shutting down one measly operation," Joe said. "He's rampaging against the whole industry. That's the way these environmental crazies are. If Early ever had to do real work for a living, he'd be singing a different tune."

"Someday you're gonna regret the rift with Early," PJ said.

Joe snorted. "Fat chance."

"You ought to make up while you still have the chance. Your brother looks terribly skinny and yellow. His kitchen's chock full of pill bottles. I think he has cancer."

"You're gonna be mighty disappointed if you expect me to start boo-hooing," Joe said.

"He wrote up a will. I had to notarize it."

Joe took a step closer, his nose wrinkling. "A will—what's in it?"

"Sorry, it's confidential."

Joe looked over his shoulder and spat on the ground. "He's still leaving the farm to me, isn't he? Who else has he got?" He paused to think it over. "He isn't giving our land away to some charity, is he?"

"If Early wants you to know what's in his will, he'll tell you himself. Go mend fences with your brother before it's too late."

Joe stood stock still for a few seconds, huffing like a boar, then turned on his heel and left.

"I bet he'd change it again if you make up with him," PJ yelled at his back, but she didn't think he heard. Joe slammed the door of his sedan and took off.

How could two brothers, both fine men in their way, very different men, allow their relationship to fall out like this? PJ regretted encouraging Joe to assign his mineral rights to Fairhope. Both Joe and Boomer had flipped $2,500 her way, compensation for her role in the negotiations. But she couldn't have foreseen the trouble the transaction would cause. She shook off the guilt. Natural gas exploration was good for the local economy and good for national energy independence. It was her duty to promote the welfare of the county even if it meant some friends got hurt.

As for the will, PJ didn't know who this hairdresser was to Early or why he'd leave his farm to her when he knew the family land meant the world to his brother. She didn't expect anything herself. The special friendship's benefits only extended so far, and the benefits part had all but disappeared this past year. Her dear friend was dying.

~

FIFTEEN MINUTES INTO THE RIDE back, Ty turned down the radio. Finally, Summer figured she would find out why he had dragged her up to Amwell Township.

His eyes cut over to her momentarily before shifting back to the two-lane highway leading back to I-79 and over the border to West Virginia.

"Two years ago Jennifer's cousin—the one who owns the camper—contacted me through my website. He was desperate for help and wanted to know if other farms outside Amwell Township had trouble with Fairhope Energy."

"Have other farms experienced problems?" she asked.

"Absolutely. Thousands have."

Thousands—Summer wouldn't believe his figure without seeing a scientific study. People on both sides scattered numbers around like confetti—and they had about as much substance.

Ty added, "I wanted you to understand it's not only my family suffering from energy company accidents."

Ah, the hurt that wouldn't heal. The loss of his parents, missing their funerals, Grace's disability—those wounds were more traumatic than the leg injury he suffered in combat. He couldn't save his own family, so he sought out others injured by the energy industry and tried to save them instead. Survivor's guilt was something Summer understood.

"Jen's cousin confided that little Annie is still sick," Ty said. "He doesn't think she'll make it through the rest of the year, but Jen's in denial."

How did anyone know what to say to news so awful? Summer could only come up with a cliché. "No child should have to die."

"Children die all the time. At least half a million kids have died in the Iraq War, and over a million have been orphaned. All these deaths because of fossil fuel. Someone has to stop them."

Ty, she knew, had decided he was that someone. Summer pretended to study the wisps of clouds out the window while she stewed over his intense drive, which surely would lead to more trouble. "So you organized a protest against Fairhope and got arrested."

His jaw twitched. "Didn't realize you knew."

"Dayita."

For a moment, he remained quiet, processing this. "I should have realized she would research me. She's a good friend. I hope you know how good."

She knew, but did he? "You have no idea what she went through to get the information for Corky about FloMoshun." Summer detailed the out-of-town trips, the all-nighters Dayita had pulled.

"If you give me her phone number, I'll thank her personally." Ty flicked the blinker on to signal the turn onto the Interstate. "What else did she find out about me?"

Summer waited until he'd merged into the high-speed traffic before answering. "You were a Navy SEAL, then a mercenary."

He jumped in quickly to justify his becoming a mercenary. "Because I needed the signing bonus."

"For your mother's cancer treatment—yes, I know." This meant, in a way, he had sacrificed his leg to save his mother from the illness caused by an energy company. There really was no limit to what Ty would do to stop them.

"Is there anything your friend can't find out on the Internet?" he asked, only half-joking.

"You must have been close to your mother."

"There was absolutely nothing she wouldn't have done for her kids. We were her life."

Summer felt an ache, that familiar sense of loss she always felt watching Mrs. Patel fold Dayita into her arms after a Frisbee match as if she were the most precious thing in the world. "You're lucky to have had such a devoted mother." She couldn't keep the bitterness from spilling into her voice. "My mother pretty much doesn't care. Never has."

"You're wrong."

"How would you know?" she asked. He didn't answer. How could he? He'd only spent a few days last spring in her mother's house while he recovered from the gunshot wound. Summer had spent years living in her dead sister's shadow. Even before the accident, Jordan Cassidy had been more focused on the daughter who had spent her short life in and out of the hospital as surgeons tried to repair congenital heart problems. Though Summer loved Chrissie, increasingly she had come to realize she'd always resented her twin. As a nine year old, Summer had even known a smidgen of guilt-tinged hope that after the funeral Jordan Cassidy would finally notice the daughter who was healthy. Didn't happen.

After Summer was injured by Jake Fowler, whole days followed when her mother had actually behaved in maternal fashion. During those short weeks, Summer hoped they were finally going to forge the kind of relationship Dayita had with Mrs. Patel. But Jordan Cassidy had quickly returned to popping pills after Summer healed.

No, Ty didn't understand anything about her family.

They drove in silence for a short while.

At the Morgantown exit, Ty put on his blinker again.

"Where are we going?" she asked.

"While we're up this way, you ought to see Coopers Rock. Geologists are supposed to like rocks, right?"

They drove through the university town and accelerated onto another Interstate highway. Soon the landscape grew more rural. She knew their elevation was increasing from the way her ears popped.

For some reason, Ty had decided to play tour guide. "We're passing over Cheat Lake. The Cheat River is a great place for white water rafting—should be on your must-do list for next spring. Got its name because it has cheated so many people out of their lives."

Ty exited the Interstate, and soon the van wound its way along a paved road traversing the state forest. He resumed his touristy narration. "This area gets its name from a fugitive whose hideout was in these parts. He was a cooper who made barrels and sold them to folks who lived nearby."

After parking, he led her toward a long wooden bridge. Intermittent wind snaked its way up her sleeves and under her collar as their feet thumped along the boards. When she reached the overlook, she stopped breathing.

For miles in every direction, the view was glorious: magnificent cliffs, massive boulders, the stunning river gorge, and Cheat Lake itself. The underpinnings of the planet lay in front of her, stark and beautiful.

"I've wanted to bring you here ever since we first met," he said. "I'll bring you back another time with proper gear if you'd like to go caving."

"Would I ever!" One reason they'd bonded so quickly after they met was their shared love of outdoor adventure, but could he really go caving with his prosthetic? Of course, she chided herself. He could do everything else—kayak, hike—why not spelunking? She admired his determination not to let the loss of his leg hold him back.

"This isn't the best time of year to visit," he said. "It's prettier when everything's leafed out in spring and summer or in early fall when the hillsides are blanketed in orange and gold."

She breathed the words, afraid to break the spell. "It's spectacular just as it is."

"Thought you might appreciate it."

An overwhelming sense of connection to everything washed over her. The hills, the river, and Ty standing beside her. "Did you know the soft, sugary sand on our Florida Panhandle beaches is almost all pure quartz carried away from these hills by rivers?" The gorge was a testament to the power of water, and the persistence of time. "Thank you for bringing me here, for understanding what it would mean to me."

Ty slid one arm around her waist and pulled her around to face him. "There's no one else like you in the whole world. Not even close. I've missed you, Summer."

His words were ones she'd waited for, but why had it taken so long?

His hands cupped her hipbones and her backside bumped against the railing. As he pressed his body against hers, a muffled sound rose from his throat so softly she thought she might have imagined it. He nuzzled his face into her hair, and she wrapped her arms around his shoulders, pulling him closer. He tunneled under her jacket, lifted the bottom band of her sweater, his fingers pressing into the channel of her spine, and finally he was kissing her, kissing, kissing, and the world outside them disappeared.

But then he drew back, his head turned away, his hands keeping her at a distance. "We have to talk."

Talk—now? "What about?"

"Your mother."

A volcanic woman madly in love with him was about to explode from the strongest desire she'd ever felt in her life—and he wanted to talk about her mother? *Her mother?*

But he was still talking. "She's not the way you think she is at all."

You had to be kidding. She shrugged his hands off her shoulders. "Yeah? How is she?"

"Remember when your mom let Grace and me stay at her house after you—" He broke off.

"After I shot Jake Fowler. It's all right to say it."

"Your mom and I had a long talk," he said. "She told me your exceptional intelligence would be wasted if you didn't get your PhD. Said you'd resent anyone who sidetracked you. I tried not to buy it at first, but the more time I spent with you, I knew she was right."

This was her mother's idea of caring? At least now she understood why Ty had grown so distant after he returned to West Virginia.

"I'm smart, but not smart enough to make my own choices—is that it?" she asked.

Ty said he'd asked her mother the same thing, but she had an answer even for that: Summer possessed boatloads of IQ, but not nearly as much EQ, or emotional intelligence and maturity. "She said you take too many risks—and I think she's probably right," Ty said.

How dare her mother, who couldn't get out of bed in the morning without anti-depressants, accuse her of emotional immaturity. "Take me home," she said. When Ty's mouth opened as if he intended to argue, she added, "Now," and stalked off toward the van.

"Don't be like that," he called to her back.

"Why not? You and my mother think I'm emotionally immature. I'm trying to meet your expectations."

For the duration of the drive, Summer turned NPR up as loud as it would go. She wanted ain't-no-mountain-high-enough kind of love from a man. It should take more than a measly warning from her fractured mother to turn an ex-SEAL into a world-class wimp.

What ticked Summer off more than anything—her mother was partly right. Eventually Summer would resent anyone who kept her from her doctorate. The challenge of absorbing new material was her addiction, and a major reason she hadn't jumped on Kit Corbett's money pile. Yet.

As soon as Ty's van turned down her dirt road, she asked him to let her walk the rest of the way, said she needed the exercise. Arms hugged to her torso, she tramped toward the cabin. She was twenty-two frigging years old, for God's sake. Her mother had no right to interfere in her life.

She picked up her phone to call Dayita but set it back down. Her mother's betrayals were just too humiliating to share. Dayita had a mother who supported her in every way. How could she possibly understand what this felt like? She slumped onto the sheet-covered couch, empty, hollowed out, hungry.

That lasted three minutes, tops. Sitting here feeling sorry for herself was beyond ridiculous. She jumped to her feet and grabbed her truck keys. Ty was one guy out of about three-and-a-half billion in the world. She was healthy. Young. And smart enough to have a rewarding career ahead of her. Maybe as a university professor. Or she could make her fortune with Kit Corbett or another company like his. She had the world by the frigging tail, way more fortunate than most of the world's population.

All she needed tonight was a big plate of mac and cheese. Then maybe a few beers paid for by bets on dart games and the distraction of one of those other three-and-a-half billion guys.

~

Seven-thirty. At night. What unholy ghoul would be visiting without calling ahead at this hour? Early would live in the city if he wanted visitors dropping by at all hours.

He tramped over and peeped through the hole. A huge eye stared back, and as it withdrew, first a nose, and then the entire face became visible, one he recognized, despite the bizarre warping caused by the fish-eye lens. He was surprised to see Ms. Meth-head at his door again. She had already seen his rifle, so he didn't suppose she planned to rob him for drug money.

She stepped away and a dim, much larger figure replaced her and pressed the bell twice—rude, if you asked Early. When he saw who it was, he wasn't surprised. What else could you expect from an asshole who would grab a woman's boob while she was trimming his hair? Early's fingers itched to load his granddaddy's rifle and drill a hole through Boomer Walsh's chest. The nerve of the man to show up here. Early clenched and unclenched his fists a few times and talked himself into calming down. Walsh didn't know Sloane was Early's daughter—hardly anyone knew.

Why in the world would the two of them think they could change his mind by showing up at night?

"Wallace, you'd better go hide in the bedroom," Early suggested. "This is likely to get ugly." The hound looked up with soulful eyes and huffed before padding down the hall, the golds and browns of his coat rippling as he passed under the incandescent floor lamp.

Early flung the door open. The redhead positioned herself well behind Walsh. Early was struggling to remember her name. "What do you want?"

Walsh laughed. "That's no way to greet your neighbors, Early."

Her name came back to him. Rhymed with Fucker. "You aren't my neighbors. You live out in one of those fancy new subdivisions, Walsh. I don't know where Ms. Tucker is from, but I suspect she was spawned in one of those swamps down south."

"Don't be such an old grouch," Boomer said. "You gonna invite us in?"

Early had half a mind to slam the door, but relented. They were up to no-good, and if he knew the nature of it, he could foil their evildoings. Or at least aggravate the hell out of them.

Once in the living room, they settled onto the couch at considerable distance from each other. Couldn't blame them. Early wouldn't want to sit near either one of them.

He eased into his favorite chair. "Well?"

Boomer leaned forward, clapping a calloused hand on each knee. "Our lawyer would be one mad sumbitch if he knew we were here, but I got to thinking how everyone would be better off if we could keep the courts and the lawyers out of this. Surely, as neighbors we can come to some sort of agreement, Early. Tell me what it will take to make this legal action of yours go away, and we're gonna do our best to make it happen. Anything reasonable. You name it."

"Replant the top of my hill—"

"Okay, you've got it."

"And then pack up all your equipment and go away."

"Be reasonable, Early."

"You asked what it would take and I've told you, real neighborly and polite-like."

Walsh and the redhead exchanged looks. She took the lead. "Here's what we were thinking, Mr. Glover. I heard from some of your neighbors you had cancer—"

"That's none of anybody's business."

Ms. Meth-head Tucker scratched at an arm. "Well, that's what we heard."

Walsh jumped in with his version of sympathy. "And we were really sorry to hear it, Early. We might be on opposite sides of this fight, but I sure never wished for you to get sick. Now, I know those treatments can be expensive and tiring."

Ms. Tucker broke in. "Especially when you're trying to keep up such a large farm."

Walsh acted as if it were the first time he'd heard this, as if they hadn't rehearsed. "You need to concentrate on getting well, Early. Think how much easier your life would be if you didn't have to feed animals and keep all your pasture cut."

Their concern was so touching Early felt obligated to help them out, his voice toting a bucketful of sorrow. "I do get so exhausted, especially—" He paused, staring down at his feet, noticing for the first time his big toe had poked its way through his sock. He wiggled it, studied the length of the nail, which could use a clipping, then decided he'd let the suspense build long enough. "Especially what with trying to run all the truckers off who are stealing my water. I get real tired of all you frackers."

Walsh's face cracked into what might have been an exasperated smile. "You take great pride in being a card, don't you, Early?" Boomer modulated his expression, trying, Early guessed, for earnest sincerity. "We are prepared to offer market value for the land and take the burden of upkeep off your shoulders—or we can offer you $50,000 to make the injunction go away, and you can keep your land and the mineral rights. The offer's more than fair, don't you think?"

The woman added, "Either way, the money would cover a lot of medical expenses. If you don't have your health, you don't have anything." Early was tempted to respond that Ms. Meth-head should know. He felt quite proud of his restraint. It really wasn't like him to be so tactful.

"Come on, Early. What do you say? Let's do this without lawyers."

"Or rifles," Ms. Meth-head joked.

Early had heard enough. His knees cracked as he rose and stood, arms akimbo. "You wouldn't be here if you didn't know you were going to lose in court. And you will. I've got depositions from former employees and more important, I've got the guidebook where you admit you trick people into signing over their rights. I mailed copies this morning to the newspaper and every government official around. My lawyer's initiating a class action suit. We'll halt drilling all over this state. So here's what I've got to say: good night, neighbors."

Walsh got to his feet. "Sorry you see it that way. Fracking's giving a lot of people around here good jobs. What's gonna happen to all those families without paychecks?"

"What's gonna happen to them when you poison all the land and water?"

"Come on, Darlene. There's no reasoning with this moron."

Early could hear them as they walked to Boomer's SUV.

"You sure he didn't get that damn guidebook from you?" Boomer asked.

"No way. Do I look that stupid?"

"You don't want me to answer that. I don't see where else he could've gotten it."

"Not from me."

"Well, you can believe this: if I find out it was you, I'm gonna personally beat the living shit out of you."

Wallace emerged from hiding and sidled up beside Early's stocking feet. Early shut the door and stooped to rub the mutt's lumpy head.

"Wallace, buddy, I almost feel sorry for Ms. Tucker. Men like Walsh give our gender a bad name."

10

November 23

HAD THE RINGTONE OF HER MOBILE always been this loud? Summer yanked the covers over her head. She wanted nothing more than to go back to sleep, but the previous evening darted about in her mind. By the time she'd chased down a big plate of mac and cheese, she hadn't arrived at Knuckleheads until around nine. She had dropped in, hoping to run across Hank, but he wasn't there. Last night the atmosphere hadn't been much fun because this guy named Marky was bellowing about not being able to work because of an injunction. All the men had been in a sour mood. None presented even a remotely pleasant distraction from Ty.

Summer had only half listened to the bickering until Corky Rogers' name came up. Marky said it was too bad Corky hadn't died in the spill since the traitor was participating in a class action lawsuit. The viciousness animating Marky's face shocked her.

When another man suggested Marky lay off Corky, it started one of those male pissing contests with the predictable make-me, think-I-can't exchanges that brought the bartender over to separate them. Almost as soon as he stepped back behind the bar, the men were at it again, their friends jumping in on both sides.

To avoid becoming collateral damage in their argument, Summer left after only one round of darts.

That night as she lay rolled up in quilts, if her mother's latest betrayal wasn't bouncing around in her head, the memory of Ty's kiss was. And when he wasn't on her mind, the controversy over Corky Rogers tormented her. The lawsuit was riling up neighbor against neighbor. When she knocked on doors, she might encounter not just indifference but outright hostility. It must have been nearly three in the morning when she fell asleep.

And now, before the sun had even dared to show its face, her phone wouldn't shut up. If she could endure a few more riffs, whoever it was would go away. When silence finally sifted over the cabin again, she burrowed more deeply under the blankets, her feet numb with cold despite woolen socks. She must plug the drafts in the cabin walls with something Rocky couldn't pick out of the cracks. Must build a fire. Not now. Later. Much later. She drifted back toward sleep.

The obnoxious song on her mobile jolted her awake again.

"Yeah?" she croaked.

"Gee, I'm sorry. I didn't mean to wake you. I pegged you for an early riser. I'll call back later."

She shoveled her hair away from her face and propped herself up on an elbow. "I'm awake now anyway. Who's this?"

"Early Glover."

"You're early, all right."

He chuckled. "I found something you might find interesting, Ms. Cassidy. A Fairhope Energy landman's guidebook marked 'proprietary, do not distribute.' One of those legal thieves accidentally dropped it on my property."

She remembered how he had first greeted her at his door. "Your rifle have anything to do with your acquisition?"

"Not exactly."

She pushed herself all the way up off the quilts on the floor. "Actually, Mr. Glover, Ty Franceschi let me read his copy yesterday."

"Good, I hope you found it as informative as I did, but actually I discovered something else pertaining to you in particular. Loose copies of an addendum to Fairhope's contract were tucked into the back of the book. Fairhope is now offering free water testing with the promise of bottled water delivery if certain chemicals are present. The offer is void if water is tested by third parties other than their chosen lab or government agencies responsible for water safety. That would eliminate you, Ms. Cassidy. This document was drafted right after you came to town."

Finally—an explanation of why Fairhope clients were turning her down. Any doubt she still had that the company might be innocent evaporated. "I'll stop by to see the addendum later today if that's okay."

Only when the conversation ended, did Summer realize Ral probably heard every word.

~

AFTER EARLY'S PHONE CALL, Summer consumed several cups of coffee and fixed herself some oatmeal. It was Sunday, and Summer was determined to get some exercise while she tried to make sense of her life. The more she thought about Fairhope's sneaky efforts to undermine her study, the angrier she became.

A dead pine stood near her driveway. Summer had never thrown a hand ax before, but the ax by the fireplace and the dead tree were handy outlets for her frustration.

From experience, she knew a wide stance provided the best stability. She pointed her leg at the dead pine. Like throwing a Frisbee, the trick was to hold the arm still except for the elbow. With a grunt, she let the ax fly. It thudded into the dirt. She'd misjudged the heft of the ax head. It pulled her elbow down, which made the spin wonky. The elbow had to remain pointed at the target.

Easier said than done. She missed on the next two tries. On her fourth attempt, the blade thwacked into the trunk and bits of bark showered down.

She practiced for an hour, increasing the distance and working on the position of her thumb, which controlled the spin. When her biceps began to complain, she stopped for the day. This was definitely a different sport than the darts or Frisbees she had mastered, but if she practiced half an hour each morning, it would be a cool addition to her repertoire.

Then she headed to Glover's Lake, her new phone in her pocket. She parked on the side of the road a quarter of a mile short of the water. The sun's rays, low and bright white across the horizon, blinded her as she jogged along the road, making her wish she had worn sunglasses. A hawk floated overhead. Otherwise, the road was deserted.

As she rounded the bend, two white-tailed deer, both does, teetered on spindly legs beside the water. Sensing an alien presence, one raised its head and through some silent communication alerted the other. They froze like statues. Attuned to another silent signal they fled, the soft thuds of hoofs diminishing as they vanished into the woods.

Summer ran on. Joe Glover's silver sedan motored past, carrying him to church, she supposed. As she rounded the bend, Wallace dashed off Early's porch. His coat flashed brown and gold and his ears flapped comically as he galumphed down the road to greet her. He sent up an rrr-rh-rrh to announce her. The cabin opened. There stood Early in red plaid pajamas, rifle in the crook of his arm. When he saw Summer, he set the rifle back behind the door and motioned her inside. She and Wallace jogged up the graveled driveway.

Once inside, Early said, "You coulda knocked me over with a feather when I saw Wallace running down the road after you."

You could knock him down with a feather anyway. For real.

"He wasn't *after* me. Wallace was being friendly. Joining me on my morning run."

"Wallace isn't a joining kind of dog. He's been a one-man companion ever since he found the llamas and me and decided to stay."

Summer stifled a smile. Was Early jealous because his dog liked her?

"I'm glad you stopped by to pick up the addendum, but I hope you'll stay for coffee," he said. "And if you have time, you can help me feed the llamas."

That sounded like a hoot. For well over an hour they discussed philosophy, science, and religion, one subject tumbling into another. Early Glover had earned an undergraduate degree in physics before he turned to philosophy and religion.

"I was intrigued, Ms. Cassidy, by seeking answers in science, but one day I realized as fascinating as science is, it didn't answer some of the most important questions about our universe."

"Such as?"

"Why we are here. The meaning of life, particularly human life."

Summer blurted out something she'd heard in a documentary. "The purpose of life is to produce more life."

"Then it follows that if a human has no children, his life has no purpose."

"No, my statement was only a biological explanation of the purpose of every life form." Did Early Glover have children? No framed family photos hung on his walls or decorated his credenza. Summer's sister Chrissie suffered through multiple surgeries and didn't live long enough to have children. Still, her sister's life and death had meaning, even if Summer couldn't put it into words. What meaning did Early find in his own mortality—which might be imminent if Summer correctly understood what those orange plastic pill bottles meant.

"Did you discover answers to those essential questions about existence?" she asked.

He laughed. "Only more questions."

"Questions form the basis for scientific discovery. But how can you believe in God when no one can prove he exists?"

He leaned forward, intense and earnest. "A wise man once said, 'You cannot believe in God until you believe in yourself.' Believe in yourself, Ms. Cassidy. Trust yourself. You are an intelligent young woman. Keep asking the right questions. There's more to our cosmos than what we can understand through our limited senses. Some physicists suggest the existence of parallel worlds. Ah, so many mysteries to explore, so little time."

Sometimes Summer believed she could feel Chrissie reaching out to her. Did some part of her sister live in a parallel world, somewhere beyond the waltzing of wormholes? Did her spirit surf magically along gravitational waves? She didn't quite believe it, but how she wished it were true.

~

Sunlight refracted off Glover's Lake, splitting into thousands of tiny sparkles. The graceful bare limbs of a weeping willow along the water's edge arched nearly to the surface. The setting was darn close to Corky's conception of paradise—or would be once the willow leafed out again and the surrounding meadow greened up. Even now, Glover's Lake was something special.

He moved closer to Sloane and wrapped his arms around her from behind, alternating between peering over her shoulder at the water and nuzzling her neck. "I can't believe this is gonna be ours, that your daddy is giving it to you."

"That's what the old goat says."

"It wouldn't hurt you to be nice to him, Sloane. He's real sick, you know. Did you see all those pills in the kitchen?"

"I saw. He's probably making nice now because he wants somebody to nurse him through the end. If that's what he thinks, he's in for a big surprise. He was never there for me, and I'm not about to wash his butt for him now that he has the Big C."

Corky wished she'd forgive her daddy. If she didn't, she'd fill up with regret someday. "I'd help him. I've always liked Early. He's been a real friend over the years."

Sloane grunted. "You've got a marshmallow beating in your chest, Corky Rogers."

He turned her around and whispered on her lips, "Isn't that why you love me so much?"

She kissed him. "Mmmmhm."

"I think I heard you saying 'S'more, s'more.'"

A laugh bubbled from deep in her throat and she pushed him away.

Corky clasped her hand in his and they watched light shifting on the water. "Next spring, let's come out here for a picnic under the willow. You could bake those killer pepperoni rolls."

"Okay by me, as long as you bring the beer. But honey, lunch is gonna be the second course. I'm going skinny dipping in the lake and you're coming in with me."

Corky didn't think so. He was too fat. "My skinny dipping days are long past."

"Not true, you big teddy bear, your best skinny dipping days are ahead of you because you've never been skinny dipping with Sloane Dumont."

She had a point. Dancing two steps away, she taunted him to come and get s'more if he wanted her. He did—of course he did.

As he leapt forward, he heard a blast and intended to turn in the direction of the sound. Before he could, his chest exploded. He heard a gurgle, shocked to realize the sound came from his own lungs struggling to take in air. Sloane called his name. From the angles of her bones, he knew she raced toward him, but for some reason, she barely moved, like stop-motion animation. The world downshifted, grinding into low gear, each second dragging out, defined. What had she been saying—skinny dipping? Too cold to be naked. Very cold, he wanted to warn her, but his lips seemed frozen.

He heard cascading water, a noise which grew until it engulfed his entire head in an enormous and painful roar. Sounded like his tanker when it pushed or pulled fluids, but that couldn't be right. He was grateful when the roar was silenced, replaced by a deeply satisfying and amazing peace.

~

NAILS, BOARDS, HAMMER—everything Summer needed to fix the rotten third step lay on the porch. It simply had to be done before Dayita's visit. She had brought both her phones outside because she was expecting a call from Dayita to firm up plans for her visit. Swiping through tunes on the old phone, Summer chose a peppy number from a hot indie-alternative band, Neighbourhood. When the song came to lines about a lover's hands pressed into the holes of a sweater, her skin tingled, remembering Coopers Rock, the sensation of Ty's fingers touching the base of her spine.

She blew off the memory, humming along with the music, letting it lift her spirits. The prospects for continuing her research had improved. Because of the guidebook and Fairhope's restrictions on water testing, the dean was sending a check to cover minimal expenses, and he would chair her committee himself in Jennings' absence.

Light was fading from the sky as she positioned the first board. Darkness fell so early this time of year. Scuffling sounds caused her to turn around, hammer clutched in hand. Two squirrels clawed their way up the nearest pine, sending a hailstorm of bark to the ground below.

She slammed three nails home and had steadied the fourth between her fingers when a phone jingled. The old one—so not Dayita.

"Summer, honey?" PJ Wine's resonant alto greeted her. "My friend Early is in dire need of your assistance."

"Why? What's happened?"

"The sheriff hauled him into the jail for questioning. All a misunderstanding I'm sure they'll clear up soon."

"Why's he being questioned?"

"A truck driver was shot out near Glover's Pond."

Totally freaky—Summer had jogged right by the lake that morning. "What happened?"

PJ continued, "The man was shot with Early's rifle, I'm afraid. It doesn't help that he's been waving it around so much lately."

No, it didn't. And Summer remembered how upset he'd been when she mentioned the water haulers down the road from his farm. He had accused the truckers of stealing his water.

"He told me that rifle was never loaded," Summer said.

"Exactly. Early even breached the barrel recently to prove it to me. But the sheriff pointed out how easy it is to load a weapon. Honey, I've known Early all my life. He may be eccentric and a bit of a curmudgeon, but he's not a liar. Or a murderer. I believe him."

So the police thought the shooting was intentional rather than a hunting accident. Summer believed Early innocent, but she could see why suspicion immediately fell on him. "You mentioned he needs my assistance. What can I do to help?"

"Whoever stole the rifle bashed up that mutt of his. Early wants you to take the dog to the vet."

Poor Wallace. Still, she didn't think she was the best person to deliver him to the vet. "I'm sure the police would make sure the dog was cared for."

"They tried, but when Early heard which vet they'd taken Wallace to, he said to get his dog out of there right away and take him to—" Summer could hear paper rattling. "I've got the name right here—David N. Cone."

Summer had only seen the dog a couple of times. He might not be as friendly if Early wasn't around. "Couldn't you do it?"

"Not a chance. That mutt's as cranky and set in his ways as his owner. Early said you're the only person Wallace likes besides him."

Really? All she'd done was scratch the dog's ears a few times. "Okay, sure, I'll go get Wallace."

"What I can't understand is why anyone would think Early would shoot Corky Rogers. They were friends."

A fog of dread settled over Summer. That homely bear of a man in the hospital bed—murdered? Surely, there had to be some mistake. "Who did you say was shot?"

"Corky Rogers. Why—you know him?"

"I met him in the hospital when he was recovering from the spilled fracking fluid."

PJ clicked her tongue against her teeth. "That spill might have a connection to the shooting. Do you suppose the sheriff's thought of that? I should mention it, in case it might help free Early."

Summer bet the sheriff had already made the connection. Anyone furious about that spill might go after Corky. Early and Ty topped the list. But remembering Boomer Walsh's barely repressed anger when he learned Corky intended to file for worker's comp and Marky's rants in the bar, Summer thought those associated with Fairhope might possess even stronger motivation for murder.

~

PJ EYED THE SKY OUTSIDE THE SHERIFF'S OFFICE. The weatherman had been right, for once. The morning's sunny skies had given way to light mist, and if the temperature plunged any further, roads could ice.

She made a mental note to remind Summer to stock up on firewood. The old heater didn't work too well once it got much below freezing. And that young lady's truck better have good tread. Southerners had no idea what black ice or a heavy snow could be like.

Sloane Dumont screeched into the only empty parking spot, one marked with the blue handicapped sign, and trotted across the sidewalk in a pair of high-heeled faux leopard boots. PJ tsk-tsked. She wouldn't have worn such ridiculous boots even back in the day when she could have stood upright on them.

The streaks of mascara smeared beneath Sloane's eyes warned PJ that this might not be the time to ferret out how the young woman came to be in Early's will. Sloane, PJ knew, was engaged to the murdered trucker. The woman's nose was swollen, tissue-reddened. She'd thrown an unbuttoned coat on over pajamas and hadn't combed her hair. Not much of an advertisement for her beauty salon. PJ's church circle considered Sloane a bit of a slut, unkind gossip PJ had been inclined to dismiss as jealousy.

"Where the hell they holding him?" Sloane demanded.

"Who?" PJ asked, though she knew the answer.

"Early Glover—who else?"

Once again, PJ questioned what this woman meant to Early. "He says he had nothing to do with your fiancé's death and I believe him."

"I want to see him." When PJ didn't hop to it, the young woman added, "Now."

PJ stiffened. You didn't become county commissioner by letting folks run roughshod over you. "They're questioning him. You can't see him."

"Bullshit."

PJ glanced at the handicapped spot. "You better move your car. There's more parking behind—"

The stylist flung tears from her face. "Bullshit. Someone shot my fiancé and arrested my father—"

Father? It took PJ a few seconds to figure out she meant Early Glover. Early—a father? Even though PJ had lived here all her life, people continually surprised her.

Sloane was still talking. "—so if I'm not deserving of a handicapped spot, I don't know who is. Let those assholes give me a ticket. Now, where is that old grumpy-butt? I'm not leaving here without him."

"Let me find someone who can help you." PJ preceded Sloane into the building where she apprised Deputy Turner Skidmore of the situation. Skidmore disappeared for a few minutes, then returned and signaled they could follow him.

PJ led Sloane down a corridor to a small conference room, furnished with a rectangular table and six chairs. A deputy rose so Sloane could sit next to Dave Giovanni, Sheriff of Harrison County.

Standing behind Sloane, PJ introduced her but decided Early had better be the one to explain their relationship. "She'll tell you Early's innocent." At least, PJ hoped she would.

Sheriff Giovanni glowered. "Appreciate it, PJ, if you let me handle this. I'd like to get her statement without your prejudicing her answers."

The sheriff inclined his head toward the door. PJ considered playing the county commissioner card, but decided she'd already pushed the limits of Giovanni's patience by delivering Ritzy Lunch hotdogs for Early's lunch. But Early looked so scrawny these days he was gonna disappear altogether if he wasn't careful.

She waited outside, pacing the hall, her practical boots scuffling along the hard floor. What would the young woman say? Turner Skidmore had already produced complaints from people Early had threatened, but PJ reminded the sheriff Early had sworn he'd never used the rifle. What would he use it on, for Pete's sake? Years ago, PJ and Early were going to a high school bonfire at Hite Field. On the way, a truck with a deer lashed to the roof passed by. Early, the damn fool, got so upset he almost cried. You'd never know he'd been raised on a farm. Early wasn't capable of killing anyone or anything. Joe got all the hunting and farming genes in that family.

PJ's thoughts turned to Sloane's mother. She had known her, though not well. Pretty girl with a reputation. A year or two behind her and Early in high school. Moved away, and when she returned a decade later, she brought the child along. Had Early known about the girl all these years?

Finally Sloane emerged from the conference room, and PJ hurried down the hall. "They going to let Early go?"

Sloane lifted one hand. "Who knows? I told them Corky and Early been buddies for years. Early leads Corky's Bible study group."

A uniformed deputy passed by, shoving a poorly dressed fellow confined by cuffs in front of him. A whiff of the unwashed lingered in his wake. PJ accompanied the younger woman past the front desk, taking note of the genuine worry on her face. Sloane pushed through the front door, then turned, holding the door wide open, letting cold air rush in. "You're a commissioner, Ms. Wine. Make the bastards let him go. That old man might not have been much of a father, but he's not going to get out of being there for me this time. I want him beside me when I—" she swiped at her eyes angrily— "when I have to say goodbye to my Corky."

PJ felt sick to her stomach. If only she were half as smart as Early Glover, she might have a clue what was going on in her community. A murderer walked her streets. She didn't like the idea at all.

~

THE PLUSH RED CARPET LINING the walls of The Wonder Bar struck Summer as whacked out—though how would she know what was normal? It wasn't as if she had ever dined in a fancy steak house before. Framed posters of '50s stars like Sinatra and Monroe gave the restaurant a retro feel. The fragrance of seared beef made her mouth water.

She yanked her blouse hem down, making sure the safety pin replacing the missing button on her only pair of dress slacks stayed hidden from those at her table. She had forgotten all about Kit Corbett's dinner invitation until he called for directions to pick her up.

Corbett and the company vice president sat across from Summer, while Corbett's finance director and his wife took seats beside her. Lord help, she'd already forgotten their names. Every time she thought of Early Glover spending the night in jail, she felt sick. Had anyone taken his medications to him?

And that poor dog. Wallace's eye was swollen shut. Dr. Cone had laughed, though, when he learned Early had said delivering the dog into his hands was a matter of life or death. The doctor said Early had exaggerated faith in his veterinary skills and held some strange notions about certain other vets' ill treatment of animals. "Truth is, he likes me because I'm cheap," Dr. Cone said. "Wallace's injury isn't serious. He's going to be fine."

Summer made an effort to concentrate on the people she was with. Looking over the menu, she located the filet mignon and baked potato Corbett recommended.

She read through the other entrées. "Crab cakes," she blurted out.

"You like crab cakes?" Corbett asked.

"Love them." But no way the ones in West Virginia could measure up to fresh crab on the Florida coast.

"You have to try them here then."

"Oh no, I couldn't." Everything was so expensive. She'd ordered a petite fillet to keep the costs down.

"Three orders of crab cakes for us to share as appetizers," he told the waitress, who was dressed in black slacks and a white blouse. Kind of like Summer. She fit in with wait staff far more than these power suits she was with. She didn't belong here and couldn't stay focused on the conversation. How long would they hold Early? Did he have a change of clothes?

Her cell vibrated in her right pants pocket. That would be the new one, Dayita calling. Well, she couldn't talk now, could she?

"—to school?" The finance director was leaning around his wife to address her. His head resembled a beach ball with wire-framed glasses perched in the middle.

She had only caught the end of his question, and hoped her answer would be appropriate. "I earned a master's from Florida Sci-Tech, Mr.—" What on earth was she going to call him? Did panic show in her eyes?

"No need to be formal. I'm just Barry."

Summer swallowed. At least now she had a name. Just Barry.

"I'm working on my doctorate. My current research is on water quality near drill sites."

"How's it going?" Corbett asked.

"Terrific." She tried to convey enthusiasm, optimism, traits an employer would value, though she wasn't sure why she cared. She didn't want a job, right?

Judging by the way Corbett's head tilted, he questioned her response. His gaze shifted to Just Barry, and Summer realized these two knew something.

She opted for honesty. "Except for Fairhope's people. The company is trying to restrict testing of their wells by any outside labs. And we lost a funding source."

"I might be able to help the university financially," Corbett said.

"That's very generous of you." How could she put this so she didn't offend him? "We've tried to avoid direct funding from either energy companies or environmental groups. It's important to avoid even the appearance of bias."

Just Barry leaned in. "There are ways around that problem. We could write a general check to your college rather than funding a specific project. No strings attached to the funds, of course."

That might work. The dean would know more about how funding was handled than she did. They were being so helpful, she wanted to do something in return. "A petition is going around to drum up public support for a ban on fracking." She hastened to add, "I didn't sign. I wouldn't do anything to jeopardize the university's research."

Corbett smiled at his vice president. "LaShonda, didn't I tell you she's the one we've been looking for?"

Now she had another name. LaShonda, whose beautiful head was nearly shaved clean. Two down, one to go.

"You did," LaShonda agreed. "And she is."

Corbett raised his wine glass. "Here's hoping she says yes to a long and fruitful relationship with our company."

Summer feared her face matched the cabernet, but she raised her glass and pinged it with Kit Corbett's, LaShonda's, Just Barry's, and Mrs. Just Barry's.

Thank God, the crab cakes and salads arrived and diverted everyone's attention. The Mickster salad, with blue cheese crumbles, was as divine as Corbett had promised on the drive over. Summer speared a garbanzo bean and chunk of tomato. Surprisingly, the lump crab cakes were also well-prepared and dished up with a tasty remoulade. Right on cue as they finished, two waiters appeared.

The filet mignon and baked potato with sour cream were done to perfection. After two more glasses of good cab, so was she. Good thing she wasn't driving. Corbett had stopped at two glasses, though he'd refilled her glass before it was empty.

After they ordered end-of-the-meal coffee, Summer slipped into the bathroom and called PJ to make sure Early had medications and clothes. She needn't have worried: PJ was taking care of him. Summer rejoined her table companions.

While the waitress cleared the table of all but wine glasses, the bread basket, and Mrs. Just Barry's still half-full plate, Corbett shared tidbits about Clarksburg's history with Summer. "Once, there were over thirty different glass factories in this area, making everything from optical glass to window glass. The most famous, the Hazel Atlas factory, made tablewares. Factories closed when the natural gas supply tightened and became too expensive. Coupled with cheap labor available overseas, the industry couldn't compete."

He leaned across the table, one slim finger flicking out to touch hers as she fiddled with the stem of her glass. The gesture ended as quickly as it began, but she felt her face flush. Had the others noticed?

"We have a chance to revive an industry that's been a vital part of our state's history, Summer. I plan to be a major driver behind that change."

Corbett nodded to LaShonda, who raised a briefcase to her lap and withdrew papers and passed them to Summer with a wide smile.

"I hope you've been thinking about my job offer," Corbett said. "This is the contract we prepared."

Summer bet he'd been told more than once that he had a nice smile. Was it genuine or did he only bring it out when he wanted something?

"Since you didn't jump on my offer right away, I sweetened the deal by $15,000. Generous benefits and vacation time are built into the contract, but if anything doesn't meet your needs, we can discuss it. Don't be afraid to negotiate the details."

She made eye contact for a second and quickly looked back at the papers. The last page was already signed by Kit Corbett, Barry

Baldwin, and LaShonda Thrush. She flipped back to the front page and settled both hands on top. "I . . . I *have* been thinking about it, but . . . I never considered leaving school without my doctorate."

Mrs. Baldwin dimpled. "Who's to say you can't do both? Start the job now and earn some money. Finish school later."

Summer ruffled the edges of the contract with her thumbnail.

"Talk it over with your family and friends," Corbett suggested.

That would be Dayita and Mrs. Patel. Her mother would tell Kit Corbett he was making a huge mistake hiring an immature, unstable person.

"Call if you have any questions or concerns," Kit was saying. "I want this deal to work for both of us."

Light rain was still falling as Corbett held the door open for her to leave the restaurant. He took her elbow and guided her to his truck. Instead of turning left toward her cabin as they reached old Route 50, Corbett swung right and pulled off the road at the top of the hill.

Corbett gazed straight ahead, where the windshield wipers sounded like a metronome as they brushed the drizzle away at slow intervals. "We locals call this view the 'champagne glass.' See how the lights lining the hill look like a stem?"

Twinkling lights of houses in the valley formed the bowl. "It's a lovely view," she said. "Magical."

"My mother claims Clarksburg is 'the jewel of the hills.'" As he turned his head to smile at Summer, she caught the scent of woodsy cologne.

He pulled back onto the road and executed a U-turn. "I wanted you to see this isn't such a bad place to live. It's a good town to settle down and raise a family."

When his hand brushed against hers briefly, she forced herself not to shrink against the truck's door. He drove on to the stoplight at the top of the hill. While they waited for the light to change, the way he looked at her unsettled her again.

On the rest of the drive to the cabin, he described what it had been like growing up in Clarksburg and what her life might be like if she accepted the job and decided to stay here. She only half processed what he was saying because of the earnestness in his voice.

Corbett's face was too thin to be handsome exactly, but he was attractive. And smart. Well off, too. No ring on the finger. He could have a wife stashed at home, though it didn't seem likely. But he was too old for her, wasn't he? At least ten or twelve years older. And besides, she was chasing a PhD, not a husband. But was the academic path the only life she could choose?

By the time his truck made the necessarily slow trek down the dirt road to the cabin, she felt light-headed and heavy in the stomach—and the cause wasn't only wine and rich food. At the end of her driveway, the truck stopped, and Corbett moved his head toward her.

She dashed out of the cab. "Thank you for everything tonight. Great meal and good company."

Once inside the cabin, with the door locked, she felt like a foolish child. He would think she was an idiot. In the truck, he'd only turned his head toward her.

No, he leaned his head toward her. Definitely leaned. Sometimes she didn't understand herself. She wasn't the kind of girl to run like a scared rabbit because a guy wanted a kiss.

She heard him again: *It's a good place to settle down and raise a family.* The way he looked at her. No, she ran from Kit Corbett because he was trying to persuade her to change her life. His connections in the community could help her enormously, but she didn't want to encourage romantic notions. Their relationship must remain strictly business.

~

WHEN KIT ARRIVED HOME, MALLEYCAT was mewling piteously and brushing persistently against his pants leg. He bent down and stroked her fur.

"Sorry, old girl. You're hungry, aren't you?" The tiger-striped cat followed him into the pet pantry. A tap of his shoe released a latch and the cat's food bowl sprung out from the baseboard. From the small refrigerator, he removed a poached salmon the cook had prepared for Malleycat earlier in the day and dumped it into the bowl.

"There you go, pretty kitty."

The feline circled his legs and sniffed, but wouldn't eat, he knew, until he left the room. Prissy little creature. To think four months ago, she was caged on a concrete floor at the shelter. She'd certainly adapted to her role as Queen of the Mansion.

On the way into the media room, he loosened his tie and poured himself a brandy. As the seductive voice of Nina Simone filled the room, he settled onto the lounger and contemplated the evening. He didn't quite know what to make of Summer Cassidy, but she intrigued him in a way no woman had for a long time. He had always liked the athletic type and she had this long, lean body, every muscle toned to perfection. Then there were those amber highlights in her hair and healthy glowing skin. The physical attributes, stunning as they were, paled beside her mind—that mind! Jam-packed with an amazing breadth of information, the result, he supposed, of those years of self-directed reading in a university library. Over dinner, he could tell she'd researched his company, grasped its scope and finances.

On the drive from the restaurant, he shared a few anecdotes about his childhood. The jealousy he'd often felt for his older brother. The parents who frequently left him in the care of hired help. He was surprised when Summer failed to contribute personal stories.

From the background check he had run on her, he knew she was the active, outdoorsy type. She enjoyed kayaking and camping, and there'd be plenty of opportunities for that in West, by God, Virginia. She'd love hiking with him at Dolly Sods and the Cranberry Glades. They could ski Canaan Valley and Snowshoe.

What a knock-out she'd be with a stylish haircut and decent wardrobe. Say a red jacket and charcoal slacks at the office. Or an emerald green cocktail dress after hours—which might be a stretch. She didn't seem like a girly-girl, but he recognized a young woman in need of a better wardrobe when he saw one.

Having seen the shack where she was living, he wondered if hunger had been her main motivation for accepting his invitation to dinner. When everyone in their group had slipped on coats and stepped into the restaurant's lobby to exchange goodbyes, she'd returned to their table using the pretext of a missing glove. A moment later, he'd followed, thinking to help her search. He watched her slip the two remaining pieces of Italian bread on the their table into a plastic baggie, which he would have blown off, but he was stunned when Summer pilfered another piece of bread and a large chunk of untouched steak from Sally Baldwin's plate. She sealed the bag and tucked it into her jacket pocket. Before she could catch him watching, he stepped beyond the archway.

Surrounded by wealth all his life, he'd never known hunger. He had always assumed if people were hungry, they were lazy or drug addicts or mentally ill. That such an intelligent, lovely young woman could be reduced to sneaking scraps from people's plates affected him in a way panhandlers along the roadways never had.

Maybe poverty would make her hungry enough to accept his job offer. It could be a win-win. She would have a substantial income and a job befitting her skills and education. And he would gain a valuable employee, one with guaranteed loyalty. He sensed she wanted to say yes, but something held her back. The prestige of a doctorate? Surely the prestige of money at your disposal would trump collecting one more degree.

What impressed him more than anything: she didn't immediately accept the job offer. Money, he suspected, would never serve as Summer Cassidy's main motivation.

She had flinched when he touched her hand. He drew back immediately, though her reaction was unexpected. The report on her college years indicated a healthy sexual appetite, a proclivity that didn't concern him. It wasn't as if he was a virgin or expected his employees to be. Perhaps the age difference made her edgy. Or a distaste for mixing business and personal affairs.

He entertained no similar qualms. Tall, lithe, brilliant—she could be exactly the woman he needed at his side. Both on the job and off. What other subtle pressures could he bring to bear to gain her signature on the contract and keep her in Clarksburg? It had to happen soon. He couldn't drag out the search for a new geologist forever.

11

November 24

EARLY GLOVER'S KNEES CREAKED as he rose from the edge of the jail bunk. "You mean I can go?"

The corners of Turner Skidmore's mouth puckered as if he'd sucked on a sour ball. Early suspected it was the deputy's natural disposition erupting like a belch. "Your rifle done the killing, so I'd as soon keep you here. But the sheriff says we've got ourselves another suspect."

"Who?"

"None of your business."

"I believe you're supposed to phrase it as 'I can't discuss an ongoing investigation.'"

Skidmore's nose twitched. "It's a free country. You can believe any damn thing you want."

On his way out Early deliberately passed close enough to brush Skidmore's uniform. "Thank you for such an enlightening civics lesson, Turner. I might ask the university president to invite you as our commencement speaker. You can wear that McGruff crime dog costume."

Skidmore shoved his boot into Early's calf. Early stumbled, skinny arms flailing until he could recover his balance, and he snickered, imagining how much he must have resembled the scarecrow stumbling down the yellow brick road.

"What the hell you laughing at?"

Skidmore's snarly expression kept Early amused all the way down the corridor to the lobby where he was touched to see PJ Wine waiting for him in a rose sweatshirt decorated with rhinestone flowers.

"What's so funny?" PJ asked.

"Nothing. I just like irritating Deputy Skidmore."

PJ sniggered as they collected Early's belongings from the processing officer, and then turned sober. "Take care. Skidmore's not a man you want for an enemy. Don't you want to know why I showed up here?"

"I figure the sheriff told you they were letting me go because they have another suspect, and being my friend for fifty years, you came to give me a ride home because you know I'd do the same for you."

Laughing again, PJ held the door to the outside world open and insisted Early go first. "How's it feel to be a free man?"

"'Stone walls do not a prison make, Nor iron bars a cage,' Richard Lovelace tells us, a man whose outlook jibes with my philosophy: true freedom comes when you stop worrying about what other people think, a state I clearly reached years ago. But in reality, no man is free. We all are chained to our past and to our future, and, no matter who we are, my friend, our future is moldering in a grave."

"That's depressing. You shouldn't joke about it."

"Imagine how my students feel, having to listen to me for a whole semester." He slid into the passenger seat of PJ's SUV and buckled up. "If you don't mind, swing by Doc Cole's place out on old Bridgeport Hill so I can pick up Wallace."

"If you're sure he won't bite."

Why was she so scared of dogs? She wasn't afraid of any human, far as he could tell. "He won't bite you if I'm here."

"Sure about that?"

"Not real sure."

"Doggone it, Early—"

"I was teasing. He grumbles a little, doesn't bite."

PJ pulled out into traffic.

Early timed his kicker until the vehicle was securely on the right side of the yellow line. "Unless he knows you're a Republican."

PJ sniffed. "Now I know you're pulling my leg."

"Always said you were smarter than you look."

They passed by Minard's, one of the oldest and best known Italian restaurants in the area. The parking lot was empty at this hour. Early retrieved Wallace from the vet's and paid the bill while PJ waited in the car. Her eyes gave away her nervousness when he opened the rear door to let the dog in. Silly—wasn't as if the dog had ever bitten anyone.

She asked, "You plan to retire any time soon?"

"Nope." He had no intention of confessing he hadn't signed a contract for the next semester. Spare him the pity, please. "Plan to die at the podium. Seems only fair. Been boring my students to death for years. You? Retiring soon?"

"No way; having too much fun."

Those formative years in Clarksburg schools must have done a bang-up job instilling a work ethic. As they approached Glover's Lake, his throat tightened at the sight of yellow tape blocking off the crime scene. He would never look at the lake again without thinking of Corky. Who could have killed that gentle soul? Why? His poor daughter—after two failed marriages, she finally finds the right man, only to have him taken away so violently.

Would Sloane want to live on the farm after this? The memory might well be too horrible.

It was nice of her to come to the jail and put in a good word for him. He would call her as soon as he got home and tell her so. He hoped he and Sloane were becoming a family of sorts, even though she harbored resentment.

Once he and PJ reached his home, he announced he would write the sheriff and demand an apology for his staff's needless brutality. "If one isn't forthcoming, my lawyer will be happy to take appropriate action. I might suggest the jail upgrade to memory-foam mattresses, too." He wasn't one to complain, but he didn't feel so good. His leg still ached from Skidmore's kick.

He strode into his office and pulled up short. "What the hell? Look at this mess."

Peering over his shoulder at the scattered papers, PJ exclaimed, "Oh my."

You could bet he was going to add a paragraph complaining that the deputies were a bunch of hoodlums. How dare they tear through his desk?

Wallace barked, as if to say he was offended by the invasion of privacy too. The poor dog's eye still wouldn't open all the way. When Early found out who was responsible, he would—well he didn't know what he would do, but it would be drastic.

Early peered at PJ intently. "Now, who's this other suspect?"

"I'm not supposed to talk about it."

"Sure you can. I'm your oldest friend."

"I have friends older than you."

"Name one."

PJ's brow rippled as if she were actually going through a list of names.

"Come on. I won't tell anybody."

PJ seemed to consider this an adequate rationalization. "They found someone else's prints on the rifle. I'm sure you've met him because you both show up every time fracking is on the agenda at commission meetings. He's that agitator, Ty Franceschi."

"Those simple fools. Franceschi handled my rifle the day he picked up the guidebook," he told PJ while he called the sheriff's office. "They'll have to find someone else to pin this murder on."

~

Summer's first instinct when Corbett had invited her to a birthday party for an old high school friend had been to turn him down. She didn't want him getting any ideas. But when he mentioned his friend Nadine was married to Boomer Walsh, the man behind Fairhope Energy, she accepted the invitation. Corbett said people who could further Summer's research would be at the party, and that might be true, but with any luck, she might learn why Fairhope was trying to block her research.

The upper middle class home, red brick with black shutters and trim, looked as if it were clinging for dear life to the side of a cliff in this Bridgeport subdivision. Did you ever get used to these hills? She supposed if you were born here you took them for granted, the way she barely noticed Spanish moss and camellias.

Homes here, nearly all two-stories with basements, sat on smaller lots than those in her hometown, probably because it was expensive to level sites out of these rocks and hard clay. In Loblolly Lake, the ground was flat as milled lumber, the soil loose and sandy.

Corbett's woodsy cologne and the pressure of his hand against her waist as he ushered her through the door made Summer uncomfortable. Under the pretext of removing her jacket, Summer inched away from him and discreetly studied Nadine Walsh. What looked like a very expensive silk tunic over black leggings flattered her gym-toned body. She was about thirty, Summer guessed. Nadine's throat seemed exceptionally long, drawing attention to a slightly under-sized head and the flat contours of her face.

Summer peeked around the hostess into the great room and groaned inwardly. All the guests, as she'd feared, were dressed in upscale casual. Ones near Nadine's age mirrored her taste in clothing. The older women trended toward boiled wool blazers or sweaters with Thanksgiving-themed embroidery paired with tailored slacks. Summer smoothed the new-to-her red sweater over the same-old black slacks. Thank goodness she'd rushed to Gabe's discount store to buy another sweater after Corbett called. Her duds weren't as fancy as the other women's, but she looked passable for a grad student.

Lasagna, eggplant Parmesan, chicken Alfredo, fresh veggies artfully arranged on a tray, olives, fancy cheese—the chow here would more than compensate for the price of the sweater.

Corbett returned from the bartender with a glass of cabernet for her, an eyebrow lifting as he noticed her plate. "You must be hungry," he suggested gently.

Looking around, she became aware other guests were only sipping wine and nibbling on cheese or celery sticks. No one else had filled a plate yet.

One side of the room had five linen-topped card tables arranged at angles. Corbett escorted her to the closest one and pulled out a chair.

"I'll give you a chance to eat undisturbed, and then I'll introduce you around." He strode off toward men clustered near the bar. A massive stone fireplace provided warmth and ambiance along one wall.

Though she was eating far too fast to be polite, she devoured two pepperoni rolls, stopping only to gulp swigs of water. Her initial hunger staved off, she proceeded more slowly, observing the guests.

She recognized County Commissioner PJ Wine and Corbett's co-workers Barry Baldwin and LaShonda Thrush from the Wonder Bar. Boomer Walsh had his back turned to her, but his voice carried across the room. As she watched him, she could tell he was one of those "too much" guys. Drank too much; talked too much; laughed too much and too loudly. Corbett was shaking Boomer's hand, and it struck her how different the two men were: one so polished and smooth, the other rough around the edges. Still, he'd been thoughtful enough to visit Corky at the hospital. Yet she recalled Boomer's expression when Corky said he was filing for worker's compensation. He'd been furious. Furious enough to kill him?

Summer's speculation was interrupted when PJ detached herself from Corbett's group and trotted over, belly-fat shaking visibly beneath a fuchsia floral sweater. "How's it going, Summer?" Her eyes gleamed. "You might have already heard, but they let Early out this morning."

"Thank goodness," Summer said. "He's quite a character, but I'm sure he's harmless. Besides, whoever took the rifle also injured the dog. Wallace was defending his home."

"Thanks again for taking the mutt to Early's vet yesterday. Both man and dog are happy to be home again."

"Glad to help."

"By the way, I meant to warn you that deer season opens a couple of days before Thanksgiving, and you shouldn't walk in the woods unless you're wearing orange. Some hunters'll shoot anything that moves. It's chaos out there with everyone trying to bag a deer. Every year there's accidents."

"Warning duly noted." Summer's father had given her the same advice on her first and only deer hunt. By the next season, her parents had divorced.

PJ's eyes cut over to Boomer Walsh entertaining Corbett by the bar. "I'm surprised this little party wasn't canceled. I heard Nadine is mad enough to spit nails because Boomer made lewd advances toward Corky Rogers' fiancée."

"So soon after his passing?" Summer couldn't stop herself from staring across the room at Boomer.

"No, no, it happened about a week ago, but apparently his fiancée chased him off again yesterday morning in front of a friend of mine, Nelly Maphis, and she's a big gossip. I bet half the town has heard about it by now."

Then PJ's chubby face dimpled. "I see you and Kit hit it off."

Summer liked Corbett, but she didn't *like* him, if that's what PJ meant. Summer tilted her head to one side—which could mean anything.

"He tells me you might be sticking around these parts." PJ's eyes roved over her face. "You're frowning—that mean you're turning down the job?"

Summer guessed she failed to disguise her reservations. "Haven't decided anything yet. Big decision, you know."

"Yes, indeed, but you could do a lot worse than working for Kit." PJ glanced across the room to where Corbett was regaling their host with what must have been an amusing tale, because Boomer Walsh was laughing too loudly again.

PJ winked at Summer. "You could do a *lot* worse," she repeated. "He's a good-looking fella and I think he likes you. He'd be a good catch."

She could feel her cheeks reddening. "I'm not fishing," she said. When one of the guests pulled the commissioner away, Summer was grateful.

Spearing a piece of chicken, she wrapped a strand of fettuccine around her fork and watched four women who, from their easy familiarity with each other, were obviously friends. With a pang of homesickness, she wished she was with Dayita. Summer felt so out of place at this party—the youngest person present. At least Dayita would be joining her in just three more days. She would take two days to drive up, arriving on Thanksgiving around noon.

The doorbell rang and Nadine detached herself from the women. Summer shivered as cold air spilled inside, and though she couldn't see the new arrival, she heard a male voice respond to Nadine's greeting.

As Summer recognized the grey suit and the thick black-framed glasses, the chicken stuck in her throat. Elliot Ral caught her hostile glare and made his way toward her. She put down her fork and stood, her voice shaking with barely repressed rage. "How much does Allied Consulting pay you to run people off the road these days, Mr. Ral?"

His lip curled with amusement. "Why? You looking for a new job, Miss Cassidy? I can see why you'd find your present work frustrating."

"The only thing frustrating about my job is that you're trying to undermine everything I do."

"Look, Summer—is it okay if I call you Summer?"

"No." Summer resumed her seat and was pleased to note Ral looked flummoxed by her response.

"We're both doing our jobs. No reason to take it so personally."

"It's personal to me." If reading her email and listening in on private conversations wasn't considered personal, what was? She wished she could slap that smile off his face, but Dayita insisted he couldn't know they had uncovered his intrusions yet. Summer still was uneasy about keeping the hacking evidence from police. Ral might be a suspect in far more violent crimes. After all, if he had run her off the road, might he also have shot Corky Rogers?

When Ral continued to hang around her, she became annoyed. "For the second time, let me suggest that you can piss off."

"I guess we aren't going to be friends."

She smiled insincerely. "Not a chance."

To her relief, Boomer waved Ral over toward the bar. Did Allied Consulting work for Walsh—was that why he was here? But then Ral was shaking hands with Kit Corbett, cornering him as if they had important business to discuss. She would have hoped Corbett would have nothing to do with a lowlife like Ral.

A few moments later Nadine slid fluidly into the chair next to Summer. She interlaced her fingers, drawing attention to gold polished nails decorated with silver moons and stars. "I couldn't help noticing you getting all over Elliot like a rash. Men can be such jackasses. 'Fess up. What's he done?"

Summer knew she should keep her mouth shut, especially with Boomer Walsh's wife, but let residual anger override caution. "Mr. Ral is doing his best to wreck my research."

Nadine prompted her to explain her project. Summer described her project but limited her revelations about Ral to his harassment at meetings. When she mentioned Fairhope's restriction on outside testing, Nadine's frown deepened, her eyes frequently cutting toward the group of men by the wet bar where Boomer was wiping up a drink he'd spilled.

Nadine's lips peeled back to reveal sharp little teeth. "I'd bet my backside that Boomer is in this up to his stinking eyeballs." She sounded as if she'd like to stick a fork in one of said orbs. That old blowhard on the other side of the room would be foolish not to appreciate an attractive young wife like Nadine.

Abruptly Nadine's voice shifted into silky politeness again. "Women can sign these permission forms of yours, right? As long as they own the property jointly?"

"Sure."

Nadine's voice became conspiratorial. "I was born and raised here and I know almost everyone—and if I don't, my mother does. I can help you."

Those advances Boomer made to Corky's girlfriend must have been pretty rotten to merit such a significant betrayal. Even so, Summer figured Nadine had little intention of following through until her hostess invited her to join her the following day for lunch.

Nadine tilted her head, sending a blond cascade over her shoulder. "Cheer up. If I can smile tonight, you can too!" She flashed a sixty-watter to demonstrate it could be done. "When a man's pissed you off, it's best to let him think you're over it. Then as soon as he reaches inside the cookie jar, smash the lid down on his fingers."

Summer decided to risk one more request. What could it hurt? "Any chance you can find out what Ral was doing two days ago around 4:30 in the afternoon?"

Nadine drew back, no longer smiling, her small head bobbing first in Ral's direction, then turning toward a modern art print on the opposite wall as if she'd never seen it before, her mouth slightly ajar. As the silence extended, Summer decided she'd pushed too far. "Never mind. It's not a big deal."

Nadine glared at her. "I might be blond, but I'm not stupid, you know. It *is* a big deal. You think Elliot might have something to do with that mur—you're wrong. Surely he couldn't have. He's eaten at my table." She shook her head. "I'll see what I can find out."

When the doorbell rang. Nadine leapt gracefully to her feet, smile back in place. Summer dug into the fettuccine, listening to the smooth welcomes joined by the rise and fall of a half dozen new voices, both male and female.

She jammed another forkful of pasta into her mouth.

Someone touched her shoulder and exclaimed, "Summer?"

Another guest knew her name? For once, she wished she'd listened to her mother and only taken a small bite. She swallowed the glutinous mass, barely managing not to choke. She swiveled on her chair and looked up. Her mouth fell open. "Hank?" she said, barely believing that her dart partner could show up here.

Nadine joined them, smiling brightly, her polished nails resting lightly on Hank's shoulder. "You've already met my stepson, I see."

~

HANK COULDN'T HAVE BEEN MORE SURPRISED when he spotted his one-time dart partner at the Wicked Stepmother's birthday party. Apparently Summer was taken by surprise too, judging by the way her mouth fell open and a strand of fettuccine fell off her fork and landed on her lap. As her eyes shifted between him and his father, her forehead grew increasingly furrowed. Hank realized learning that he was Boomer's son disturbed her. What had his dad done to offend her? Not that it was a surprise—his dad had never shown much skill in navigating social occasions.

Looked as if the birthday gig might not be as dull as Hank had expected. He dropped into an empty folding chair beside his dart partner. Not wanting to stare while she picked up the wayward pasta and used a napkin to scrub at the spot on her slacks, he watched Nadine instead. She mingled, refilling this one's drink, laying an expensively manicured hand on that one's shoulder to acknowledge a clever anecdote, air-kissing the mayor as he let himself in the front door. Always a top-notch hostess, that Nadine. *Just don't leave your husband unattended, ladies.*

"I gather you don't like your stepmother."

With a start, Hank realized Summer had stopped scrubbing her slacks and was observing him.

"Is it that obvious?" He should do a better job of hiding his feelings. "Mostly I try to avoid Nadine. She's probably not all that bad." He looked down at the floor. Yes, she was—every bit that bad. Why lie? In Knuckleheads, he'd sensed Summer had been deeply wounded by something—no idea what—not the kind of stuff you talked about over darts. But he had a feeling she'd understand his resentment.

"I take it you have reason to avoid her," Summer said.

He slumped against the back of the chair and crossed his legs and arms, tried to look casual. "Nadine has known my mother forever, since way back in high school. So when Mom needed chemo, we all thought Nadine was sweet to drive Mom to the hospital for her sessions. During those long hours while poison dripped into Mom's veins, Nadine comforted my father. Rumor has it, they amassed enough reward points through a motel chain's loyalty program that their honeymoon flight to Las Vegas was practically free."

"Ouch." Summer let a few moments pass before asking, "Your mom okay?"

"Yeah, she survived—the cancer and the divorce. Now, my father says I should suck it up. Everyone gets divorced—no big deal."

Summer seemed to withdraw to a dark place, an inner universe far from this noisy party. She'd done the same thing in the bar. He'd been watching her for some time before he'd invited her to play darts.

Finally she said, "Divorce is always a big deal. But you're here at this party, so you and your dad have apparently gotten past it."

"He's the guy who taught me to hit a baseball, catch a fish, and bag a deer. He's a bastard when it comes to women, but he worked his ass off all his life so he could send me to MIT and I'm grateful."

From her expression, Hank sensed the conversation had struck a particularly painful nerve in Summer. "Hey, I'm not usually such a downer. This is supposed to be a party—so what brought you here?"

"That would be me."

Hank hadn't noticed Kit Corbett gliding toward them. Hank stood and shook hands.

They seemed an odd pair—her living in that shack and Corbett in his mansion; him, the snazzy dresser; Summer, favoring the Cinderella look the day before the ball. Not to mention he must be more than a decade older. But then, an even bigger age difference hadn't stopped Nadine from sinking her claws into his dad, and Corbett, unlike his dad, looked as if he stepped from the pages of a magazine. Not a hair out of place.

Hank hoped Corbett hadn't overheard him complaining about Nadine. At one time, the two of them had been tight.

"How do you like working for your dad, Hank?" Corbett asked.

"S'awright."

Corbett smiled. "That's not exactly a glowing endorsement."

What was he supposed to say? Fairhope's history of shoddy practices had led to the recent spate of accidents, and his dad had no money to prevent the next one from happening. Hank couldn't wait to move on. "Got my heart set on putting my education to use."

"Engineering, right? I'm sure Fairhope would be delighted to put that education to good use." Corbett's eyes gleamed. "But if it's a matter of you'd rather not work for your father—many sons want to be their own man, so to speak—I'd jump at the chance to hire you."

"Thanks, but oil and gas is not really what I have in mind." Hank then added, more for Summer's benefit, than Corbett's, "I majored in structural engineering, studying seismic loads particularly. I've applied for positions at several companies specializing in bridge and tunnel design."

The light in Corbett's eyes dimmed. He was used to getting what he wanted. And from the way his hand was massaging Summer's shoulder, she had made his Most Wanted List.

Funny thing, though. Summer looked queasy and excused herself to visit the powder room.

He had a feeling she might say yes to another round of darts after all.

~

WHEN SUMMER RETURNED FROM THE BATHROOM, Corbett's hand glommed onto her waist, and he said he wanted to introduce her to some people. She strode forward, disengaging herself in a way she hoped would seem natural. She wished his attentions were directed more toward their common interest in geology. He wouldn't be touching her all the time if she were a man.

Dutifully, she met the mayor. Slicked back hair, coal black—natural or dyed? His handshake: damp and limp as leaf lettuce. His eyes quickly dismissed her as unimportant.

It was okay. She felt the same way about him.

Next up, Boomer Walsh. "Boomer owns controlling interest in an oil and gas company," Corbett said.

"Actually, we've met." Summer accepted Boomer's hand, noting the sandpaper texture of a man accustomed to hard work.

"At the hospital," Boomer said. "I remember."

"You might be able to help her out," Corbett said.

"How's that?" Walsh asked.

"Put in a good word for her with the landowners you're working with at Fairhope." Corbett said, his hand resting on Summer's shoulder. She needed to get him alone, muster the courage to say *How about a hands-off policy since we're business associates*, but now was not the time.

"I wrote a letter to the landowners whose mineral rights I own,"

Corbett said. "You could do the same. Let them know she's offering a valuable service."

"Sure, I could do that."

Yeah, right. And the sun was going to explode tomorrow. Summer suggested Boomer should state in the letter that it was okay for people to have their water tested by outside labs. "Officially revoke the addendum to Fairhope's contracts."

Boomer's smile thinned, and Summer could see he had no intention of writing that letter. He didn't want Fairhope's problems exposed. If he showed any inclination to fix the issues, she'd be willing to cut him some slack. After all, most problems started before Walsh bought the companies, and he couldn't be expected to turn around their operations overnight.

"Why don't I send someone over to your office to pick up that letter tomorrow?" Corbett said.

"That's okay. I'll send it over first thing."

The two men stared at each other, one of those pissing contests guys got into. Which one would blink first?

She didn't find out because her cell rang. When she saw Ty's number, she excused herself and rushed to a corner of the room for privacy. Had he grown a set of balls and decided to ignore her mother's advice?

Ty's voice held an edge she'd heard only once before. "You have to get Grace."

"Get? Why? Where is she?"

"The sheriff's holding me for questioning in Corky's murder, and they turned Grace over to social services."

First they were after Early, now Ty. Neither one would have harmed Corky, but now Summer was sure the sheriff was checking out everyone known as an anti-fracker. He thought the spill was connected. "Do they have any evidence linking you to the murder?"

"My prints are on the murder weapon."

"Early's rifle."

"Yeah, I checked it out the day I picked up the guidebook."

"Couldn't Early tell them that?"

"He did. They said it only proved I knew where the rifle was and saw an opportunity to use it to commit a crime."

"For Pete's sake, that's ridiculous." Ty had gone to a lot of trouble on Corky's behalf after the spill. She could testify to that if it would help.

"Grace is all that matters right now, Summer. We can't let this happen to her again."

That *we* annoyed Summer, because it wasn't her fault Ty got arrested, but as she envisioned the child's sloppy pigtails and stubby fingers grasping a crayon, her throat contracted. Grace had been in foster care for several weeks after her parents died in a car accident. She was a turtle finally daring to poke its head out of its protective shell to test the air. Being ripped away from her brother now could undo all her progress.

"Tell me what I can do."

"Find out where they've taken her and get her out. I wrote a letter giving you permission to keep her until I'm released. It's at the front desk of the sheriff's office."

"What if they won't let me have her?"

"Tell them whatever you have to. Say you're her mother."

He had to be kidding. "But—"

"Do it. Please."

Summer swallowed her misgivings. "Okay."

"Make sure she gets to school in the morning."

"You got it."

He hung up.

She couldn't bear to think of Grace in foster care, but she really didn't have the time or knowledge to play surrogate parent either. Everything had been swinging back her way now that she had convinced the dean her research was critical to the community's well-being.

It looked as if she'd graduated from rescuing dogs to kids in less than a day. What was she going to do with a five-year-old child? But it was Grace, a child she'd taken into her home once before in Loblolly Lake. A child who'd already suffered enough.

Hank tapped her sleeve. "Everything okay?"

"I have to go. A friend is in trouble. I've got to rescue a child."

"I'll take you. I was leaving anyway."

Summer looked for Corbett, but Nadine had cornered him. Her laughter carried, all breathy and seductive, her painted fingernails clutching his arm.

"I should—" She cut her comment off, not wanting to interrupt whatever was going on between the two of them.

Hank's eyes followed hers. "I'll tell Mr. Corbett what happened. Put your coat on. I'll be back in a jif."

She couldn't leave with a man she wasn't sure she could trust—even if he seemed kind. However, the way Ral had been schmoozing with Corbett, she didn't know if she could trust him either.

As she retrieved her jacket, she realized there was only one person in this room she did trust—and what's more, she had the influence to make things happen with those children and family service folks. So she approached PJ Wine, who readily offered whatever assistance she could.

Hank looked surprised when she told him she had found another ride, but gave her his phone number and asked her to let him know how the rescue mission turned out.

As Summer suspected, PJ knew exactly who to call and where to go to rescue Grace. Before long, the hysterical child sat next to Summer in the back seat of PJ's vehicle. On the way to the cabin, Summer had to restrain Grace's arms so she wouldn't hurt herself. She wailed that bad men had taken her brother, and no matter how many times Summer repeated that the police weren't bad men, that they had made a mistake, that Ty would come and take her back home soon, that she and Grace would have fun together like when they stayed together before, the child's screaming was relentless.

Clearly flustered, PJ unlocked the cabin so Summer could carry the sobbing child inside. "Will she be all right?" PJ asked.

Though hampered by Grace's clinging to her leg, Summer tore into her backpack and found paper and a set of highlighters. She wrapped Grace's hands around a green one. Soon the child's fingers tightened on their own around the crayon-substitute and the crying subsided into occasional sniffles. She drew a parallelogram and divided it into triangles, coloring each area a different shade.

Summer said, "She'll be all right now."

PJ declared her a miracle-worker with children.

That was so not true.

12

November 25

Summer dropped Grace off at school before stopping for supplies at the grocery store, foods she hoped Grace would eat. Not too many—the sheriff had to release Ty in forty-eight hours unless they pressed charges. Fingerprints alone wouldn't serve as probable cause, since Early had explained how they got on his rifle. Then she chopped wood to make the cabin toasty for the child.

Summer planned to keep that lunch date with Nadine Walsh even though Hank had dished up enough dirt on his stepmother that Summer didn't consider her trustworthy. Nonetheless, Nadine might serve as a tool for unraveling the Fairhope conflict.

With no time to shower or wash her hair, Summer brushed it into a fresh ponytail and drove over the speed limit to reach the Walsh residence by noon.

"Mmmm, you smell good." Nadine sniffed, her long neck extending in Summer's direction, as Summer handed over her coat. "Kind of woodsy."

The heady scent of firewood underlaid with hints of sweat—yeah, that would make great copy on a perfume bottle. She followed Nadine into the kitchen and perched on a bamboo-backed barstool at the counter while Nadine put the finishing touches on lunch. The kitchen was done in soft greens and tans with an Asian design theme.

Nadine tossed a mixed green salad topped with blueberries and candied walnuts, placing it on the glass-topped kitchen table along with luncheon plates, floral napkins, and a basket of cheddar cheese biscuits stuffed with thin slices of honeyed ham. Last, she brought out a pitcher of sweet tea and set it on the table between them.

They made small talk about Florida, Nadine's favorite vacation spot, while they ate. Summer, of course, had never been to the ritzy Palm Beach or Marco Island resorts Nadine chattered about, but she contributed tidbits about the Panhandle beaches not far from Loblolly Lake. Summer scarfed her lunch down and declared the food some of the best she'd ever eaten.

Nadine brushed off the praise, but Summer could tell the comment pleased her.

"Did you bring the list?" Nadine asked, spearing a blueberry.

Summer retrieved the computer print-out from the backpack at her feet and slid it across the table.

Nadine scanned the papers. "I went to high school with Johnson's wife. She'll sign for you." Nadine put a check by that name. "Mrs. Kearns goes to church with my mother." Another check. "Dated Holden Young back in the day." Check.

By the time Nadine had gone through the list, thirty-four names were checked and eleven more had question marks because her mother knew them or knew their cousin twice-removed. "If you leave forms with me, I'll have them signed by tomorrow night."

No way. "That's a lot of people to contact in one day."

Nadine dismissed her concerns with a wave of the hand. "I'm inviting them all to lunch with me tomorrow at the Clique Club after Corky Rogers' funeral."

Summer could feel herself blanch. "That would be horribly expensive."

The observation provoked a snide laugh. "Boomer's paying. He just doesn't know it yet."

Although the offer to obtain the permissions seemed generous, Summer still didn't trust Nadine. "Why are you doing this?"

Nadine leaned back in her chair and bared those perfect small white teeth. "Honey, I'm not doing this for you. I'm doing it because no man's gonna make a fool of me in public and get away with it. Boomer's been undermining you ever since you came to town. Now I'm going to undermine him."

Her smile was anything but kind. Knowing how Nadine had stolen Boomer away from Hank's mother, Summer didn't think she had much claim to outrage, but at least now Summer understood her motives.

"What did you find out?" she asked.

"After you left last night, I overheard Elliot Ral telling Boomer that you'd visited Patty Kirby."

Chills ran down Summer's spine. How had Ral known? Was he following her? Or eavesdropping in some additional way she hadn't discovered yet?

Nadine continued. "Boomer cursed, as if that had some special significance to him. Patty's a friend of my grandmother's, so I called her up. I bet you anything Boomer knows exactly what caused the odor in Patty's water. Gotta be all those chemicals Fairhope's dumping in the ground."

Seemed likely. "Any luck finding out what Ral does for your husband?"

"Just consulting. I asked consulting about what, but Ral was vague."

"Who hired him?"

"Probably Boomer. And your date."

Summer protested, "It wasn't a date."

"Looked that way to me."

Nadine made a show of inspecting Summer, her eyes roaming from the ponytail to the well-worn hiking boots and back to her eyes. "Kit lost interest in the local women a long time ago. We're all too . . . local for him. You hail from way down South, and with your wholesome looks, youth, and education, you'd be a good catch."

"I'm not a goddamn fish."

The words flew out before Summer considered how rude she sounded, but Nadine howled and raised her palms in surrender. "Okay, I get it. Kit wasn't your date and you're not that into him. I get it."

Summer recovered her composure. "Anyway, it's not likely that Kit would have hired Ral. Kit's a small operator."

"Small?" Nadine squealed, her little head bobbing backwards. It made her neck look even longer. "Honey, Kit Corbett comes from old, old money. Though he only allows his good family name to be associated with Corbett Energy, his deep pockets seeded half the businesses in this county. Kit loaned my husband a ton of money to buy Fairhope, and now poor old Boomer's damn near bankrupt. No, honey, Kit's not small potatoes. His finger is deep in every pie."

Nadine's thumb was certainly stuck in every pie—or every eye. So who was right—Nadine or PJ Wine who'd told her Corbett was a small operator? Hank's stories revealed how sneaky Nadine could be. Maybe she had invited Summer to lunch to do some fishing of her own, to find out how involved Summer was with Kit. If Nadine planned to leave her husband, she might be after Kit.

Summer was still digesting what she'd learned. The day she'd met Corbett, he already knew a lot about her. Was that Ral's research? She suddenly felt sick. Had she let Corbett's flattery go to her head? What if he didn't really wanted to hire her? The job offer might have been another part of a campaign to stop her research. But if so, it didn't make sense that he'd turn around and help her.

She shook off her misgivings. No sense in getting all paranoid. Corbett had offered Hank a position at the party, too. He was probably trying to grow his business with young employees.

As Summer prepared to leave, Nadine pledged to spend the rest of the afternoon arranging the post-funeral luncheon. "I'll work on it until about 4:30. Then I have to get my hair done for Corky Rogers' funeral. If I don't go, everyone will think I'm avoiding Sloane Dumont, and that's not going to happen."

Summer wasn't following. "What's the connection between Dumont and Rogers?"

"They were set to get married at Christmas. Old Corky got his hands on the hooters every man in Harrison County lusted after."

Recalling PJ's gossip, Summer realized Sloane was the woman Boomer had offended. Summer had never been to a funeral before, but she decided to attend this one. The service was slated for an hour after Grace would be off to school. Summer had liked Corky, the one time she'd met him. And if Summer watched and listened carefully, she might learn something that would get Ty out of jail and uncover the identity of the real murderer.

~

WHILE SUMMER WAS ON THE WAY HOME from picking up Grace at school, a metallic cacophony beneath the truck demanded immediate attention. She pulled into a parking lot and discovered rust had caused the front bumper to come loose on the right side and drag the asphalt. With duct tape she kept in the glove box, she crouched on the blacktop to reattach the bumper to the front grille, a temporary solution at best since the grille was rust-riddled itself. That's when she found a GPS tracker attached underneath the bumper. How many ways were these jerks spying on her? She removed it and she got back in the truck. Grace requested the duct tape. Absently, Summer agreed, thinking that the GPS explained how Ral knew about the visit to Patricia Kirby. Dayita was taking too long setting up her trap. Summer had to know if Corbett Engineering had connections to Allied Consulting. Back at the cabin, she deactivated the caller ID on her new cell and called AC headquarters. She identified herself as Mr. Baldwin's assistant in the finance department at Corbett Energy. "Mr. Baldwin asked me to check on a possible billing error. Could I speak with Mr. Ral?"

"I'm sorry; he's out of the office."

No shit, Sherlock.

"But I'm Mr. Ral's assistant, Maureen Black. I'd be happy to help you." The woman possessed a telephone voice that conveyed genuine empathy. "Who did you say you worked for?"

"Corbett Energy." A company Summer hoped AC had never heard of. A rather long pause ensued while Summer was on hold, growing more and more certain every minute there was no file to be found. Ripping noises came from the kitchen. Grace was kneeling on a kitchen chair, her back toward Summer. What in the Sam Hill was she up to?

Maureen came back on the line. "Sorry it took so long. Another call came in, but I found the account. Which month's billing did you have a question about?"

Taken aback, she hung up. She had been so sure Nadine was wrong about Kit. Had he hired Ral himself or was it arranged by someone on his staff? She should have tried to find out if Ral had an alibi for the time of Corky Rogers' murder.

She hit redial. "Sorry, we got disconnected. Our records don't show what services Mr. Ral provided November 23."

Maureen's voice lost its lilt. "But that was only two days ago. He wouldn't have submitted a bill yet."

Only fast talking would get her out of this corner. "Of course not, but we had computer issues and lost our records before they were backed up. Mr. Baldwin said to make sure the services Corbett Energy requested from Mr. Ral for that date were completed.

He insisted I verify the charges. What's so urgent, I asked him, and he about bit my head off. Said to do it. You know how head accountants can be. Sticklers for details no one else cares about. Between you and me, Mr. Baldwin is not the easiest man to work for. But I do my best to be a good soldier."

Summer held her breath. Had the Bad Boss story worked?

"Let me see if any expenses have been submitted for that day." Maureen sounded peeved, and maybe she realized it because she shifted into customer-service mode. "Mr. Ral usually snaps photos of receipts each day and emails them to me. Encrypted, of course. All our data's secure."

Summer could hear the soft click of computer keys in the background—along with rips coming from the cabin kitchen.

"I'm sorry but the only items Mr. Ral has submitted in that time frame would be a hotel bill in Ohio from November 22 through the 23 for work he did for another client."

If Ral had been in Ohio, he couldn't have killed Corky Rogers. She was no closer to proving Ty's innocence and restoring Grace to his care. But she was sure now that Corbett's company used Allied Consulting.

"Yes, Maureen, I'm looking at the memo right now—oh, no, you're right. It was for November 24, I'm sorry. Has Mr. Ral submitted expenses on that date?" The night of Nadine's birthday bash.

"Whew—that's better. I was afraid we'd failed to complete an assignment. We pride ourselves on impeccable service. Mr. Ral submitted a hotel bill in Clarksburg for $120, three hours billed for a business meeting with Corbett Energy clients, and $26.48 for gasoline."

What a great job that jackass had—billing by the hour for going to a party. "Thanks, Maureen. This should keep the boss off my case." She laughed ruefully. "At least for a few days."

"Glad to help," Maureen said.

Scriiitch. Scriiitch. What *were* all those ripping sounds? Summer trotted over to the kitchen. Strips of silver duct tape criss-crossed the table top in a geometric pattern.

"Grace, what on earth are you doing?"

The child startled and slipped sideways from the chair onto the floor, her eyes brimming with unshed tears. Her thumb arced into her mouth and garbled her speech. "You mad?"

Summer became aware of how stiffly she stood, hands on her hips, ready to save the world from an invasion of duct tape. No sense being angry at Grace. When she asked to use the tape, Summer should have asked what for. Chalk it up to her lack of experience with kids.

"No, honey, I was surprised, not expecting . . ." Well, what had she expected—adult behavior out of a five year old? "What are you trying to do with the duct tape?"

The thumb popped out of the mouth long enough to mumble. "Cover the ugly." *De ug-wee* is how it came out. Summer assumed emotional stress had caused the speech problems to resurface.

"Oh." Ugly was a fair enough description of the wet glass rings and cigarette burns that marred the wood surface.

"Don't you like it?" *Wike it*. Moist brown eyes beseeched Summer, in a rare moment of eye contact that would have softened a hunk of granite.

"Absolutely, it's a work of art. A very cool idea. How about if I help you? I can tear off strips and hand them to you."

The child climbed back onto the chair, settling onto her knees. "No, thank you. You don't know how."

"Gotcha."

On the new phone, Summer sent Dayita a message describing what she'd learned about Corbett Engineering and its connection to Allied Consulting and about the GPS tracker on her truck. *Still unsure if Corbett is the one who hired Ral to derail my research*, she messaged. *Ral and Walsh seem pretty tight too. Any luck finding out more on your end?*

Her old phone jingled. When she answered, Hank Walsh asked if he could come over. "I need to talk to you."

"This isn't a good time," she said. "How'd you get my number?"

"Nadine gave it to me. She told me about the roadblocks you've hit with your research. I think I can help."

Help—or feed information to his father? "I appreciate that, but my schedule is really full right now."

During a pause, she could hear him breathing. "Look," he said, "I'm not my father. I really am trying to be your friend."

She wasn't sure if anyone here was her friend. Maybe Dayita could help her figure it out when she arrived the day after tomorrow.

"I appreciate that, I really do. We'll try to get together soon." She disconnected before he could argue.

Somehow, she had to figure out who she could trust. Fast.

13

November 26

AT THIS SPEED, DAYITA FIGURED they wouldn't arrive in West Virginia until after Christmas. It was, after all, nearly a twelve-hour drive even if you drove the speed limit.

Dayita's mother put on the blinker to enter the northbound ramp to I-75 and merged with a ridiculous degree of caution into light traffic: a few truckers setting out before dawn.

"Sure you don't want me to drive first?" Dayita asked.

"You drive too fast," Mrs. Patel said. "It makes me nervous."

A snail would make her mother jittery.

Jordan Cassidy peeked over her shoulder to the back seat at Dayita. "Summer's going to be so surprised."

No kidding. Dayita had no idea how to prepare Mrs. Cassidy for the reception she was likely to receive. Ever since Dayita's mom proposed this scheme, Dayita had been imagining the horror on Summer's face when she opened her cabin door to find the three of them standing there. She sure hoped Summer didn't blame her for this—not her idea!

Mrs. Cassidy turned back toward Mrs. Patel. "I've tried to call a dozen times to talk to her, but it always goes straight to voicemail."

"Maybe her battery's dead again," Mrs. Patel suggested.

Summer, Dayita knew, had blocked her mother's calls and messages. Calls went straight to a voicemail section marked *blocked*. Messages from Mrs. Cassidy would look like they were delivered, but Summer would never receive them.

If only Dayita had kept her mouth shut. She never should have told her mother that Summer had learned something devastating about Mrs. Cassidy. So devastating Summer had gotten choked up on the phone and couldn't—or wouldn't—tell Dayita what exactly had happened. And Summer never got choked up. About anything.

So what does her mom do when Dayita worries aloud about Summer? Picks up the phone and invites Jordan Cassidy to share their ride to West Virginia for Thanksgiving. *Their* ride. And her mother insisted they should keep the visit a surprise.

Summer doesn't have room for all of us, Dayita had argued.

We'll stay in a hotel room, her mother replied.

You don't understand. You think all mothers and daughters are like you and me.

They should be. We will build a bridge between them so they become like us.

Dayita didn't know how to convey how wide and deep the chasm between Summer and Jordan Cassidy was.

As they approached Macon, the sky lightened to soft gray with hints of rose. A semi whizzed by on their right.

"Mom, you should be in the right-hand lane."

"I'm going the speed limit."

"Yes, and everyone else is going at least five miles faster than that."

Her mother's eyes met hers in the rearview mirror. They were smiling, a sly little wrinkling and twinkling. "If I slow them down a little, I may save their lives."

"Safety is more important than speed," Mrs. Cassidy said. "I think your driving is fine, Anika."

Dayita shuddered and closed her eyes. Again, she tried to picture the moment when Summer would throw open the cabin door, tried to fathom any way this trip could develop into something other than a total frigging disaster. Summer's mom would be about as welcome as a snake bite. Maybe less so. Summer would know how to handle a snake bite. And they'd be a day earlier than Summer was expecting any company. What if she wasn't home at all?

Dayita had already enough to worry about without these additional family complications. She planned to confront Ashoka after they reached West Virginia. Elliot Ral was going down.

~

THE SUN BROKE THROUGH THE MIST over Glover's Lake the morning of Corky Rogers' funeral, its rays slicing the surface with a thousand tiny silver cuts that shivered in the wind. The lake's outer edges were liminal, neither liquid nor solid, meshed into a fragile glaze. Yet when a cardinal ventured to hop along the rim, the surface held against its feathery steps. The ice was stronger than it appeared.

Summer was, too. Stronger than her mother believed her to be. She stayed near the rear of the gathering of perhaps fifty people, but when the minister called for personal stories about the deceased, she threaded her way through the crowd for a better vantage.

Early helped a young woman from one of the folding chairs and led her to the podium. This, Summer realized, must be the much-lusted after Sloane Dumont, the object of PJ's gossip. Much to Summer's surprise, the woman wore a red sequined dress, the top covered only in a black woolen cape, which she shimmied off into Early's waiting hands. She spread her arms wide, nearly knocking Early over.

Audible gasps rose from the mourners, a scolding from those setting their eyes for the first time on Sloane Dumont's attire.

"Go ahead. Gawk." Sloane wiped her face with a black-gloved hand. "This was supposed to be my wedding dress. Instead, I'm wearing it to the funeral of the sweetest man that ever walked these hills. For months I worked on my vows so they'd be extra special. What Corky deserved. I wanted to surprise him." She sniffled. "If he was right and there's an afterlife, his spirit is hovering over this lake and he'll hear them today. The man of my dreams died right here in my arms."

She swayed and might have collapsed if Early hadn't roped his arm around her shoulders.

"You don't have to do this," he croaked.

She sniffled. "Yes, I do." She thrust her considerable chest out. "Me, I think this life is all we got, but I hope to God I'm wrong and I'll see Corky again one day. Here's the vows I wrote for my man." She unfolded a sheet of paper and began to read. "I love you, Corky Rogers, because I can see into your heart, past the outer husk to the tender spirit within. I pledge to cherish you all the . . ."

When Summer's eyes started to water, she tuned out Sloane's voice. She had to suck it up; show the world—and herself—Summer Cassidy was strong enough to handle a funeral. Instead of listening, she studied the crowd. Among the mourners Summer spotted

PJ Wine and that deputy she'd met when she went to see Ty in jail. Skid Marks Skidmore. That's how she remembered his name. Was he casing the mourners for possible suspects?

Behind the folding chairs a pod of men in jeans and jackets stood, ball caps in hand, eyes on their own well-worn shoes. Corky's co-workers, Summer surmised. Or his bar buddies. Each one appeared stricken by his death. The only co-worker she would have recognized was that Marky fellow who'd bad-mouthed Corky in the bar and he wasn't present. Had he been angry enough to kill Corky?

Her eyes roved over a number of older women with beautifully coiffed hair partly hidden beneath dressy hats. Surely Sloane Dumont's loyal customers. Next to them, Nadine Walsh. She looked slick and rich. As Summer shifted her position slightly, she could make out Boomer, and Hank on the far side of his father. After Sloane Dumont finished, Boomer stepped forward to speak the sort of things expected of a boss. Corky was a good worker. Always on time. Quick to buy his buddies a beer. Give a friend or even a stranger the shirt off his back. Though most of the gathering stared at the ground or at the casket to the right of the podium, Boomer's attention seemed focused on Sloane while he spoke. Was his desire for this woman sufficient motive for murder? And was Boomer Walsh the only one hoping to prevent her marriage to Corky?

So many people had come to pay respects, most unknown to her. None had expressions that gave them away. She had been foolish to think she might find the killer this way.

Besides, none of these people would have taken Early Glover's rifle to commit the crime. To hear Early talk, everyone around these parts was all about God and guns. Folks had easy access to weapons. That left two possibilities. First, everyone in town had heard about Early leaving that rifle beside his door to chase off landmen, so grabbing it was a crime of opportunity. Or someone hoped to frame Early by exploiting his reputation as a crusty old curmudgeon.

Another possibility occurred to her. If folks knew Early had cancer—and secrets like that were hard to keep in a small town—maybe the killer figured Early would die before he could be tried. The case would be closed and the killer would get away. It also struck her that if someone had seen a man at Glover's Lake, they might have assumed it was Early. What if he had been the intended victim?

She was probably over-thinking this. To quote Dr. Seuss, sometimes the questions are complicated and the answers are simple.

Early spoke next, the gist being that Corky Rogers was the next-best-thing to a saint for making his daughter so happy. And now so sad. The words washed over Summer, mostly unheard, until Early used a quotation that got her attention. "The great poet Thomas Campbell wrote, 'To live in hearts we leave behind is not to die.' Corky Rogers will not die. He will live on in the hearts of those who loved him and in none more so than the heart of this beautiful woman who was to be his wife."

Recognition of truth washed over Summer. In a previous conversation with Early, they had considered the possibility of parallel worlds, and Summer had pondered the possibility of her sister's spirit living on in some nebulous place. Probably wishful thinking. The revelation didn't leave her any sadder. Because Chrissie did still live in Summer's heart. She loved her sister. Love complicated by resentment, guilt, and regret is love nonetheless. And like Sloane, Summer couldn't quite relinquish all hope that she'd see her sister again so she could tell her so.

A motion under the pines along the lake caught her eye. Summer turned and recognized the wiry outline of Joe Glover. She eased behind the crowd, hoping to speak to him at the end of the service.

Early's words reached out to her again, as he publicly acknowledged Sloane as his daughter. "Until a few months ago, I didn't know I had a daughter, so I missed out on all the things a father should have been there for, and I'm deeply sorry. Her wedding was supposed to be our "coming out" party. That wasn't to be. But I'm here for her today and as long as I'm able, I'll stand by her side, sharing her sorrow over the loss of my friend Corky Rogers. He will live long in our hearts."

During that acknowledgment many emotions flashed over both Early's and Sloane's faces—not "love as simple as shaving soap"—words Summer remembered from an Anne Sexton poem she'd read in English class. Complicated love. It seemed to her that love always swirled in a cauldron of other emotions. Certainly that was true of her mother and father's relationship. True also of her own feelings for Ty.

As Summer drew close enough to Joe to see his face, she halted mid-step. With a frisson of shock, she realized if looks could kill, Early wouldn't have to wait for cancer to claim him. Joe was already moving away from her, headed toward the road. Summer remembered the sadness in Early's voice when he spoke of the rift: *You see Joe, tell him "hi" from me.* If only she could get Joe alone for a few minutes, maybe she could help him see he would regret it the rest of his life if he didn't make peace with his brother before he died.

The thin strands of "Amazing Grace" marked the end of the service, each note of the soloist visible in the chilly air. Then Early invited mourners to his church for food and fellowship.

Joe, she saw, was already hobbling down the road toward his farm, his gait choppy as if he had pulled a muscle.

She hurried to her truck, but a slew of cars and trucks were attempting to turn around for the ride back to town. How many were joining Nadine at the Clique Club? By the time Summer negotiated her way through the congestion, Joe was already on his porch. She drove past just as his front door closed. With her windows up, Summer couldn't hear the slam, but the wreath of orange and yellow plastic daisies told the story. It arced outward and rebounded against the center panel. One of the flower spikes broke free and fluttered to the ground.

Obviously, he wasn't in a good mood, so she didn't stop.

That afternoon the test results from Patricia Kirby's well were completed. Debbie Romano, who had been processing Summer's samples in the lab, called with the news.

"I thought something was up when I saw you'd written a personal check to cover the expense," Debbie said, "but I didn't jump you ahead in the queue. I should have. There were higher than expected concentrations of benzene, toluene, arsenic, and diesel range organics. I emailed you a copy of the full report and sent a copy to the appropriate officials."

After thanking Debbie, Summer called Early. Kirby's house was not that distant from his farm—if you considered how a bird flew—and he might know where the water in the creek that ran behind Mrs. Kirby's house came from and where it merged into something larger. It would save time if she didn't have to follow its path on foot. Most maps wouldn't include details on mere trickles. Neighbors would know of it, though. It probably disappeared altogether during dry spells in the summer, but would be prone to flash flooding if the ground became saturated from snow melt or heavy rains.

Early did know of the creek. "Run-off from way around the mountain feeds into it. It snakes through the back of the properties on Windy Hollow Road, runs through my farm, and eventually meets up with Little Tenmile Creek."

When she'd visited Mrs. Kirby, she'd only considered the closest fracking site as a possible source of contamination and believed it was unlikely because of the terrain. But a creek could carry contaminants long distances from an operation on the other side of the mountain.

"Why don't you come over for a chat today?" he asked. "I could use the company."

She explained her time would be limited since a friend of hers was due to arrive on Thanksgiving morning.

"You can't celebrate Thanksgiving in that tiny cabin. You must all come over here and join us for a proper feast."

"Oh no, we couldn't."

"I insist. Otherwise, it would just be Sloane, PJ, and me. If you all come, it will be more like a proper celebration than a continuation of the funeral."

Summer agreed, stipulating they would bring over part of the meal.

How sad that Joe and his wife wouldn't share the holiday with Early. This would probably be his last Thanksgiving. That sallow skin meant his liver was nearly overwhelmed.

~

BOOMER, AS SUMMER HAD PREDICTED, hadn't come through with a letter of recommendation from Fairhope, but four new landowners had signed up for testing with the help of Kit Corbett's letter of introduction.

Grace actually smiled when Summer picked her up from school—and smiles from this child were rare.

As they held hands walking toward Summer's truck, Grace announced, "Now you really my mommy."

Summer felt a crushing weight in her chest. "No, honey, more like your big sister, remember? Your brother will be back soon and take you home." Summer desperately wanted this to be true.

"He didn't go away forever like Mommy and Daddy?"

"No way. He'll be back tomorrow at the latest, and we'll celebrate, won't we?" Unless they filed charges. Then Summer had no idea what would follow.

After all Grace had been through, she needed stability more than anything. Last spring Summer had found Grace sitting alone in a hallway outside a meeting room. Summer had scolded Ty for leaving the child by herself. When she threatened to call family services, Ty revealed they were homeless, living in his van. Impulsively, Summer had invited them to stay in her apartment. Ty had refused the offer, but Summer had convinced him to let Grace sleep in her apartment until she recovered from a cold. No wonder the poor kid was confused by the constant upheavals in her life.

When they got back to the cabin, Summer set out to fix their dinner, but Grace objected to the blue box of macaroni and cheese.

"This not the right kind."

"Come on, you love mac and cheese, and this is my favorite." Summer's voice became a syrupy sing-song. "Really yummy stuff. Wait until you try it. You're gonna love it. "

"It not the right kind."

Summer's voice lost the song. "It's the only kind I have."

"It not the right kind."

Was this all part of Asperger's—if that's what Grace had?

"The box is orange," Grace said.

Summer blew out air. "The right box."

"Orange," Grace repeated.

Summer had the sneaking suspicion Ty had been buying Grace the organic brand. Summer couldn't afford that luxury for herself.

She slipped into her jacket. Armed with truck keys and Ty's debit card that she'd picked up at the jail earlier, she was ready to brave the rain that had started half an hour earlier. "Okay, it's off to the store we go. Gotta have the right kind of mac and cheese."

She helped Grace zip into her pink puffy parka. Summer held out a pink mitten. Grace stuck out her lower lip and hid her hands behind her back. "Those not right."

Summer counted to three, trying to be patient. "Which are the right ones?"

"Purpoo."

The purple ones. Summer dug through Grace's duffel bag and found the purple mittens. The pink ones, Grace explained, were for school. The purpoo ones were for everything else.

A motor rumbled in the distance. The decibels slowly increased. Great. A visitor—right when she'd gotten Grace ready to leave. God, she hoped it was Ty, sprung from jail. She had no idea how to handle Grace's demands. Was giving in the right thing to do? Or was she reinforcing unacceptable behavior?

Peering out the window, Summer watched the headlights enlarge until the vehicle parked behind hers. Car doors slammed, followed by voices. Female. Not Ty. She sighed, then found a new reason to hope—maybe Nadine had arrived to save the day with a freaking boatload of signed release forms.

She crossed to the door, hobbled by Grace, who was hanging onto Summer's leg.

"This can't be the right place. It's a shack!"

Her mother's voice. No, no, no. What was she doing here? This couldn't be happening. Absolutely not.

"Of course this is it." Mrs. Patel's lumpy shape waddled up the road.

"It's Summer's truck," Dayita, her form last in line, pointed out.

Summer flipped on the outside light, illuminating the path for the approaching group. Mrs. Patel stumbled on the porch steps. Too late, Summer realized she'd forgotten to warn them about the uneven boards.

Her mother reached the porch. "I bet you're surprised to see us!"

You think? Summer wanted to say, but her tongue froze.

"Well, that sure was a long drive," her mother said. "And terrible weather. We drove through snow in the mountains. Slip-sliding away."

Her mother sounded chirrupy. Must have taken some good drugs. "Aren't you going to invite us in?" she asked.

When she extended her arms, Summer mechanically returned the hug.

Suddenly Grace let go of Summer's leg, bounding onto the porch, arms stretched out. "Dee-tah! Miz Nee-kah!"

Any other time the child's enthusiasm would have amazed and pleased Summer, but she couldn't shake the feeling that none of this could be happening. Every second weighed on her, each a stone that kept her from articulating what she felt as her mother loomed in front of her. What words did you say to someone who tried to crush your most cherished dreams? Especially when that someone was your mother.

Her mother broke the silence.

"Oh my Lord, that's Grace! You're shacked up with *that man!* In this . . . this . . . *shack!* No wonder you don't answer the phone. You've been too busy—"

"For God's sake, hush up!" Summer hissed, her eyes cutting to Grace. The child had turned from the Patels, startled by the disapproval in Jordan Cassidy's voice though too young to understand the accusation.

Absorbing the rebuke, her mother's lips trembled. She fumbled through her purse, probably already looking for pills to take the edge off, Summer thought bitterly.

Standing back from the doorway, she allowed the group to move inside. Glaring at Dayita, Summer whispered, "I don't understand how this could have happened."

Dayita held her palms outward denying responsibility, but her eyebrows and shoulders hunched, telegraphing guilt.

"Don't blame Dayita, the surprise was all my doing," Mrs. Patel said, slipping off gloves, her cheery voice surreal, magnifying the sensation that this was only a bad dream and any moment Summer would wake up. But no, Mrs. Patel continued. "Since Dayita was coming anyway, I thought we could take turns driving and get here sooner and what could be nicer than a real Thanksgiving holiday in the mountains."

Nicer was not the word Summer would have chosen. When her phone rang, she was grateful for the distraction. It was Nadine, wanting her to pick up signed permission forms. Thirty-eight total, a phenomenal accomplishment that Summer wasn't capable of properly appreciating while watching bodies swarm inside her cabin. Why, they could barely turn around without stumbling over each other. They stomped sleet off their shoes. Rubbed hands together for warmth. Piled coats on a kitchen chair because there was nowhere else to stash them.

In no hurry to deal with her guests, Summer let Nadine blather on with biting commentary on Sloane Dumont's red sequined dress and Boomer's eulogy for Corky Rogers. "The insincere bastard. If you could've heard him bitching last week about Corky's filing for worker's comp, you wouldn't believe he was talking about the same person," Nadine said.

Eventually Summer thanked Nadine and hung up. First, she bussed Mrs. Patel's cold, chubby cheek. Then she grasped Dayita's arms long enough to whisper, "How could you do this to me?"

Dayita turned away—but not before Summer saw tears form in her friend's eyes. Oh, now she'd done it—she didn't want to hurt Dayita—but damn it, she knew Summer wasn't even speaking to her mother. And where were all these people supposed to sleep? On the roof with Rocky? Unable to look at her mother, Summer said to no one in particular, "I guess by now you've noticed I don't have room for extra guests. Grace is staying with me until her brother gets . . . back." She was trying to avoid mentioning police in front of Grace. The child was traumatized enough already.

"Now, don't you worry about that," Mrs. Patel said. "Your mother and I have a motel room, so we won't be in your way. Unless the weather turns bad, we plan to do a little sight-seeing after Thanksgiving, isn't that right, Jordan?"

Her mother didn't answer. With sidelong glances, Summer noticed her mother watching her. "What's wrong, Summer? We haven't seen each other for months. Don't you have anything to say? Why can't you look at me?"

Tension vibrated in stillness so pervasive that the tiny room seemed to be holding its breath. A dizzying lightness overtook Summer. "I don't know how to talk to you anymore. Not since I found out you wrote those awful letters. How could you? Do you hate me?"

Her mother's face grew slack as if she'd had a stroke, her body swaying, hands reaching blindly for the back of a kitchen chair. The front legs lifted, teetered, and clacked as they resettled. Summer was vaguely aware of Mrs. Patel helping her mother sit down.

Dayita prompted, "What letters, Summer?"

"How did you . . ." Her mother couldn't finish.

The dizzy moment passed. "It doesn't matter how I found out. We'll have to deal with it. Later. Right now I have an important errand to run for my research. Dayita is coming with me." Summer clutched Dayita's arm. "Mrs. Patel, could you please take Grace to a grocery store and buy her the right kind of macaroni and cheese? It comes in an orange box. Buy three. I'll fix some for all of us when I get back."

A blur of motion and words. "Yes, honey, of course, we will go shopping for you." Mrs. Patel hustled Jordan Cassidy from the chair and redistributed the coats. "We will have dinner fixed when you get back." She grabbed Grace's mittened hand. "A nice, hot dinner." Cold air drifted past the open door. "I'll pick up some roasted chicken in the deli, too." Soft thuds of shoes on the creaking floor. "You like chicken, Grace, right? I remember you like it."

On the porch Mrs. Patel paused, looking over her shoulder. A tear rivered down her cheeks. She made no effort to wipe it away. Her mouth was moving but Summer couldn't make out the words. She felt as if she were underwater, sounds muffled, light and color distorted.

The door closed.

Summer's head felt weightless. Emptied out. Her knees folded and she fell into the chair her mother had vacated. She bent over until her forehead rested on her knees.

Dayita was calling her name. Summer supposed she had to face her. *Deep breaths, slow them down. Count them.*

"Should I call for help? Summer? Talk to me."

She felt Dayita's breath against her forehead, felt hands cupping her shoulders. She took one more measured breath. When she stood, her legs felt sturdy.

"I'll be fine," she said, and meant it. "Let's run that errand."

~

IT SEEMED AS IF THEY WERE ONLY CREEPING ALONG, but still the rear wheels of Summer's truck fishtailed as they rounded a curve, sending Dayita's heart flying and her fingers digging deeper into the cracked leather bench seat. The truck righted itself. Good thing Dayita wasn't the one driving. She definitely would have over-corrected and sent them hurtling into the guardrail. Summer, though, took the road conditions in stride.

But she shouldn't even be driving so soon after that major freak-out. Lordee, lordee! Dayita thought she was going to have to dial 911. For real. When was Summer going to explain that bomb she'd dropped on her mother? Dayita yearned for details.

As Summer drove, she explained why Grace was staying with her. "Ty's fingerprints were on the murder weapon, but it's all a stupid mistake. They should release him any moment."

Dayita closed her eyes as they navigated a winding steep road lined with luxury homes. If you could afford one of these mansions, seemed as if you could find flat land to build on—but maybe there wasn't any. Summer pulled next to the curb in front of a red brick two-story.

"I'll just be a sec." Summer got out and scampered toward the house.

Orange and gold globe lights lined the walkway. Hay bales and corn stalks were arranged near the door and in several clusters in the yard. Looked as if the owners got into Thanksgiving in a big way.

When Summer returned with a folder, Dayita asked, "What was so urgent about picking up those papers tonight?"

Summer started the engine. "It could have waited until morning, but I needed time to figure out how to deal with my mother."

"Want to talk about it?"

"Not really."

As the silence extended to the point it became uncomfortable, Summer finally shared the appalling tale of her professor's visit and her mother's letter. "I'm sure Ral hacked the university system to find it," she said.

"Holy crap, I can't believe someone's trying to blackmail you! Why didn't you tell me?" It would have sped up setting the trap to snare Ral, but no matter: she had found a way to slam him back into the rat hole he had crawled out of.

"It's somewhat degrading to find out your own mother doesn't believe in you," Summer said.

"What your mom did sucks. I know how much you wanted to go to MIT. But there's a silver lining here if you're willing to find it. At Penn State you're closer to Ty and you have an excuse to visit him often in Clarksburg."

Summer choked on a laugh. "Funny thing, my mom managed to mess up things with Ty, too. Last spring she told him to back off and the big wuss listened to her."

"What!" Dayita couldn't imagine her mother interfering that

way—but then her mom thought she had Dayita's future all mapped out. She was supposed to marry a cousin she hadn't seen since she was a toddler. What would her mother do if—no, when—she refused?

Summer sighed. "Yeah, can you believe it? It pisses me off to admit this, but my mother was partly right. Ty keeps asking me to join his nonprofit, but no man is going to come between me and my doctorate."

Dayita hesitated. How would Summer take this? "Your mother's wrong about your being fragile, but admit it—you've pulled some crazy stunts."

They had passed through town and were back on less traveled roads again where thin patches of slush were accumulating.

"You talking about my hitchhiking to the Slave Canal? Dayita, for heaven's sake, I was fourteen!"

"You can quit telling that fib. I know you stole your mother's car."

When Summer didn't respond, Dayita worried she'd made her mad.

"How'd you find out?" Summer finally asked.

"Your mother called mine, of course, hunting for you. She was frantic."

"Mom promised she'd never tell a living soul. Why am I not surprised she lied?" Summer explained the compact they'd made concerning public school. "Did you know I was gone a whole day before she even noticed?" The bitterness in Summer's voice was painful to hear. She added, "I've told that hitchhiking lie so long I kind of believed it myself. I never wanted anyone to think of me as a criminal."

If you asked Dayita, Jordan Cassidy was the criminal. Police should have charged her with child neglect. Dayita recognized the convenience store they'd passed on the way to Nadine's. Soon they turned down the narrow road to Summer's cabin and parked beside the Patels' car. As she jumped down from the truck, Dayita blinked. Had something moved on the roof? Probably shifting shadows, nothing to worry about. But as she peered into the pitch black void, something definitely moved. She shrieked and hopped back inside the truck.

"What's wrong?"

Dayita pointed with a shaky hand. "Something's on your roof."

Summer laughed. "Meet Rocky, my resident raccoon. He's inquisitive. Wants to check you out."

That *thing* had scared her half to death. Dayita huffed, "Geez, couldn't you get a dog or a cat?"

"It's not like I invited him. He was here first."

Dayita was reluctant to get out with that beastly thing up there. Summer could go first, in case it jumped down. When Summer stayed put, Dayita sensed she had something else to say.

Summer's tongue clicked against her teeth. "Figuring out why we do the things we do isn't easy."

Dayita suspected Summer was talking about more than the Slave Canal now. "What are you going to do when you go inside?"

The truck door creaked open. "Find a way to forgive her. It's the mature thing to do."

~

BOOMER'S WHOLE DAY had sucked royally. Having to give that speech at Corky Rogers' funeral would have been depressing all by itself. The day only went downhill from there. Turner Skidmore showed up at Fairhope headquarters to tease Boomer about getting kicked out of Sloane Dumont's salon. At first, it seemed as if Turner was being friendly, snickering with Boomer about the size of those hooters. But then, the deputy wondered aloud if Boomer and Corky had words about the whole thing. Boomer wasn't stupid. He saw where Turner was trying to go, so he excused himself to head out to a job site.

Who could blame him, then, for having a drink or two with the guys before heading home—a little stress relief? But Nadine refused to cut him any slack. Yelled at him about that temporary license—said it was against the law to drive anywhere else besides going to work. Nag, nag, nag. Made him sorry he'd called to tell her he'd be late getting in.

By the time Boomer steered into his driveway, it was nearly two in the morning. He clicked the garage door opener. Nothing happened. He pressed again. Damn battery had to pick now to die. Rain was already coating the windshield. He got out of the SUV, tromped toward the front door and stumbled over one of those stupid hay bales. He was freezing his nuts off out here. He took off his gloves and fumbled through his key ring. It had been so long since he'd used the house key, he wasn't sure which one it was, and he couldn't see a damn thing in the dark. When he found what looked like the right one, he inserted it. Didn't work, damn it. Why couldn't he get a break—just once? He tried another key. And another. His back itched as droplets trickled down his neck.

He really didn't feel like waking Nadine and facing her ire, but he couldn't think of any other option short of breaking a window. He rang the doorbell and stood there for what seemed like forever, trying to be patient. He knew she was in there. The light in the guest bedroom was on. Maybe she'd fallen asleep. Exasperated, he punched the doorbell five or six times. Why didn't the bitch answer the door?

He screamed, "Nadine!" Lights blinked on across the street. Christ, next thing you knew the neighbors would be summoning the cops. He called Nadine's cell. When she answered, he bellowed, "You fucking deaf? I been ringing the doorbell for twenty minutes. Get your ass out of bed and let me in."

"No need to yell. I can hear you fine."

He could picture Nadine's little head bobbing, her face a portrait of self-righteous indignation. God, she annoyed the crap out of him. He swiped at raindrops that bleared his vision.

"Boomer, I had the locks changed today. My lawyer will deliver divorce papers to your office tomorrow. Please sign them promptly. There's no need to drag this out."

Divorce—after that great birthday party? But now he recalled she'd been laughing with Corbett. Boomer didn't think he could stand it if she left him for Corbett. As devastating as that would be, a third alimony payment would be even worse. Through the alcohol haze Boomer remembered how Wife Number One and Number Two screwed him over. Much as it galled him, he had to make nice.

"Nadine, honey, I know you're angry, but let's not throw away everything we have. We should try counseling." God, the idea of listening to her gripe to some stranger made him want to stick a nail gun to his head. "We can work this out."

"Too late. By the way, I helped that little researcher out; you know the one I mean."

"You did *what*? You better be kidding."

"Nope. I collected gazillions of release forms for water testing and handed them over to her tonight."

He felt blood drain from his face. After all his efforts to make sure those researchers went away, his own wife fucked him over. If they blamed anyone's funny-tasting water on his wells, regulators might halt drilling. God only knew for how long.

"Geezus, Nadine, what have you done?"

"You screwed over the wrong woman this time, buster." She disconnected.

Soaked through to the skin, he needed to sit down or lie down. He staggered toward the SUV and tripped over another of Nadine's stupid hay bales and landed on his knees. His teeth bit into his tongue, leaving a metallic taste in his mouth. Musty odors curled into his lungs. His stomach heaved but nothing came up. No wonder. He hadn't eaten since lunchtime.

When he stood, his legs wobbled like Slinkys. A couple of deep breaths steadied him.

He had to get those forms back.

~

THE FRAGRANCE OF ROASTED CHICKEN and the right kind of macaroni and cheese filled the tiny cabin, but Summer's stomach churned until she felt as if she couldn't eat a bite. She studied her mother as she lay on the couch. Her eyes had blinked open once when Summer and Dayita returned. They had remained closed since. Heavily medicated, no doubt. Summer sent Mrs. Patel a questioning look, which prompted a head shake and worried frown.

Dayita flopped onto one of the two kitchen chairs next to Grace, her long legs extended. For the first time, Summer noticed she wore gold sequined tennis shoes with platform soles. Dayita was a hoot.

Mrs. Patel bustled around in the kitchen, cutting up vegetables for one of her unique salads. This one had grated carrots, orange segments, raisins, chickpeas, and almonds. She measured oil and spices into a bowl.

"I need an assistant chef," Mrs. Patel said. "Someone who is very good with their hands."

Grace raised her hand. So did Dayita.

Mrs. Patel studied them as if she couldn't make up her mind who to choose. "It must be someone really special, someone willing to work hard."

Grace stood on the chair and waved her whole arm in the air so franticly it warranted support from her other arm. Mrs. Patel awarded the bowl and fork to her with the command to thoroughly blend the ingredients without spilling any. "Dayita can be the assistant to the assistant."

While everyone else was busy, Summer attached a sheet of paper to her clipboard and found a pen. This would only get harder the longer she waited. She jostled her mother's shoulder until her eyes opened. "Mom, I understand why you asked Ty to stay away from me. You were right. I need to focus on getting my degree. Even so, I wish you'd talked to me instead of him."

Her mother pressed a hand across her eyes. "Do we have to do this now?"

"I think we do. I understand why you wrote the letters, too. You believed you were protecting me." Inside, Summer was wound so tight she thought she might explode, lobbing bits of shrapnel across the room. She forced herself to rein it in: the potential destruction would be irreparable. You only had one mother, and like it or not, Jordan Cassidy was hers.

Her mother glanced at her tentatively, before closing her eyes again. "I wrote them before, you know . . . before last spring. Before I realized how much you'd grown up."

Summer's fingernails bit into her palm. As if anything could excuse a mother filleting her daughter's heart like a fish.

Mrs. Patel turned, waving a paring knife in the air. "Yes, Summer is very strong, very grown up. We're all very proud of her."

Very, very, very. Summer needed all the superlatives she could get to pull this off. Dr. Jennings' letter of recommendation had given her the idea. She could never use his letter because it might jeopardize his family. But a letter from her mother could be even more mitigating.

"You can help me now," Summer told her mother. "Someone is threatening to use one of your letters to discredit my research. You can write a letter explaining what a strong, stable young woman I am. You could say you are proud of the way I've overcome obstacles to pursue my dream of becoming a research scientist. If these people make the other letter public, I will offer the new letter immediately to counteract the damage."

Her mother rolled her face against the back of the couch, which made her words even more muffled. "I don't feel up to writing a letter right now. Tomorrow, when I feel better."

Experience had taught Summer that her mother, like most addicts, rarely felt better tomorrow, or the tomorrow after that.

Dayita's eyes opened wider, asking the unspoken question: what would Summer do now?

"Let's try," Summer said. "I'll help you."

Dayita jumped up. "The assistant to the assistant will help too."

Summer lifted her mother into a sitting position while Dayita shifted her feet to the floor. Jordan's features retained the vague confusion of someone awakened in the middle of the night, but she remained upright.

Summer and Dayita sat on either side—bookends if she slipped over.

"You're stronger than you think," Summer said. "We both are." She put the pen in her mother's hand and dictated what needed to be said. The handwriting was spidery but legible enough.

Summer bit her lip, turning her back on everyone while she placed the letter in a manila folder.

Her mother clutched at Summer's arm, preventing her from walking away. "Can you ever forgive me?"

What was she supposed to say? Early's words came to her: *It takes strength to forgive, but it's the only path to peace.* She steeled herself against the tears that threatened. She absolutely refused to show weakness. "I'm trying to."

"Of course she will," Mrs. Patel said. "Give her a little time. You both will be okay. Supper's ready. Everyone come get your plates."

Grace directed Mrs. Patel on exactly what food could go where on her plate. "Don't let anything touch."

Watching her mother slump over on the couch again, one arm thrown over her eyes, Summer said, "I'm not really hungry."

Mrs. Patel waved her wooden spoon like a magic wand. "Yes, you are. You have to eat to stay strong."

Summer filled a plate and found she was hungry after all.

~

After dinner, it took both Dayita and her mother to hold Mrs. Cassidy steady on the way to the car. For the first time, Dayita fully realized what Summer had contended with all these years. Why she escaped to the Patels' home so often. Why she never wanted any kids in high school to visit the Cassidy house. Until this trip, Dayita figured Summer's reluctance stemmed from her mother's slovenly housekeeping and the creepy candlelit shrine for Summer's twin in the living room.

After they got Mrs. Cassidy settled into the car, Dayita's mother came back inside and cradled Grace in her arms, saying, "The little one can stay with us so you two girls can stay up late catching up."

Grace was already halfway asleep when they bundled her into the car for the drive to the motel. The rain had stopped.

Dayita waved goodbye until the car was out of sight. This trip made Dayita appreciate how lucky she was to have such a good mother. Nothing excused Jordan Cassidy's hatchet job on Summer, not even losing her other child. Maybe Summer could forgive her, but Dayita couldn't.

She shivered and stamped her feet.

"Go on inside and get warm," Summer said. "I'll bring in extra firewood."

She didn't have to ask twice. Dayita pulled one of the kitchen chairs next to the fireplace. She shrugged her arms out of her jacket, but left it draped over her shoulders. Though burning brightly, the logs didn't put out enough heat to keep the whole room warm. The scent of burning wood near the chimney was pleasant.

Thwacks came from outside. She hadn't realized Summer had to chop the wood herself. When Summer had told her she'd rented a cabin, Dayita had imagined a mountain view retreat, not a retreat from civilization. She should have asked questions. She knew Summer's project was underfunded, but Dayita never imagined how it impacted her lifestyle. Not that it would bother Summer that much. The cabin door opened and cold air rushed in. Rosy cheeked, Summer propped the ax against the wall next to the door.

"Can't you leave that thing outside?" Dayita said. "Makes me think of ax murderers."

"Puh-leeze, girl. Get over it." Summer trotted back outside, returning with an armload of logs and kindling. She spread the whole mess out near the fireplace—to dry the logs, she said. "In the middle of the night, it gets really cold in here."

This wasn't already really cold? Geesh, you could fill a glass with ice and in the morning the cubes would be intact.

Dayita screamed and rocketed out of her chair. A huge spider was crawling up the sleeve of Summer's jacket and had almost reached the bare skin of her neck.

"What on earth?" Summer asked.

Dancing from one foot to the other, Dayita pointed at the spider. Rolling her eyes, Summer flicked it off her coat into her other hand and relocated it to the porch. "Happy now?"

"Much better."

"You can have the bed or the couch," Summer said, "but they both suck. I usually pull blankets onto the floor."

Tiny claws clattered on the roof, and Dayita tensed again. "It's too early for Santa's reindeer. I suppose that's the raccoon."

"Watch this." Summer stood on a kitchen chair and tucked a tissue into a crevice between the ceiling boards. More steps pattered overhead and the tissue wiggled, then inched upward, eventually disappearing. Paws drummed and claws clicked in the direction of the kitchen, followed by a noise resembling a vacuum cleaner.

"What's that?" Dayita asked.

"Rocky purring. He's pleased with himself. Pretty clever, don't you think?"

Dayita snorted. Only Summer would think a raccoon was cool. She dragged the quilt off the couch and laid it on the floor. She folded her legs and dropped down, patting a spot for Summer to join her.

Dayita couldn't keep a Mona Lisa smile from creasing her face. "The trap is ready."

"Thank God! Wait until you get a load of this." Summer tramped to the kitchen and fished around in the drawer. Summer tossed the black case onto the quilt. "Ral has been spying on me with this GPS tracker. Even without the phone, he knows everywhere I've been and has been listening in on conversations that took place near the truck. It's creepy."

Dayita filled Summer in on how she had studied Ral's blog posts on Internet security, and then followed a hunch that a guy like him would dig the Dark Web.

"And?" Summer prompted.

"He's been crawling all over the virtual world in places a White

Hat hacker wouldn't be." If Dayita started talking about how TOR worked and how difficult it was to trace encrypted activity, she knew Summer would accuse her of Geek Speak, so she simplified what had been a complicated task. "Ral couldn't resist bragging about his exploits in online chats. I found enough evidence to convince a cyber-sleuth I know at the FBI to do some searching for me. We found Ral had hacked a health care provider's database to steal people's private records like birth dates and Social Security numbers. So I created an online identity using a pseudonym and posed as a buyer for his stolen information."

Summer hi-fived her. "You are way beyond cool!"

"I am, aren't I?" Dayita couldn't help but smile. "We get to interrogate him after the FBI agents take him down."

Firelight flickered over Summer's face. Her features blackened, leaving the impression she had merged into the shadows. "I can't imagine how many people's lives have already been harmed by data he stole."

Dayita looked off into the fire, her braid wrapping anaconda-like across her shoulder and down her back. "Loss of personal information is a serious problem, Summer. People are posting so much about themselves on social media, they've given up their right to privacy without a fight. They don't even realize there's been a war and they lost. I've decided to start my own company, a cryptography firm offering user-friendly encryption so ordinary people can take back their privacy and in the process, fight against all the surveillance big government and big corporations are doing."

"Keep fighting against Black Hatters like Ral, too, Dayita."

"Always." But the promise held a huge rush accompanied by a sliver of terror. A very thin line separated the kind of Gray Hat hacking she'd used to access Signal-Muller from Black Hat activity. The temptation to make yourself rich or simply pay off your bills pulled many a hacker across the line. And the adrenaline rush, for many, became addictive even without the promise of wealth. Is that what had corrupted Ral? She hoped she'd always be strong enough to stay on the right side.

~

A DISTANT MOTOR was growing louder, but half asleep, Summer decided it was only a trick in the way sound carried from the highway on a quiet night. But then she definitely heard something unnatural—a car door? She sat up.

"The raccoon?" Dayita asked.

"No, stay under the quilt."

Summer tiptoed to the door and slid her feet into her boots. A thump was followed by crunching gravel and cursing.

She tied the bootlaces and picked up the ax.

Someone thudded up the steps onto the porch.

"What're you doing?" Dayita whispered.

Summer put a finger to her lips.

Who stood on the other side of the door—and how much would the firelight allow him to see?

Could be local kids who used the cabin as a party spot, but surely they would realize the cabin was occupied when they saw her truck. Inches away from her, the doorknob turned. Had she remembered to lock up after bringing in the logs? When the knob turned back without opening, she let out her breath.

Footsteps bumped along the porch toward the larger kitchen window.

Gingerly she turned the lock mechanism on the door. With the ax handle, she flipped on the porch light, simultaneously opening the door with her free hand. She stepped outside.

A yelp of surprise escaped the intruder's mouth as he whirled around. He held a semi-automatic rifle. She gripped the ax handle tighter, ready to throw if necessary. She took in the ball cap and brown jacket of Boomer Walsh. The sickly sweet odor of bourbon wafted her way. He swayed and she realized he was totaled.

"Kind of late to come calling, Mr. Walsh. I think you'd better leave."

"My wife shoulda mind her own bidnez. I want dem papers back."

Summer should have known Nadine would relish telling her husband what she'd done.

"Not going to happen," Summer said. "Those forms belong to me. You'd better leave now."

He brandished the rifle. "Maybe you din't notice but you're not in position to call duh shots."

She thought he was mostly bluster, but drunks could be unpredictable. They started bar fights even when they could barely stand up.

"Maybe you didn't notice, but I'm armed with an ax."

"Lil gurl like you wouldn't know what ta do wid—"

The muscles in her throat tightened. "It would be a serious mistake to underestimate me. I never miss my target—ask your son."

"Whas Hank . . ." He swayed but recovered his balance. His arm moved as if he intended to point the rifle at her.

"Raise your arm one inch more and I'll bury this ax in your neck. You won't get off a shot, and you'll bleed out before an ambulance can get here."

His arm was already lowering when Dayita's voice came through the open door. "She'll do it, too, Mister. She killed one man already this year."

Boomer Walsh's glassy eyes darted to the door. His weight shifted to his back leg and he looked less certain. "Jus' gimme da damn papers. Nadine had no right, no right ta go behin' my back like dis."

Summer was ready to retort, but Dayita beat her to it. "If she doesn't kill you, I will. Safety's off and I got a bullet aimed right at your heart. Drop the rifle."

That computer genius wouldn't have a clue how to use a gun even if she had one, but Summer was grateful when the bluff proved effective, and he lowered the weapon to the porch.

"I'll be back," he muttered. "Gonna . . . court order. Get dose papers back." His eyes shifted to his rifle. "Gun too."

Court order, her ass. They weren't his papers to begin with, but you couldn't reason with a drunk. "I'll leave the gun at your house or office tomorrow." She didn't want him returning, drunk or sober. Summer eased backward into the doorway to let him leave by the steps.

Behind her truck sat a dark SUV. What if it wasn't Ral who tried to run her off the road? As a scientist, she should have known better than to jump to a conclusion without solid evidence. Could have been Boomer Walsh. Or anyone else who drove a dark SUV.

Walsh slipped on the wet leaves and went down on one knee. He came up cussing. "Fuckin' stupid bitch. Couldn't hit duh broad side a barn wid dat ax. I'm gonna come back . . . my .30-06 an' fix her ass."

With one quick step forward on her left foot and a full body thrust, she uncocked her right arm. The ax whipped through the air and thwacked into the pine.

Walsh staggered. "Whad da?" He turned to face her. "You crazy muthafuckin bitch! You almos' . . ." He couldn't finish. His panting breaths puffed into the cold air. He tottered two steps backward, and then let loose a deranged laugh. "But you missed!"

"No, Mr. Walsh," she called out. "I hit my target. That pine's already dead. I wouldn't break the bark on a live tree and risk killing it. But I won't have the same consideration for your sorry skin if you ever come back here."

His eyes roamed over the pine, confirming it was, indeed, dead. He stared back at her, muttered something she couldn't hear, and skedaddled the rest of the way to his SUV. Without turning to see, she sensed Dayita had come outside in her stocking feet, standing behind her. They waited on the edge of the porch until his tail lights disappeared.

Icy fingers of night air slipped through Summer's sweatshirt. The scent of smoke, sweet and pungent, soothed her. Reminded her of good times camping with her father. He never could have imagined the ways the skills he'd taught her would be put to use.

There came a noise like Grape-nuts hitting the bowl. With a sharp hiss, Dayita grabbed Summer's wrist. Her touch pulled Summer entirely into the present.

"Relax. That *was* Rocky."

They went inside, welcomed by the warm fire. Summer dialed 911 and reported Boomer's threats and drunken behavior. The dispatcher thanked her.

Until now, Summer had felt safe out here in the cabin. But tomorrow, she had to get Dayita and Grace out of here. It wasn't safe for any of them any longer.

14

November 27

BOOMER ROLLED OVER IN BED, half awake but overwhelmed by the sensation something wasn't right. It was more than the sledgehammer pounding inside his head, which was about average. No, it was the stench of urine that terrified him. He had never pissed himself before, and if that's what had happened, he was giving up the bourbon. Right now. Forever. He would never take another drink. He cracked open one eye and felt dizzy when he realized he was in jail. As he pushed the length of his body up, his stomach roiled. He made it to the stained toilet before he upchucked.

He staggered over to the bars and bellowed, "I want my fucking lawyer." When no one appeared immediately, he screamed, "Noooow." He added, "Pretty please."

Turner Skidmore pimp-walked in.

"All the goddamn taxes I pay I oughta be getting better service than this," Boomer fumed.

"Don't get your panties in a wad, Boomer. It's not like you're our only customer this morning."

If Boomer had been on the other side of the bars, he'd have wiped the floor with that asshole. "Good morning, Turner. Think we could get my lawyer over here, so I can be on my way?"

Turner looked so cheerful Boomer wanted to slap him.

"Doubt it, my friend," Turner said. "It's Thanksgiving."

Thanksgiving—he'd completely forgotten about it. He'd better call Hank. They usually watched football together after his son feasted with his mother. He groaned and rubbed the stubble on his jaw. "What are they charging me with?"

"For starters, driving drunk on a suspended license."

"Bullshit. I want my lawyer."

"Let's give him time to have a cup of coffee before we disturb him, okay? It's not seven yet."

"How about the morning paper?"

"Can do." Turner strolled out and took his good old time returning, but at least when he did he held the *Exponent-Telegram* in one hand and a cup of coffee in the other. He passed both through the bars.

Boomer's stomach lurched at the urine odor rising from the mattress when he sat down, but holding the coffee cup beneath his chin improved matters. It wasn't the best coffee he'd ever had, but it was hot. He unfolded the newspaper, skimming the usual boring political headlines. On page three, he smiled as he read the local Town Talk column. Headline could have been larger, but the timing couldn't have been better.

The column throwing doubt on the Cassidy bitch's stability could be his get-out-of-jail-free card.

"Turner, I need to talk to my son."

"I already called him and your wife. Funny thing is, neither one wants to speak with you. They both suggested you should use your time in here to think about where your life is headed."

Boomer's hands shook. Neither one would have a thin dime between them if it weren't for all his hard work. Damn the both of them.

~

"Your boy's been behaving badly." Elliot Ral squared his feet and tapped at the ball. It rolled a few feet down the artificial turf of Kit Corbett's indoor putting range and dropped in the hole.

"Nice putt." A fat tiger-striped kitty slunk into the room and purled around Corbett's leg. "He's hardly my boy."

Maybe not, but Corbett pegged who Elliot was talking about fast enough. "Last night he got stinking drunk and paid a visit to Ms. Cassidy's cabin."

Corbett was already into his swing when his head jerked up at the mention of the girl. First lousy shot Elliot had ever seen him make.

"What happened?"

"It was hard to piece together from the video. Some stuff happened out of camera range and rain degraded the picture quality.

Best I can tell, Boomer wanted to get something back from her. He made his request at two in the morning. With a rifle in hand."

Corbett's grip tightened on his club.

"No worries," Elliot said. "Ms. Cassidy hurled an ax at him. It missed by a few hairs and I believe old Boomer about pissed his pants."

Glassy-eyed as if picturing the scene, Corbett's mouth spread slowly into a smile, and then he laughed out loud. The kitty darted at the laces on his golf shoe, untying the bow. "Cut it out, Malleycat." He picked the cat up, scuffing its fur a few times before depositing the little nuisance in the hallway and closing the door. It mewled on the other side.

"I don't think you need to worry about her," Elliot said. "She seems more than capable of taking care of herself. And she wasn't alone in the cabin." He had Corbett's full attention. "A friend of hers from Florida is visiting."

"Male or female?"

"Female. She and her mother arrived with Ms. Cassidy's mother yesterday for dinner." Everything else about Dayita Patel would remain Elliot's secret. His prize in a little cyber-competition. "The mothers took the little girl with them to a motel."

"Figure out who the kid is?"

"Got the story from PJ Wine." The commissioner had pretended reluctance, but she could hardly wait to race into the tale after she'd returned to Walsh's party. "The kid is Franceschi's sister."

"The protest organizer?" Corbett's gaze seemed to turn inward, as if recalling all he knew about Franceschi. "A good-looking fellow."

Corbett looked as if the knowledge gave him indigestion. Elliot had been suspicious for some time that Corbett was keeping an eye on Ms. Cassidy for reasons other than the one he gave about vetting and protecting a possible future employee.

When Corbett bagged his club, Elliot followed suit, and added something he suspected would please Corbett. "Cops are questioning Franceschi about Corky Rogers' murder."

Corbett surprised him by asking if he thought Boomer shot Rogers. Elliot offered no opinion. It was against company policy to talk about any of its clients.

"Are you going anywhere for a big feast later today?" Elliot hoped for an invitation to dinner, but it wasn't forthcoming: Corbett was eating at his aunt's home, a big family gathering.

Early Thanksgiving morning, Summer made coffee, anticipating the hot breakfast Mrs. Patel had promised to deliver from the motel's restaurant. Around eight-thirty, Mrs. Patel arrived with Grace and Jordan Cassidy.

"Mumsy, you have no idea what an exciting time you missed last night," Dayita said before Mrs. Patel even had a chance to set down the containers of egg and bacon sandwiches sided by hash browns.

Summer tried to catch Dayita's eye, to hush her up, but before she could be stopped, the details of Boomer's drunken foray onto the cabin porch popped out.

As Summer feared, her mother became hysterical, insisting Summer move back to Loblolly Lake.

"No worries, Mom," Summer said. "Dayita threatened to shoot him with a nonexistent gun and I hurled a real ax at him. He went away. We called the cops. Problem solved."

"Such smart girls," Mrs. Patel said, patting Dayita's shoulder. "So capable."

Those observations and a breakfast sandwich calmed her mother down some. Then Hank Walsh called to apologize for his father's behavior. It was really decent of him. She could hardly hold him responsible for his father's actions anymore than she wanted to be held responsible for her mother's. He pressed her to meet up with him the following day, but she begged off with the excuse of hosting company. When her mother learned who she'd been talking to, she freaked out all over again.

Fortunately, another distraction came a few minutes later when Ty arrived. Summer felt weak-kneed with relief.

Grace ran to him, her fingers digging into the cloth of his jeans. "I thought you went away like Mommy and Daddy and you weren't coming back for me."

Ty tried to lighten the moment by playfully punching her shoulder. "Afraid you're stuck with me, Sugarpop."

With a start, Summer realized she needed to alert Early Glover that her one guest had mushroomed into five. She needn't have worried. He told her to bring them on.

For most of the morning, Grace held onto Ty's jeans, clinging to his side. At times, he would gently disengage her fingers so he could move freely. Summer was dying to know whether he had been cleared completely but couldn't ask and risk upsetting Grace. Around eleven, he announced he and Grace were going home to shower before the big gathering. Grace disengaged from him long enough to hug "big sister" Summer and then while she exchanged goodbyes with the Patels. Summer asked Ty whether he was in the clear.

"I think so, but with these guys you can never be sure," he said. She squeezed his hand before he and Grace drove off.

By noon Early's home was filled with friends of Summer's, both old and new. Sloane made sure everyone had drinks. Summer thought Sloane looked at her rather strangely while handing her a glass of wine.

A thread of tension had developed in the kitchen, as both PJ and Mrs. Patel vied to assert authority. Despite disagreement as to who was in charge, soon the fragrance of reheated smoked turkey had Summer's mouth watering. Grace stood on a chair spooning cranberry sauce into a china serving bowl under Dayita's supervision. Summer's mother reclined in Early's favorite chair in the living room.

Early read aloud a copy of a letter he'd sent to the sheriff complaining of ill treatment. Summer agreed with everything he had written until he got to the part about needing memory-foam mattresses for the jail. She had to laugh—what a crazy, lovable old coot.

The moment PJ Wine arrived, she whispered something to Early. They both glanced at Summer and quickly looked away when she noticed. Summer decided it was her imagination until it happened again between PJ and Sloane. The secretive stares made Summer feel awkward.

Grace arrived with Ty, who seemed unusually tense. He held a folded newspaper against his leg. "Summer, is there somewhere we could talk?"

When Early saw the newspaper, he grimaced. "What'd you bring that damn thing here for? I hid mine."

"She'll find out anyway," Ty said. "Might as well be now."

Summer's chest caved inward. "Find out what?"

"Bah humbug. If you must spoil the holiday, take her in the guest bedroom over there." Early motioned to a door off the kitchen.

"There's a chair. She's going to need one."

She followed Ty into a minimally furnished guest room: brass bed, antique wooden chair, mirror, and one lovely watercolor on the wall. A large window let in natural light. Summer sat in the chair. Ty presented the newspaper, folded to page three. Seated on the bed, he watched her read the column.

She hadn't known how they would use her mother's letter, but it was almost a relief to have it in the open. Now she could counteract it.

"You already knew about this, didn't you?" Ty said. "I can see it in your face."

His eyes seemed to lose focus for an instant, and then flicked toward her, his features softening. "I'm sorry. I didn't understand until now how difficult, how . . ."

"How messed up things are between my mother and me," Summer finished. She filled Ty in on the blackmailer's attempts to stop the research. "I have a new letter from my mother in my backpack. I'll take it to the newspaper office tomorrow and demand a retraction."

"Needs to be sooner. This column shouldn't go uncontested a minute longer than necessary," he said. "We'll get the retraction in the paper tomorrow. Sit still, I'll get your backpack."

He retrieved it from Early's living room.

"Let's keep this column from my mother," Summer said. "It'll upset her all over again."

Ty called a reporter friend and read Jordan Cassidy's letter aloud. He listened for a moment and put the reporter on hold. "Alexis wants to speak with your mother."

Summer shook her head.

Ty told Alexis he'd call her back. "Summer, I know you're trying to protect your mother, but she's the only one who can undo the damage."

Knowing the reporter was only doing her job by verifying the accuracy of a source, Summer reluctantly agreed.

Jordan Cassidy blanched when Ty laid the second letter she'd written on her lap. "All you have to do is tell Alexis you wrote this retraction. I already read the contents to her, but she has to verify that you actually wrote it."

Sloane, Early, and PJ stayed on the couch, not even pretending indifference. Summer supposed they'd all read the newspaper.

Jordan Cassidy took the phone and admitted she'd written both letters. "Please try to understand—I wasn't well when I wrote the first one. I was desperate to keep my daughter from leaving home and didn't know how else to stop her." She poured out the whole sad story of Chrissie's death. When she finished, she took two pills and swallowed them with pinot noir.

Summer let her fingers graze her mother's shoulder, thanking her, fully intent on retreating to the kitchen, but her mother seized her wrist. "I love you, Summer."

She had a strange way of showing it. Not knowing how else to respond, Summer echoed the words, but damn it, love didn't begin to adequately define their relationship.

Ty was still on the phone with Alexis, pacing and filling her ear about Boomer Walsh's shenanigans the evening before.

Summer trotted over, wiggling her fingers for the phone. "Alexis, here's some real news, much more important than this family soap opera of ours, news the oil and gas industry would like to suppress." She described the contaminants found in Kirby's well, and the intent of the addendum Early Glover had found in the back of the guidebook.

The reporter promised to publicize Summer's findings.

Soon after the phone call, Mrs. Patel supervised Grace in using an old-fashioned hand masher on the potatoes while Summer stirred flour into caramelized onions with broth to make turkey gravy. PJ carved the turkey and received a swat with the towel for stealing so many pieces from the platter. "Save your appetite for the table," Mrs. Patel said. "To the dining room everyone."

Summer shook her mother's shoulder gently to rouse her. "Time to eat."

When everyone had gathered around, PJ raised her wine glass. "Happy Thanksgiving. I am thankful we could be together today."

Her toast was repeated around the table, but as shadows passed over faces, Summer knew that some of those present, especially Sloane Dumont, were thinking about the one not at the table. When all the dishes had been passed, Grace told Mrs. Patel about the way she'd covered up the ugly on Summer's table.

"I used duck tape," she said.

"Duct tape," Summer corrected.

"No, duck." She made a scritchy sound like the tape tearing and insisted it was exactly how a duck sounded.

PJ Wine's eyes narrowed for an instant, perhaps disturbed about the defacing of her table, but then she laughed out loud and sipped a little more of Early's fine whiskey.

While Summer and Dayita cleared the table, Summer noticed Ty and Sloane off in a corner of the living room having a heated discussion. Carrying the turkey platter to the kitchen, she caught one clear glimpse of Ty as he turned away from Sloane, his jaw line rigid, a warrior's face. What in the world had those two been arguing about?

After the meal Early apologized for needing to lie down. Sloane held his arm and walked with him to the guest bedroom. Summer could hear him fussing at her for treating him like an old man.

"Let me take you to the hospital or call hospice or something."

"It's not time yet. All my life I've been Early, but this is one occasion when I won't be."

"I'm trying to talk sense to you, old man. This is not the time for another one of your early jokes."

"It is exactly the right time. Laughter's the best cure for grief and other pains." Their voices faded as the bedroom door ticked closed.

A moan broke the silence in the living room, and PJ Wine fled to the bathroom.

15

November 28

GRACE, SUMMER NOTICED, WAS STILL HANGING onto Ty's leg as they mounted the steps to the cabin in the morning. Once inside, the child sat on his lap, a new development in response to his sudden disappearance with the police. Summer hoped this episode didn't set back all the progress Grace had made since starting school.

Summer poured Ty a cup of coffee and gave Grace some juice.

"Be careful where you set your cups down," she cautioned them. "Where the duct tape overlaps it's a little uneven."

"Quite the little artist, aren't you, Sugarpop?" Ty said.

Summer tugged lightly on one of Grace's pigtails. "The Amazing Grace."

Ty pushed the morning paper across the kitchen table to Summer, pointing to the bottom story on the front page. With satisfaction, Summer read a moving article Ty's friend had written to counter the previous day's column. The reporter dredged up Jordan Cassidy's battle to cope with the loss of the daughter she'd fought so hard to keep alive. Summer came off as a hero who had helped Patricia Kirby when no one else would. The story was exactly what Summer needed—the community was no longer likely to dismiss her as a kook.

Summer flipped through the pages. "Nothing about Boomer Walsh yet." She supposed the reporter had to verify every lead.

Ty frowned. "Boomer was released this morning."

"You're kidding."

"I heard his lawyer used yesterday's column to suggest you were unstable and an unreliable witness."

"Overlooking the rifle pointed at me."

"Lots of guys around here carry guns in their vehicles, especially during deer season. He said you misunderstood."

"Hard to misunderstand intention when he brought a rifle onto my porch."

"What can I say? A judge saw fit to grant bail." He leaned into the table, his fists resting on Grace's duct tape. "The rules don't count for these guys. If we're going to beat them, we can't play by rules either. We've got to avail ourselves of every means possible to get away from fossil fuels.'

"Look, I'm all for green energy. It's where our government should spend research dollars and make infrastructure investments. But our dependence on fossil fuels isn't going away overnight. I'm trying to make sure we obtain them safely."

"There is no 'safely' with these guys. Even with every safeguard at their disposal, spills are inevitable."

His single-minded certitude annoyed her. "Maybe spills are inevitable, but every form of energy poses its own risks, has unintended consequences like killing birds or acid leaching into groundwater when batteries are disposed of, or effects we haven't even discovered yet."

He took her hand. "Summer, come to work for me at Water Warriors. We've got to fight back against these guys with every tool at our disposal."

His eyes were drawing her down a dark well, dragging her into a place where she could lose herself, where his need to right the world would dominate every waking moment. How easy it would be to give in, share his obsession, but if she did, it would swallow her dreams, consume her life the way it had his.

"You have your way of fighting," she said, "and I have mine. Same cause, different methods." An image surfaced unbidden to her: a chiseled fierceness she had noticed after the dinner at Early's, when Ty and Sloane Dumont huddled in a corner. It had troubled her at the time. "What were you and Sloane talking about yesterday?"

A wall slammed down in his eyes. "Were we? I don't remember."

You didn't forget conversations as intense as that one. Why was he lying?

He removed Grace from his lap and stood. "I knew you'd turn

me down. You wouldn't be you if you hadn't. I wish it could be different." When he leaned over and kissed Summer softly, it felt like goodbye.

She sat still, listening to the sound of the van's engine fade away. He was gone.

Summer drove over to the motel to say farewell to the mothers, who were leaving for Florida because a major snowstorm was forecast for the evening. Dayita planned to stay on and ride home with Summer before Christmas.

"The holidays will be here before you know it," her mother said. "Something for me to look forward to."

Summer planned to enlist the Patels help in persuading her mother to enter rehab after the holidays. No telling whether her mother got out of bed most days or bothered to fix meals for herself. The pills had to go.

After Mrs. Patel drove out of the parking lot, Summer plopped onto one of the double beds. Dayita was keeping her mother's motel room since Boomer had been released. Summer refused to let her stay at the cabin any longer.

"If it's too dangerous for me, what about you?" Dayita asked.

She avoided the question. Unlike Dayita, she could shoot a real gun and throw a mean ax. "I'll come back to get you before we meet your FBI friend. I have water samples to collect." Summer's cell had been jingling all morning with calls from people who'd told her they'd get back to her about tests and hadn't bothered to until they had read that feature story making her out to be some kind of hero. Not that she was, but she'd take all the help she could get.

~

ENSCONCED IN HIS EXECUTIVE CHAIR, Boomer clenched the pages of the morning paper. If he had hold of that double-crossing reporter, he'd throttle her. What a sappy piece she'd written.

"Oughta be something we can do to stop that smartass Cassidy girl from causing any more trouble," Marky Markowitz said from the seat across from Boomer's desk. "Everybody says the little bitch's been beating the pants off all the guys in Knuckleheads. Well, she ain't come up against the likes of Marky Markowitz. I'd send her ass scooting back to Florida with a dart stuck right between her eyes. Seems like we can't get a break, boss. First Corky screws up and we get blamed, and now they might blame us for Kirby's water."

A bit of a hothead, Marky was, but Boomer liked him because he was reliable in a crisis. He had taken charge of containing Corky's spill, and he'd picked up Boomer that morning when he was released from jail. Cops had yanked Boomer's temporary license and impounded his vehicle on account of a second DUI, so he couldn't drive himself, and his own son refused to pick him up.

So no one was more surprised than Boomer when Hank strode into the office and asked Marky to give them a few minutes alone.

Took some nerve waltzing in here after not picking him up. When the door closed behind Markowitz, Hank stared at Boomer in silence for a full minute before taking Marky's vacated chair.

"Dad, you need help."

"I'm not in the mood, so spare me the lecture."

"Dad, you got drunk and threatened an unarmed girl with a rifle."

"You're misinformed, smartass—she threw an ax at me. Barely missed." The logic of his defense didn't make sense even to him. He shouldn't have taken the rifle out of his SUV at the girl's cabin, but he didn't need his kid to tell him so.

Hank continued as if Boomer hadn't spoken. "Two DUIs in a month, your third wife has kicked you out of the house, your life is falling apart. Come on, Dad, you have to start going to AA meetings, or if you don't want to go the spiritual route, see a doctor—they have meds to help you back off the alcohol. This can't go on."

Rearing back in his chair, Boomer felt blood rush to his head. "Have you lost your fucking mind—talking that way to me?"

"You need to see a bankruptcy lawyer, find out if you can restructure your debt."

Hank didn't know squat about debt. Boomer had always protected his family from financial concerns. He earned it, they burned it. How dare his son issue ultimatums!

And Hank hadn't finished. "One more thing: I know something's wrong out at the Domico site. Let's fix it before it becomes public. Tell me what I can do to help, and I'll do it."

Boomer stood, thrusting his torso forward, fingertips pressing into the wooden surface of his desk. "You done?"

Further surprising Boomer, Hank's gaze remained steady.

Shaking with rage beyond his control, Boomer repeated, "You

done? Because I'm going to say this only once. Ever since I was nine years old and got my first job, I been handling my own problems, and considering the roof I put over your head, the college education I provided, and the company I run, I've done a pretty damn good job. I don't need advice from a boy who's never held a job except for the one he holds now working for me."

Hank stood. "I love you, Dad, and I'm trying to help. I want you to remember that later."

After his son left, Boomer sank back into his chair. *Later*—what did that mean? Something wrong at the Domico site—what did he know—or think he knew?

Boomer didn't have much time to dwell on their confrontation because the phone rang, and Sloane Dumont reminded him of his standing appointment for the following week. At last—life was cutting him a break, a small one. Though she hadn't said so in words, she was forgiving him for his indiscretion.

Tearful, she cried in his ear for a while about how much she missed Corky. He commiserated, grateful for a reason to calm down. His hands were still shaking.

"I appreciate all the nice things you said about him at the funeral, Boomer. I really appreciate it, I really do, you know what I mean?"

"You're welcome, honey, I meant every word." He could hear the whiskey in her voice. "You been drinking, Sloane?"

"Yeah, I'm a regular badass, huh?"

"Aw, you've always been a badass gal, but that's what everyone loves about you." In the background, Boomer could hear occasional voices and the clink of glassware. "Where are you?"

"The Greenbrier. I deserve a drink after all I been through."

She had named a restaurant and bar attached to a motel, not fifteen minutes away. After the load of bullshit Hank had dumped on him, he deserved a drink, too. "You want some company?"

"I don't know, Boomer. I should probably go home."

"Doesn't sound like you should be driving anywhere."

"You're probably right." She waited a beat before adding, "Not even a badass gal like me should drink alone."

Boomer blew out of his office into the parking lot before he remembered his SUV was still impounded. He rushed back inside and rifled through his desk drawer for keys to one of the company's

SUVs. Fairhope owned two SUVs and three trucks.

Bastards might have confiscated his personal vehicle, but luckily Boomer had plenty of others at his disposal. One of the many benefits of being the boss.

~

THE CRIMINAL JUSTICE SERVICES DIVISION of the FBI was housed in a modern glass-rich facility that impressed Summer. "The building's humongous," she said, estimating it took up about the same space as three football fields. "How'd a little town like Clarksburg snag an operation like this?"

"Pork-barrel politics at its best," explained Special Agent Jimmy Wong. The national fingerprint database had moved here while Robert Byrd wielded power as the legendary senior senator from West Virginia. Wong drove Summer and Dayita through the property to show it off, but the FBI didn't conduct interrogations or hold prisoners there, so afterward they rode downtown to a rather dreary tan stucco building behind the post office. "It's convenient since the federal courthouse is above the post office," he said.

From the attention he showered on Dayita, Summer assumed Wong's interest extended beyond cybersecurity issues. Biracial, he was a well-dressed young man with a trendy hairstyle characterized by deliberate cowlicks. Wong held the door open to a secure interrogation room for Summer and Dayita to meet with Elliot Ral.

Hands folded before him, Ral appeared relaxed, not at all nervous or defensive. The deal the FBI was offering must be awfully good. He didn't seem like a man worried about his future.

"These women have questions for you, and I expect your full cooperation," Jimmy Wong told Ral.

Immediately Summer asked whether he had run her off the road the night of the church meeting. If he wouldn't come clean about that night, she couldn't put much stock in anything else he said.

"No." If he was lying, he hid it well. No emotion tainted his voice; nothing in his expression gave him away.

"Do you know who did?"

"Some people around here see your activities as a threat."

An evasive response, so she pressed him further. "Like?"

"Boomer Walsh mouthed off about outsiders destroying local jobs. Your name comes up frequently."

"Walsh knows I'm not here to kill jobs. What's he really scared of?"

Glancing at Jimmy Wong, Ral hesitated, as if deciding how much he was required to reveal. Wong's unwavering features granted no reprieve.

"Fairhope owned a lease on John Cunningham's place," Ral said. "One of their impoundment ponds leaked for six months before anyone discovered the liner had rotted. Effluent leached into a creek that eventually feeds into the West Fork. More than one of Walsh's other impoundments have similar aging liners."

No one had told her about the Cunningham leak. "Go on."

"You know about Corky Rogers' spill."

"Did Walsh shoot Rogers?"

"He's capable of it."

Summer considered the wording of his response, and then asked, "Did you shoot Rogers?"

The whites of Ral's eyes mushroomed behind those hipster glasses, the first sign of nerves Summer had noticed. "Of course not! I'm not a violent criminal."

He looked at Jimmy Wong specifically while he answered, leading Summer to believe their deal only covered cybercrime.

She pulled the GPS tracker from her jacket pocket and pushed it across the table. "But you are a criminal. Taping people without their permission is a criminal activity."

He had the good graces to flush. "You must realize in my line of work—"

"What *is* your line of work? Your office staff and website are vague."

He had the company drill down pat. "The consulting firm performs intelligence gathering and computer security for corporations."

Dayita, who'd sat silent until now, made no effort to keep the sneer off her face. "So a company hires you to spy on competitors, you hack their computers to steal secrets and gather information they can use to blackmail people—and you turn around and sell your services to stop people like you from doing the same to their company."

Ral shrugged.

"Did you access the university administration's server and download Summer's student file, including private letters?" Dayita asked.

"Yes."

"So you tried to blackmail me," Summer said.

"No, I found and provided the letter to my client. I have no way of knowing what use was made of it."

"Who are your clients?"

"AC never reveals a client's name. It's a promise we take seriously."

Wong broke in, "Real ethical of you, I'm sure. The deal is you answer every question. No exceptions."

Ral's lips clamped tight and looked as if he would refuse, but in the end, eyes trained on his folded hands, he gave up Walsh.

Thank God it wasn't Corbett after all. Summer wanted to believe the term *ethical businessman* wasn't an oxymoron. She had one more question. "Who hired you to plant the tracker on my truck?"

"Walsh."

Dayita broke in. "The phone and computer hacks—also Boomer Walsh's request?"

"Yeah."

After a few moments of silence, Jimmy Wong ended the session and escorted Summer and Dayita from the building.

To Dayita, he added, "I'll be in touch."

Summer elbowed Dayita on the way to the truck. "I saw the way he was looking at you. What's that mean—he'll be in touch?"

Dayita only smiled.

"What kind of deal do you think Ral cut?" Summer asked.

"Reduced prison sentence if he answered all Wong's questions about how he hacked the health care provider's site and who he sold the info to."

Summer dropped her at the motel.

"You coming back?" Dayita asked.

"I might."

"*Might.* That means you won't."

"Not necessarily," Summer said as she left, but in truth, Dayita knew her too well.

~

WHEN SUMMER RETURNED to the cabin a little after six, Ty's van was parked in her driveway, and he was leaning against one of the rough-hewn posts supporting the narrow porch roof. What was this?

She would have sworn he'd written her off for good when she turned down his job offer again. She pulled in front of the van to park.

"I wasn't expecting you. Hope you haven't been waiting too long."

"Not long. What have you been up to until after dark?" he asked.

"Thanks to the story your reporter friend wrote, I've been taking water samples most of the day." Ty knew nothing about Ral, and it was far too cold to launch a long explanation out here on her porch.

He held up a couple of grocery sacks and a bottle of wine. "I brought you dinner. Hope you didn't have other plans."

"Nothing definite. Where's Grace?" Summer stopped fumbling with her keys, peering around him to see if his sister was still in the van.

"I dropped Grace at the motel. Dayita's babysitting."

A surprising turn—Summer figured he wouldn't be able to pry Grace loose after the scare with the police. Summer unlocked the cabin and turned on the lights. "Make yourself comfortable. I'm going to bring in more firewood. Supposed to snow tonight."

"I'll do it."

She considered arguing but knew he'd think she was dissing his prosthetic leg. Instead, she offered to open the wine while he was outside.

She found a corkscrew and poured two glasses of a decent Zinfandel scented like blackberries. The take-out dinners of lasagna and salad from Oliverio's soon filled the cabin with the scent of basil, oregano, garlic, and tomatoes. Grocery sacks held a loaf of whole wheat bread, a dozen eggs, tubs of yogurt, butter, peanut butter, cans of soup, rice, beans, and a pound of bacon. What was up with all this sudden thoughtfulness?

She heard his footsteps on the porch and hurried to open the door. A rush of cold air preceded Ty and the firewood. He added it to the stack beside the fireplace and stoked the logs with a poker. She brought the wine to him. Firelight sparkled through the glass and swirled through the wine.

She touched his nose, reddened from cold. "You look like Rudolph the—"

He interrupted her with a kiss. A fierce kiss. Needy. His fingers tangled through her hair; grappled their way under her sweatshirt, traveling up her spine.

"Your mother's head isn't on straight," he said. "I'm sorry I listened to her. Forgive me?"

She answered by sucking his lower lip into her mouth. For so long, they'd fenced around this moment, and she'd given up believing it would happen. Yet here he was, and this time he wasn't walking away.

16

November 29

BOOMER WAS USED TO HIS HEAD POUNDING in the morning, but this felt different. It came from outside his head: like a fist banging on a door. If he kept his eyes shut, maybe it would stop. Someone called "Open up" from far away.

Suddenly an officer he didn't know, this short chunky dyke, demanded he sit up. He did, but where was he? There were two double beds. A motel room, then. An empty wine bottle lay on the floor near the wastebasket. The dyke shook her head, speaking to Turner Skidmore at her side. "Look at him, drunk as a skunk."

Boomer knew he wasn't drunk. It was coming back. He'd had a glass or two of wine with Sloane. They'd been in the bar. Sloane said she was dizzy, needed to lie down. She decided to get a room, so Boomer went into the motel and registered and paid with his credit card. He steadied her on the way to the room, even had to open the door. He remembered thinking he wasn't gonna take advantage of her condition. He would help her inside and leave. But after he got the door opened, she started crying again and begged him to stay. Said she needed something to eat and didn't want to eat alone. So he called over to the restaurant and ordered her dinner. Stacked steak sandwich. Salad. Bottle of cab. He couldn't remember a thing after the first glass of cab. No one could have the bad luck to blackout and forget the taste of those sweet melons of hers. He refused to believe it.

Skidmore knelt down. "Boomer, you hear me?"

"Of course I hear you. I'm not deaf. What's going on?"

"There was an explosion at your office last night. Much of the building was destroyed in the fire."

"Jesus." Boomer raked his finger through the stubble of his crew-cut. Fairhope headquarters, a four-story structure, was completed only a month after Boomer had taken over control. "It's practically new. How could this happen?"

"We were hoping you could tell us. We'll do a full investigation, but it looks like arson."

Why were they staring at him?

"We called your house," Tuner said. "Your wife says you have been sleeping in your office.

"So?"

"You didn't sleep there last night." The dyke offered that brilliant observation.

"You're a genius—how'd you figure that out?"

"It would help if you could explain why you decided to get a hotel room." Turner suggested.

"Tired of sleeping on the couch."

Their disbelief was thinly disguised. What was this—they thought he blew up his own office? Why would he do that? The answer came to him before he finished the thought. Insurance.

"All right. I'll tell you the truth even though it's not nice to blab a lady's private business. I was here with Sloane Dumont."

Turner snorted. "Boomer, you're gonna have to do better than that. Everyone knows you've been trying to get in her pants. Rumor's all over town she threatened to dismember you."

"But it's the truth. The lady said she was lonely."

They weren't exactly rolling their eyes, but he could see they didn't believe a word of it.

"The room was paid for with your credit card," Turner said, "and only one dinner was on your tab."

"Can you think of anyone who might have done this?" the dyke asked.

Damn right he could. "Ty Franceschi—he's been causing trouble for Fairhope for months. Years. He's been arrested for trespassing on our property before. Check him out. And Early Glover. That bastard's filed one injunction after another against us. His lawyer's drumming up a class action suit now, from what I hear. It was probably that crazy bastard."

Turner was taking notes, a good sign.

"We'll check them out." Turner looked deliberately at the suitcase on the luggage rack. "Meanwhile, don't leave town."

How had his suitcase gotten here, the one he was living out of? It should have been in his office.

~

STRETCHING LIKE A CAT, SUMMER AWOKE in front of the last embers of the fire, feeling every inch of skin had been loved and cherished. Since Ty was not beside her, she waited, assuming he was using the facilities. She waited under the quilt, but the absence of noise as time passed, gave her to understand she was alone. Her throat constricted with a new fear: he might have slipped away without telling her, their night together hadn't meant anything to him after all. Vaguely she remembered waking up in the dark, groggy from wine, and he was fooling around with his C-leg where it had been plugged into the wall. His restlessness hadn't alarmed her. She knew he rarely slept well. But where was he now?

Grabbing a blanket, she padded toward the front door, her feet barely registering the chilly boards. Relief washed over her as she spotted Ty's van parked behind hers.

She hugged the blanket tighter around her body, rocking in a feeble effort to generate heat. Icy air crept past the battered weather-stripping goose-pimpling her bare flesh, but she remained at the window, amazed.

Every inch of the world sparkled with a blanket of white diamonds. Her truck, Ty's van, every tree, every bush, the ground—snow covered all. A miracle.

She threw on layers of warm clothes and stepped onto the porch as he was returning with an armload of firewood. She scampered past him.

"Hey, careful," Ty said. "This stuff can be slippery."

But it wasn't soft or slippery—it crunched. Ice crystals crusted the snowfall. She stretched her arms wide, turning around and around. Ever since leaf fall, the unmitigated greyness of the landscape had doused her spirits. The glory of this morning made up for every depressing moment. "Snow's totally awesome—even better than duct tape. It covers up all the ugly."

He waited at the door, arms log-jammed, watching her. "Don't tell me this is the first time you've seen snow."

She stuck her lower lip out like a child. "Of course I've seen snow. A few flakes fell once in our yard and melted as soon as they touched the grass, but we all went outside to watch. All the neighbors, grown-ups and kids alike."

Evidently amused by the idea of snow generating excitement, he shook his head and took the wood inside.

When he returned, she walloped him with a snowball that fell apart on impact.

"Dumb move, Cassidy." He scooped up a handful of snow, pressing it between his palms, scooped up more and pressed again. "You started a battle you can't win. I was born making snowballs. An expert with years of experience. You, on the other hand, are a novice." He blasted her with what felt like a cannonball. It didn't even shatter, so she picked it up and whipped it back at him.

She ducked behind her truck, gathering handfuls and rolling them together until they hardened. "Pride goes before a fall, Franceschi. I'm a fast learner." The next ball smacked him on his bare neck while he was bent over collecting snow.

They pelted each other, taking cover behind trees until they were frozen to the core.

"Truce," he called out. "How about I fix you bacon and eggs for breakfast?"

"Perfect," she panted. The only thing that kept her from total joy was concern that her mother and Mrs. Patel might not have made it past the mountains before snowfall. She hoped they were safe.

Once inside, Ty insisted he didn't need her assistance in the kitchen, but the hearty aroma of bacon made her realize she was starved, and she kept slipping in behind him to pilfer strips just as it crisped. Soon they were savoring fried eggs and toast. Ty's cell beeped. He listened for a moment, and then gave directions to her cabin.

She couldn't imagine who might be coming. "Who was that?"

"Sheriff's office."

She set her fork down. "What did they want?"

"To talk to me." He continued eating his eggs.

"What about?"

"Didn't say. Guess we'll find out when they get here."

A knot of dread settled in her chest. The only explanation she could think of for his not asking what they wanted was that he already knew. She got up to clear away the mess on the table. Breakfast dishes, last night's wine glasses—the place was a disaster.

Ty tugged her toward him, wrapping his arms around her waist. "Leave it. Mmmm, bacon tastes even better on your lips."

She pushed him away, unable to quell her apprehension. When the knock came, even though expected, her nerves reacted as if they'd been electroshocked. She grabbed a coated elastic band and was fastening her hair into a ponytail as Ty let deputies in.

There were two, a man and a woman, who identified themselves, the woman apologizing for tracking in snow. Summer remembered Deputy Skidmore from an encounter at the jail.

The deputies' eyes roved over the room, taking in the quilts on the floor, the empty wine bottle, stemmed glasses in the sink.

"A couple of questions for you, Mr. Franceschi," the woman said. "Where were you last night?"

Skidmore stage-whispered, "You trying to embarrass the lady, Reeves?"

Summer shot him a dour look. "He was here with me. Why? What's happened?"

"All night?" Deputy Reeves persisted. "I have to ask for the record."

"Yes, all night."

"Sure about that? He couldn't have slipped out?" Reeves persisted.

"I'm sure." But after she answered, she wondered if that was completely truthful.

Reeves looked at Ty, who arched an eyebrow.

Skidmore flicked his head toward the door. "Come on, Reeves. Franceschi's a bad ass and we'll get him for something one of these days, but look around." He gestured at the empty wine bottle, the quilts on the floor, aiming his index finger specifically at the condom wrappers on the hearth. "Boomer's sent us on a wild goose chase trying to save his own skin."

"What's happened?" Summer asked again.

"Ongoing investigation," Skidmore said. "Can't say."

Summer listened as the deputies' footsteps navigated her porch steps. If they had Boomer in custody again, this meant she and Dayita could stay at the cabin without worrying that he would show up armed and drunk. She had to know if they were arresting him. She put on her boots again and grabbed a jacket.

"Where you going?" Ty asked.

"I want to find out if they are holding Boomer."

"Forget about Walsh. Why let him ruin our day?" Ty followed her onto the porch, but she was already sprinting down the driveway.

Because the only space to turn around was occupied by the truck and van, the deputies had to back down Summer's road. She waved her arms overhead and they stopped. Deputy Reeves rolled down her window.

Summer asked if they planned to arrest Walsh.

"Not enough to hold him," Reeves said.

"Yet," Skidmore added while Reeves raised the window. They continued to back down Summer's drive.

It wouldn't be safe for Dayita to stay at the cabin. Summer supposed she should join her at the motel—unless Ty planned to make a habit of spending the night. She glanced up at the porch where he waited. Not likely. He wouldn't always have a willing babysitter to keep Grace and get her off to school in the morning.

Summer crossed behind Ty's van, watching her footing, when she noticed tread marks braiding the snow. They aligned directly with Ty's tires and continued under them, a detail the police apparently had missed. She stared, refusing at first to believe what those tracks meant. Had she lied to the police? What had Ty done?

Suddenly he appeared beside her, both of them studying the tracks, then each other. She tried to skirt past him but he seized her arm. "Summer, wait."

She tried to pull away, too distraught to look at him again.

"You're too damn smart for your own good."

She didn't know what she would have said if her throat hadn't closed up. She could hardly breathe. Again she tried to pull away. When he wouldn't let go, she found her voice. "Last night you were in mission-mode, weren't you? You planned every detail, right down to how you would use me as an alibi."

"But you have to know how much I love you," he said, still clinging to her arm. "If I had any idea how disturbed your mother was I wouldn't have listened to her. I would have driven up to Penn State every weekend to be with you."

How she wished it were true, but now she'd never know for sure.

His eyes were dark, sad. When she pulled away, this time he let her go.

~

PJ WINE WAITED OUTSIDE the United Hospital Center's ICU "Oh Ms. Summer, I was afraid you'd be snowed in and couldn't get here. They tell me Early may not make it through the next twenty-four hours. He has a do-not-resuscitate order." Her voice thinned to the breaking point, and Summer clasped the older woman's hand to offer what little comfort she could. "I don't know what I'm going to do without the old fool," PJ said. "We've been friends for over fifty years."

"Is he conscious?" Summer asked. "I'd like to see him."

"No, but Sloane is in the room with him now. They'll only let one of us in at a time. They say the cancer has metastasized and flooded his body with blood clots. Caused a stroke. To think we all were eating Thanksgiving dinner with him less than two days ago."

"Anyone could see he hasn't been well for some time."

What the girl said was true, but PJ hadn't thought Early's body would betray him so utterly, so completely, so soon. Now that death was here for Early, she felt her own expiration date was stamped on the back of her neck, like a pack of questionable lunchmeat destined for the landfill. If she didn't think about something else she'd start boo-hooing again.

"I suppose you heard about the explosion at Fairhope headquarters," PJ said.

"Read about it a few minutes ago in the newspaper."

PJ steered Summer to the other side of the room for more privacy so she could share what she'd heard from Turner Skidmore. It would make what was happening a little less scary. What if Boomer tried to cut a deal? What if he mouthed off about things he shouldn't? Like PJ's appointing one of Boomer's friends to the Local Emergency Planning Committee to make sure enforcement of safety regulations didn't infringe on fracking operations. And a little kickback on a sweet real estate deal PJ had arranged for Boomer. The kind of thing she did for constituents all the time, but it might be misunderstood.

She lowered her voice. "Between you and me, I heard they've

been questioning Boomer Walsh. Said he might have set fire to his own building for the insurance."

The girl looked real pale like she might pass out. PJ had the impression the young woman didn't like hospitals much. Few people did, but she seemed extra upset, ready to hightail it.

"There doesn't seem to be anything I can do here," Summer said. "Did you call Joe? He should know about his brother."

PJ dabbed at her eyes with a handkerchief. "When I notarized Early's will, he made me promise not to line Joe up for any deathbed visits. Said if his brother wouldn't talk to him while he was alive and kicking, he sure didn't want him hanging around like a ghoul." It was a crying shame to see brothers feuding like this. PJ and Early had tangled more than once over the years, especially over fracking, but they'd always made up.

Early's will was gonna surprise a few people. PJ wasn't sure how this unusual connection to the Cassidy girl and her boyfriend had come about, but PJ would carry out Early's wishes. Eventually a lawyer would take charge, but for now the duties fell to her as executor.

She waited until a trio of hospital workers passed, and then cleared her throat. "Ms. Summer, I called you here today because Early has made a bequest you need to know about sooner rather than later."

It fell on PJ to deliver the news that Early was leaving custody of his dog to Summer. That miserable cur made this guttural noise low in its throat every time PJ visited. Not quite a growl, but close.

"Wallace? Really?" The pupils of he girl's eyes enlarged, and she seemed unsteady on her feet. "I can't take him. They don't allow pets in my apartment at the university."

The old fool had foreseen that problem. The girl wouldn't get rid of the dog so easily. "Early's will stipulates a generous allowance for Wallace's upkeep," PJ said. "You should be able to find a suitable spot to live with a pet."

She didn't look convinced.

"It's enough to pay for your books and tuition," PJ added. "Early took a shine to you, said you're kindred souls."

Warmth stole over Summer's face, clearly taking his approval as a compliment. PJ took it to mean they both buried their noses in books too much. You could miss out on a lot of living that way. Anyway, of course Summer would be pleased that Early was essentially awarding her a scholarship. She gave the girl a key to Early's house and told her where Early had stashed instructions for the dog's care.

The contents of his will, though, still troubled PJ. "Look here, you must be close to Ty Franceschi or he wouldn't have asked you to take care of his kid sister."

At the mention of Franceschi, the girl tensed. PJ wondered if they had quarreled, but she had to finish now that she'd brought him up. "You might warn him. Early's leaving his granddaddy's rifle to him—once the police are done with it. Joe's liable to get his dander up. He always felt that rifle should have come down to him since Early doesn't hunt." Some inheritance—a murder weapon.

Summer's fingers toyed with the key, but she didn't rush off. "Guess when Joe inherits Early's land, that'll be the end of the lawsuit against Fairhope."

"I'm not supposed to discuss what's in the will," PJ said. Summer bestowed a look she guessed she deserved, and she relented. It'd be public knowledge soon enough. "You didn't hear it from me, but he's leaving all his property to his newfound daughter as long as she continues that blamed lawsuit."

The girl looked spaced out. A maintenance worker ran his floor polisher practically right over her boots and she didn't step aside. "Does Joe know he's been cut from the will?"

PJ looked away. "Notaries have to respect people's privacy and not talk about their business."

"Seriously, PJ, did you tell Joe? It's important."

Oh Lord help her, she'd always had a big mouth and her foot was usually in it. "I might have let it slip, sort of."

~

Summer phoned Ty from the hospital parking lot. "You better find a way to fix this so Boomer Walsh isn't blamed for destroying Fairhope headquarters."

"Why would I do that?" Ty asked.

"Because I'm going to tell the police you left during the night if you don't. You were an explosives expert with the SEALs. I know you caused that fire. That's what you and Sloane were plotting on Thanksgiving, isn't it?"

"You don't know that."

"I do. Boomer tried to use her as an alibi and she denied being with him."

"Walsh commits crimes against the environment and Sloane believes he killed Corky, too."

"So the two of you did this to punish him, to punish Fairhope."

"Walsh deserves to go to prison."

"Can you hear yourself—setting yourself up as judge and jury? Ty, if you can't let go of your anger, it's going to destroy you. Have you stopped to think about what will happen to Grace if you go to prison? Look how upset she was when they held you for questioning."

She could hear him breathing during a tense silence. Finally she said, "Fix it."

And that, she had no doubt, severed their relationship irrevocably. It was over but not over. She couldn't stop her fingers from remembering the ribbons of muscles across Ty's back and mourning the loss.

She started the engine and headed to Early's to retrieve Wallace. The poor dog slobbered all over her as a greeting while she rubbed his velvety head. His water bowl was empty. She filled it and he slurped a long drink while she found his leash. She was sure he could use a walk before she took him to her cabin. Preoccupied by Ty's betrayal, she found herself leading the dog toward Joe's. Last night's snow had mostly melted from the roads, even out here in the country where less traffic spoiled its purity. Fresh snow was beautiful for a short time; it quickly turned gray and yucky—or yellow, as in the puddle Wallace was making.

As they rounded the bend, she spotted Joe shoveling his driveway. Wallace growled. She grasped his leash tighter and scolded him. No matter what Early had told PJ Wine, Joe deserved to know his brother was dying.

She headed down his driveway. With a muscular lunge, Wallace nearly dislocated her shoulder. He snarled, snapped, and growled, tugging her forcefully toward Joe Glover.

Understandably freaked out, Joe backed up, holding the shovel over his shoulder with the clear intention of whacking the dog over the head if Summer failed to restrain him.

"Wallace, stop." She leaned in the opposite direction, throwing her one-hundred-twenty pounds against what she judged to be his seventy. "Wallace, cut it out." She hauled him back to the beginning of the driveway and tied him to a fence post. She trudged back to Mr. Glover.

She apologized. "I don't know what's gotten into him."

"Dog's as mean as a rattlesnake. Just like his owner."

"Mr. Glover, I know you and your brother have had your issues—"

He stabbed the end of the shovel down so hard it must have jarred his bones. "Issues! He's tried to ruin my life since we were boys. Always took the best of everything for himself. Took the best piece of our land and didn't even bother to farm it."

"Look, I didn't come here to argue with you." Hearing was one of the last senses to leave the body. Even if Early was unconscious, he would know if Joe visited. "Your brother's in the hospital. He's dying. This is your last chance to make peace. It's hard to forgive yourself when a family member dies and you've left hard feelings unresolved." Summer would give anything to have her sister back long enough to tell her she was sorry for every unkind word, to say *I love you* one more time.

"The only peace I'll ever have from Early's meanness is when he's six feet under where he can't do any more harm."

"I'm sorry you feel that way." She untied Wallace and walked him back to Early's. She let him hop into the passenger seat of her truck while she went inside the house to gather his supplies.

In Early's desk drawer she located a neatly labeled envelope: "Care of Wallace." Beside it lay an envelope labeled Last Will and Testament. She resisted the temptation. For less than two seconds. The first item in the list of bequests willed his land and llamas to his daughter Sloane Dumont. Early apologized for the land's condition. He warned her that the way the frackers clear-cut the hill would make the valley prone to flooding. He said not to drink the water without testing it at least weekly when active drilling began.

Summer found her name and Wallace's, linked there in black and white—along with an enormous sum to devote to his care. Early noted that since he didn't expect his dog to live on a diet of ramen noodles, the dog's caretaker shouldn't be expected to either. Therefore, he was providing a generous allowance for food for the caretaker's plate, with plenty left over to nourish her brain in the way of books and tuition. His grandfather's rifle went to Ty, and several pieces of artwork and his liquor cabinet and contents were left to PJ. The last notation in the will stated that if the death of any of the above-named individuals preceded his own death, the property bequests would go to his only brother, Joe Glover.

She returned the will to the drawer and gathered Wallace's supplies. As she loaded them in the back end, Joe's silver sedan blew past.

The way things were playing out nagged at her. The feud between the Glovers went deeper than the current fracking fracas. Until now, she figured Ty and Sloane were right about Boomer shooting Corky Glover. He had meanness. He had motive. But why would he steal Early's rifle to commit murder? Joe might have taken it though, especially if he felt it should have been his to begin with.

And Wallace's reaction to Joe had been off the chain. If he had bashed the dog's eye in while stealing his granddaddy's rifle, no wonder Wallace was ready to tear off his limbs. Summer wouldn't be at all surprised if PJ had let the contents of the new will slip out in Joe's presence. Even if PJ hadn't, Joe might have found the will at the same time he stole the rifle. What if Corky Rogers hadn't been the intended victim? It might have been Sloane. To hear her talk, they had practically been body-locked before he died in her arms.

She thought it might be prudent to at least mention her theory to Sloane. Summer called PJ at the hospital, only to find Sloane had already left for either her salon or home, PJ wasn't sure which. Summer headed for the salon which was closer.

When she arrived at A Cut Above, a tinkly bell announced her entrance. The baby-faced receptionist was attaching a stick-on fuchsia sequin to her ring fingernail. She didn't look up.

Summer cleared her throat. "Could Sloane find a minute to talk to me?"

The phone rang but the girl chose to pull a chartreuse sequin from the strip of decorations and apply it to her middle fingernail instead of answering it. "She stopped by but canceled her appointments for the day. Said she was too upset."

"Was she going back to the hospital?"

The girl peeled off a turquoise sequin. "No, home." The phone quit ringing, and the girl looked at Summer for the first time. "Gee, you're the second person who's come in here asking the same stuff."

A sick feeling came over Summer. "Who else was here?"

The girl shot her a why-do-you-care look and turned her attention to a magenta sequin.

Summer snatched the strip away. "Sloane doesn't pay you to ignore phone calls and clients. Now, who else was here?"

Babyface looked ready to cry. "Some old man. He said he had important business with her, so I told him same as you. She went home. He limped out of here and that's all I know."

Had to be Joe. "Where's she live?"

The girl rattled off an address a block from Ty's apartment, and whined, "Can I have my stick-ons back?

Summer tossed them to her with orders to call Sloane and warn her of the danger, then to call 911 and give them Sloane's address. She sprinted toward her truck. As she drove past Ty's place, she spotted his van. She didn't want to involve him, but for Sloane's sake she stowed her personal feelings. When he answered his phone, she gave him Sloane's address and told him to come armed.

A few seconds later Summer located Sloane Dumont's house, a task made easier because Joe's silver sedan hugged the curb in front. She lived in a tidy little house painted cream with Wedgewood blue shutters. Summer deliberately backed up until her bumper tagged Joe's. Summer only hoped the ditzy receptionist had gotten a message to Sloane.

"Wallace, you stay here. I'll be back in a few minutes."

The dog cocked his head as if he understood. She rolled the window down an inch so he'd have fresh air.

Avoiding the front porch, Summer trotted down the small expanse of dormant grass that passed for a side yard. The windows were too high to provide a view of the first floor. Crouched like a frog, she could peer into the basement through narrow windows set four inches above ground level. She could make out a workbench, a jumble of paint cans, and sacks of potting soil and fertilizer. Sloane's car was parked inside the garage. She tiptoed toward the back of the house and discovered an alley. Garbage cans were set out at intervals for collection. The grind of a truck compressing trash drifted over from a few blocks away. A hand clamped over her mouth, suppressing the scream that rose in her throat, but she quickly relaxed. She knew the hand and its scent. Ty held a finger to his lips and let go. They turned the corner, now facing the rear of the house. Seven steps of poured cement led to a tiny porch partially obscured by lattice work. Ty pointed to a missing glass pane in the back door, and she could see shards inside on the kitchen floor. He signaled her to follow him to the alley.

"What's going on?" he asked.

She explained why she believed Joe intended to harm Sloane. "I'm pretty sure we got a warning to her."

"Did you call the cops?"

"Told Sloane's receptionist to."

The front street was quiet, no sign of law enforcement. "I'll go in through the back door and check things out. Stay here in case he tries to escape."

"No way. We both go in. I called you for back-up, remember?"

He frowned. "We clear the first floor, then I'll go upstairs. You can check the basement."

She knew he'd assigned her the basement because she had already seen neither Joe nor Sloane was down there. Ticked her off. He knew she could shoot—hadn't she saved his life once before?

Ty gave her a 9mm handgun. She checked the clip, a practice her father had instilled in her when he'd taught her to shoot. It held fifteen rounds. Ty carried a larger gun, a make she didn't recognize, possibly military grade.

"Be careful," she said.

He touched his knuckles to her cheek. "You too."

~

Much sooner than Dayita had expected, Jimmy Wong got in touch. He had learned that Elliot Ral hadn't been forthcoming about additional surveillance equipment he'd employed. Under further questioning, Ral admitted he had mini-cams placed outside Summer's cabin and another woman's home and described their locations. The FBI had already recovered Ral's phone, which he used to monitor the video feeds.

"He was trying to avoid mention of a second client, one with more money and clout than Walsh," Jimmy said.

"Who's this other client?"

"Another oil and gas firm, Corbett Energy."

"Summer's mentioned Corbett." The news would disappoint Summer. She'd spoken favorably of Kit Corbett as an oil man with good ethics. He wasn't as squeaky clean as she'd thought.

Wong suggested Dayita ride along to retrieve the cameras since she was familiar with Summer's road, which might make locating the devices easier. She readily agreed.

Attached to a pine next to the highway, the first camera Dayita discovered would record any vehicles pulling into Summer's driveway. The other one, more difficult to locate because numerous trees might have worked for Ral's purpose, was aimed toward the porch. But in time they found it and headed back toward town to find the cameras outside Sloane Dumont's.

"You know her?" Jimmy asked.

"Not well, but I spent Thanksgiving with her and her father." She turned on Ral's phone, and she saw the battery was nearly exhausted. She clicked on Sloane's name, figuring she might as well check out the video feed coming from the Dumont house—at least until the phone died, which might be any second. It was both amazing and more than a little scary what technology could do. Those cop shows where police had to sit in vans outside a mobster's house to pick up audio and video were so yesterday.

The feed from the first camera streamed onto the screen. "Hey, that's Summer's truck," Dayita said. What's she doing there?"

She switched to the second camera, which appeared to be aimed through one of Sloane's windows. "Holy shit, Jimmy. Some guy's creeping through Sloane's living room and he's toting a big-ass shotgun."

Trying to get a look at the video, Wong swerved into the left lane.

"Better keep your eyes on the road and get there as fast as you can," Dayita said, as she called 911. She reported the armed intruder at Sloane's but before she could offer more details, Ral's phone cut out.

~

THE DUMONT HOUSE WAS QUIET except for the thrum of a furnace. Summer watched Ty's back as he slunk through the living room and began to creep up the staircase to the second floor. Where was Sloane? Had she locked herself in the bedroom or run to the neighbor's house when she got the warning? Her car was in the garage so she hadn't driven off. Maybe the stupid receptionist hadn't even called her.

The door leading to the basement creaked as she opened it.

She grimaced—might as well announce her presence to the whole neighborhood. Holding the gun in front of her, she crept down steps carpeted in a hodgepodge of colorful remnants, which kept them from creaking. The odor of mildew intensified as Summer descended. A wavy dark stain along the base of the wall served as a reminder of previous water intrusion. She took the last two steps slowly, allowing her eyes to adjust to the dim lighting provided by those narrow ground level windows she'd peered through earlier. The basement was divided into three separate rooms. This one was semi-finished and contained a washer, dryer, and ironing board. A garment rack shared a side wall with a utility sink and dehumidifier. No sign of Joe Glover.

The door on the far wall had a small window, the hood of Sloane's car visible through the glass. Summer tiptoed over and peeked through. Unless Joe was hiding behind the car, he wasn't in there. She backtracked to search the third room, the one with the paint cans and workbench. She cracked the door open and entered, leading with the gun.

A dizzying miasma of machine oil, paint thinner, and gasoline assaulted her senses. She turned halfway around, disoriented, and found herself facing the workbench. A wrench hung from a peg at eye level. Its edges wavered. The ground beneath her feet undulated. A click sent her heart leaping into her throat. As the world folded in on her, she crouched and pressed her hands over her ears so she wouldn't hear the shot that came after the click. She took deep breaths, trying to defeat fear with logic. It was only the heater coming on, not a gun. The wrench was only a wrench.

But the shouts of "police" and pounding feet overhead sounded real. She closed her eyes. If she opened them, she knew—just *knew*— she would be back in Florida, back inside the nightmare. Jake Fowler would be sneering down at her.

~

WHEN THE UNIFORMED OFFICERS BURST through the front door, Ty was upstairs, checking the first bedroom. He trotted down the steps. Deputy Skidmore screamed, "Drop your weapon, drop it now."

Ty lowered it to the step behind him and jogged down the last two steps. "Thank goodness—"

"Stop where you are," Deputy Reeves shouted. "Do not come

forward."

Ty froze. "But there's—"

"Shut up and put your hands on your head."

Ty slowly raised his hands and clasped them on his head. Why hadn't Summer run upstairs when she heard the police?

Turner Skidmore bellowed as if Ty were in another room, "Turn around slowly."

Ty did as he was told. "Okay, okay, but I'm one of the good guys. Joe—"

"Shut up and follow orders," Turner said. "You can't get out of this one, Franceschi, armed breaking and entering—caught you in the act."

These clowns were actually going to arrest him. Where was Summer? She would set them straight. "Wait a minute—we're the ones who called you to—"

Turner reminded him to shut up and recited the Miranda rights.

Sloane Dumont stumbled down the steps. "What the hell? I know this man. He's a friend."

Turner shoved Ty toward the door. "Ma'am, we got a call about an armed intruder in your house and here he is. You're safe now."

Sloane said, "I think you're mistaken."

"No mistake. We're well acquainted with Mr. Franceschi. He has a string of priors."

"Summer?" Ty yelled. "Where the hell are you? Summer?"

"Summer's here?" Sloane asked, looking around.

"Shut up, Franceschi," Turner said.

"Summer?" Ty yelled.

Turner Skidmore pulled out his baton and smashed it against Ty's skull.

~

Dayita Patel and Jimmy Wong dashed toward the Dumont house. With relief, Dayita spotted Sloane, peeping through a window facing the front porch. The curtain swished into place and she met them on the porch.

Jimmy flashed FBI identification. "Ma'am, a man was stalking through your house with a weapon."

Sloane crossed her arms, shivering slightly. "I know. The police left right before you got here. They arrested Ty."

Dayita shook her head. "Why on earth?"

Sloane waved her hands in the air. "Crazy isn't it? I tried to tell them I knew him, but he was armed and I guess he did break in. They said he had a string of priors."

Dayita's hands formed fists. "For unlawful trespass at environment rallies—hardly what you could call violent crimes." She looked around. "Where's Summer?"

Sloane's brow wrinkled. "I don't know. Ty was yelling for her too. You think she's here?"

"We saw her go through a doorway in your kitchen." Elliot flicked his head toward the curb. "Her truck's right there."

"She must be in the basement," Sloane said. "Wait, how the hell could you see inside my house?" Sloane's face reddened.

"Agent Wong will explain later," Dayita said. "We have to find Summer. Can we look in your basement?" Not waiting for approval, Dayita hurtled down the porch steps and raced across the dormant strip of lawn between the houses. She squatted down, resting her bum on her sequined tennis shoes, so she could peer through a low window. Her eyes roamed over piles of junk. No sign of Summer. Dayita was ready to try another window when movement on the floor caught her eye. It was Summer! Dayita rapped on the glass.

Legs hugged to her chest, Summer didn't respond. Dayita yelled and knocked again. Jimmy braced himself against Dayita's shoulder as he peered in the window, too.

"She's in there?" Sloane stood behind them, disbelief saturating her voice.

"Something's wrong." Dayita said. Even from a distance, she could see Summer was shaking uncontrollably.

"Friend of mine came back from Iraq and freaked out like that sometimes," Wong said.

"I guess it could be PTSD," Dayita's voice carried doubt. "Pretty traumatic stuff happened to her last spring, but she's tough . . ." Dayita trailed off, because in all honesty, Summer had never been as tough as she pretended to be.

"You two can stand around here jawing, but I'm going in after her," Sloane said.

Wong grabbed her forearm. "Wait."

"The guy in the video definitely wasn't Ty," Dayita said. "He was much older and short."

"You're trying to tell me there's another man with a gun in my house?" Sloane asked.

"Did the police search the house thoroughly?" Wong asked.

Sloane frowned. "Didn't bother—they were so sure they had their man."

"Then I go first." Wong drew his weapon. "If it was a burglar, he's probably long gone, but you two wait out here until I make sure."

Dayita watched him disappear around the front of the house. Through the window, she could see Summer shivering on the floor. Jimmy was right: any burglar would have fled when the police arrived. She was going in after her friend.

"Is there another way into the basement?" she asked.

"The garage," Sloane said. "Let's go get her."

~

SUMMER HUGGED HER LEGS tighter. Her heart pumped so forcefully she could hear its roar in her ears. Why wouldn't they go away and leave her alone?

But no, Dayita was bringing her back, her arms everywhere, octopusing her body, stroking her head, rubbing her arms, rocking her, whispering meaningless sounds, enveloping her in a web of safety. Summer's breathing slowed and she snapped out of the terror that had overtaken her.

"Come on, honey." Dayita's fingers slipped under her arms. Sloane stepped to the other side, supporting her.

"Through the garage," Sloane said. "This is the fastest way out. The cold air will do her good."

At the front street, Summer shook off their assistance, insisting she was fine.

"You're not fine," Dayita said, "but it's good to know you've found your voice again. What happened?"

"It smelled like the shed." She looked at Dayita, who would know right away what shed she meant. "I got woozy, then I saw a wrench, and thought I saw—" She had defeated him once. She could defeat his ghost, which was nothing more substantial than the memory of the evil she'd witnessed. "I thought I saw Jake Fowler—and I lost it."

"Can you drive her home in her truck?" Sloane asked.

"Sure," Dayita said. "Jimmy should be out soon. Sure is taking him a long time."

"I can drive," Summer said. Last time Dayita had driven her truck, she'd had to replace the transmission.

Dayita frowned. "No way."

Summer was about to ask what had brought Dayita and Jimmy to Sloane's, when Dayita drew away from the truck and asked, "What's a dog doing in there?"

"You remember Wallace, Early's dog." Poor mutt had been shut up in the truck for—how long? An hour? "My dog now," she amended. She opened the passenger door. "Hey, pal, how you doing?" For an answer, he hopped down, raised a leg, and sprayed the curb.

Summer's jacket felt lopsided. She patted the pocket. The Smith and Wesson wasn't a heavy pistol, but she still knew it was there. They could drop it off at Ty's when they passed his apartment. Where was he, anyway? She turned to Dayita. "I guess when the police came, they got Joe. Did Ty go with them as a witness?"

Dayita looked at her as if she were tripping on strong drugs. "They arrested Ty. Who's Joe?"

You had to be kidding—how could the cops have screwed this up so badly? "You two get in the truck, lock the doors, and call the police."

Summer pulled the pistol from her coat pocket.

Dayita freaked. "Where'd you get a gun?"

"Ty gave it to me." Summer bounded up Sloane's porch steps. "Get in truck—now!"

"What're you doing?" Sloane said.

"Jimmy's in there." Dayita's concern hung in her voice.

Wallace followed closely at Summer's heels as she stalked the length of the front porch, peering through both windows. She stopped short when she saw Jimmy Wong sprawled on the living room floor. Shit, shit, shit. Summer prayed he would be okay.

"Call for police and an ambulance," she yelled.

Thank God, Sloane already had a phone out and was tugging Dayita to the truck.

Summer slid the safety off and went in through the front door, Wallace at her side. She knelt by Jimmy Wong and touched his carotid. He had a pulse. Sticky blood massed on his scalp. Looked as if he'd been whacked on the head, not shot.

She tried to think where Joe might be. Not in the basement. Had Ty finished searching the upstairs before the police had arrived and managed such a monumental screw-up? Unless she had this figured all wrong, Joe had killed Corky Glover by accident. The target was Sloane, and he planned to finish the job.

A creak came from the second-story staircase, which ascended along the far wall of the living room. Was Joe going up or coming down? He had to be aware someone was here, she realized. The voices, the door opening—no way he could have missed all the commotion.

She stole across the room, and body pressed against the wall, she waited and listened. Another cautious step came down the stairs, definitely down.

She would wait. She would see his feet first long before he could see her.

Another creak. A boot edged into view beneath the angled wall of the staircase. Before she could react, Wallace snarled and leapt at Joe's calf.

Joe screeched and tumbled down into view, his shotgun discharging into the plaster ceiling and walls. Debris rained down in hail-like chunks. He scrambled back onto his feet, shaking his leg, trying to back away, but Wallace had locked on.

"Drop the weapon," Summer said, training her gun on him.

"Get this damn mutt off me." Joe raised the stock of the shotgun, clearly intent on smashing it into Wallace's head.

With all her might, Summer delivered a sharp kick to his knee. Screaming, he collapsed to the floor, the shotgun falling aside. Summer kicked the gun away.

"Off, Wallace," she said in a firm voice. She was somewhat surprised when the command worked since she had no idea what kind of training Early had given him.

Her pistol still trained on Joe, she ordered him not to move. Sirens announced the belated arrival of law enforcement and ambulances. Joe would face prison time, a terrible outcome for a man who'd loved the outdoors all his life. Summer couldn't imagine anything worse. Why couldn't he have been happy with what he had? Did people always want more and more and more?

Summer was relieved to see Jimmy Wong stirring and sitting up on the floor as she met the officers and paramedics at the door.

Sloane was right behind them. "Before any of you idiots bash another of my friends on the head, I want you to know that dog—" Sloane pointed at Wallace—"and that woman—" she pointed at Summer—"are my friends. You plan to hurt them, you're going to have to go through me first."

"Me, too," added Dayita, who'd followed them in.

Deputy Reeves apologized for the mix-up. "Sheriff Giovanni's on the way here himself to apologize." To a paramedic, she asked, "Any serious injuries here?"

The paramedic shook her head, and Joe Glover, though limping badly, was cuffed and led away. Another paramedic cleaned and bandaged Wong's scalp while Dayita worried over him. Wong seemed chagrined that Glover had gotten the jump on him, and Summer figured he'd take a lot of guff from law enforcement colleagues.

A nose bumped Summer's leg. She stooped down and cradled Wallace's head in her hands. "You done good, old boy."

She rubbed his velvety ears and felt a moment of profound connection. If there was such a thing as a soul, it was that spark of life, of a sentient being burning in the depths of the dog's eyes. That spark, so precious, so fragile, would soon be extinguished in her friend Early Glover. This time, no matter how hard she tried, she couldn't stop the tears.

17

November 30

WHAT WITH ALL THE DISTRACTIONS of the Thanksgiving holiday and the arrests of Ral and Joe Glover, Summer hadn't had time to pin down the source of Patricia Kirby's water problems. Following up on the leak on Cunningham property seemed a good place to start. Could that leak have resulted in Patricia Kirby's tainted well?

First thing in the morning, she drove to town, parked in a public lot, crossed Pike Street, and headed toward the library on foot. As she passed by Waldomore, a voice called out, "I'm looking for a bodacious dart partner tonight. Know where I can find one?"

A cheerful Hank Walsh dodged traffic to cross the street. He was dressed in jeans and a camo jacket, with a knitted cap pulled down over his ears. No gloves, though, and as he came closer she noticed his hands were reddened by cold.

"How about tonight?" he asked, wiggling eyebrows barely visible beneath his cap. He must have sensed her reluctance because he added, "I have papers I think you'll want to see."

If he was trying to sound mysterious, he'd succeeded. "What time?" she asked.

"Pick you up at eight if it's okay."

"Works for me."

A truck drowned out his next words, but maybe he said something about being glad he ran into her. If he was serious about helping her, he could find out why his father seemed determined to derail her water tests and convince him to stop.

"Any word on the fire at Fairhope headquarters?" If anyone would know, Hank would.

"Believe it or not, Sloane Dumont told the sheriff she spent the night at the motel in Dad's room," Hank said.

"I'm sure you're relieved." And Summer was too: she wouldn't have to take her suspicions to the police, though her stomach was still tied in knots over Ty's involvement. It wasn't a victimless crime. Not only Fairhope would suffer. An insurance company would lose money. "Do they know how the fire started?"

"No other suspects yet, but they're sure it was arson." He said they'd talk more later and jogged off toward the bank.

If Ty was arrested, Grace would be swallowed again by the foster care system. Summer couldn't bear to think of it, so that was one more reason she was keeping her mouth shut. But if Ty continued this vendetta, sooner or later someone would get hurt. If that happened, she would share the blame because of her silence now.

She hurried into the main library, where she located a news article about the leaky wastewater impoundment constructed by Fairhope Energy in 2009 back when Harewood controlled the company. During that period, Boomer Walsh had overseen operations at several Fairhope sites, including that one. But from a map, Summer determined it was nowhere near the Kirby property.

In the article, a deputy secretary of the DEP's Office of Oil and Gas Management acknowledged leaks had occurred at other impoundments, particularly older ones like Cunningham's. The official indicated public safety had improved since the Cunningham open pit had been installed because of a shift to closed systems for holding wastewater before it was either treated or shipped out of state. He added that when companies did use impoundments, double-lined walls and spill detection devices were required now.

No cases of well contamination from the Cunningham impoundment had been confirmed, according to the article, but from 2009 to 2013, the state received over a hundred complaints of water wells contaminated by fracking. Only in four cases did evidence compel a driller to take corrective action.

A whole section quoted Ty.:

"If you want to know how dangerous it is when government agencies tasked with protecting us look the other way because they are controlled by the energy industry, ask the people of Buffalo Creek." Franceschi referred to the 1972 disaster, when a waste containment pond owned by Pittston Coal Company burst, allowing 135 million gallons of water, sludge, and mud to form a thirty-foot high wall of debris. It rushed through the valley below, killing 125 and displacing thousands.

"Ask the 300,000 people of southern West Virginia who were without water early this year because chemicals used by the coal industry leaked into the Elk River," Franceschi said. "Our Local Emergency Planning Committee (LEPC) needs to assess the potential hazards associated with wastewater disposal from fracking operations. Since the LEPC is appointed by our county commissioners, the responsibility for public safety lies with them."

The last paragraph made the hair on her neck stand up. She hadn't known about the role of commissioners like PJ Wine. If election campaigns were funded with money from energy companies, commissioners were likely to appoint LEPC members friendly toward the industry. The potential for conflict of interest and lax oversight struck her. It was all too easy to trust elected officials to do the right thing in the public interest—and later express shock when they didn't.

She left the library and drove off to visit another landowner who had agreed to testing. She parked in front of the house, a tidy story-and-a-half wooden structure. Her phone jingled with an incoming text from Dayita: *Forgot to tell you why Agent Wong and I were at Sloane's house. Ral confessed he had placed mini-cams outside Sloane's house and outside your cabin. We were there to take them down.*

You might as well archive privacy as a thing of the past.

~

AT KNUCKLEHEADS BAR, SUMMER was enjoying a dart match pairing Hank and her against two young women. Her third dart whizzed toward the target, its point piercing the 19, her third throw nailing that number.

"Whoo-hoo! We own it now," Hank cheered.

Summer grinned as he executed a little happy dance, which reminded her that Dayita had gone dancing tonight with Jimmy Wong. How weird was that? Dayita never went on dates because she was engaged to a cousin in Bangladesh.

The petite woman Hank had introduced as Holly Stone frowned suspiciously. "Didn't you say Summer was a newbie?"

"New to town, not new to darts," Hank said. "Next time, ask more specific questions. We're thirsty and you're buying, right?"

Holly and her partner Trish good-naturedly ponied up.

"I demand a handicap next round," Trish said.

Hank carried his and Summer's beers to an empty table in a corner away from the action. Was he about to get romantic or what? Summer couldn't get a read on him, but she knew he had some purpose behind the evening. He had such an easy way about him, and when he asked about what she'd done after she left the library, she explained she'd gathered a couple of water samples. Hank's warmth drew her out in a way few people did.

After a few more sips of beer, he took a folded paper from his parka. "I was serious when I said I wanted to help you. You might find this interesting."

It was a copy of a check from his father made out to Alfred Chambers for a thousand dollars. The memo at the bottom said *wedding gift*. What did it mean?

He handed her another paper, this one a well inspection of Site 198 on Domico property. It was signed by Alfred Chambers.

"You're saying the check is a bribe," she said.

"I'm not saying anything, but it's a reasonable conclusion. My dad's secretary, Holly Stone, says the original inspection contained a citation for a leaky impoundment. That document disappeared, and Dad gave her a new inspection form to file, only this one showed the Domico site was clean. Something's wrong at that drill site."

"Any idea what?"

Hank shook his head. "Could be anything. Bad cement. Inadequate casing. Leaky wastewater holding pond."

If a second leaky pond became public, pressure could build to reexamine Fairhope's handling of fracking waste. Why would Hank bring these documents to her—what was his angle? "I know you feel your father deserted your mother when she was undergoing chemo—"

"Our disagreements go way beyond that, Summer. Dad's disappointed I don't want to continue to work for his company."

"Why would Holly . . ." She didn't know how to phrase her question nicely.

Hank tipped his mug and gulped down an enormous quantity of beer, avoiding eye contact. "I asked for her help. She was willing because my father has a way of offending people."

No kidding. He'd certainly turned Nadine against him.

"Since Holly's first day on the job, he's been harassing her," Hank said. "At first it was small stuff. How well she filled out her sweater, how pretty her eyes were, that sort of thing. Then he suggested they take a weekend trip together."

Summer winced.

Hank traced a line through the condensation on his glass. "Holly explained her lack of interest was irreversible, that she was gay. The next day he gave her a weeks' notice, which she's just finishing up. He said he couldn't afford to keep a secretary any longer." Through half-lidded eyes, he seemed to be watching Summer apprehensively.

"Outrageous—she should file a lawsuit." Maybe it was Summer's imagination, but she thought he looked relieved.

"Not her style," he said. "Besides, he really can't afford a secretary. He's way behind on his bills and loan repayments."

Summer sighed. Early Glover would have filed suit in a heartbeat, the old curmudgeon. "How did you come to know all this stuff about Holly, that she'd rejected your dad?"

"We became friends through the LGBT community. Which is another area of contention with my father. He doesn't approve of my lifestyle."

Summer's mouth fell open. How had she missed the signals? No wonder he hadn't hit on her.

He added, "I have lots of friends who are girls, but not girlfriends. I hope I can count you as a friend."

"You bet." She held up her fist and they bumped.

Summer hated pushing him further but felt she had to. "Are you giving these documents to me to get even with your father for . . ."

She couldn't think of a word to cover all the areas of disagreement Hank had expressed.

He winced. "Believe it or not, I don't want to hurt him or his business. He's worked hard all his life. He took a big risk and overextended himself by acquiring control of Fairhope. He dreams of being a big man in the community like Kit Corbett. But Dad doesn't have the organizational muscle or financial strength he needs to manage the company. He's giving the job one-hundred-and-twenty percent of what he does have. It's not enough, Summer. Dad was the site manager at the Cunningham property and knew that pond was leaking for months and didn't do anything about it. He argued that by the time the wastewater got to the creek, the chemicals would be so diluted they couldn't hurt a fly. Nothing would convince him it might endanger people's health. The blowback against Fairhope Energy after it became public was ferocious around here. I don't want to see a repeat at this other site. The sooner he fixes any leak, the better."

It took considerable courage to place public good over private loyalties. Hank was a damned decent guy, and there were too few of them.

"Let's check out that Domico site," he suggested. "My last name will gain access to anything we want to see."

~

THE DOMICO DRILL SITE COVERED A mountain top that had been lopped off. Summer judged the concrete pad big enough to accommodate a shopping mall. Hank's truck snailed the incline in a queue of a dozen other trucks up a narrow dirt road. A similar convoy passed them going downhill. Two wastewater impoundments twice the size of Olympic pools were terraced into the hillside. Floodlights turned night into day, erasing the stars and the moon altogether. Besides the rumbling engines, the beep-beep of equipment backing up assaulted her eardrums. She couldn't imagine how the people who lived in the cluster of frame houses along the country road below managed to sleep. This was what Early's place would be like once drilling started.

Hank gave her a hard hat and donned one himself.

"Bring along your lantern, too," she suggested. "We may need to explore areas beyond the lights."

When a pot-bellied workman approached, Hank flashed his ID card.

The workman, recognizing the name of the boss's son, pumped Hank's hand. "Always happy to have a Walsh visit. Be happy to show you around."

"We'd rather wander around on our own for a while," Hank said.

Summer couldn't read the man's expression, whether his eyes flashed puzzlement or concern. "I don't have to tell you, safety first," he said. "Be careful with your lady friend."

After the workman strode away, Hank asked, "What do you want to see first?"

She waited to respond until one of the hard hats finished shouting directions through an electronically enhanced bullhorn. She suggested they walk across the drill pad and get a general feel for the overall operation. At least twenty trucks were lined up on each side of the pad, all with engines revving in a steady drone. This operation was much larger than the one Summer had toured with Corbett. Another dozen transport vehicles waited their turn to offload chemicals or sand or haul off waste.

If the problem was faulty well casing, they weren't going to find out by walking through the site. Her mind kept returning to the wastewater impoundments and the way they were situated on the terrain. If they leaked, they would mingle with groundwater runoff and end up in a stream or creek.

"Do you know if these impoundments have double-lined walls and spill-detection devices?" she asked Hank.

"Not sure, but I think they were built before that was required."

She set off downhill, off road, dodging roots and underbrush, Hank following behind, calling for her to wait up.

The liquid in the first impoundment was relatively clear. Summer took the lantern from Hank and aimed the light toward the ground, working her way around the perimeter. Corners and seams would be most vulnerable for leaks, but she saw no evidence of deterioration.

They traversed the hill toward the second pond, skirting several boulders, their boots crunching across a patch of rubble and construction remnants. A hundred yards out, she detected a chemical odor, a foul smell intensifying the closer they got. It reminded her of something she couldn't put her finger on. A metallic taste began to annoy her. Swallowing did little to alleviate the sensation. Made sense—all smell was particulate. The closer they got, the more her eyes watered. *The body's natural cleansing defense against toxins,* she thought. *We're being poisoned.*

Hank coughed and waved his hand in front of his face. "Let's get out of here."

"Soon," she said, shining the lantern over the wastewater. Tinged burnt orange, the hue reminded Summer of North Florida clay. A cursory inspection of the liner's corners didn't turn up any obvious breaches, but this pond was considerably less full than the other one.

If the liner leaked underground, where would the water go? Enough light escaped the floods to reveal the major geographic features of the land. Groundwater would travel along the slight depression channeling southeast into the forested area below.

"Which way now?" he asked.

"Wherever groundwater would go."

She plunged downhill, entering terrain untouched by bulldozers and land movers. Initially they encountered scrub and brush, the occasional sapling. They passed the tree line and moved through the forest, where Hank's lantern proved inadequate to penetrate the dark. She tripped when she tangled with a thick vine. Gingerly she released the vine's grip and discovered, much to her chagrin, that thorns had ripped the fabric of her jeans.

Several times, she detected a trace of chemical odor layered beneath the far more pleasant vegetal scent of decaying leaves. Midway down the hill, the grade gentled, a change her calves welcomed. She stopped so suddenly Hank stepped on her heels, apologizing profusely. She heard him but was preoccupied. Something wasn't right. She directed the beam of light at the base of a white pine. Sap rot—those fan-shaped growths her father called turkey tails—crept up a deep crack in the trunk. She aimed the light toward the canopy. Brown needles clumped together from snapped branches. She turned in circles, throwing light at the deciduous trees. The abundance of dangling branches confirmed her fears. These trees weren't simply dormant. They were dying.

She led the way along the concavity, moving more slowly now, stopping periodically to peer at the ground. At one point she paused and inhaled. "Smell it?"

Hank's neck canted upward as he sniffed. "Isn't the odor drifting down from the impoundment?"

"I don't think so." They were well below both ponds now. "Look at this." She aimed the lantern low and pointed out a ribbon of rust staining the leaf mold.

"We should come back in daylight when it's easier to see," Hank said.

"But we're so close now. The creek—I can hear it."

They stood still, listening to the faint trill of water kissing pebbles. She cantered toward the sound as fast as she dared.

She reached the creek first. Air that should have been rainwater-fresh reeked like the impoundment. She could taste the chemicals in the air again, this time remembering the medicine her father administered when she'd had croup as a child. The pharmacist tried to mask the odor with cherry or grape flavoring, but the ploy had never fooled any kid.

She shone the lantern around the riparian zone near the creek, determining the vegetation was, for the most part, dead or dying.

"How did you know this was where the creek would start?" Hank asked.

"I've been studying water systems and terrain for years, remember? It's what hydrogeologists do."

"Guess I never asked why you wanted to do these tests. I figured you might be a chemistry major."

She aimed the lantern where run-off gathered in a pool before trickling on in the general direction of town.

Hank knelt down and poked a stick into unnaturally dark water. "Same rust color as our impoundment waste. Pretty conclusive evidence even without tests."

"Crap." She stomped the ground.

"What?"

They had come straight from the bar. "I don't have my gear to take samples."

Hank agreed to come back with her the next day. They retraced their journey uphill, Hank taking the lead. The climb felt anti-climatic. Chilled to the bone and exhausted, she longed for the warmth of a fire and the simple pallet on her cabin floor.

"Tomorrow I'm going to follow the creek and see where it goes."

Was this leaky pond responsible for Kirby's polluted well? She would soon find out.

"Count me in. My father needs to get ahead of this problem because the press will have a field day when they find out."

Summer couldn't promise she'd keep their discoveries quiet forever, but since Hank had helped her, she owed him a chance to gain his father's cooperation. If the company showed it was tackling the problem with all its resources, it would make a huge difference in public perception.

They reached the brightly lit roadway, panting from the long climb. Summer's throat ached from inhaling cold air and chemicals, but the trek would become easier along the road's shoulder.

"Better keep the lantern on so trucks see us." She had no desire to be flattened by a sleepy driver veering off road.

Hank jerked to a stop, and she noted elevated tension in his stance.

"What's wrong?" she asked.

"The foreman must have called my dad. That's the company SUV he's been using, and it's blocking me in."

~

HANK SUSPECTED THE FOREMAn had reported his presence on the property, and didn't like what it meant: his father and the crew knew about the leaky impoundment. Why else would visitors concern them?

He trudged up the hill toward his father, whose backside had been resting against the hood of Hank's truck. At Hank's approach, he slid a flask into an outer pocket of the quilted nylon vest he was wearing and raised up to his full height.

"What the hell you trying to pull, Hank?"

"Pull? Nothing." Hank winced inwardly at the way the pitch of his voice rose. Why did he always let his father put him on the defensive?

"I get a call from my men that you're out here with some broad. I get to thinking it's a mighty funny place to take a date—and then I think, oh wait—my son don't date the girls. So I get to wondering why you might be out here, and I don't much like the answer I come up with."

Eyes closed, teeth clenched, Hank counted to three, embarrassed all to hell that Summer witnessed his father dressing him down. But he would not rise to gay-bashing bait. Not this time. He opened his eyes and told his father a truth he needed to hear. "Dad, we need to haul off the wastewater before news of the leak becomes public. If we're proactive, we can control the message."

"Here's a message for you, sonny boy: there ain't no leak on Fairhope property, and if you and your little tree-hugger friend go around telling some cockamamie story that there is, I'll sue both your asses for slander. She's poisoned you against your own father."

"Dad, that's not true." Hank wanted to bring up the falsified well inspection, but didn't know how without exposing Holly as his source. "Something's poisoning the creek at the bottom of the hill. It reeks of chemicals and the water was—"

His father bashed his fist against the truck, the metallic thunk jarring Hank's nerves even further.

"There is no goddamn creek on Fairhope's site," Boomer roared.

Hank reminded himself to stay calm, to avoid escalating his father's rage. "Maybe not on the site, but in the woods below there sure is. Why don't you walk down there with me and Summer tomorrow? Take a look for yourself."

"Neither of you are coming near this property again. Son or no son, you're fired, hand over your ID."

Summer, who'd been quiet until now, broke in. "Sir, you surely don't mean that. I asked Hank to help me find the source of pollution in a creek below this mountain. My fault—I dragged him along."

Hank appreciated the lie meant to deflect his father's wrath, but he doubted his father would back down. In two more weeks, Hank would be gone anyway. Firing him would allow his dad to save face. When Hank took off for the engineering job in San Francisco, the community wouldn't think Boomer had been snubbed by his son.

"I meant every word of it, Ms. Cassidy," his father said. "My son escorted an enemy onto Fairhope property. So here's what's going to happen: if either of you set foot on this mountain again, I'll bring trespass charges against you—or worse. Consider this the only warning you're going to get."

"Come on, Summer." Hank got in his truck, executed a U-turn and headed down the mountain. In time his dad would cool off. He always did, because Hank was the only constant in his father's life.

18

December 1

Summer sat on the bed in Dayita's motel room and apologized profusely for not being able to spend the evening with her. "Tonight Hank and I are on a mission to collect samples connecting his dad's impoundment to pollution in this tiny creek out near Windy Hollow Road."

Dayita knocked on Summer's noggin. "Hello? Is anyone home in there? You might have noticed that Boomer Walsh is a loose cannon, bound to hurt somebody."

"Can't be helped. I need those samples."

Dayita sighed. "Promise me you'll be careful."

"Aren't I always?"

Dayita huffed.

"I'll be with his son," Summer added. "How safe can I get?" She changed the subject. "So how was your date last night?"

"It wasn't a date, merely an exchange of information and techniques with a colleague."

"More likely an exchange of saliva and tango techniques. So is Jimmy a good dancer?"

Dayita smiled. "The man's a world-class computer whiz and has more moves than *Dancing With the Stars* contestants."

"So is the information exchange complete or are you meeting again?"

Dayita admitted they were meeting again in a few hours.

"You stinker—you let me go on and on, apologizing for not spending the evening with you."

"If you hadn't, I'd have had to apologize to you."

Summer laughed and then drove back to the cabin to eat and change into warm hiking clothes. Hank had asked her to park where their vehicles couldn't be seen from the access road. At dusk when she arrived on Windy Hollow Road, Hank was already out of his truck, leaning against the hood.

"I checked out the Domico site with these." Hank touched the cord retaining the binoculars at his neck. "A couple guys were standing around with rifles. I've never seen weapons out at any site before."

That sucked. "We can get the creek sample, but we're going to have to ask state inspectors to obtain samples from the impoundments."

"We can't wait, Summer. Freddy Chambers signed off on the inspection. My dad owns him. Months could go by before we could convince someone else to take a look. Meanwhile, the leak could make people sick."

Maybe it already had. Patricia Kirby's respiratory issues might stem from exposure to chemicals when she showered. Benzene would disperse into the air, and breathing it was as harmful as drinking it.

If Hank was determined to get impoundment samples, they'd have to wait until dark and sneak up the hill.

"We'll get the easy sample first," Summer said, "but those guys are just supposed to scare us off, right? Your dad wouldn't let them shoot at you, would he?"

Hank's silence did nothing to boost her confidence.

They hiked an easy mile over relatively flat wooded land to reach the headwaters of the watershed. After talking with Early, she'd traced the water system on a map. Run-off from these hills eventually emptied into Little Tenmile Creek, which merged into Tenmile Creek, which merged into the West Fork of the Allegheny, which joined the Monongahela to become the Ohio River, the largest tributary that dumped into the Mississippi. Some of the water evaporated and rained back onto the land, draining again to this watershed; some was withdrawn for agriculture or drinking; and some flowed all the way to the Gulf Coast of Louisiana.

She explained to Hank the lab had already sent the analysis of Patricia Kirby's well to local water district authorities, and they had accepted Summer's offer to help trace the source of the carcinogens found. Meanwhile, they were working to pinpoint how far downstream water might be tainted.

Obtaining the rust-tinged sample from the headwaters proved easy. Summer tightened the lid on the bottle and secured it inside an insulated foam carrier. She had Hank record the GPS coordinates on the bottle.

It was still daylight as they set off through the woods. They reached the edge of the tree line as the last light faded from the sky.

They stood for a few moments peering at the hill ahead. In the distance, floodlights marked the Domico drill pad. The convoy of trucks delivering supplies to the pad appeared as a tiny string of twinkling lights winding up and down the hill. Engines rumbled like distant thunder.

The last hundred feet of the approach had been clear cut, and floodlights would make them easy targets.

"No sense in both of us going up there," Hank said. "Why don't you take the creek samples back to your truck? I watched how you did it. I can fill a few bottles myself."

"You sure you don't want to let the state take over from here?"

"I'm sure."

"Then I'm coming with you."

Summer started up the steep incline.

~

Dayita laughed at a joke Jimmy Wong told. They were sitting next to each other, his arm casually draped over her shoulder, at the Fifth Floor martini bar. Dayita loved this place. From the windows sited above the skyline, the town's lights twinkled like a galaxy of distant stars.

The waiter brought their martinis and a food menu.

"You sure you don't want to call Summer and invite her to join us for dinner?" Jimmy asked.

"No." There was only one thing Jimmy could have said to kill the mood and he'd found it. "She's kind of busy."

"So what's she doing?"

"Maybe she wouldn't want me telling her business."

"Why not—she robbing a bank? What's the big secret? Come, on. No secrets. Tell me everything."

He touched the dimple in Dayita's chin and she felt floaty. What could it hurt if she told him? She wanted his opinion on Hank Walsh anyway.

"She's going with Boomer Walsh's son to get evidence his dad's polluting a creek."

Jimmy tensed, withdrawing the arm he'd draped across her shoulders. "Where are they going?"

"What difference does it make?"

"It's important."

She tried to remember. "Windy something or other. I thought she said holler, but that can't be right."

"Ral told me Kit Corbett was monitoring Summer's cabin because Boomer seemed increasingly desperate. Desperate men are dangerous. She could be in trouble."

"Summer scared him off once already."

The anxious look still creased his forehead—unsettling Dayita even more, especially considering the whole crazy PTSD episode in Sloane's basement. "You really think she's in danger? Even though she's with this guy's son?"

"Corbett says the father and son have a strained relationship, says Boomer's not behaving rationally. Hard to say what he'd do."

"Then we have to let Summer know." She tried Summer's number, but it went straight to voicemail.

"If she's trekking out in the countryside, her phone might be out of range."

Jimmy canceled their food orders and escorted Dayita to his sedan.

~

A PALE QUARTER MOON GAVE off enough light for Summer to make out the terrain as they clambered upward. They had no choice but to move slowly. From here on, the land was pimpled with rubble and deep cavities. Floodlights on top of the flattened mountain served as the North Stars by which they would set their course.

As the grade steepened, Summer's legs ached. "This mountain climbing stuff's about to do me in."

"Mountains?" Hank scoffed. "Not even close. They're mere foothills."

"Tell that to my calves."

She noted the absence of insect music she was accustomed to in Florida. Too cold for them this time of year? Or had the leaky impoundment killed off all living things? There'd be no way to hear creatures even if they were present, she supposed, over the rumble of machinery, which grew stronger with every step they took.

Hank stumbled, his boot sliding on scree. He went down on a knee, cursing softly.

She whispered, "You okay?"

"Fine." He flicked dirt off his palm.

Even in dim light, she could see the skin was broken. "Bet that stings."

"No big deal." He stepped around her, trudging upward. Had he insisted on collecting the samples to prove something to his father—or to himself? It was hard enough for any guy to meet the cultural expectations of manhood. Being gay must make it even harder. Especially with a father like Boomer Walsh.

They hiked on. Summer could smell the chemicals now. They were nearly to the area the floodlights illuminated. Her next step started off fine, a firm footfall, but when she tried to pull the right leg forward, her boot caught and she pitched forward. She tumbled down, her elbow absorbing the brunt of the impact. She hissed as pain stabbed her arm and leg. She pushed up to sitting and rocked back and forth, rubbing her ankle, swearing softly. A quick assessment told her the elbow would only hurt a short time. The ankle sprain was more serious. From her position on the ground, she could make out the tree root, a thick loop exposed during clear-cutting, that had snared her foot.

Hank dropped beside her. "This is all my fault. I should have let you contact DEP."

"No, you were right. Chambers wouldn't have done anything about it. Your dad would have insisted."

"How bad is it?" Hank asked.

"Help me up."

Hank hauled her to her feet. "Can you put weight on your leg?"

With his support she tried, but pain rocketed all the way to her hip.

"I'll go get help," he said.

"Hold onto me while I take a few steps. I can walk this out."

They were so close now. They couldn't quit.

They paused to readjust his support of her right side. "Even if you make it to the impoundment, how are you going to walk back down?" he asked.

"We're going to get the samples. We'll figure out what to do about my ankle later."

"If you say so."

The impoundment lay about one hundred yards ahead. The sun at noon couldn't have lit the slope up any brighter than those lights did.

"We'll take the right side," Hank said. "See the shadowed areas?"

She wouldn't have called them shadows, exactly, but the glare was softer there. She hobbled along with Hank's help. At last, they reached the lower impoundment. She tried to breathe through her mouth but it only made the medicinal taste worse. She uncapped the collection container and secured it inside a metal ring. A pipe extended eight inches above the ring. She lowered the pipe into the impoundment and let fluid fill the bottle. She withdrew and capped it. While she centered a second container in the ring and repeated the process, Hank wiped the first container with a sterile cloth, applied a label she had prepared in advance, adding the GPS coordinates, and secured the sample in the foam transport. When they had five samples, she said it should be enough.

"You go ahead and get these back down the hill," she said.

"No way I'm leaving you."

"Yes, you are. I'll wait a little while and then call Dayita to come and get me." She could bring Special Agent Jimmy Wong along. He carried a weapon.

Hank gauged the distance to the access road. "I don't think you can make it to the road by yourself."

"Sure I can."

He shifted his weight from one foot to the other, clearly uneasy about leaving her alone.

She flopped to the ground to show him her decision was made. "All this will have been for nothing if you don't get those samples down the hill. Everything will be fine. Dayita will get here in no time. Now go."

Hank zigzagged downhill, avoiding brush and boulders, looking back at her from time to time. Once she judged he'd reached tree cover, she pulled out her cell and turned it on. For several anxious minutes she waited, until the screen reported the news she dreaded—no service available. She must be in a dead zone, sandwiched between thickly forested hills that blocked the closest tower's signal.

Well, she sure wasn't hiking up to the site where they probably had a signal amplifier but also men waiting with guns. She'd have to hobble downhill on the road until her phone located service. She pushed to her feet and took two wincing steps. A single shot rang out.

She dropped back to the ground, her eyes darting around frantically to find the man who'd fired the weapon. Had he aimed in the air or directly at her?

Two men in hard hats scuttled down the hill. Even if she threw something—a phone, a rock—she could only take out one man. But these were working men. Not killers. They probably had wives. Kids. The thought only consoled her for a moment—the Mafioso were big on family and that didn't stop them from killing.

"What have we here?" the tall one said.

The second man, a stout little rooster, poked the barrel of his rifle in her direction. "Believe this must be one of them intruders Boomer has us watching for."

As he drew closer, Summer recognized him from Knuckleheads—Marky. The monster who had wished that Corky had died from FloMoshun exposure. If he was so hateful toward a co-worker, she couldn't expect any kindness.

Boomer Walsh's company SUV streaked down the access road and parked as close to them as possible. As he stalked across the rocky terrain, Summer's heart plummeted. What would he do when he reached her? But she had an even more pressing worry. Marky's rifle was aimed at her torso and his trigger finger seemed so twitchy, it was altogether possible he might shoot her accidentally.

Trying to conceal how much his carelessness terrified her, she said, "First thing my daddy taught me about guns is not to point them at anything you don't intend to kill."

"You don't know nothing about our intent," Marky threatened.

"You would've already shot me if that's what the bossman had ordered. Speak of the devil, here he comes."

"You got a smart mouth on you for a girl hopping around on

one leg," Marky snarled.

Boomer's boots crunched toward them, his neck rotating to scan the area. On the final four yards, his arms extended as if asking WTF. He drew so close she could smell his bourbon breath.

"Where's my goddamn son?"

"No idea."

He seized her arm, which transferred her weight to her injured foot and she gasped, nearly collapsing from pain. When he let go, she shifted all her weight to her intact leg, keeping her eyes focused on Boomer.

"What are you doing up here?" Marky asked, poking the barrel of his weapon within inches of her hip.

"I'm a geology buff," she said. "I came up here to see if there were any rocks I could add to my collection."

"After dark?" Marky said.

"Shut up, Markowitz," Boomer snapped. "Don't show her you're fucking stupid enough to take her seriously." He slipped his weapon off his shoulder and angled the barrel in her direction. "No more games. Where is he?"

"I swear I don't know, but I'm glad you guys came along because, as you can see, I hurt my ankle. I need help getting over to the road to wait on my ride."

Boomer ground his teeth, then ordered the two men to search the hill for Hank.

As soon as the dark night swallowed them, Boomer prodded Summer with the rifle. "Move that cute little ass over to my SUV."

"You could at least thank me for returning your rifle."

"Could be you're gonna regret returning it. There's a lot of hunting accidents this time of year when some fool goes wandering around in the woods."

Recalling PJ's warning about wearing orange, Summer damn near forgot about pain in her ankle. Boomer might actually be crazy enough to shoot her. Could she flag down a trucker? Would one help her if he saw Boomer Walsh holding her at gunpoint?

Not likely. Boomer cut their checks.

~

HANK HAD BACKTRACKED HALFWAY to the truck when he heard the shot. Bloody hell. Should he dash back up the hill to rescue Summer? He looked at the container of samples and back at the distant floodlights. No, the best course of action was to get back to his truck. Then barrel ass up the road and make sure she was all right.

He turned on his flashlight and sprinted as fast as he dared through the trees. Still at top speed, he turned on his cell. If he could get a signal, he could summon the police. Or his mother. She could talk sense into his dad even when he was drunk. A few yards later, he paused to check the phone. No signal. He ran on.

Hank's mother had raised him to be a true believer. He prayed the samples would remain intact while he plunged through the forest. He prayed he wouldn't fall and sprain his own ankle. Most of all, he prayed Summer would be safe.

When he reached the truck, he set the samples on the ground, hiding the container behind a bush. No way was he taking them up the hill where his father could confiscate them. His back wheels fishtailed as he peeled out on the asphalt. He turned onto the access road. The huge chunks of gravel were meant to hold up under the duress of heavy truck traffic. They were not intended for speed, and his head banged into the roof repeatedly. He kept going.

His father's vehicle was headed downhill, Summer clearly visible in the passenger seat. Unable to think of a better option, he yanked the steering wheel hard left in front of his father. He'd be forced to stop—unless he was too drunk to react in time. In which case, he'd tee-bone Hank's truck.

~

"**Look out!**" **Summer screamed** as Hank's truck dived in front of them.

Boomer slammed on the brakes, and Summer's forearms smashed into the dashboard. She flung open the passenger door. Her ankle gave out as soon as she put weight on it. She dropped to the ground and rolled away from the SUV.

Hank raced from his truck and lifted her up. "You okay?"

"Nothing broken, only bruised. Where's—"

Hank shook his head, a warning not to ask about the samples in front of his father. A tanker was idling behind Hank's truck, the first of many vehicles they'd be blocking if they didn't move soon.

Boomer's big form lumbered past the hood of his vehicle, the rifle held ambiguously. Not exactly pointed at them. Not exactly *not* pointed at them either. A bit dazed, Boomer scratched at his nose, staring at the rifle as if he wasn't quite sure why he was holding it. That uncertainty disappeared when his gaze shifted to Hank's face. Boomer had found a target for all his frustrations.

"What brings you out here this time of night, son?" Rage steamed visibly from his mouth with each breath. "Aren't you usually diddling one of your fairy friends by now?"

Before Hank could respond, Summer tried to stem the eruption of long-simmering generational, familial conflict. "He came up here to look at the rocks, like me. It's a really cool place. Or it used to be before someone blasted the top off the mountain."

Boomer barked off a half-laugh. "A girl one trigger press away from dying ought to keep her mouth shut."

Hank stepped between them. "Dad, there's not gonna be any talk about dying. Why don't you give me the rifle?"

"Tell you what. Give me whatever you took offa my property and I'll let you have this rifle."

"I don't know what you're talking about," Hank said.

Boomer slipped off the safety and Summer's heart nearly stopped. Though he wasn't as smashed as the night when he came to the cabin, she had detected bourbon on him—and an even stronger whiff of desperation.

He swung the rifle in the direction of the truck. "Let's have a look."

When Hank didn't move, his father pointed the rifle into the air and fired a single shot. The sound seemed to bounce off every nerve in Summer's body.

"Okay, take it easy, Dad. I'm going."

She stayed put since Boomer hadn't included her in his command.

Hank loped along, his gait and demeanor way too calm, Summer thought, if the samples were actually there. What would Boomer do if he didn't find what he was looking for? The first shot had been to scare them into compliance. Next time they might not be so lucky.

A sedan was hurtling up the hill—friend or foe? And even if it was help, it didn't look as if it could arrive before Boomer discovered the samples were missing. She couldn't risk their lives by betting that Boomer would behave rationally. He might actually shoot Hank. Or her. Stooping down, she seized a hunk of gravel they'd used to surface the road. Must be busted up cement. The chunk had decent heft, much larger than ordinary gravel: a suitable weapon—if her throwing arm hadn't been screwed up by slamming into the dashboard.

When Boomer swung the rifle away to look in the bed of the truck, Summer cocked her arm and hurled the cement at his head.

Instinct must have alerted Boomer because he turned and ducked. His rifle was already on the way up when Hank grabbed the barrel. The two wrestled, grunting, teeth bared. Summer stooped for another chunk of cement, calculating how difficult it would be to find a clear target while they were struggling. A moot point a minute later when Boomer regained control of the weapon. Panting, he stepped back from his son and the rifle wasn't yet aimed. Summer saw her opportunity, maybe the last she'd have.

She whipped the rock toward Boomer's arm and he lost his grip. The rifle clattered as if fell onto the gravel.

The car had arrived, and Jimmy Wong sprinted their way, weapon drawn, Dayita not far behind.

"Special Agent Jimmy Wong," he shouted at Boomer. "Leave the rifle where it is."

In the distance sirens announced the approach of additional law enforcement, a welcome sound since several truckers had climbed out of their vehicles to see what the holdup was. It was hard to guess how many of them might be armed and willing to defend Boomer.

But with Jimmy Wong already present, it soon became apparent the truckers only wanted to watch the show. Summer imagined they'd all be telling their families later their own versions of what went down on Domico's hill, each story containing various inaccuracies since eye witness testimony was notoriously wrong. When deputies arrived, they took a belligerent, cursing Boomer into custody. As they drove off with his father in cuffs, Hank looked so defeated Summer ached for him. He had tried so hard to get his father to do the right thing, only to have Boomer point a weapon at him.

Over the next hour, deputies took statements from Summer and Hank, with Dayita and Jimmy Wong verifying what they'd seen while riding up the hill. Summer told Deputy Reeves that Marky Markowitz and the Stick Man had disappeared into the dark night and weren't likely to reappear while the law was present. Reeves assured Summer they would track them down and charge them with unlawfully detaining her at gunpoint.

Officers also questioned truckers waiting to get back on the road.

When the deputies finished with Hank, he retrieved the samples and passed them over to her.

"I'll get these delivered to the lab right away," she said. "I can't thank you enough." Words seemed inadequate to express everything she wanted to say to this dear new friend. "I hope everything works out for you in San Francisco. Promise you'll stay in touch."

He offered her a fist and they bumped, but then, feeling it insufficient acknowledgment of all he'd been through, all they'd been through together, she kissed his cheek.

An engine revved, and the foursome moved out of the roadway as the first tanker in line resumed its journey down the hill. No matter how many Deep Water Horizons blow-outs, Exxon Valdez spills, and Big Gumbo Creek leaks occurred, Americans would demand and get their cheap energy.

But for now, maybe only for this one night, no more tankers would journey up the hill. Deputies had shut down the Domico site.

She hoped there would always be scientists and some good people in government trying to ensure all energy, whatever its source, was obtained as safely as possible. And, she hoped activists would keep opening people's eyes to the ways we all kept destroying the only habitable planet around. Thankfully, most found effective methods less violent than Ty's.

19

December 4

A LIGHT BREEZE CAUGHT the last of Early's ashes, snowing them across the sunlit surface of Glover's Lake. Gathered on a tongue of land extending into the lake, a small crowd watched somberly.

As Summer remembered Early's will, she sucked in her bottom lip to curb a smile. Early insisted he wanted no service. If life had value, he wrote, it lay in how it was lived. People had never held back their true feelings about his behavior while he was alive; there was no need to tell pretty lies once he was gone. His will urged Sloane to be a good steward of the land and the llamas he was passing into her care, because in the end that is how we should be judged. He'd left PJ Wine his second best bed. The allusion to Shakespeare, who'd left his wife the same, tickled Summer.

As Sloane lowered the urn, it rattled. "Early Glover, you cantankerous old goat. You messed up the timing on your entrance into my life, and now you're messing up your exit too." Laughing through tears, she turned the vessel upside down and shook out the remainder of his bones. Summer regarded Sloane as a woman of true courage. She'd experienced the most difficult year imaginable—losing her mother and her fiancé, finding and losing her father—yet she was still able to smile.

Wallace, who had sat passively at Summer's side, tipped his nose into the air and sniffed. Did he understand Early was gone? She thought so. When she had tucked one of Early's shirts into the dog's bed for comfort, Wallace had whined and nuzzled the cloth.

Sloane addressed the gathering. "Folks, I tried to convince Early to have a wake, but he requested a church supper, and assured me he'd be there in spirit because he loves PJ's pizza casserole. So come on over to the church basement where Patty, Katie, Elma, Toddy, and Midge will have rounded up enough food for an army."

Summer touched Sloane's coat sleeve. "I'll be there after I take Wallace back to the cabin."

"You'll do no such thing," Sloane huffed. "Early loved that dog and you'll bring him along. I dare anyone to fuss about it."

"That's right, we dare them to fuss," PJ added, but Summer couldn't help but notice both women gave the dog a wide berth as they linked arms and returned to their cars.

The church where Early had taught Bible studies was a red brick structure with white trim resembling frosting over two arched doors and the large arched window between them. The basement was nothing fancy: folding chairs set up on a cement floor. The ladies had covered long tables with white cloths and loaded them with comfort food.

Her plate piled high with casseroles, Summer slipped into the seat beside Ty, who had opted only for coffee.

"Deputy Skidmore assured me Boomer Walsh will stay behind bars this time, no bail," Summer told Ty.

"Unless he hires a clever lawyer who gets him out again," Ty said, "which would be a shame." His fingers grazed her hand, lingering only briefly. He left without drinking the coffee.

The real shame was he couldn't let go of his anger toward those he blamed for his parents' deaths and his sister's disability. He would never be free or whole until he did. Forgiveness is the path to peace, Early had said. A peculiar philosophical musing for a man who greeted folks at the door with a rifle, but Early had been an unpredictable eccentric. One of the few people who refused to cloak his true feelings with good manners.

PJ slid in next to Summer to let her know she had called for a halt to drilling on all Fairhope sites until the state could conduct a thorough safety review. "I hope this won't damage your research project," PJ said.

Summer assured her she could randomly select new sites from other companies to replace Fairhope's. Had PJ realized Early's cancer might have been triggered by Walsh's leak at the Domico site? If so, that suspicion might have spurred her to buck the oil industry and the many constituents who would be outraged by loss of income.

As if intuiting the direction of Summer's thoughts, PJ said, "I heard Boomer is declaring bankruptcy, and Kit Corbett plans to take over Fairhope. He was reluctant to assume all of the company's problems, but he says someone needs to run the good sites, fix those that can be salvaged, and with the EPA's help, clean up the messes Isaac Harewood and Boomer Walsh have left behind."

Summer seemed to be continually revising her opinion of Corbett upward. "He really is a good man, isn't he?"

PJ shrugged. "Sure, but don't kid yourself. Kit's an astute businessman first and foremost. He has what most oil men don't: enough money to wait until the flooded market corrects itself."

"You think it will?"

"It's in everyone's best interests to form a consortium like OPEC to control supply and demand."

Summer knew that wouldn't happen overnight. While the oil glut was causing pain to companies like Fairhope in the short term, she thought it could bring about a measure of good. If everyone slowed down the rush to frack, they could consider how—and whether—it could be done safely. She hoped it happened before fracking caused a major quake, or seriously damaged the limited supply of fresh water.

Dayita joined the table, with far less food on her plate than Summer had piled onto hers. That girl never did eat enough.

Digging a fork into the chicken-rice casserole, Summer pondered the nature of food after funerals. The gift of food affirmed the essential goodness of fellow humans, while the act of eating affirmed life and demonstrated the intention to move forward after loss.

Dayita's ankle bracelet tinkled insistently, which meant, Summer knew only too well, that a scolding was coming. What had she done this time?

"Summer, girlfriend, this time you are getting help even if I have to drive you to a counselor myself."

Oh, that. "Thanks, but no thanks."

"After that freak-out in Sloane's basement—you gotta get professional help. You might be able to kick butt, but you are a woman in need of a support group."

A bunch of people sitting around in a circle moaning and whining to each other? Not for her. But she'd read about a Bio-Acoustical

Utilization Device that targeted emotional scars. Under the guidance of a neuropsychologist, the hand-held gizmo helped reset the brain's fear circuits through biofeedback and audio signals. Research-based, the therapy appealed to her. She believed in science. In asking questions. In finding truth through a verifiable process.

Right now, she looked forward to shoveling distractions out of her way to focus on her dissertation again—but since Early's death, she'd been thinking about taking a detour to expand her horizons. She'd seen so little of the world outside of books. Living in West Virginia these past few weeks made her realize photographs and textbook illustrations weren't the same breathtaking experience as being there. A photograph of the gorge at Coopers Rock was no substitute for standing on the precipice where the wind whipped your face. Where the immensity of time and space stretched out in front of you as far as you could see.

"I have a better idea than a support group," Summer said. "I'm thinking about trading the truck for a van, taking the summer semester off, and heading out West. There's a bunch of cool rocks out there I haven't seen."

"You can't do that!" PJ protested. "What about your research?"

"The first round of water tests will be done and I won't need to retest until next fall. I'll teach some undergrad classes in the spring, so I'll have a little income." Not to mention the bequest from Early. As one who had struggled to pay for college himself, he had known what a difference a bank account would make in her life. Briefly she closed her eyes and sent yet another thank-you winging toward the ether. Maybe his spirit lingered out there somewhere—waltzing near a wormhole—or suing one—and he could sense her gratitude.

To Dayita, she said, "I was kind of hoping you'd come along. You could start up your company from the road, couldn't you? I could help set up spreadsheets, research the competition."

Summer could almost see the pistons in Dayita's mind fire.

"Omigod, that would be so cool!" Dayita said. "As long as we can find decent WiFi, I can work anywhere. The two of us on the road. What a hoot!"

Summer's lips twitched: it would be cool until Dayita realized she'd be using campground bathhouses and hiking in places where she might encounter a bear or a moose or a snake. Exposure would be good for Dayita; it might help her overcome her fears, using the same principle as the Bio-Acoustical Device Summer was considering for herself.

"I guess this means you're turning down Kit's job offer," PJ said.

"Afraid so. I told him yesterday." Summer dug into PJ's pizza casserole, rich with mozzarella, basil, tomato sauce, and pepperoni.

"Because of the surveillance cam?" Dayita asked. "Cut the guy some slack." She explained Boomer had mouthed off about putting an end to the water testing. "Corbett was only trying to protect you."

She supposed she should be flattered, but if Kit was worried about her safety, he should have explained the danger and trusted her to handle the situation. "Sloane and I are both big badass gals," she said. "We didn't need his protection."

"Corbett was only responsible for the camera at your place," Dayita corrected her. "He used Allied Consulting primarily for background checks on employees and computer security. Ral told Jimmy Wong the camera at Sloane's was installed at Boomer's request almost a year ago because he was obsessed with her. Ral thinks he was trying to catch a peep at her boobs."

Okay, now that was totally creepy. Poor Hank—no wonder he wanted to escape to San Francisco.

PJ cast a suggestive sidelong look at Summer. "I got the impression Kit was interested in you personally."

Corbett made no secret of wanting more than a business relationship. He had assured Summer a job—and maybe more—would be waiting if she changed her mind later. After she finished her research and earned her PhD, she might think about it.

"Right now I need lots of friends, both boys and girls," she said, pirating Hank's phrasing, "but no boyfriends."

PJ rose, preparing to take her paper plate to the trash can. "That's too bad. We'd like to keep you here in Clarksburg."

Once she'd left, Dayita asked, "What's going on with you and Ty? I noticed he didn't stay long."

"It's complicated."

"Why? You two love each other."

"I wish it was that easy." If you ever fall in love, savor that first enchantment, Summer wanted to tell her. All intoxicating moments in life flashed by too rapidly, like the riotous color of autumn leaves and the purity of fresh fallen snow. Even to her best friend, Summer couldn't explain how deeply Ty's choices hurt. She empathized with his rage, understood why he felt impotent to stop the destruction through the legislative process because money had corrupted the system so thoroughly. Government agencies responsible for oversight would always be hamstrung by miniscule budgets. Even so, she couldn't condone what he'd done. A heaviness had settled deep within her bones. She would never be sure that he would have come to her that night had there been no mission to destroy Fairhope. Though she wanted to believe touching another person with such exquisite tenderness was impossible unless love fed the fingers, niggling doubt remained.

"I can't trust him," she said. True, but not the whole truth. Because Ty would always have her back, would risk his life for her. Like she'd said before, it was complicated.

"Who can you trust after all that's happened?" Dayita asked.

Good question. All of Summer's relationships had grown more complicated this semester. People were like science: the more she learned, the more she realized how little she understood. But even if you could never know all the answers, and sometimes not even the right questions to raise, Early was right: you had to keep asking.

"I trust myself," Summer said. "And, of course, I trust you."

The joy in Dayita's smile touched Summer enough to withhold this small secret: she also trusted the mutt nosing her knee for a bite of chicken. With the love of a good friend and a loyal mutt, she was more than ready to journey out into the world.

Acknowledgements

First and foremost, this novel owes so much to my mother, Patricia Stanley. Not only did she share her concerns over hydraulic fracturing and the effects it might have on West Virginia's environment, she clipped hundreds of articles from the Clarksburg-Exponent Telegram and mailed them to me. And those contributions pale next to the constant encouragement she gave me to continue writing.

Other family members and friends contributed ideas and support, as well—my thanks and love to each of them.

The plot and characterization received an incredible boost from Heather Whitaker, a truly gifted editor. Liz Jameson's line edits also contributed to the final manuscript.

Judie Mulholland provided invaluable background information that strengthened the computer security portion of the story. In addition, several geologists and workers in the oil and gas industry provided their perspectives for the story.

These books provided useful background: *The Power Surge: Energy, Opportunity, and the Battle for America's Future* by Michael Levi; *2013 Complete Guide to Hydraulic Fracturing (Fracking) for Shale Oil and Natural Gas: Encyclopedic Coverage of Production Issues, Protection of Drinking Water, Underground Injection Control* by the EPA; *The End of Country: Dispatches from the Frack Zone* by Seamus McGraw; *Hydrofracked: One Man's Mystery Leads to Backlash Against Natural Gas Drilling* by Abraham Lustgarten, *Shale Gas: The Promise and the Peril* by Vikram Rao Ph.D.; and *Cold, Hungry and in the Dark: Exploding the Natural Gas Supply Myth* by Bill Powers.

Countless websites also provided background on fracking.

I am so fortunate to have my critique group members in my life—Marina Brown, Rhett DeVane, Peggy Kassees, Hannah Mahler, Claire Matturro, and Susan Womble. I'd never finish a book without their encouragement.

I would also like to thank these early readers for giving generously of their time: Doug Alderson, LC Fiore, Penny Gilmer, Ursel Homann, Peg Holmes, Norman Julian, Phyllis Wilson Moore, Edwina Pendarvis, Sanford Safron, Pat Spears, and Meredith Sue Willis.

And finally, thanks to the Tallahassee Writers Association and Florida Writers Association for the continued inspiration and camaraderie they offer.

All errors that remain in the novel are purely my own, and no reflection on the contributions of the many kind people who helped to nurture this book into existence.

While I made every attempt to present all sides of the issues surrounding hydraulic fracturing, no doubt some will take offense. I hope they will remember a novel has to develop a story that is entertaining. If it proves informative or educational as well, that is all to the good.

While the novel is not meant to accurately portray any actual events, in some cases, I constructed scenes similar to real-life occurrences. All characters and fracking sites are fictional inventions. Stansbury, Ohio, and the environment group Water Warriors are entirely fictional. I also took liberties in describing the weather in Clarksburg in 2014. It was as cold as depicted, but it didn't snow on the dates mentioned in the story. Deviation from truth was necessary for plot development.

Donna Meredith

lives in Tallahassee, Florida. Her articles have appeared in various newspapers and magazines, and she frequently contributes book reviews to *Southern Literary Review*.

Her award-winning novels include *The Glass Madonna*, *The Color of Lies*, *Wet Work* and *Fraccidental Death*. The nonfiction title, *Magic in the Mountains: Kelsey Murphy, Robert Bomkamp and the West Virginia Cameo Glass Revolution*, tells the amazing story of a determined and talented couple who revived the ancient art of cameo glass in the twentieth century in West Virginia.

Donna holds degrees from Fairmont State College, West Virginia University, and Nova Southeastern University, and studied creative writing at Florida State University. She taught English, journalism, and TV production in public high schools in West Virginia and Georgia.